A Night Made for Love . . .

Her dress had fallen off one shoulder, baring it and the top of one creamy breast. With her hair tumbling down her back, her mouth moist from his kisses, she had never appeared more seductive.

"I am ravenous for you, sweet. Are you ready for me?" he asked.

Aimee met his smoky eyes and hesitated. She longed to give in, to end this conflict between them and answer the needs calling to her by the sight of his hard male body. As if he sensed he was influencing her decision, Luke stepped back two paces and left her standing alone.

Aimee folded her arms over her bosom to still its frantic pounding. Her eyes dropped to the floor in shyness as she stunned him with her reply.

"Yes, Luke. I want to be yours."

Luke's blood ran through his veins in a torrent. He walked forward slowly, eyes on her face, afraid he had heard her wrong . . .

COLLEEN SHANNON
Nominated as Best New Historical
Romance Novelist
for 1986 by Romantic Times

The Tender Devil

Colleen Shannon

CHARTER BOOKS, NEW YORK

THE TENDER DEVIL

A Charter Book / published by arrangement with
the author

PRINTING HISTORY
Charter edition / October 1987

ISBN: 0-441-80221-4

Charter Books are published by The Berkley Publishing Group,
200 Madison Avenue, New York, New York 10016.
The name "Charter" and the "C" logo are trademarks
belonging to Charter Communications, Inc.
PRINTED IN THE UNITED STATES OF AMERICA

*In loving memory of my mother, Vi Jean,
my first and greatest fan.*

PART I

⤜⤛

Your mad, unending play of passion in eye, in gesture, mood and limb is all of Satan's restless fashion; your luring laughter is from him.

—Bjørnstjerne Bjørnson,
"I Love You Ha! You Brown-Skin Devil"

Chapter One

AIMEE LINGSTROM DREW her carriage to a halt in the hills above Bergen. She took in deep breaths of the fresh mountain air, vowing nothing would spoil her enjoyment of this perfect summer day, not even anger at her father. Like a sensuous cat, she lifted her face to bask in the sun. The call of a ptarmigan feeding her chicks, the joyous rush of the stream at her feet and the rustle of the wind-tossed trees soothed her like a lullaby. Nature's gifts were too bountiful, summer's joy too brief to waste in anger. She turned to admire the city below.

Bergen was always beautiful, but after a daily rain, she emerged in her full, eight-hundred-year-old glory. There were crumbling Gothic churches, winding streets, narrow alleys and steep stairways. The fish market bustled as usual, as shoppers hurried from *smack* to *smack* to select the freshest, cheapest fare.

Vessels of all types, from tiny shore boats to majestic clippers, bobbed in the cobalt water of the port. At the Tyskebryggen, the quay built centuries ago by Hanseatic League merchants, workers unloaded goods into old warehouses. Some of the warehouses, with their oddly angled roofs, overhung the water so that crates could be winched into them from docking boats.

This part of Bergen was like a city frozen in a time far removed from this year of 1873, Aimee thought dreamily. From here the cobbled streets lined with ship ribbings, the

Rosenkrantz Tower and the Bergenhus fortress, guarded the harbor entrance like aged but fierce mastiffs. They reminded her of a harsher age when roles were clear-cut. How wonderful it would have been to live in Norway's glory days when the world trembled at the mere mention of the name —Viking!

Sighing, Aimee urged her pony higher into the hills. No matter how she might wish otherwise, those glory days were long gone. For centuries, Norway had been dominated first by Denmark, and then after the Napoleonic Wars, by Sweden. This bitter fact made it harder for Aimee to trust her father's wisdom to align their family business with a wealthier, more powerful family. Aimee feared the Americans would try to interfere in their family affairs as arbitrarily as the Swedes tried to limit Norway's self-governance.

But try as she might, Aimee could not sway her father, Ragnar. The shipping business he'd spent his life building was ailing, threatened by stiff Swedish competition. An alliance with a remote American relative was a godsend. He would not only have access to new capital, he could eventually achieve a cherished dream: conversion of his wooden fleet to sturdy iron steamers. In return, the Americans could open a passenger line between Norway and America, and they would gain a beautiful daughter to wed their son to.

Aimee suspected Ragnar was eager for the alliance for other reasons. He had helped put Bergen on the map as one of Norway's busiest ports. Fueled by iron will and ambition alone, he had parlayed a single rickety wooden ship into a successful fleet, one of Norway's most prosperous. Then an ailing economy and tough Swedish competition had forced him to curtail his dreams of expansion. Capping those dreams was another he perhaps yearned for most: a male heir to inherit his business. A grandson born of a strong, successful father to the wealth and position Ragnar craved for his descendants. If obtaining these goals meant separating his older daughter, Sigrid, from Gere, her childhood love, then so be it.

Aimee knew Ragnar had never approved of the handsome young sailor. He leaped at the opportunity to wed Sigrid more "suitably." He paid no heed to their objections, his fatherly point of view being vastly different from their own. Aimee's mouth tightened grimly as she remembered one of their many arguments on the subject.

Legs braced in his habitual commanding stance, he demanded, "Why should I squander Sigrid's future on a penniless young man whose only prospects are ambition and a winning smile?"

Aimee looked him straight in the eye. "Perhaps because you were once such a man yourself. *Mor* has had no cause to regret her marriage. Would you deny Sigrid the same chance to find happiness in her own way?"

Ragnar scowled. "Yes, I would, for I know the trials that await her."

Aimee's set jaw quivered. "Why must he be so stubborn," she muttered to herself. She had no idea how much she resembled him when she rebelled. "The bonds that are forged in hardship are often much stronger than those forged in plenty," she said, her chin lifting. "Besides, why won't you believe that material comfort is of little concern to me or Sigrid? Our lives are comfortable compared to most. We have no need of fancy jewels and gowns. Happiness and peace of mind are far more valuable commodities. Sigrid will have neither if she is separated from us and the only man she could ever love." Aimee watched him hopefully, rather proud of her steadfast reprimand.

But Ragnar was equally adamant. "Sigrid is too young to form such an attachment. It's easy for you two to scoff at wealth when you know nothing of the trials of accumulating it. You don't seem to understand that if I don't raise some capital, the way of life you and your sister enjoy now may come to an end. You don't know what it's like to have nothing."

Steaming, Aimee had then flown from the house, to seek this refuge.

Now, as she navigated her carriage through the hills, Aimee wondered yet again how her father could be so blind. Aimee knew no two people who were kinder, more deserving of happiness than Gere and Sigrid. She couldn't understand how Ragnar could entrust the sweet, gentle Sigrid to a wealthy, arrogant American who would care for nothing but himself. Sigrid was a shy, frail homebody. She would be desperately unhappy as the future mistress of the far-flung Garrison empire. Why couldn't Ragnar see that?

Aimee tossed her head angrily as she remembered more of the confrontation that had sent her from the house. He had ruthlessly cut off her entreaties by scoffing, "Since you refuse to have anything to do with our young men, I am determined that Sigrid, at least, will wed sensibly. She thinks she loves Gere now, but I'll wager when she meets young Garrison, she'll change her mind soon enough. I've heard he has quite a way with the ladies."

Infuriated, Aimee had retorted, "Sigrid will never forget Gere! And I'll do everything in my power to stop you from separating them. If Sigrid isn't strong enough to fight you, I am."

Ragnar had risen to his feet, towering above his willful younger daughter. But Aimee had held her ground, foot tapping impatiently. "If you want to help Sigrid, it's easy enough to do so. You can wed young Garrison instead," he boomed.

Aimee lifted her chin. "You know me better than that. I'll never marry. All men care about is compliancy. If you don't admire their muscles and hang on every word they say, they think you're a radical. No, threaten all you like, *Far,* but you'll never force *me* to wed a man I don't respect. And since you and Gere are the only men I admire, I'm in little danger of marrying at all. Aimee stormed to the door, and turned for a parting shot. "You and Gere—but I'm beginning to wonder about *you.*" She slipped out, ignoring her father's outraged roar.

Aimee reined her cream-colored pony to a halt and jumped down from her carriage, ignoring the twinge in her leg. The voice of her conscience sounded. Was she being selfish? Should she agree to wed the American to save Sigrid and her father's business? Aimee kicked a tuft of grass for relief. She was friends with many young men, but she had no desire to tie herself to any of them. Invariably, they failed to live up to her dreams, or match her father's blustery strength or Gere's quiet tenderness. The American would be no different. Worse, perhaps, for—being a man who had known nothing but privilege—he would no doubt expect unquestioning obedience from his wife. Sigrid could offer that to a man; Aimee could not. Perhaps she was simply too independent to give herself so completely to another, as her mother often moaned.

But why should she conform, she asked herself rebelliously. There was more to life than marriage and having babies. It was time women threw off the shackles men had chained to them. Marrying a wealthy, arrogant man was not the way to keep her freedom. No, she told herself yet again, there had to be another way to save Sigrid. She could never marry the American, for she would never be dominated by anyone, regardless of the emotional, physical or social toll.

Aimee set her worries aside and strolled about to admire the scenery. A waterfall tumbled a frothy silvery trail over a flower-decked cliff. From her aerie in the hills, she could glimpse her favorite fjord, the Hardangerfjord, 170 kilometers of the prettiest scenery she'd ever seen. Steep mountain walls, some jagged with imposing rock, some lush with vegetation, were yet snow-capped at the top. The sun struck the ice and danced on the indigo waters of the fjord's narrow inlet, dazzling Aimee's eyes.

As usual, her temper was calmed by nature's grandeur. When a pair of foxes erupted from a hollow log to wrestle playfully in the grass, Aimee stood stone still, watching in delight. She absent-mindedly tossed her long braid over her shoulder, alerting them. They froze, then scampered away. Aimee smiled after them, envying their freedom and lack of care.

Her parents never understood her deep love for nature. These wanderings didn't make her lonely; they rejuvenated her, gave her peace as crowds and parties never could. Aimee admired the flowers; she giggled as they seemed to curtsy grandly before the wind. She put a finger to her chin and curtsied back, picking several blooms with which to decorate her braid. The flowers complemented the colorful embroidery on the sleeves and neck of her white blouse. Aimee held her green skirt up so that her ankles showed, and she whirled in an exuberant dance until she was dizzy. She collapsed onto the grass, laughing with youthful joy, the merry peals of her mirth sounding as melodious as birdsong that suddenly stopped in midrefrain.

The laughter died on her lips. Her head lifted like a wary doe's as her instinct warned her an alien approached. The back of her neck prickled. She started to turn her head when an anguished howl distracted her from the source of her unease, a man riding a magnificent white Arabian, a breed very rare in Norway. He so blended with his animal that the blur of muscle and movement formed a uniform silhouette against the sky.

Oblivious, Aimee dropped her braid, her eyes searching frantically as another cry seemed to shatter the crystalline air. She knew that sound. God, not again!

Rushing toward its source, she spied a tawny-colored splotch under a birch, and raced to her carriage to remove her knapsack. She hurried toward the trapped animal, too upset to notice the tall rider dismount, his black hair gleaming in the sun like a raven's wing.

Aimee circled the trapped animal. It was a lynx, baring menacing fangs. It struggled to escape, whimpering again and again as the small trap cut more deeply into its paw with every movement. Panting, it watched warily as Aimee inched closer, but made no movement toward her. She circled to see how she could spring the trap open. She found a gnarled tree limb nearby, and an idea flashed to mind. She would use it to wedge between the trap's jaws and then pry the animal's foot free.

She'd managed to do as she planned, when a horrified "No!" sounded behind her. "Are you insane? Get away!" the booming voice startled both her and the animal. She turned. A shadow blocked the sun. A shadow of a man holding a menacing club. . . .

Hissing in anger and pain, and taking advantage of the distraction, the lynx limped rapidly away. Aimee turned on the intruder, a snarl very like the lynx's twisting her beautiful mouth. Her pale green, gold-flecked eyes narrowed and sparked.

"You won't be satisfied until you've drained these mountains of life, will you? Did you know she was pregnant? You should wait a few months, then you'd have more hides to barter."

The stranger seemed torn between fury and amazement as he glared back. "Have your brains gone soft, girl? I'm no trapper. I was trying to save you. Don't you know a wounded animal is dangerous?" He spoke in a slightly accented Norwegian, but Aimee was too angry to notice.

"I was trying to save the cat, and at this distance I was hardly in danger. Not that it's any of your business," she added scornfully.

"I'm making it my business," he retorted. "You've obviously little sense if you roam about the countryside freeing trapped, dangerous wild animals. You *need* a keeper."

Aimee's mouth set stubbornly. Who did he think he was? Her eyes wandered over him, and caught the braided, formal uniform of a captain. A sailor cap topped his thick unruly black hair. He was tall, well over six feet. His skin was bronzed, his lashes lush and curling, his eyes deeply, magnetically black. His looks were alien to everything she knew and admired, but she was bothered more by the inner man she sensed inside his dark, dangerous self. Legs braced, feet apart, eyes challenging, he dared her to cross him. Aimee, however, was not bothered for long.

After her battles with her father, she was in no mood for another confrontation with an overbearing male. If her heart beat a little faster, she told herself it was because he'd frightened her. With a haughty toss of her head and a scorching look, Aimee dismissed him, scooped up her knapsack and turned to leave. The knapsack contained some medical supplies she had planned to use on the cat's wound.

She was unaware of the stare that followed her. She didn't realize what a strange contrast she was; a girl with a bone structure delicate as a kitten's, but the will and strength of a lioness. Her ferocity gazed out of her face, through yellow-flecked eyes. Her features were more piquant than beautiful, but they endowed her with hypnotic power. Her wide, intelligent forehead and determined cheekbones tapered to a tiny nose. Her willfull mouth was, at the moment, tight with anger. When she flung her silver-blond braid over her shoulder and turned disdainfully away, the stranger accepted her unconscious challenge. White teeth flashed in a taunting smile as he tossed the club aside, snatched Aimee's wrist and whirled her to face him.

"This is my first visit to Norway, but I've been told how courteous and friendly your countrymen are. Apparently that's not true of your countrywomen," he needled. She stiffened at his touch and jerked her wrist so furiously that he let her go to avoid hurting her.

She backed several paces, clasping the knapsack to her breast like a shield. "You expect courtesy from me when you frightened me to death and scared away the animal I was trying to save? Now she'll probably catch an infection and die, thanks to your interference," she hissed. The man towered over her as he advanced. Chin high, Aimee refused to retreat again.

She met him look for look when he drawled, "Pardon me. Next time I come up on a young girl about to be savagely mauled, I'll stand by and watch."

His sarcasm found its mark in Aimee's flush. Irritated, she

shifted from foot to foot. "I told you, I was not about to be mauled. If you were truly trying to help, then I apologize." Her tone, however, held little of apology. When she tried to step around him, he blocked her retreat.

She bit her lip to stifle a scream. Inhaling, she flung back her head to demand he move aside, but the breath caught in her throat at the expression in his eyes. His eyes dropped to her Cupid's bow mouth, and she was suddenly self-conscious, as strange new feelings awakened within her. He looked delighted, amused, interested, but there was something else in those hot eyes, something that bothered her. It was almost as if he'd seen her before, as if they'd been friends. No, more than friends. Lovers . . . Her heart tripped at the thought. He smiled then, a friendly smile, an unthreatening smile, and she told herself she'd imagined that hungry gleam.

He responded easily, "No apology necessary. I hope the cat doesn't become ill. Tell me, do you perform these rescue missions often?"

Aimee hesitated. Head cocked on one side, eyes coaxing, the winning smile emphasizing the spare, handsome planes of his face, he encouraged her confidence. Since he no longer tried to browbeat her, she decided to at least treat him with the courtesy due a newcomer to Norway.

"I release what animals I can. To the chagrin of the trappers and my parents, I might add." She grimaced wryly.

The stranger's nod was sympathetic. "I can imagine you're not popular with the trappers. But I understand your concern. We've already hunted too many animals into extinction."

Aimee's eyes narrowed suspiciously. She'd never met a man who sympathized with her radical views on nature. Even Gere thought she was silly to worry about creatures put on earth for man's use.

"Perhaps," she said noncommittally. "I only know that animals are not merchandise to be slaughtered and sold. They feel pain, joy and misery, as we do. This indiscriminate slaughter is not right. We're not masters of the earth. We're tyrants. Someday, if we're not careful, we may spoil everything not just for animals, but for ourselves as well."

"Indeed, I know how you feel. I was a crew member on a whaler once. They harpooned a cow who had just given birth, and I've never before or since heard such a mournful wail as the cry that calf emitted. It's a sound I'll never forget." He shuddered in memory.

Aimee searched his face, trying to gauge his sincerity. "If I may ask, sir, what are you doing here in the hills?"

"I just arrived in Bergen today. This is my first visit to Norway and I wanted to see the scenery I've heard so much about. And I must say, I'm not disappointed. The guide-books can't do this coastline justice."

"*Ja*," she muttered, noticing the stranger communicated in almost perfect Norwegian.

They both turned to look at the Hardangerfjord. The wind was rising, and the waters of the inlet were no longer serene. The restless, white-capped waves crashed against the cliff walls. A female raven shrieked in irritation as the nest she was constructing blew out of its tree. Even the waterfall seemed agitated as the wind caught the hem of her gossamer water-skirt and sent it drifting outward in a gentle display.

"Is there anything you recommend I see while I'm here?" he asked after a moment.

"There's much to see in Bergen. Part of the city dates from medieval times. I would especially recommend the fortress and St. Mary's church."

He turned his head to smile at her. "Thank you," he said softly. He touched one of the flowers in her braid. "You know, when I was riding up, I saw you dancing in the clearing. You curtsied to the flowers, and you seemed so vital, so attuned to your surroundings, that for a moment, I thought I'd ventured into a strange world where Odin held sway and you were queen of the fairies."

He gently lifted her braid to his face to smell the same flower he'd fondled. "You remind me of a fairy pictured in one of my storybooks when I was a child. At least in appearance. I suspect that in all the ways that matter, you're very much a woman."

Aimee burst out laughing, missing his second comment. "I've been called many things, but a fairy isn't one of them."

His mouth quirked, and he used the tip of her braid to tickle her cheek. "By a man, I'll wager."

"You would definitely call my father a man," she agreed.

"Has trouble with you, does he?"

"So he says. Personally, I think he's the one who causes all the problems." She eased the braid out of his hand and inched away from him.

The quirk broadened into a grin. "Naturally. I take it

you're not committed to a young man, then."

Aimee wrinkled her nose distastefully. "No, and he won't let me forget it. He thinks women are constructed for two purposes: having babies and serving husbands."

His eyes sparked into that strange expression that made her tingle. "And it goes without saying, of course, that you don't agree."

"Of course." Uneasily, she watched him span the gap between them. Her vague sense of alarm returned.

He stepped so close she could feel the heat of his body. "Don't you think some lucky man might be able to change your mind, one day?" His voice was a soft, purring rasp across her nerves.

She eased farther away, retorting, "No, I don't. All men care about is having someone to take care of them and accede to their every demand." Wariness descended on her full force as he shook his head and stalked her steps.

"You do men an injustice, pretty lady. We don't all want timid little doves. Some of us admire women with spirit. . . ." His voice trailed off, but the expression in the gaze caressing her mouth reverberated with meaning.

Aimee's eyes widened as she struggled against the spell he cast. Inexperienced though she was, she recognized the attraction he felt toward her. She also understood why he made her so uneasy. She sensed that his urge to dominate was as primitively masculine as her urge to rebel against his arrogance was feminine. He wouldn't be content with less than total, absolute possession. She pitied any woman he chose for his own, she told herself. But even as she commanded her feet to move away, she was riveted by the fascination of his approaching mouth. So full, it was, so mobile and seductively male . . .

This time, when he spoke, his lips brushed her ear. She quivered as he coaxed, "Please, tell me where you live. I want to get to know you better."

Aimee watched helplessly as that mouth came closer, and closer. Before his lips brushed hers, they opened. His strong white teeth grew into fangs, glistening as they bared to crush her will. The vivid imagery snapped the bonds that held her. She whirled to flee, but the knapsack knocked into her leg and tripped her. He flung out his arm to catch her. They were both off balance, and crashed to the ground, Aimee landing on top of the stranger.

For a moment, startled gold eyes stared into widening black ones, then she shoved angrily at his shoulders with small fists. "Let me go!" she demanded, squirming until he seemed less and less inclined to comply.

Instead, he whirled them about until their positions were reversed. Pinioning her arms above her head, he surveyed the fascinating little face that again shone with life. That killing smile hovered on his mouth, but this time, anger gave her immunity to his charm.

"I saved you from a nasty fall, and this is the thanks I get?" he chided teasingly.

Her mouth dropped open at his audacity. How dare he blame her when he had been the one to pull her down? When she searched for blistering words, his eyes lowered to her white throat. As though compelled, he lowered his mouth to the sweet, throbbing hollow that seemed to beckon. Aimee felt his heart begin to pound as heavily as her own. Humiliation and alarm mingled in her confused mind, but then all was swamped under a wave of fury. She went limp.

He grinned against her velvety skin when her struggles ceased. Trailing a path of kisses to her pointed little chin, he drew back to smile at her, giving her room to squirm away and leap to her feet. She rubbed the spot at her throat where she could still feel a tingle, her mouth trembling in outrage.

"What gall! Are you in the habit of forcing yourself on defenseless women?"

He rose gracefully, onyx eyes caressing the flush in her cheeks. "Defenseless? You? The wild-animal doctor?" He threw back his head and laughed.

The sound set her teeth on edge. She propped her hands on her hips to still her urge to slap him. "That lynx is harmless compared to you. At least she attacks only in self-defense or for subsistence." She raked a scathing look over him. "You obviously know little of mercy or kindness."

He snatched her wrist and pulled her close to him. "Do you need mercy or kindness, woman-child? Something tells me you'd never be satisfied with that from a man. . . ." His voice trailed away suggestively.

Aimee swallowed at his sweeping examination, but she refused to let him see her nervousness. Outwardly, she defied him; inwardly she wondered how she could have dropped her guard, even momentarily. His very appearance of granite, chin and straight indomitable spine, warned of a man who would master every challenge. Loss was not a word in his vocabulary; he would wring triumph out of defeat if he had to mold circumstances to fit his cause. Here was a man who would win, no matter what the cost to himself or his opponent.

Aimee squelched any sense of admiration. She was no conquest to be won. She would fight the devil himself if he tried to bend her to his will. And she had never met a man who reminded her more of a seductive devil. . . .

As they stared at one another, the man and the girl, it seemed the heavens themselves darkened with the portent of things to come. Black clouds brooded and frowned as if in disapproval of the two contrary mortals below. Lightning flickered on each stiff face like a warning from Thor, but the humans knew nothing of his anger. They were aware only of each other.

Black eyes challenged green, but neither figure wavered in determination; he, to master, she, to defy. The air resounded with Thor's fury as jet eyes coaxed, "Stay with me, let me hold you and protect you." Sea-foam eyes blinked an absolute refusal. "Leave me alone, I want nothing of you."

She tried to pull away, but he tightened his grip and purred, "No, little sprite, you can't run from yourself. You need much more than kindness from a man. You're destined for passion. . . ."

"And you're destined for worse if you don't release me immediately!" she spat, infuriated. No decent Norwegian man would speak to an unmarried girl so familiarly.

He arched an eyebrow and intertwined their hands to inspect the vast difference in size. "Really? Now that would be interesting indeed. You can barely reach my chin. Shall I bend down?" He did so, and his eyes locked with hers in a mocking challenge.

He obviously didn't believe she'd dare strike him. The arrogant beast! Aimee wondered if his advances had ever been rejected before. If not, it was time they were. . . . Blood boiling, Aimee doubled up her free hand and knocked the smirk from his mouth. Simultaneously, she jammed her foot over his instep.

He grunted in surprise. His grip went lax. She darted away like the fairy he called her, leaped into her carriage and lashed her pony into a gallop, her blond braid flying in counterpart to the pony's tail.

Had she seen the stranger's reaction, Aimee would have been even angrier. He rubbed his tingling mouth, his eyes sparkling—but not with rage. What a girl, he marveled to himself. Fire, intelligence, compassion, prettiness all in one lovely little package. Intrigued, he moved to mount his horse and follow, only to realize he hadn't taken time to tie down Polaris in his haste to save the girl. Polaris was gone. The thought made him laugh out loud. Save her, ha! *He* needed protection from *her*.

Horse fetched, Luke Garrison mounted, determined to pursue her. In all his twenty-eight years, no woman had rejected him. He'd seen a gamut of emotions in his various female companions: cajolery, flirtation, coyness and flattery as they tried to win him, then anger, pride and vindictiveness as, bored, he eased them out of his life. Never, not once, had a single one of those women failed to be enraptured by his charm or seduced by his wealth. And strangely, never, not once, had he so longed to charm a woman.

He was reining his stallion to follow and make her tell him who she was before he came to his senses. For the first time since seeing her dancing in the glade, remembrance returned to him like a rap on the head. He was committed elsewhere. He had no right to force himself on an innocent who disdained him. Luke tried to visualize his stepmother's reaction if he brought such a girl home instead of the docile, proper young lady she was looking forward to dominating. His mouth took a wry twist as he turned Polaris toward Bergen. Raindrops hurled like recriminations on Luke's head as he reluctantly traveled back to his ship.

His word had been given, and he would keep it, no matter how much his instincts urged him to do otherwise. Their verbal fencing had stimulated his mind as much as her look and smell stimulated his body. He found most women boring intellectually, but she had seemed as charming inwardly as she most certainly was outwardly. Duty, honor, loyalty had become elusive as dust motes swirling in the brilliance of her appeal. Even after one meeting, he suspected she matched him in will and pride. What a challenge it would have been to win her.

But it wasn't to be, so he'd best put her out of his mind. In the end, he told himself, she probably would have bored him like all the rest. Urging Polaris into a trot, he decided to spend his last nights of freedom between the warm, willing thighs of an undemanding wench if he had to search every dockside tavern to find one. And he'd look for a plump, dark-haired *frøken* who smiled and lifted her skirts with equal facility, he resolved firmly. However, as he hastened toward the docks, it was a very different image that filled his mind.

Aimee, flushed with anger, was pacing up and down when Sigrid joined her in their bedroom. Sigrid went to their dresser to straighten her neat topknot in preparation for luncheon, but she was distracted by her sister's restless strides. It was unusual for Aimee to be so flustered. Her blue eyes widened with curiosity. Usually it was she who was emotional, Aimee who logically suggested a way out of her dilemma.

Sigrid turned to face her. "What on earth is the matter, sister?"

Aimee's rosy flush bloomed crimson. "Nothing, Sigrid," she muttered. She went to the window seat, sat down and folded her arms about her upraised knees. Sigrid sat down beside her.

"*Kom, søster,* I know I've been distracted lately, but I can still see something is troubling you. I burden you with all my problems, so now it's your turn. Did something happen to you today in the hills?"

Gnawing at her lip, Aimee nodded. "Yes, I met a man. . . ." She turned her head away, but Sigrid caught the fire in her eyes.

Sigrid's eyes narrowed with interest. A man! It was high time! Sigrid thought it unhealthy that Aimee took no interest in the young men who called on her, for she was more conservative than her rebellious young sister. Aimee was friendly enough, but there were invisible barriers around her that only Gere had been able to breach. At the thought of Gere, a knife twisted in Sigrid's stomach, but she took a deep breath and forced herself to concentrate on Aimee. For once, their roles were reversed. She could be comforter and advisor now in small recompense for all Aimee's support of her.

She probed cautiously. "Yes, what happened?" And, with sudden alarm, she exclaimed, "You weren't attacked, were you?"

Aimee's mouth tightened in memory. "Yes, but not in the

way you mean. A man . . . kissed me. He tripped me, too, but caught me as I fell. But that's not why I'm angry." She put a betraying hand to her throat.

"You mean he kissed your throat, not your lips? And then he let you go?" At Aimee's jerky nod, Sigrid almost smiled. Sigrid had always been a little awed by Aimee's aggressive, bright intellect, but there was one subject about which she knew more than Aimee—men. Sigrid also knew better than to voice her thought: a kiss on the mouth could mean many things, and not all of them indicated physical attraction; a kiss on the throat meant the stranger must have liked the look and feel of her. Aimee's reaction was just as telling. The rosy flush and refusal to lift her eyes meant Aimee was prey to many more emotions than anger. Sigrid was so delighted she couldn't resist teasing her sister.

"Just think, *kjaer,* you've had your adventure! Wasn't it exciting to be desired by a man? I'll bet he was as handsome as he was masterful," Sigrid teased.

Aimee glared at her, but the memory of the sailor's heavy length crushing her into the grass was still too vivid for her to appreciate Sigrid's humor. "I did not mean I wanted to be assaulted by a . . . devil of a foreigner, either, as you well know."

"He couldn't have been too much of a devil or he wouldn't have released you. But why are you so angry, then?"

"Because he dared to criticize me and to force his attentions on me even after I made it clear I wasn't interested."

Sigrid smiled wryly. "He sounds like a man like any other, Aimee."

Unable to dispute the point, Aimee took to pacing again in an effort to steady her nerves. She muttered as she walked, "But he was so exasperating. He was enormous, even taller than Gere, and he's so dark he must be Spanish or Italian. He was certainly more arrogant than any man I've ever met." As she remembered his gall in blaming her for stumbling, her dark brows slanted together in a frown.

"You've wished you could meet a man like one of the characters in the Dumas novels you love so much, and now you have, all you do is complain. You wanted gallantry, and you found it—did he not save you from a fall? You wanted passion and daring, and he certainly seems to possess both of those attributes in abundance." Sigrid was exasperated at her sister's refusal to appreciate what sounded like a very attractive man. Would she never cast off her ridiculous notions of being an equal, rather than a helpmate, as God intended?

Stung, Aimee shot her sister a reproachful glance. She clasped her elbows and retorted, "If he's an example of such a man, then no thank you. I'll keep my illusions as they are."

Shaking her head in despair, Sigrid rose to finish straightening her hair. Why must Aimee be so stubborn? If only she would try to conform more, maybe *Far* wouldn't be so set on this marriage, for then he would have two daughters to marry into good families. Sigrid bit her lip in self-reproach. She must try to understand Aimee's feelings instead of brooding constantly about Gere. But try as she might, Sigrid could not understand Aimee's need for independence. It seemed natural to her that women should be dependent on the men they loved. Sigrid trusted Gere with her very life, and she pitied Aimee a little that she would never know that same comforting sense of protection and belonging. At least she wouldn't if she continued to evade all the young men who admired her. . . .

Aimee, in her turn, worried about Sigrid. She wondered if the American would be anything like the stranger in the hills, and she shivered with fear for her sister at the mere thought. The sweet, gentle Sigrid would be crushed by the will of such a man. Sigrid needed someone both strong and gentle, someone kind and patient. Someone like Gere, Aimee thought wistfully. Sigrid needed a man who would not speak harshly to her, for Sigrid cringed from all conflict. And life with a man such as the stranger would be nothing but conflict. She could maintain her identity in such an atmosphere; Sigrid could not.

Then marry the American yourself, her conscience suggested slyly, but Aimee silenced it. Instead, she reflected on how odd it was that she, the sister who had borne such physical hardship at an early age, was the most determined. Perhaps her physical disadvantage had forced her to conquer challenges Sigrid had never faced. That early bout with rheumatic fever had left her with a weakened leg that made it hard for her to participate in normal childhood activities. She refused to be deterred, however. When the children went skating, Aimee tagged along, skating awkwardly, falling often, pulling herself to her feet to try again and again until she at last achieved an odd rhythm.

When her parents forbade her to learn to ride, she ignored

them and practiced secretly. She scoffed at their worries and spent many happy hours in the hills alone. Aimee knew now that her wanderings had strengthened her leg until it was as strong as her good one. Was it those same wanderings that had blessed—or cursed—her with a will her father called as unyielding as any man's and a bone-deep need for independence? Aimee didn't know, but, in an odd way, she was glad of those early years of pain. They had taught her much about life.

As long as she could remember, she had been the confidante of her sister and friends. She was trusted to keep a confidence, listen closely and objectively, and offer advice when she could. Consequently, she was sought after by the other children, and, as she grew older, Sigrid told her all the young men were drawn by her intuitive understanding of human nature. She seemed so much more mature than the other girls, they said. Aimee was warmed by their respect, but more determined than ever to be friendly, though cloaked in reserve. She had no intention of encouraging any of the young men she genuinely liked into a relationship she could never fulfill.

It was ironic, Aimee thought, that the same qualities lauded in her as a child were now causing her parents such consternation: respect for the individual, emotional strength, independence, compassion for others. She couldn't put her destiny in the hands of a man who could not share what she treasured. None of the young men of Bergen, nice as they were, understood her values. If she bowed to Ragnar's demands and married one of them, she'd make him and herself miserable. Were all men like that? Even the man she'd met today had admired her spirit only as long as she didn't use it to defy him.

Aimee rubbed her leg. It never bothered her anymore, so why must it choose today, of all days, to give way? If only she hadn't stumbled, the stranger wouldn't have caught her. He wouldn't have held her arms above her head . . . Aimee rejected the memory violently. Oddly, though she'd seldom been kissed before, and never by force, she felt less anger at the stranger's physical trespass than at his arrogance. She didn't pause to wonder why she hadn't found his touch distasteful. She only knew she was relieved at the knowledge that she'd never have to see him again.

Aimee walked to the mirror to examine her wind-swept

appearance. Examining her image of disarray, she realized she should change her damp clothes before luncheon, but she hadn't the energy, and they were almost dry. The blast of her father's anger at her earlier impudence would dry them fast enough anyway, she thought humorously.

Aimee touched her sister's shoulder lovingly, worried by Sigrid's brooding look. "Come, *søster,* let's eat lunch and put our problems in perspective. A full stomach can make the head think more clearly, *ja?*"

Sigrid shook herself a little and smiled into Aimee's warm eyes. *"Ja,"* she agreed with calm Norwegian practicality, "let us eat. Hunger always makes the world seem darker." The two sisters hooked arms and walked down the stairs.

Their maid Marthe was just serving the soup when they entered the dining room. After one sour look, Ragnar didn't react to Aimee's straggly braid, wrinkled skirt and smudged blouse. Ingrid, their mother, was not so forbearing.

"Datter, if you must roam the countryside, against our wishes as we have repeatedly told you, then you will at least sit at the table like a lady. Go at once to your room and change."

Aimee flushed, but rose to comply. To her astonishment, Ragnar waved her back into her chair with a meaningful look at his wife.

"Today is a day for celebration, Ingrid. Let the child alone." And he beamed at his daughters. Ingrid sighed, but a smile lit her fine-boned face as she let the matter drop.

Aimee plopped back into her chair, surprised by her mother. She was seldom so understanding. And Aimee had expected a chastising from her father for her earlier rudeness, but he seemed to have forgotten the incident. What was going on?

Ingrid's appearance was as neat as usual. The rich golden hair she'd bequeathed to Sigrid coiled in symmetrical braids atop her head. Her beige linen dress with the white collar was one of her best. Only a careful eye would have noticed the neat patch at her elbow.

It was the suppressed air of nervous excitement emanating from the assured Ragnar, however, that made both girls stiffen. Their eyes met as their thoughts meshed in the communion their parents could never understand.

"He's here!" flashed Aimee.

"Dear God, what will I do?" returned Sigrid. Then, with mutual dread, their eyes returned to their mother.

"Eat, children." When the girls picked up their spoons, Ingrid looked inquiringly at her husband. He nodded and cleared his throat.

There was not a sound at the sturdy oak table when Ragnar voiced the expected news. "Your betrothed has arrived from America, Sigrid. He lunches with us tomorrow."

Both girls had braced themselves, but the news still shocked them. Paled and subdued, Sigrid applied herself to her soup, and Aimee sensed her misery. Aimee gripped her spoon to keep herself from flinging it at her father.

Her parents were so accustomed to her refusal to conform that they had long since given up trying to mold her into the proper Norwegian girl. Sigrid, however, was not even allowed to choose the man she wanted to wed. Perhaps because one of their daughters was so recalcitrant, they expected the other to give them blind obedience.

Aimee hung her head in shame and vowed to do anything she could to help Sigrid escape this soulless alliance so that she could wed Gere. A sigh escaped her lips. She started guiltily when her mother spoke to her.

"And what mission of mercy did you perform today, Aimee?" Her mother's voice was dry, but Aimee heard the subtle reproach in it. Ingrid nodded at Marthe as the main course was placed in front of her.

"I found a lynx caught in a trap and released her," she admitted, swallowing. She waited wearily for her mother's explosion.

Ingrid became flushed and reprimanded her daughter, "Aimee, why must you shame me so? You know the trappers' wives have been complaining about you. Sometimes I think you deliberately do all you can to humiliate me. When will you take your proper place instead of wandering about the hills like a wild thing?" Ingrid took an exasperated bite of her crisp, flat *grøvborod*.

Aimee glanced at her father to see his reaction. When she glimpsed his reproach, she dropped her eyes. It troubled Aimee to disappoint her mother, but her throat ached with regret at the confused pain she found in her father's eyes. Was she always to be a burden to him, someone to worry about, instead of someone to rejoice in? She wished passionately she could do something to redeem herself in his eyes; something that would prove her to be a responsible and mature woman instead of the willful child he believed her still to be.

"*Far*," she began hesitantly, "won't you please let me take over the books? I know things are getting difficult in the business, and I want to do anything I can to help. I've proved myself capable by now, surely."

Ragnar pursed his mouth in disapproval. "I regret giving in to your wheedling. You are competent, yes, but such occupation is not proper for a young, unmarried woman. If you truly want to help, you'll make an advantageous marriage." He looked at her challengingly.

Aimee wanted to scream with frustration. She took a measured bite of potato, chewing slowly to calm herself. When she answered, her voice was cool and even. "That is out of the question, and it serves nothing to argue again about the subject. It is Sigrid's future we're concerned with, not mine. Is there truly no other way to get the capital you need, *Far*? Can't you merge the business with a Norwegian or Swedish shipping company that doesn't require a marriage? Wouldn't that be even more profitable? Surely you wouldn't lose as much control over decisions that way, and then Sigrid would be free to marry Gere."

Ragnar looked as irritated as she had expected. "Swedish and Norwegian shipping companies know little more about steam than I do. The capital investment is too great. Besides, what motivation would they have to join with me? If we go under, it's less competition for them. No, this is the only way. It's a marvelous opportunity, both for our business and for Sigrid. She'll be a member of one of the most influential families in America. Instead of . . ." He trailed off and took a bite of herring, but Aimee and Sigrid both heard his unspoken disdain of Gere. Sigrid bit her lip and looked down, troubled, as always, by her father's disapproval of Gere.

Aimee clenched her hands to hold on to her temper. "The Garrisons might be wealthy, but they must have problems of their own. If their son is so eligible, why must they go halfway around the world to find a bride for him?"

Ragnar choked and looked at her under his creased brows. "Their reasons are none of your concern, miss. . . ."

Aimee pounced on the words. "So they have a reason, then? What is it?"

Ingrid twisted her napkin between her hands. Her laugh sounded false to Aimee's ears. "Why, they consider Sigrid perfect for their son. The Garrisons have less to gain from this match than do we, and it's only because of the family ties and the marriage that they even consider assisting in our conversion to steam. When the two companies merge, your father will run and retain most of the control of the Norwegian branch. They will obtain a small fleet of wooden ships, the connections to open a passenger line between Norway and America, which I understand they have been wanting to do. They also get a beautiful daughter-in-law."

When Aimee cast her mother a skeptical glance, Ingrid snapped, "Yes, there are other reasons. Hedda Garrison was betrayed by her former husband, Samuel Mayhew. . . ."

Ragnar interrupted, "Enough, Ingrid. The story is not fit for their ears."

Aimee folded her elbows on the table and leaned forward. "We're not innocents any longer," she scoffed. "And if the Garrisons are not even fit to talk about, why are they fit to marry?"

Ragnar's jaw clenched as he searched for ways to repudiate his daughter's words. "They were victims, not perpetrators, and the story is very ugly, even to someone as mature and knowledgeable as yourself." His sarcastic emphasis on the latter part of his sentence made Aimee flush with anger.

She retorted, "We know more than you credit us with, no thanks to you. . . ."

Ragnar slammed his fist down. "Quiet! I'll have no more arguments about this. Why can't you understand how much our whole family will gain by this alliance? We get not only the means and know-how to convert to steam, a large flow of capital we sadly need and a strong, intelligent son-in-law, but, most important, our grandson will one day inherit everything."

"That only makes it even more strange. Since they have so little to gain, why have they selected a small, ailing Norwegian line to bestow their munificence upon?"

When Ragnar merely scowled, Aimee insisted, "We have a right to know. You can't expect Sigrid to give up Gere without even knowing why."

Ragnar shifted in his seat, unable to deny the truth of her words. "It is not my story to tell. Sigrid will learn the truth from her husband when he sees fit to tell her. All I can say is that it is a private affair involving Hedda and the Mayhews that . . . influenced her decision to unite with us."

Sigrid paled even more at the hint of mystery. Aimee clasped her hand nearby and leaned to whisper, pleadingly, "Sigrid, why don't you say something? Are you going to let them separate you from Gere?"

But Sigrid looked defeated. "What else can I do? *Mor og Far* would never forgive me if I ran away with Gere now. Besides, how could I be happy with him knowing I'd betrayed my parents?"

Aimee looked at her sister tenderly and squeezed her hand. How thoughtful she was. She knew nothing of subterfuge or cruelty. She'd be a lamb among wolves in the Garrisons' world. Aimee had to find a way to break up this marriage! "Don't worry, Sigrid, I'll find some way to get you out of this," she encouraged softly.

Aimee leaned back in her chair and fixed her father with a cool, unflinching stare. "I think you're being both callous and unreasonable. You've never even met the Garrisons, yet you approve of them over a man who has proved himself kind and reliable. For all we know, Luke Garrison could be a defiler of innocents. . . ."

Ingrid and Sigrid gasped in shock. Ragnar leaped to his feet and roared, "Enough! I'll have no daughter of mine speak so indelicately. You shouldn't even be aware of such things, much less voice them. Leave the table. Go to your room and consider your manners. . . ." But he spoke to an empty chair. Aimee had already gone, though not to her room. The front door slammed with enough force to rattle the knob.

Ragnar slumped back into his chair and clasped his head in his hands. "What are we to do with that girl?" he asked his wife wearily.

The answer came from an unexpected quarter. For once, the gentle Sigrid's voice was harsh. "She's only trying to help me. Is that wrong?"

Ragnar looked at her in astonishment. "And what do you think I'm trying to do? I love you, and I want you to be well-provided for. I don't want either of you to have to struggle as your mother and I have. Why can't you and Aimee see that?"

Sigrid's reply was barely audible. "Perhaps because we both think other things are more important than material comforts. Aimee understands how much I love Gere. You don't. I guess there's nothing else I can do but try to understand that you'll never accept him, now."

Sigrid rose to leave the room, but she turned at the door, her curvaceous figure taut with control. "I will marry Luke Garrison, but I do so only because I could not bear to marry Gere without your approval. I know you'd never forgive me. I hope I can eventually find it in my power to forgive *you* for separating me from Gere. . . ." The sentence trailed off into the shocked silence. Ragnar and Ingrid looked at one another uneasily. Could it be she truly loved the penniless young man?

Sigrid mounted the stairs like an old woman, her steps dragging and weary, leaving a pregnant silence behind her. Her face felt numb. Her lip bled where she had bitten into it, and she felt a great, yawning chasm where her heart continued to beat.

As the door to her room closed behind her, a gentle whisper echoed in the corridor. "Good-bye, my Gere. *Farvel,* my love."

Out above Bergen, in the gently sloping hills, Aimee walked, trying to calm herself, to no avail. Her parents would never accept Gere. They were set on this marriage and nothing short of a scandal would change their minds. Why must they be so rigid in their ideas? They acted as though she and Sigrid should believe babies came from cabbage patches. What did they think girls whispered about, their latest sewing projects?

Many a night she and Sigrid had stayed up late talking about how Gere's kisses excited Sigrid. Gere was always careful never to overstep the bounds of propriety and never pressed beyond their sweet embraces. Aimee had tried to talk to her mother once, about intimate relations with the opposite sex, but Ingrid shushed her and told her such a subject was improper. Their strict Lutheran upbringing occasionally frustrated both girls.

Much as she loved Norway, sometimes Aimee longed to escape its social restrictions. Why couldn't she be accepted as she was instead of urged to fit the demure role her parents believed was natural? She had long ago accepted the fact that the qualities she considered her best merely confused her parents. Her compassion for animals was unhealthy; her longing for knowledge, inappropriate in a girl; her yearning to visit other lands, see other peoples, was foolish; and above all, her refusal to encourage suitors was willful. She sometimes thought she was nothing to her mother but a constant reminder of her failure in conceiving such a rebel.

Her father loved her unconditionally, but he didn't understand her, either. It hurt that he patted her on the head and smiled indulgently if she revealed her intellect to him. She was a sweet child who shouldn't trouble her head about such matters as astronomy, history and mathematics. Someday, she'd marry and find true happiness, appropriate for her as a member of the female species.

Why couldn't he respect her intelligence and right to decide her own future? She longed to win his respect and love, not as his daughter, but as a person worthy of admiration, as strong in her way as he was strong in his.

Gere respected her for what she was . . . Gere. Aimee didn't have to close her eyes to picture the young officer. Hair of an even brighter gold than Sigrid's, eyes just as blue, but manly as a young Viking warrior. He was always laughing, always eager to live life to the fullest, always kind, but never judgmental.

It was Gere who had schooled her in the art of riding. It was Gere who smuggled her the novels and books her parents forbid her to read. It was Gere who stayed up all night and helped her minister to the sick baby deer that had wandered into their pasture. He was the only man she would ever. . . .

Aimee sighed and slumped to the ground, weary of the endless cycle of thoughts. Sigrid must never know how, despite her efforts to stifle her feelings, she longed to have Gere watch her with the same glimmer that he cast on Sigrid. Besides, even if Sigrid did marry the American, Aimee knew Gere would never consider her more than a dear sister.

For a long time, Aimee sat, quiet, thoughtful and anguished, but as she remembered all she owed to Sigrid and Gere, her resilient spirits bounced back. Sigrid and Gere were perfect for one another, and if any two people deserved happiness, they did. How were they to rid themselves of the very large obstacle that prevented it, in the person of the wealthy American? Aimee frowned, pondered and brooded until her head ached. Finally, slowly, she smiled, her face aglow with the vivacity the foreigner had found so mesmerizing. Humming softly, Aimee headed for home.

Chapter Two

SUNLIGHT STREAMED THROUGH the porthole, flooding the jumbled bed and its rumpled occupants in a merciless pool of light. One of the figures stirred, wincing at the rays that immersed him in liquid fire. Luke Garrison tried to turn over, but, strangely, he couldn't move. Groggily, he swallowed the lump of foul-tasting cotton in his mouth, but gagged and realized he had just attempted to ingest his own tongue. Again, he tried to move, but he was pinned down by something—a plump, smooth thigh? Startled, he felt under the covers to explore the find, then grunted as the memory of last night burst into his aching brain.

After that fiery encounter in the hills, he had come back to the *Mercury* in a surly mood, less resolved to his marriage commitment than ever. He snapped at his crewmen for a good two hours before his simmering temper cooled. Then, disgusted and eager to get things over with, he quickly dispatched a note to the family of his fiancée letting them know he would call tomorrow. The die cast, he ignored his feeling of impending doom and accepted his first mate's invitation to go ashore and taste the strong Norwegian ale.

He lost count of the number of tankards he drank. Somewhere past six, but with his loss of memory, a welcome relaxing of inhibitions washed over him. He vaguely remembered confiding his encounter with the girl to the crew. How they had roared at his discomfiture!

"Lusty Luke let one get away, eh?" cried Jimmy, the mate

and a veteran of many voyages with Luke. He felt comfortable using the sobriquet the captain's men had given him.

Luke flashed him a shriveling stare, but since his eyes were hazed with drink, he looked like a ruffled, slightly cross-eyed owl. "Never intended to take the wench. Obviously an innocent. But damn it, why was she so defiant?" He was more bothered by his inability to charm her than he would admit.

Potter, the engineer, opined, "Aw, cap'n, what's it matter? Virgins is more trouble than they's worth. Give me a gal who knows the score any day, right, buckos?"

There were rumbles of agreement and, encouraged, Potter continued, "Now see that wench over there? She's a likely armful if I ever saw one." He nudged his captain, sending Luke's sip of øl down the wrong pipe. Luke gagged and choked.

"Hell's bells, cap'n, don't you know how to drink?" Potter complained. He grew red at his own temerity, but Luke was too busy coughing to hear the remark.

Tears in his eyes, Luke's cough subsided. He wasn't so drunk he forgot to move down the bench away from Potter before taking another sip, however. He listened with half an ear as Potter rambled on.

"That pretty frøken is just what you need to lift your, er, spirits, eh, mates?" The other sailors chuckled at his sly wink, but when Luke just stared into his ale, Potter slapped his shoulder. The half-full tankard tilted in Luke's lax hand and dumped its contents into his lap.

Cursing, Luke slammed the tankard down on the table, missed, and hit his knee instead. Grunting in outrage, he tossed the tankard to the table and reeled to his feet, his breeches wet in a most embarrassing place. He settled his cap on his head, shrugged on his jacket and fixed his men with an angry stare. He was bewildered when, instead of appearing respectful, his crewmen stifled their grins. He had no way of knowing that, cap askew, jacket buttoned haphazardly and smelling like a brewery, he presented far from an intimidating appearance.

"Don't need my crew to procure my women for me. But you're right, what I want is a wench." He looked blearily around, spotted a voluptuous brunette barmaid and belatedly remembered his earlier resolve. Nodding his head in satisfaction, he moved toward her—and stumbled over a table leg to land his full length on the floor.

His men roared, then helped him to his feet and out the door. Potter, however, stopped and spoke to the brunette.

Remembering now, Luke gritted his teeth at the fool he must have made of himself. His crew would never let him forget. He should have known better than to drink so much ale. His system could absorb half a bottle of liquor with few effects, but ale and champagne yielded explosive results. At the time, avoiding thoughts of tomorrow and obliterating a certain image had seemed more important than maintaining his dignity, but now he was furious with himself. Shaking his head, he turned to stare at the disgruntled face of the brunette barmaid.

"Well?" she snapped, apparently waiting for something.

He stared at her stupidly. "Well, what?"

Muttering to herself, she hopped out of bed and pulled on her clothes. "For a man who looks like a stallion, you act like a gelding," she said mockingly. Casting him a pitying look, she stalked to the door and slammed it behind her.

Luke winced at the bang. He was tempted to pull the covers over his head and hide, but as her meaning penetrated his befuddled brain, he jackknifed to a sitting position. He was so mortified at the realization that he hadn't been able to perform that, this time, he barely noticed the pounding between his temples. Ignoring the pain, he cursed roundly, condemning the fairy in the hills. Then he maligned his parents and his unknown bride, and then, for good measure, he swore at Potter most loudly of all. Feeling only slightly better, he eased out of his large bed.

Thus, as he held Polaris to a steady walk on his way to the Lingstrom house several hours later, his mood was black. He would have gladly traded the *Mercury* for the freedom to turn around, go back to Bergen and sail away to any destiny other than that of husband to a giggling, insipid Norwegian girl. Only the deep love he felt for his parents, the honor his father had embedded in him since babyhood and his desire to best Jeremy Mayhew gave him the will to go on.

Eyes slitted with hostility, he glared at the neatly fenced fields and orchards as if the beautiful countryside was the source of all his problems. Damn Hedda anyway, and damn her obsession with securing an heir to the family empire. After her mistake in mixing her blood with Mayhew's and producing a son like Jeremy, she was determined her adopted children—Joshua's children—should wed into untainted families. And what better way of securing a noble bloodline than by arranging a marriage with her own remote but "blueblood" relatives?

Luke had laughed at her idea. But since it made life easier not to thwart her, he had not vetoed her plan. He also half-suspected the Lingstroms would not sell their daughter to a man they'd never seen. By the time he found out he was wrong, it was too late. Even his father was enamored of the idea by then.

The talk that had capped the decision would always be branded in his memory. He and Joshua had been having their usual after-dinner brandy when Joshua broached the subject. "It's high time you quit tomcatting about and settled down, boy. Sooner or later one of your gals will turn up pregnant and you'll have to pay support for the rest of your life. I don't want any bastards running around my neighborhood. Time you spent a few of those energies in the marriage bed and produced a son. Hedda and I aren't getting any younger. We want to enjoy our grandchildren before we're too old to get about."

Luke had snorted. "Try another approach, Father. I can't imagine anyone less deserving of pity than you and Hedda. Old indeed!" And he calmly circled the brandy in his snifter held between two large, tanned hands.

Joshua slammed his glass down on the Duncan Phyfe table beside his leather, high-backed chair. "Dammit, boy, I'm through asking. If it's left up to you, you'll never marry. I can think of half a dozen fillies who would have made fine additions to the family, yet you were bored with them after only a few weeks. What's the matter with you? I never would have believed any son of mine could be so flighty."

Luke could not meet the steady, black-eyed gaze that mirrored his own. He dropped his eyes, and remained quiet at first. How could he explain something he didn't understand himself? From the time he lost his virginity at fifteen to the seductive wife of one of his father's business associates, he had gone from conquest to conquest much like some of New York's debutantes flitted from flirtation to flirtation. He had enjoyed each relationship with lusty enthusiasm while it lasted, but invariably his interest in each woman waned.

Was it because he'd never found a woman strong, beautiful, intelligent and independent, like Hedda? She had been a wonderful stepmother for a lonely little boy, even in the bleak days when society spurned her because of the illicit liaison with Luke's father. Or perhaps his conquests had always been too easy. The women who hadn't been enchanted with his physical attributes, or his aggressive but charming personality, had been seduced by the hope of winning his love, and thus his fortune.

Shaking his head, Luke admitted, "I honestly don't know why I've never loved a woman, Father. Perhaps it's simply not in me to feel so deeply."

Joshua's eyes were dark as he studied his son's bent head, but he was still ruthless enough to take advantage of the moment. "If that's the case, then you should have no objection to making Hedda and me happy then, hmm?" he pounced.

Luke's head snapped up to glare. Joshua returned a bland smile. Poker-faced, Joshua used his last ace. "I heard something at the docks today you may find interesting."

The lack of emotion in his father's face alerted Luke, and he braced himself. Only when Joshua was scheming for advantage did his face become expressionless.

"It seems Jeremy Mayhew is going to try to save his fortunes by doing something that's never been done before. Did you know he plans to open a passenger line between Norway and America? Then, if it's successful, he'll expand the line to other Scandinavian countries. It's risky, but could be quite lucrative, what with the amount of immigration coming from these countries."

Joshua calmly filled his pipe, tamped the tobacco down with his index finger and lit it, ignoring his son's reddening face. "No doubt this venture will save him, unless, of course, someone else should beat him to it. Someone with better connections, shall we say?" Joshua's teeth clamped down on his pipe to hide his smile at Luke's low curse.

Luke sprang up to his feet. "You bastard!" he growled. "You're determined to win if you have to blackmail me to do it. Guilt didn't work, so now you've come up with your best card. You know I'll do almost anything to thwart Mayhew. You old fox!"

Joshua blew a wreath of smoke, watched it rise, then observed his son, whose tirade left him unperturbed. He had won, and he knew better than to press the issue.

Luke collapsed into his chair, shaking with mirthless

laughter. "I agree," he droned, his voice weary but rancor-less. "But if this marriage—no, this *alliance*—doesn't work, then let it be on your head." He stomped out of the study without another glance at his triumphant sire.

That moment of weakness had led him to Bergen. He crossed his hands on his saddle pommel and studied an attractive, large and white-painted frame house. Green, carved trim lined the peaked roofline and window ledges. A handsome, ornamental gate with slatted, swinging doors seemed to stand in welcome near the roadway. The gate had its own little shingled roof with lifelike farm animals carved across the top.

He dismounted and tied Polaris to a tree on the side of the house. He straightened his shoulders under his elegant, tailed blue jacket, dusted off his matching linen waistcoat, straight-ened his narrow tie and smoothed the tan breeches that tapered down each leg. Deciding he was as ready as he would ever be, he strode through the gate with his usual confident air and banged the reindeer head door knocker.

A maid answered the door. He entered a wide foyer with a worn but valuable oriental carpet covering the floor. A narrow staircase rose to the upper stories; doors exited off the hallway on each side.

After one startled, wide-eyed look at his tall dark good looks, the maid ushered him through a left doorway. There, he found his host and hostess awaiting him in a large, sunny parlor. Heavy empire-style furniture, old but comfortable, lined the room. A huge rolltop desk crouched between the bookcases near the window. The green damask-covered couch and chairs looked slightly frayed and the gold drapes at the window were beginning to fade. But the wooden floors gleamed with polish and scattered bowls of flowers gave the room a cheery, welcoming atmosphere.

The Lingstroms rose, Ragnar advancing with hand out-stretched. *"Velkommen,"* he boomed heartily. "We are glad to meet you at last." After they shook hands, he introduced Ingrid.

"God dag," she nodded, her small body stiff with a tension Luke didn't understand.

"And how is dear Hedda?" Ragnar asked jovially. A little too jovially, Luke decided. Something strange was amiss. Where was the girl?

They conversed about his voyage, the hopes of success for

the opening of the line, his family, and even the weather, but all the time Luke was conscious of the nervous shifting of Mrs. Lingstrom. She grew more tense with each tick of the mantle clock. Perhaps the girl didn't want to wed either and had fled, Luke speculated with a sudden surge of hope. Just as he searched for a polite way to ask, the front door slammed.

He heard feminine voices arguing, low but fiercely. The eruption was in the hallway. With a sickly smile, Ingrid excused herself. Then when an apologetic look creased Ragnar's brow and he followed suit, Luke's curiosity got the best of him. He strode toward the source of the commotion, then froze in the doorway. Shock flooded through him.

Two young women dressed in similar gray skirts and white blouses were now arguing with their parents instead of each other, but Luke paid little attention to the conversation. His eyes were riveted to the stunning features of the girl he had met near the fjord, though those features were now distorted by fury. She was the girl he was to wed? A thrill shivered through him.

Ingrid hissed to her, "How could you humiliate me so?" in Norwegian. "You knew he was to arrive this afternoon, yet you deliberately dawdled. . . ."

Ragnar glared even more fiercely at his daughter. "If you've ignored my wishes, Aimee, I'll . . . ," he cried. He took a deep breath in an obvious attempt to stifle his fury, because of the stranger's appearance. But the effort failed. A tirade erupted again.

But Luke wasn't listening. His mind was besieged by his feelings. He told himself it was anger, but it felt perilously close to elation. He had never thought he would see the nymph again, so he had tried to put her from his mind, only to discover he was bound to her in the most intimate way. Now he would get his only half-admitted wish: a chance to break through that wall of hostility and make her as enamoured as all the others. Oh, what a challenge, what a glorious contest it would be.

Luke was so lost in his pleasurable visions of the future it took him a moment to realize his fiancée had noticed him. She had opened her mouth to retort when a flash of blue caught her eye. Turning her braided, wind-tossed silvery head to ferret out the source, her fiery eyes collided with his. He relished the change in her expression. Her cheeks, rosy with anger, blanched, her eyes went saucer wide and her small breasts rose as she gasped.

When he lifted an eyebrow suggestively and stared at her throat to goad her to remember their last encounter, she whirled away from him. The Lingstroms turned at her odd reaction. Varying degrees of dismay and embarrassment colored the other three faces.

Ingrid took each girl by the elbow and trooped them to the stairs. "We'll discuss this later. Dress quickly in your evening clothes and come back down." She gave them a small push, then turned back to Luke full of apologies.

"*Unnskylde dem,* my daughters had an errand to run and were a little late returning. We will eat as soon as they are dressed." Regaining her composure, she led the way back to the parlor. Luke wondered vaguely if all Norwegian women were so spirited. He smiled with anticipation at the thought. Ragnar sent a glower up the stairs before he, too, returned to the parlor.

Upstairs, Sigrid scolded, "Aimee, how could you do such a thing? It will be hard enough for me to resign myself to losing Gere without having him watching my every move as I get to know my fiancé." She tugged her new taffeta, the exact sky blue of her eyes, over her head.

Aimee shrugged unrepentently. "Even if you won't take steps to free yourself, I will. This seemed a good beginning."

Aimee turned away from her sister's accusing gaze, absently unbraided her hair and brushed the tangles out. The hairs on her neck were still stiff from encountering the dark stranger again. She swallowed, fearing anew what it would do to Sigrid to wed such a man. Now that she knew his identity, it was even more imperative to break up the engagement. Sigrid would be helpless against his dominant personality.

Strangely, the memory of his disturbing embrace flashed into Aimee's mind. Her hands stilled as, for a brief, traitorous moment, she wondered what it would be like to embrace that power and strength. A picture formed in her mind, born of a subconscious struggling against itself. This vision of herself locked in passion in the stranger's arms was but a remembrance of their earlier encounter, Aimee told herself. Gritting her teeth against the memory of his encircling arms, she went to the armoire and removed her gown.

Even in the privacy of her mind, she could not admit that the picture she saw little resembled the memory. The stranger was not kissing her neck, he was kissing her full on the mouth. And she was not struggling, she was clinging to him ardently. Worse, and more potently, she and the American were both naked.

Aimee still refused to think of him by name. Somehow assigning an identity to him made him too real. And more threatening. Vigorously, she shook her dress out to avoid asking herself why she should consider her sister's fiancé a threat.

Aimee dragged the dress over her head. It was a simple yellow muslin bordered at the high neck and sleeves with a white frill of lace. She was more glad than ever she'd ignored Sigrid's plea, and Ragnar's order, and had gone ahead and invited Gere to lunch. Yesterday, when she returned from her sojourn, she had ecstatically shared her idea with Sigrid. She had been stunned to find Sigrid opposed. Ragnar's antipathetic reaction had not surprised her.

When she informed him of her intent, he ordered flatly, "You are to do no such thing. This is our first actual meeting with any of the Garrisons, and Sigrid needs to make a good impression. Inviting her former suitor will hardly assist." He then marched from the room, smug in his belief he had gotten his daughter's acquiescence.

Aimee sniffed, unimpressed by his fatherly authority. "I want to make an impression on him, all right," she muttered darkly.

The next morning Aimee found her door locked, her father's way of showing he meant serious business. But she found it easy to lower herself from the ornamented lip framing their bedroom window and drop the remaining feet to the ground. When Sigrid brought her breakfast up and found her gone, she rushed to stop Aimee before she reached Gere's cabin.

Sigrid didn't take time to explain matters to her parents. She was anguished at the thought of meeting her fiancé under Gere's eyes, but she also wanted to keep peace in the family. However, Sigrid's efforts were for naught. She met Aimee returning from Gere's cabin. The girls argued so vehemently that they returned late.

Now, Aimee's heart pounded. She wondered vaguely who made her more nervous—her father or the American. Her jaw set stubbornly. No matter what anyone else said, she had done the right thing in inviting Gere. He would fight for

Sigrid, but, more important, Sigrid was never able to spend an evening in his company without showing her devotion. Aimee doubted that any man of such wealth and power as the American would want a bride who longed for another. And this man, in particular, was such a person. With a shiver, she recalled the aggression apparent in his every mannerism, including his swagger. Again she breathed thanks she was not his betrothed. And she would do all she could to ensure that Sigrid did not become that, either.

Sigrid gave up arguing with her oblivious sister and fixed her hair in an elaborate style. Curls dangled down her back from a high topknot on her head. When Aimee threaded her hair between her fingers to braid it in her usual manner, Sigrid's temper flared in a rare display.

"Enough! You've made us all late, so at least this once you can be presentable." Sigrid ignored her sister's reproachful look and shoved her down on the red velvet-cushioned stool in front of their dressing table. Her clever fingers tugged, twisted and poked, none too gently, but she ignored Aimee's squawks as she arranged the sea of silver waves in a complicated chignon.

When she was finished, even Aimee was startled. The sophisticated style made her look older, drawing attention to her slanted eyes and long, elegant neck. Twisting her head from side to side, Aimee felt armored and ready for the coming battle.

Aimee never saw the unusual appeal of her huge eyes, expressive, stubborn mouth and matte complexion, but Sigrid did, and she smiled with pride. Sigrid touched Aimee's cheek lovingly. She could never stay mad with her for long.

Aimee hugged her in return. *"Kom,* Sigrid, let us beard the lions. Together, we will save you for Gere."

The girls stepped carefully down the stairs, single file because of the unaccustomed fullness of their crinolines. At the door to the parlor they clasped hands briefly, for strength, then they entered the arena.

They found their father pouring their guest the last glass of Spanish sherry. Sigrid and Aimee smiled into space and moved toward a vacant couch, but Ragnar stopped them by beckoning to Sigrid.

"Sigrid, why don't you serve your fiancé?" He held out the crystal tumbler. After one furious glare, he ignored his younger daughter.

Luke examined each girl through hooded eyes. Aimee was definitely the more beautiful of the two, but there was a calm serenity about her that appealed to him far less than Sigrid's spirited willfulness. He smiled at Ragnar's suggestion, expecting Sigrid to balk at waiting on him. He was stunned to see the girl he thought was Aimee come obediently forward, take the glass and hand it to him with a shy smile before seating herself on the couch beside her sister.

Luke swallowed the lump in his throat and forced a smile to his stiff features. "Well, Sigrid, do you think you'll like living in America?" He tensed, waiting to see which girl would reply.

"Indeed, sir, I hope so," the real Sigrid responded. She wondered why the smile on Luke Garrison's face suddenly looked fixed. Her eyes wandered over him. Despite her despair, she couldn't help admiring him from a deep, feminine level. He was, after all, a very handsome man.

Aimee, too, was watching him, but the bold masculinity Sigrid found so appealing made her hands sweat. He was dark everywhere: hair, eyes, lashes and brows. Even his skin was tanned a shade never found in Norway because of the short summers. What made her heart flutter in her throat, however, was the aura of power that radiated from him. It emanated not from his looks, but from the bold spirit Aimee knew instinctively no woman had ever conquered.

The thick, sooty lashes should have softened his countenance, but somehow they enhanced the magnetism of his eyes. Each feature added up to a face that fairly shouted a wild challenge to any woman rash enough to pick up his gauntlet, "Try your wiles on me at your peril. Possess me for a while if you can, but hold me you never will." Aimee shifted restlessly under that dare, nerves tingling.

Neither Luke nor Aimee were aware of the tension they created as they stared at one another. They only knew it was time for each to take the other's measure, to test the adversary's mettle. Their silent clash of eyes wouldn't have been tenser if they'd brandished foils and challenged, *"En garde!"*

Luke tried to cow with the message, "I don't know how, but somehow, someday, you will belong to me."

With a defiant thrust of her pointed chin, Aimee silently retorted, "Never. Get out of our lives."

Sigrid looked from one to the other, frowning. What was

she witnessing? Aimee was wary as a doe poised for flight and Captain Garrison seemed coiled to spring on her at any moment. Sigrid's eyes ran over her betrothed, and, unbidden, Aimee's description of her adversary in the hills rang in her ears, "Taller even than Gere and dark as an Italian . . ." Sigrid gasped, drawing her parents' puzzled gazes away from their guest and their younger daughter.

Ingrid decided enough was enough. This day had been a disaster from the beginning, and it was time someone took charge. She opened her mouth to suggest that they proceed to the dining room, but a knock sounded. Marthe ushered in Gere. Ingrid barely refrained from screaming with frustration. What else could go wrong? Surely nothing worse could happen, she moaned inwardly. The old Norse god of mischief, Loki, probably watched on, amused.

Ragnar leaped to his feet and took a menacing step toward Gere, but Ingrid pulled him aside and whispered fiercely, "Now is not the time to make a scene. Being rude to Gere will solve nothing and could, in fact, disgust Captain Garrison." Ragnar clenched his hands, then he sat back down. The look he shot at Aimee boded ill for her.

Aimee didn't even notice. She jerked her dilated eyes away from the taunt in Luke's to smile at Gere. "I'm so glad you could come, Gere. *Mor,* since we're all here, shall we eat?"

Aimee was so rattled she was truly unaware of her rudeness in not introducing Luke, but he took the oversight as a deliberate insult. His temper, already unbalanced from the numerous shocks he had received this day, began to get the best of him. Gere smiled so charmingly in Aimee's direction that Luke was too busy gritting his teeth to notice that Gere's eyes were fixed on Sigrid's downcast face.

"Thank you for the invitation, Aimee. And this must be Captain Garrison?" He turned to Luke with a measuring look, ignoring Ragnar's disapproving scowl.

Luke extended a hand to the newcomer, but the gesture was not cordial. He scented a rival and reacted accordingly. Gere's chiseled features reflected a similar reaction. The men clasped hands and pumped them vigorously up and down, both refusing to be the first to release their crushing grip.

Ingrid's patience was exhausted. A nightmare was unfolding before her eyes, but this was not a dream she was powerless to end. She clapped her hands imperiously. "Gere, release Captain Garrison this instant! And you, sir, guest or no guest, I will have no brawling in my home." Her look was so fierce that both men dropped their numbed hands.

"Now, let us eat while we still have stomach enough to digest our food." Ingrid sailed through the door like a riverboat under full steam. The others, eager to get the meal over with, followed. Aimee brought up the rear. She gulped when her father blocked the dining room door.

He pulled her aside and whispered fiercely, "You're not to think you'll get away with this, you little fiend. You're not too old to turn over my knee, and my hand is itching mightily. Keep that in mind as you eat. I'll not have you egging Gere on to be forward to Sigrid or rude to Luke. Understood?"

His eyes were so piercing that Aimee nodded, gulping down any resistence. Shoulders squared, jaws clenched firmly, father and daughter looked like replicas of one another as they entered the dining room. Luke sent them a curious glance, wondering what was going on.

Sigrid and Aimee sat across from Luke and Gere. At first, silence hung over them as they circled the table piled high with cheeses and breads, roast mutton, salted fish, and boiled potatoes.

The silence was guarded. Gere watched Sigrid, Luke watched Aimee, Sigrid watched Luke watching Aimee, Aimee watched her fish, and Ragnar and Ingrid watched everyone else until the atmosphere was as thick as the slice of mutton Ragnar slammed down on his plate in exasperation.

"Well, Captain Garrison, what do you think of Bergen?" Ingrid finally inquired wearily.

Luke had just caught Sigrid's quick, despairing look at Gere, and his reply was absent. "What? Oh, I find it charming. No port in America has anywhere near the look of antiquity. The old warehouses and offices are so close together I understand they've burned down a number of times, yet they're always rebuilt to look like they did centuries ago with their angled roofs and overhanging wooden galleries."

Ragnar nodded. "*Ja,* we are proud of Bergen's ancient heritage, and our town is, after all, the first port of call for many visitors, so we like to keep part of the city as it was long ago. You must take time to see St. Mary's Church and the cathedral. They date from medieval times when Bergen was a commercial center for the known world. . . ."

Luke nodded as Ragnar talked. He also noted that Ragnar

had not said a cordial word to Gere. It was obvious he didn't welcome the handsome sailor's attentions to his daughter. The question was—which daughter? He had at first thought Gere was interested in Aimee. But after catching that intense exchange between his betrothed and the sailor, he now wondered. Musing wryly, he admitted he felt protective of the younger sister. It didn't matter that he had no claim there. He still felt territorial every time Gere looked at her. He had to forcibly remind himself that he was engaged to the calm, quiet one.

At one point, when the parents spoke to the maid, Gere leaned across the table to whisper, "Sigrid, I must see you later." Luke's suspicions were confirmed. Luke casually glanced up to catch Aimee's reaction. He was shocked to see her watching Gere with longing.

The situation was so absurd he was tempted to laugh. Here he was engaged to a woman who wanted another man, while he himself lusted after her sister, who apparently wanted the same man. His crew, his friends back home and his parents would never believe Lusty Luke had been passed over by two provincial Norwegian girls for a pretty sailor. Luke shifted his long legs in chagrin, accidentally brushing them against soft, muslin skirts.

Aimee's eyes flew from Gere's face to his. Her soft expression hardened into disdain. She shifted away from him, heating up Luke's already simmering temper. Perhaps if she had not already rejected him when he was struggling to charm her, and perhaps if his pride had been less outraged at his actions—or inaction—last night, he could have shrugged off her scorn. As it was, this series of molehill events coalesced into a mountain.

He reached the boiling point at dessert time when they finished off the rice pudding. Ingrid piped up, looking eager.

"Shall you retire with Sigrid and me to discuss the wedding plans, Captain Garrison?"

Luke heard a voice respond, "There must be some mistake, madame. It's not Sigrid I'm engaged to, it's Aimee. Surely I should discuss the plans with her?" He was only slightly surprised to realize the voice was his own.

The charged atmosphere around the table grew thick. Gere's eyes flashed at Sigrid, Sigrid's eyes flew to Aimee with dread, and Ragnar and Ingrid gasped. And Aimee? Aimee stared into Luke's coal black eyes like an animal caught in a trap, her heart pounding with primordial wariness.

Ragnar cleared his throat of shock and suggested weakly, "You jest, *ja*, Captain Garrison?"

Fixing his eyes steadily on Aimee's ashen face, Luke retorted, "I jest, no, Mr. Lingstrom. It seems my mother accidentally reversed the names. She meant to arrange a match with Aimee. She wants me to marry someone easy to train for her future role as the mistress of the Garrison empire. Someone young and biddable, that is."

Gere choked on a sip of water and stared at Luke in astonishment. Aimee, biddable? Garrison and his family were in for a shock if they expected to mold her into any different shape than her own.

Sigrid, however, caught the irony in Luke's voice. Luke Garrison wanted Aimee precisely because she was *not* biddable. Her little sister was a challenge, even to this experienced man. Sigrid speculated briefly whether he could scale the invisible wall Aimee kept between herself and the male sex, but her sister's white face distracted her when Aimee, the strong, determined one, looked at her pleadingly.

As she always had, Sigrid leaped in to help. "Captain Garrison, I bear you no ill will if you don't want to marry me, but certainly your mother didn't intend for you to wed Aimee. She's only eighteen, surely very young for such a role. Can our families not form an alliance in business without forming wedded ties?"

Everyone at the table stared at Luke with bated breath. He meticulously folded his napkin, drawing out the tension. What the hell was the matter with him? Here was his chance to cry off, but he knew he had no intention of doing it. His parents would probably never forgive him, but if he was careful, they'd understand. The reason sat across from him, peering at him with angry green eyes, hope flickering in their golden depths as they lingered on him. He had wanted this strange woman-child from the first moment he saw her, and have her he would. He'd have to marry soon anyway, so it might as well be someone he wouldn't be bored with inside a month. He would deal with Hedda's fury if the time came. He was at least still wedding into her precious family, so she shouldn't protest too long.

Luke aligned the napkin beside his plate, rose and intoned, "No, they cannot."

Aimee reared back like a panicked filly, and Luke was so

irritated at her reaction he couldn't resist needling her. Leaning across the table until his face almost touched hers, he drawled, "My mother wants our united families to produce in more than business. She wants a grandchild. She believes your blood will mix beautifully with mine, Aimee."

His voice caressed her name, but Aimee didn't notice. The picture his words conjured up suffocated her. Gasping for breath, she leaped to her feet. He was still leaning over her, so her cheek brushed his as she rose. She put up a trembling hand to rub at the spot as though she could wipe the contact away. Luke scowled.

"I'll never marry you! Never!" At first her voice shook, but the arrogance in Luke's stance fanned her anger. She stabbed a finger at him.

"Do you think I don't understand what you want? You want to humiliate me because of what happened the other day. No one, male or female, certainly not a mere girl, thwarts you and gets away with it. Well, this time you've met someone you can't crush beneath your boot. I WILL NOT MARRY YOU. You can break my entire family, you can beat me, you can lock me up. I'll starve before I tie myself to you."

Aimee's racing heart made her bosom heave, but she remained firm as she stared into the wildfire of Luke's black eyes. The room receded; neither were conscious of the shocked observers looking on. The earlier silent battle of eyes now found voice in Aimee's softly uttered oath.

"Devil! You want my every thought, my will, my soul to belong to you. You shall not have me. I belong to no one but myself, do you hear? I give myself freely, no one takes me. And Norway will become a swamp before I'll give myself to you." Sure of herself now, Aimee raked a last disdainful look over him and calmly walked off to her room.

No one moved until the sound of her steps faded. Then, enervated, Ingrid leaned back in her chair, her head reeling with what she had just heard. As Ragnar's shock wore off, he began to hope that maybe, just maybe, Aimee had met her match. But then he frowned, wondering what had incited such hostility in his daughter. With a hard look, he vowed to confront Garrison later. Gere looked curiously at Luke's expression of almost violent determination.

Sigrid couldn't help feeling elated that Luke didn't want her. She wasn't certain he'd get Aimee either, however, for she alone understood the scene they had just witnessed. Aimee, independent, willful Aimee had just, knowingly or not, fired the opening salvo of a battle that would not let up. The violence of her reaction to Luke could mean only one thing: she felt threatened. For the first time in her life, she'd met a man who could penetrate the defenses she shielded herself with.

Sigrid was torn between worry and satisfaction that a man—and *what* a man, she thought with inward admiration —had recognized Aimee's strength and was attracted to her *because* of it. Sigrid was unsure who to pity. Aimee faced a man who would conquer her or crush her in the attempt; Luke faced a woman who would, as she said, starve before letting him own her. Either would emerge victorious only if Aimee surrendered willingly, not to Luke's possessiveness, but into his tender devotion. As Sigrid recalled the battle they had waged, she was not optimistic either would triumph. Closing her eyes, Sigrid prayed.

Chapter Three

AIMEE LOCKED HER door, her heart beating a panicked tattoo. She eased down on the bed, stiff as Ingrid's starched linen, and tried to rein in her thoughts. The logical mind she'd always taken pride in was muddy and weakened by images of Luke Garrison daring her, claiming her as his own. She was humiliated to learn that, when challenged by a will as strong as her own, she was as much a prey to primitive instincts as any foolish female. And each of those instincts warned her that she had not heard the last of Luke Garrison.

She sensed that his determination to humble her matched hers to defy him. She couldn't look to her parents for support. Sadly, for the first time in her life, she couldn't even go to her own sister for help. Sigrid's happiness lay with Gere, and if she could keep the American occupied, Sigrid would be free. But how was she to keep the marriage trap from closing about her instead?

She was expecting the knock. Still, when it came, she started. Ragnar demanded, "Aimee, open this door and let me in." Aimee grimaced, but obeyed.

Ragnar's angry glare made Aimee want to resist more. When the fire in his eyes died, the expression that replaced it disturbed her. She turned away from the weary reproach she saw there. Closing the door, he followed her into the room.

"Aimee, I don't know what happened in the hills between you and young Garrison, but whatever it was surely doesn't justify your rudeness. And as for your defiance of me . . ."

Aimee whirled around at that. "Yes, what of it? Would you admire me more if I let you condemn my sister to misery?"

Ragnar slumped down on the window seat in despair. "Nothing will convince you you're wrong, will it? Even after meeting Luke Garrison, you're obsessed with the notion that Sigrid will be unhappy. Why? He seems a fine young man."

He sounded so bewildered, so troubled, that Aimee's anger died. She sat down next to him and took his hand. "I'm more than ever convinced, after meeting him. Can't you see how arrogant he is? Sigrid needs a gentle man. And believe me, Captain Luke Garrison knows nothing of gentleness."

Ragnar frowned. "What happened between you?"

Aimee shifted away and rose to pace in front of him, debating how much to tell him. "He was . . . presumptuous. We didn't know who the other was, but I saw enough of him to realize he is totally unsuitable for Sigrid."

"But it strikes me that he is eminently suitable for you, Aimee," Ragnar said gently.

Aimee froze in her tracks. She croaked, "That's insane. We'd battle constantly. The only reason he pretends to want me is because I spurned him in a prior confrontation and he wants revenge."

Ragnar shook his head before she'd finished speaking. "You sell yourself short. I'm a man, and I recognize the expression in his eyes when he looks at you. He is genuinely attracted, Aimee. He wants you to come down and speak with him so he can apologize for his behavior."

Aimee almost folded over in laughter. He wanted to charm her into submission, and when she was relaxed and trusting, he would pounce. That fiend had never given a genuine apology in his life unless he hoped to gain something. Aimee's eyes narrowed into glittering slits. But gain her he never would. She would be so obstinate, so cold, that he'd leave Norway a bachelor and be glad of it. He was a man who lived life with gusto, and he could never reconcile himself to a loveless marriage. And so when Ragnar offered his arm, she took it with equanimity. She didn't pause to consider that her explosive reaction to Captain Luke Garrison was the exact opposite of coldness.

On that brief, fateful journey down the stairs, Aimee was vaguely aware that her family's happiness lay in her hands. She could redeem herself in her parents' eyes by helping Ragnar achieve his most cherished aims: a cross-Atlantic liason. And she could spare Sigrid for Gere in the process. But the selfless feelings were trampled by a wave of rogue fears. To tie herself to such a man as Garrison was unthinkable. He would not rest until she was a model society wife that bore no relation to the person she was or hoped to be. No, even to save Sigrid, she could not surrender.

Luke rose the moment Aimee entered the parlor, his iron resolve to make her his own masked behind a charming smile. His eyes sparkled like jewels as he drawled, "I wish to offer my sincere apologies for my behavior at luncheon. My only excuse is that I was so enthralled by your charms that I, er, forgot myself. You made a powerful impression on me the first time we met, and I fear my aggressive instincts got the better of me. Of course, I understand your reluctance to wed a stranger, and we'll say no more about it at present. All I ask for now is your forgiveness."

He cocked his head inquiringly. He knew he was sincere, but Aimee only read duplicity in his handsome, open face, and her wariness increased. She favored him with a tiny nod, for she, too, had a role to play. She seated herself on a distant chair, but Luke sat as close as he could on an adjacent chair.

"Of course, Captain, I forgive you. You are a guest in our home, so how could I do less?" Her smile was polite, but chilly as a mountain gale.

Ragnar looked from one to the other. Then, shrugging, he excused himself. Stoically, Aimee refused to surrender to her nervousness. Her pose was calm, hands folded and face remote—but the rapid rise and fall of her chest betrayed her traitorous emotions.

She felt a vivid awareness of his every movement. When he blinked, she admired the thick lashes that bordered his eyes. When he stretched his long, booted legs in front of him, she reluctantly raked over every taut muscle. He had the strange magnetism of a wild animal, Aimee told herself. He mesmerized her no more than any exotic, dangerous beast. As a man, he held no attraction for her. None whatever. But when he spoke, she was helpless against the compulsion to watch his wide, sensual mouth.

"I was wondering if, perhaps, you'd show me more of the beautiful countryside? Hedda has never forgotten the land of her birth. She brags to this day about how even our own wonderful scenery cannot match the grandeur of Norway, land of waterfalls and fjords." His smile stretched into a delighted grin when he spotted the fascination she could not hide.

Aimee nodded assent. "Of course, I'm sure *Far* will be delighted to escort you wherever you wish. I would offer to do so, but I have a weakness in my leg from a childhood illness, and I tire easily," she exaggerated without compunction.

Her mobile little face was so remote Luke almost reached out to comfort her before he saw the calculation in her eyes. The little minx! She's not above using this imagined physical flaw as a weapon when it suits her. I've seen no evidence of weakness. Doesn't she realize her apparent fragility makes her strong character all the more appealing?

Luke stared at her, trying to understand what fascinated him as much as her slim, curvacious body. Why is she so fiercely resolved to remain independent, untouched and unloved? Doesn't she know her inviolate air makes a man long to undo that prim chignon, kiss that tight but sensual mouth until it moans, caress the soft swells of her breasts until those primly positioned legs relaxed into the abandoned sprawl of desire? He shifted uncomfortably as his erotic thoughts led to undesirable results.

A frown creased his high forehead as he reflected on her intense appeal. With every meeting, she seemed more desirable. Objectively, he scanned her from head to toe, but he still couldn't explain the gnawing hunger he felt to take her, make her his. Her figure was sleek enough: a tiny waist, pert little breasts and surprisingly womanly hips. But he'd known a dozen women shaped more voluptuously. Her face was fascinating, but not conventionally beautiful. No, he was forced to the conclusion that Aimee's appeal was more intrinsic than her outer charms. It was the essence of her stubborn little mind, the loyalty of her zealously guarded heart, that he longed for. He was disturbed at the implications of this conclusion, and thence irritated with himself and with her.

Male instinct goaded him to attack the fomenter of these rebel urges, especially when her fortress of reserve was such a challenge to breach. However, he'd already tried direct assault and been rebuffed; perhaps it was time to bring more subtle arms to bear.

Aimee darted a suspicious look at him when he agreed genially, "Certainly, *frøken* Lingstrom, I will be delighted to have your father escort me. But it's a pity you shan't be with us. I did so want to show you my ship. I'd hoped to ask your advice about my stallion's foal. I brought the mare along to sell to a client in England, but I'm afraid she died shortly after the birth, and I'm having a problem coaxing the lad to eat. He's near death from lack of food."

Shaking his head in regret, Luke rose. He allowed only the smallest hint of reproach to creep into his voice. "But of course I understand your reluctance. I would not want to cause you any pain. The foal will have to take his chances, for we've done all we can think of to save him."

He moved to bow in dismissal. Aimee cut off the suave insult by surging to her feet, forgetting her intent to be cold. "Damn you," she gritted, "quit trying to trick me. If you want my help, ask for it. Don't try to play on my emotions. I was against a wedding between our families from the beginning, and as far as I'm concerned, I'd prefer to work as a scullery maid over selling myself to anyone, especially to a tyrant like you."

Satisfied, Luke was admiring her flushed cheeks and sparkling eyes. This vivacious girl on the verge of womanhood was the real Aimee, the one he was determined to reach. However, his glow dimmed the moment she voiced her closing comment.

He glared into her defiant face. "Tell me, would you have agreed to visit my ship if I'd asked you?"

She bit her lip, then nodded fiercely. "Yes, if I believed you were honestly concerned about the foal instead of with furthering your own ends. Tell *me*, do you ever do anything without calculation? Have you ever succumbed to an instinct, pursued a goal without knowing you'd receive a reward in return?" Aimee vaguely realized she was inciting him rather than disgusting him, but she was so furious that, for the moment, she didn't care. It was time he learned arrogance was not a male flaw only.

Luke's nostrils flared at her impudence. His earlier resolve to be gentle, coaxing, anything but aggressive scattered when Aimee's vow to remain cool had fled. Again they faced off like fencers. Luke advanced a menacing step, Aimee retreated. Luke took two strides forward, Aimee backed away three.

The determination in his nature, the power and potency of his manhood had never struck her with such force. Aimee's knees grew weak at the advance as well as the menacing note in his voice.

"How wise you are, my dear. You're right. I seldom do things on impulse, and never have I been more convinced of the danger of acting hastily than I have today. It was impulse that made me ask for your hand instead of your sister's, but what's done is done. I'll make you mine if I have to take us both through hell to do it."

He forced her against the arm of a chair. Before she tumbled backward, he encircled her waist and pulled her against his chest. "But strangely, I find it exhilarating to act impulsively now. You're a hard taskmaster, sweet Aimee, but a thorough one. I'm sure you'll be delighted to hear another powerful impulse is taking hold of me."

He grasped her neck and arched it back. His arm coiled about her waist like a snake. Then he leaned into her until she was nearly bent over the chair arm.

Aimee wished she'd never sparred with him. She could now feel every inch of his muscular torso rubbing against her. She quivered; her heart pounded. She told herself his touch was distressing, but underneath she knew she feared the emotions he sparked.

Luke's face came closer, closer, until he filled her world. Nothing existed but the two of them, nothing else mattered but escaping the warlock's bewitching eyes. His whispered warning completed the spell, draining her will until she couldn't cry out for Ragnar.

"You shall help me learn to be impulsive, and I shall teach you to be a woman. I've learned my first lesson. Now it's time for yours." His face was so close he only had to move an inch to capture her trembling mouth.

Aimee couldn't move, for he had her anchored securely. After a moment, she no longer wanted to move. She was both buffeted and enthralled by the storm of passion she'd aroused. His lips consumed hers, sucking as though he would draw his breath from her own lungs. His hungry, coaxing mouth and the strange sensations his hard body stirred disoriented her. Was this what it was to be desired? This hurricane, this tornado that swept her away? How soft and warm his lips were, how passionate, so different from the few chaste boy-kisses she had known. This was a man's embrace that called to every womanly instinct she possessed. Aimee's mouth trembled and began to open, but when he nibbled her lips and plunged into the tiny opening she allowed him, she was shocked. The instinct to respond was vanquished by a renewed onslaught of anger. She had been wanted, invaded and conquered, but she would not be defeated. She drew back, clamped her jaw closed, and lay motionless in his arms.

Luke used all his expertise to make her respond, but she was cold and stiff in his arms. With a punitive, gentle nibble, he released her mouth and lifted her to her feet, still holding her close. Expressionlessly, he watched her rub her mouth furiously on her sleeve, but his hands tightened into a vise at her waist.

He lifted her chin. "The ice is thicker than I realized, but whether you know it or not, you've a passion for living I've seldom seen in a woman. It shows here," he stroked her mulish mouth, "and here," he kissed each delicate eyelid. "I'll need to do little to make you melt. Your own inner fires will thaw you for me." Luke released her and stood back to await the tirade he knew would come.

Aimee breathed a sigh of relief when she was free of his disturbing contact. She backed away a safe distance, then let her frustration loose. "You've never had a woman reject you, have you? You're so accustomed to winning every battle, taking anything you want, that your conceit cannot comprehend it when someone spurns you, especially an inexperienced country girl."

His imperturbable stance, arms calmly folded, head cocked expectantly, infuriated her more. Aimee was so angry she stamped her foot. It felt good, so she did it again, flinging words at him this time.

"I'm not like your other women. Your manly physique" —she gave him a scathing glance—"appeals not at all to me. Your wealth means nothing, and your arrogant charm makes me ill. So, Mr. Almighty Captain Garrison, what have *you* to offer *me?*" Aimee waited with satisfaction for his outburst. She was congratulating herself for putting him in his place when he threw back his shiny black head and roared with laughter. Aimee stared in confusion.

He mocked, "Who are you trying to convince, me or yourself?"

Aimee didn't see the caressing, admiring look in his eyes, and she had no idea how vitally attractive she was at that moment. Her rage only drew Luke, but she had not yet recognized this irrational trait in him.

Aimee's face colored furiously. Her eyes flamed like tiny, golden suns as she parceled out the only punishment she could think of appropriate for this laughing devil. Barely aware of her action, Aimee picked up the closest object, her mother's sewing basket, and flung it. It thudded against his chest, knocking the mirth out of him. He barely had time to dodge before she hurled a tiny porcelain unicorn, her other hand already reaching for more ammunition.

The unicorn shattered against the parlor door, missing Luke's head by inches. Footsteps sounded in the hall. Aimee's eyes were so blind with fury she didn't see the playful, joyous look on Luke's face as he picked up a large sofa cushion and circled her warily.

"My fair warrior, I cry foul. If you wanted to challenge me, you should at least give me time to hold up my shield." He held up the green, tassled cushion with all the aplomb of a knight displaying his coat of arms. Aimee's latest throw, her father's pipe, bounced off the makeshift shield.

Aimee's bloodlust was pounding so fiercely, she didn't hear the door open or see her family rush in, but Luke did. He regretfully decided the fun must end. They were casting stunned, disbelieving looks at Aimee. Dropping the cushion, he corralled Aimee and pried the comfit dish from her hand. When she tried to scratch him with the other hand, he fended her off with his arm.

He hauled her close. "Enough, dear termagant. We've an audience. I've enjoyed our quiet little discussion. Let's have another soon." Forcing her coiled fists to his mouth, he saluted then kissed her.

Aimee shuddered at the warm moist touch. She tried to free her hands and strike out, but when he released her, he leaped back out of harm's way. Aimee then noticed her family, but she was still too rattled to mind.

Luke nodded courteously to his three gaping in-laws-to-be, then backed out the door, waving to the stunned group, a sly grin on his handsome face. When the door closed behind him, Aimee's knees collapsed. She sank onto the couch behind her and heaved a great, shuddering sigh, wondering what it was about this man that upset her so. She barely stifled a bitter laugh as she remembered her intent to disgust him with her coldness. How on earth was she to find a way out of this mess? Unable to avoid it any longer, she lifted her head proudly to look at her gaping family.

Ingrid and Ragnar were stunned at her behavior. She had always been polite to others, her emotions rarely aroused in company. They looked at her like they'd never seen her before. Indeed they wondered how their blood could have given birth to such an odd, multi-faceted personality.

It was Sigrid's gaze Aimee refused to meet. Sigrid would search and pry for the reasons behind Aimee's tantrum, and Aimee wasn't ready to know the answers herself, much less share them with anyone, even Sigrid.

Consequently, when Ingrid questioned her daughter warily —"Aimee, why were you so upset? What did Captain Garrison do?"—Sigrid barely listened to Aimee's evasive reply. Sigrid needed no more proof that Captain Garrison was assaulting Aimee's infamous wall of reserve, weakening it with each encounter.

Sigrid watched her sister squirm under her parents' questioning stare, then stirred. Smiling, she began to straighten the shambles Aimee had made of the room.

Luke whistled a tune as he rode back to Bergen. He doffed his hat to every woman he passed and nodded to every man. He hadn't felt so invigorated since the time the ship's boiler threatened to blow and, at immense peril, he fixed a key valve. He was amazed a mere woman could give him the same feeling. Was this what he'd missed in his relationships? This challenge to win not only a pliant, soft body, but a woman with a sharp, intelligent mind and will as strong as his own?

While his female companions had always been stunning, their characters left much to be desired. After the first flush of passion, Luke invariably became bored with their stupidity, cupidity or crudity. Aimee was the only woman he'd ever met who hadn't disappointed him. Perhaps even she would in time, he told himself. But his instincts about people assured him otherwise.

Aimee's fury had further convinced him she was a woman of repressed but strong passion. The thought of holding this girl of contradictions, fire and ice, sweetness and obstinacy, pride and insecurity, in his arms made his head whirl. He was dead certain now Aimee would never become boring unless she clung and became subservient. But if she fell in love with him? What then?

Luke shied away from the thought. He hadn't planned

beyond winning and possessing her. Every woman he'd known had eventually claimed to love him, and their anguished demands for him to stay, to make love with them once more, had only hastened his resolve to escape. He felt contempt for any man or woman who would become so humble in a relationship. Luke's stomach tightened at the thought of seeing the proud Aimee in such a supplicating position.

If she fell in love with him, this time he would not be able to escape. Oddly, when Luke pictured Aimee caressing him with tenderness in her eyes and love in her touch, he felt no distaste. Indeed, the vision seemed right. No, it seemed destined . . . inevitable. His thoughts made him uneasy, so he was relieved to be interrupted.

"Captain Garrison! And how did your meeting with Aimee go?" Sigrid's sweetheart, Gere Haugen, eased up beside Luke. He was driving a *karjol,* a single-passenger carriage that looked antiquated to Luke's cosmopolitan eyes.

Luke smiled in remembrance. "It was . . . very entertaining. But I've a way to go before convincing Aimee to wed me."

Gere was not surprised to see the anticipation on his face. He was beginning to understand Luke, who had at first seemed distant. Now he hoped to call him friend. Luke had freed Sigrid. Luke possessed many of the qualities Gere most admired, and, like Sigrid, he believed the American would be good for Aimee.

With these thoughts in mind, Gere invited, "Would you care to sup with me, Captain Garrison? Perhaps we can discuss the latest advances in steam. And if you'd like to ask about Aimee, feel free. I've known her since she was a child and she's like a sister to me."

Luke glanced at the handsome Norwegian in surprise. "I was under the impression you already had an appointment this evening."

Gere flushed. "That is much later. Sigrid cannot get away until after supper."

"Very well, then. I do have a number of questions I'd like to ask about Aimee, but I insist you dine with me aboard my ship. It's much easier to show you the latest advances in steam than to tell you."

Gere grinned. *"Flott! Mange takk.* I will be delighted to join you."

The *Mercury,* iron-clad from prow to stern, stood out among the wooden ships docked in Bergen's harbor like a shiny raven amid a flock of hawks. Gere had the natural prejudice of a sailor who had known no other form of sea travel, and to his eyes, the comparison was unfavorable. The smokestack towering amidship, the low bulwarks, the two masts that rigged a small sail, all completed the picture of a vessel that was ugly and ungainly compared to the graceful circle of clippers, schooners and brigs.

Gere saw the pride in Luke's eyes, however, so he said nothing. Once aboard ship, Luke introduced him to his skeleton crew, then began the tour. Like many of her contemporaries, the *Mercury* had been designed mainly as a liner to ferry the increasing flow of emigrants and traffic across the Atlantic. However, her hold was large enough to carry more goods than a clipper.

The appointments were more luxurious than any Gere had seen on a sailer. The smoking room, the ladies' boudoir and the dining saloon were all decorated in burlwood with stained glass light fixtures suspended from the frescoed ceilings. Most impressive of all was the grand saloon.

Lavishly carved mahogany beamed the high ceiling and lower half of the bulkhead. The upper portion was papered in green, hand-painted silk displaying a pastoral scene. Long, parquetry tables, chairs and benches abounded. An elegant piano sat in one corner. Two marble, coal-burning fireplaces abutted each end, but what amazed Gere most was the placement of the saloon. Extending the main deck's width, the cabin was situated amidships instead of astern as had been the style since the Middle Ages.

When questioned, Luke explained, "We did it for comfort, mainly. The stern is noisiest because the screw is located there. Second-class cabins, crew's quarters and of course the steerage are nearer the stern for that reason."

Gere felt a twinge of sympathy for the crew. He'd heard many horror tales involving screw-driven ships. How terrible to come back from a long watch to a rolling, noisy bunk.

Luke smiled at Gere's expression. "The *Mercury* is the latest design. She's stabler, faster and quieter than most screw-driven ships, and the discomfort the crew suffers by proximity to the propeller is minimal. Paddle wheelers are simply no longer economical."

Gere had heard the arguments in favor of screw propellers,

but he remained unconvinced. Screws were entirely sub-merged and thus each rotation was used fully in pushing the ship forward; wheels propelled only half a rotation because the paddles sliced the water as they spun. Gere preferred the quiet maneuverability of a schooner's rudder and sails over either design.

The first-class cabins were spacious and elegant. They were lined with Turkish carpets, gilded mirrors, velvet-curtained portholes and swagged berths. Gere turned on the brass tap at the marble lavatory and was amazed to see fresh water spout out.

"You must have paid a fortune for this ship. Why are the accommodations so luxurious?"

"Since the war, unfair taxes and harsh laws have hurt the merchant marine in America. It's getting harder and harder to make a profit, and the competition has become fierce. The passenger trade is more profitable than any other right now, so the more comfortable you can make the voyage, the better chance you have of attracting customers."

Gere lifted an eyebrow. "What you really mean is all this luxury is necessary to make people forget the dangers of traveling on ships with boilers."

Luke shrugged, unoffended. "I don't deny many people still harbor such fears, but they have no basis in fact. Our line has never had a major accident yet."

"Then why have you no passengers?" Gere pounced.

"We were almost at capacity on the trip from New York to London, but I booked no passengers from here to London so I could get to know my bride. Now that I've met her, I'm especially glad I did. I'll need every advantage I can get to win her."

Gere hid a smile at Luke's chagrin. He listened closely as Luke continued, "We are solidly booked from London to New York. We recently signed a lucrative mail contract with the British government, and when I pick up the mail a few weeks hence, I'll deliver timber from Stockholm to London. With the textiles and furniture I'll take on then, our investors should make a handsome profit on this voyage."

Gere was impressed as they continued the tour, especially when they reached the lower reaches of the ship and Luke showed him the boiler room. It held eight of the largest boilers Gere had ever seen. Each had two furnaces and one flue; the eight flues met at the top. Their spent emissions were funneled through the single smokestack tunneling through both decks.

It was when they reached the engine room, however, that Luke's chest really expanded. Gere comprehended little of the great array of cylinders, cogs, pistons, and pumps, but he could understand Luke's pride.

"I'm totally convinced the days of sailing ships are numbered, at least when used for commerce, and you're looking at the reason. This engine has only recently come into use, but it's spreading rapidly. It's called the compound engine and it uses sometimes forty percent less coal than the old single-expansion engine."

Gere winced at Luke's prediction on the fate of sailing ships, but he still circled the massive machinery with interest. "Why is it more efficient?"

"Because it recycles the steam through another cylinder, whereas the old engines used it but once, thus requiring more fuel for the same amount of power."

Gere shrugged. "Impressive, no doubt, but clippers can still make the Atlantic crossing in twelve days at much less cost. Few steamers can boast that record."

Luke smiled ruefully. He'd had this argument countless times with many of his friends and his father's business associates. He'd never been able to understand why so many sailors viewed steamers as behemoths of the sea. For himself, he'd trade the grace and beauty of a tall ship any day for the challenge of a boiler room. Man using his ingenuity to conquer the seas by wresting power from coal was far more interesting than relying on fickle winds.

He answered mildly, "That's rapidly changing. The *City of Brussels* made the crossing in less than eight days in '69. Now lines are building lighter ships with less displacement. We should be able to cross faster than ever. The *Mercury* can approach twenty knots at full steam. Besides, the cost of coal-powered vessels compared to sailing ones has been exaggerated. Don't forget steamers require a considerably smaller crew."

They continued their wrangling over dinner as Potter served them. The two men were different as night and day in looks and temperament, but they shared a common trait: each enjoyed a good debate. They argued at length and were pleased neither could claim victory.

By the time they began a plain but hearty fare of boiled

carrots, brown bread and roast beef, they were friends. Consequently, Luke felt comfortable raising the subject of Aimee.

"Tell me, Gere, why is Aimee so innocently unaware of her power over men?"

Gere glanced up in surprise, then narrowed his eyes. He had never considered Aimee beautiful, but knew she was alluring when animated. Even then, in his mind, she couldn't compare with Sigrid in looks. Still, she had charm. . . .

He framed his response carefully, for he wanted to give Luke insight into the complexities of Aimee's personality. "Aimee's parents love her, but they've never understood her. They want Aimee to be like Sigrid—compliant, ladylike and friendly. Aimee is none of these, as I'm sure you've noticed. She's simply too independent. When she was ill as a child, she learned to be self-sufficient. She conquered her illness by sheer force of will."

Gere's voice and eyes were so admiring that Luke had to stifle a surge of jealousy.

"Independence is fine, but why is she so wary of suitors?"

Gere studied his hands. "I'm not certain myself. She's sweet enough to the young men who have courted her, but she never lets them get too close. I think she's afraid Ragnar will try to push her into marriage. He and Ingrid are strict parents, and I'm afraid they think it unnatural for Aimee to long for anything besides marriage and a home."

Gere looked a little puzzled, but Luke nodded in comprehension. He could sympathize with Aimee. How awful it must be to be as intelligent and spirited as a man, but to be expected to act the docile, complacent female. "Why can't they admire Aimee for what she is? Would they want her to stifle all that marvelous spirit and mold her into something she is not?"

Gere shrugged. "I'm not sure Ingrid and Ragnar know themselves how they want Aimee to act. As you may have noticed, I am not exactly a favorite visitor, and most of what I know of them is through Aimee and Sigrid. Still, in fairness to them, I have to say Aimee would try the patience of a saint. Did you know she roams about the countryside letting loose any trapped animal she can find? She drags home every wounded creature she discovers, no matter how diseased or dangerous. I've seen her bandage a fox's tail and escape without a scratch, but when I helped her set the animal free, it bit me. Animals are strangely drawn to her. Perhaps they sense how she cares about them."

Gere wiped his mouth with his napkin and shoved back his plate. "Aimee is an enigma, in many ways, but she is more than the rebel or the child her parents see. She is both, and neither. She's the strangest mixture of wisdom, naïveté, strength and vulnerability I've ever known. If you win her trust or sympathy, she'll walk through fire for you. She has an intuitive understanding of people. I've seen her become friends with surly, crippled sailors and shy sheepherders in no time."

Gere's smile softened at the memories. "She can also be a little mischief when she likes. I remember when she mixed pepper in Ragnar's tobacco. She was mad at him. I believe that was the one and only time he ever spanked her. Sigrid cried and pleaded for mercy for her sister, but Aimee never said a word."

Gere's smile faded. "She's like that, honest and straightforward. She takes responsibility for her own actions, and I've never seen her lie to herself before. That's why I'm so surprised at the way she's acting toward you. It's not in her nature to deny her feelings."

Luke's eyes lit up. "You believe she is attracted to me, then?"

"She's struggling against it, but I've noticed the way she looks when you're not watching. If you persevere, I think you can win her."

Luke's face set with determination. "Oh, I'll persevere, all right. Have no fear of that," he vowed softly.

Gere searched Luke's face. He nodded approvingly at the resolve he read there. "Aimee needs a man like you. If you can be patient with that prickly side and win her trust, I can tell you from personal experience that she is one of the most loving people I've ever known."

He turned wistful. "I imagine Ragnar will assist you in every way he can. He adores Aimee, and now that he's seen how much you desire her, he must realize she's no longer a child. He'll soon see how perfect you are for her. His persuasion, added to yours and Sigrid's, will probably be enough to sway her. If you someday win her love, you could search the world over and never find a more faithful, loyal and loving wife. I wish you luck. You'll need it."

After Gere left, Luke stared into the dregs of his wine. He

was only just realizing the monumental task he had set for himself. With the old cynicism, he wondered briefly if the prize was worth the game. But as he recalled the passionate girl who had flung missiles at him a few hours past, he knew winning her was worth his every effort. Tomorrow he would visit Mr. Lingstrom to seek his aid. A bold grin creased his cheeks as Luke retired to his own luxurious cabin and prepared for bed.

PART II

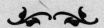

My delicate butterfly, look out, for I mean to take you! I'm weaving a net of the finest mesh; its threads are the song I make you.

—Henrik Ibsen, "Agnes"

Chapter Four

LUKE WHISTLED A light ditty as he rode to the Lingstrom home, his anticipation heightened by the beauty around him. The sky was blue as the wildflowers waving in the thick grass. Mountains loomed in the distance like benevolent giants cloaked in green velvet. He fancied they smiled down on him, as if approving of his pursuit of one of their native daughters. Luke saluted them and laughed at his whimsy. He dismounted, tied Polaris to the gate, and strode buoyantly up the walk to the Lingstrom house.

The maid led him into the library, a room walled by books and oil paintings. Ragnar was studying his business inventory in preparation for the merger, but set his papers aside and rose with outstretched hand as Luke stepped up to him. Luke didn't miss the measured look, however, behind the older man's cheerful gaze.

"*God morgen. Hvordan står det til?*" he asked.

"I'm fine," Luke responded in Norwegian, the language he employed on his stay in the country. "But I'd like to discuss Aimee with you, if you have time."

The other man's smile froze, but he pointed to a nearby chair so the two faced one another.

Ragnar released a long heavy sigh. "*Ja,* we must talk. First, though I don't doubt your gallantry, I must know what happened between you and my daughter the first time you met, apparently not in this household."

"Of course. From the minute I saw your daughter, Ragnar,

she fascinated me. We met when I was riding in the hills above town. We had something of a . . . confrontation. I let her know I was attracted to her, and she seemed angry. She stumbled, I caught her and kissed her throat before releasing her. She then ran away. That's all that happened, my word of honor upon it."

Ragnar could visualize the scene Luke described, but he didn't press the issue of Luke's forwardness with Aimee. "Why is she so disturbed by you? Do you know?"

Some of Luke's cheer faded. He shrugged and answered wryly. "I was hoping you could give me insight into that. I swear I've never hurt her, nor would I dream of doing so."

Ragnar sighed. "My daughter is not like other women. She claims to have no interest in marriage and children. She resents any limits upon her rights to make her own decisions."

Ragnar sounded as puzzled as Gere had sounded. "So I don't know if it's you, the man, she resents, or you, the threat to her freedom." Ragnar eyed Luke for a reaction.

The younger man smiled and uncrossed his legs, more thrilled than repelled by the nature described. He leaned forward.

"Do you want me to wed your daughter, Mr. Lingstrom? I can't honestly say I love Aimee, but she fascinates me more than any woman I've met, and I swear I'd treat her tenderly."

Ragnar leaned forward also, to emphasize his words. "But can you be patient? Even if we can coax her into accepting this marraige, I suspect she'll fight you every step of the way afterward. And what will Hedda think of the switch?"

"I'm aware of the need for patience, and I can only say I'll do my best. You needn't worry about my family. They'll be surprised, but I'm certain they'll accept her soon enough. It's premature to worry about that now, at any rate. The question is—will Aimee ever accept me?"

Ragnar nodded approvingly. "Ah, I'm glad to see you understand Aimee somewhat, Luke. Indeed, that does seem the greatest challenge." After another lingering look, he nodded decisively.

"All right, young man, I will add my voice to yours. After seeing you with Aimee, I realize I've misjudged my daughter. She's become a woman before my very eyes, but I was too blind to see it. She'll need a firm hand, and something tells me you're just the man."

Ragnar's voice faded. His eyes stared out the window, and Luke sensed he was picturing some cherished moments with his younger daughter. Luke was moved at the tenderness in Ragnar's brown eyes. He remained silent for a moment, then he cleared his throat. The older man turned back to him.

Smiling, Ragnar offered his hand. After they shook, Ragnar went to a pitcher of ale and poured two drinks. He offered one to Luke and winked, "Drink up, boy. Something tells me we'll need to fortify ourselves for the battle ahead."

Luke laughed and toasted, "To Aimee. May her woman's pride learn to bend, just a little."

There was no evidence of bending in Aimee that morning. She left Father Erichsen's and mounted her pony. As the family pastor, she visited him once a week besides the usual day of worship. Now free of the kindly presence, her mind reeled with fresh thoughts. Two days. Surely she could be polite to that arrogant, self-assured American for a mere two days. Remembering his glee as she hurled insults, she sighed doubtfully. She'd never known anyone who could infuriate her so, and he seemed to enjoy enflaming her.

But she hoped to be free very soon. If Sigrid would agree to marry Gere in two days, then half the battle would be won. Nothing on earth would make Aimee agree to wed Garrison then. He'd have to go home and admit to his parents and friends that he'd been rejected by two naïve, provincial Norwegian girls. The picture of Garrison confronting his family, wringing his hat in nervous hands, an embarrassed flush on his haughty face, brought a gleam to her eye that unbeknownst to her, mirrored Luke's when he took his leave of her. She bristled with eagerness at joining in a fray as old as time but as new as today. How she would relish teaching him a lesson. She smiled to herself.

The smile faded as reality seeped in. Why was it so important to best Garrison? Why had it become almost as important to win this test of wills as it was to keep her freedom? Why?

Because you're scared of him, she told herself. You fear his power to hurt you, a deep, stifled part of her whispered. She shook her head in reaction. No, she disliked him, he disturbed her, but not because she was attracted to him. He was arrogant, different from anyone she had ever known, and he had brashly tried to bend her will to his. She would let no man dominate her, no matter what the cost.

What if the cost is your father's business, that little voice whispered again. Aimee winced. Surely the Garrisons would not be so vindictive? Surely they wouldn't have wanted her as their daughter-in-law in the first place. She was European, after all. But the fear lurked in the back of her mind as she rode down the lane. She was glad to have her dark thoughts interrupted when two male voices piped up.

"*Morn,* Aimee! We were just coming to see you." The young men, tall, sturdy and fair mirror images of each other, rode up beside her.

Aimee pulled her pony to a stop, smiling. "*Morn,* Sven and Olaf. And what brings you away from your flocks this morning?"

Both brothers began at once: "We wanted to ask your opinion," and "We wanted to show you . . ." They trailed off and glared at each other.

Aimee smiled. As long as she could remember, the twins had competed, right down to who would talk first and louder. Aimee pulled her pony off the road. When she moved to jump down, she found the twins jostling against each other to assist.

Aimee crossed her arms and remained where she was, a teasing look in her eyes. "Perhaps I should stay put to avoid an argument. If you two get started, we could be here all day."

The twins reddened and grinned sheepishly. They both opened their mouths to speak and Aimee held her breath, but Olaf bowed to his brother. Sven cleared his throat and explained, "We found a gold brooch the other day we wanted to ask you about. We think it's Viking, and since you've read so much, we thought you'd know."

Aimee climbed down from her horse, helped by the brothers. Olaf dug in his pocket and retrieved a small gold object which he handed to Aimee. Aimee didn't notice that his hand lingered on hers a little too long, but Sven did. He scowled at his brother, getting a frown in return. An argument brewing was foiled by Aimee's excited gasp of admiration.

"Oh, Olaf, Sven, this is lovely. I'm no expert, but it certainly looks old. See the strange whorls on the sides that interlace and meet in the center? This is very similar to other ornaments found in ship burials." Aimee turned the brooch over in her hand and studied the other side. She didn't see the wistful, intent gazes fixed on her.

Sven shifted nervously, but when Olaf moved a little closer to Aimee he blurted, "Aimee, I wondered if you might attend the summer festival with me?"

Olaf hissed, *"Fi!* You knew I intended to ask her, you . . ."

Aimee bit her lip to keep from laughing at their antics. "It's sweet of you to ask, Sven, but I'm very busy at home right now and I don't think I'll be able to attend."

Sven looked crestfallen, but Olaf brightened. "If you change your mind, I'd like to take you, too. I'm older and can certainly dance better." When Sven's head popped up Olaf met his brother's eyes with blazing ones.

Aimee averted another war by handing the brooch back to Olaf and demurring, "I don't think I'll change my mind, but thank you anyway. This brooch certainly appears Viking to me, but you'll have to send it to Royal Frederiks University in Christiana for verification. Now, *unnskyld,* if you'll excuse me, I have several errands to run."

Olaf stepped in front of his brother and clasped Aimee's waist to lift her onto her pony. Aimee put her hands on his shoulders for balance, and, at that moment, a horse and rider rode into view. She turned her head idly and froze. Angry black eyes glared at the large hands clasped around her waist.

Luke doffed his hat mockingly as he pulled up to them. *"God dag, frøken* Lingstrom. Do you need assistance in mounting your horse?"

When Aimee flushed with anger, Olaf released her and turned curiously to glare at the intruder. Luke introduced himself, adding, "Doubtless you've already heard about me from my fiancée. Isn't that right, *kjaer?"*

Olaf and Sven blinked at Aimee. She gritted her teeth and spoke with a hiss. "No, it is not, nor will it ever be."

She then turned to the brothers, and smiled sweetly. "Thank you for your invitations. I just may decide to attend the summer festival, after all." Sven and Olaf smiled, but weakly, their eyes shifting from Aimee's rosy face to Luke's scowling one. They sensed that Aimee was more interested in defying this stranger than in attending the festival.

Aimee didn't notice their puzzled sad look because her eyes were locked with Luke's. Olaf and Sven hurried into their carriage. "Er, yes, we hope you can come. Thanks for your advice." With one last envious look at Luke, they bolted down the road.

Aimee turned a disdainful shoulder on Luke, but he stopped her with a hand on her reins. "Since we've had this propitious meeting, I'd like to invite you on a tour of my ship." Luke was angry that she seemed so at ease with the two young men, yet so wary of him, but he clamped down on his surge of jealousy and smiled at her.

Aimee stared down at his strong hands, telling herself she hated them. So why did she tingle as she remembered what they felt like on her body? She lifted her eyes to his and shuddered when she saw his gaze fixed hotly on her mouth. He watched her lips form the words, "No, I have another errand to run."

He lifted one hand to stroke her braid back over her shoulder, the movement so tender Aimee was shocked out of her anger. "Please," he urged gently. "I will make no advances, I promise. I truly want you to look at my foal. I'm worried about him."

Aimee tried to look away from his black eyes, but she was trapped in their enticing darkness. Aimee's head took on a will of its own and she nodded. "Very well," she murmured. "I'll come soon."

Luke leaned so close his breath stirred her hair when he spoke. "Thank you . . . Aimee." He let her reins go, smiled, and rode on his way, leaving the sound of the endearment he whispered ringing in Aimee's ears. *Kjaer*. Dear one.

Aimee rode on to Gere's, more confused than ever. He didn't really mean it. He didn't care about her. And she certainly didn't care about him. But even as she berated herself, she couldn't erase his face from her mind; she couldn't help but wonder why he seemed so manly next to the twins. And she couldn't quiet the pounding of her heart at the thought of meeting him again.

"Sigrid will never agree, Aimee. I tried to talk her into it last night, and she refused." Aimee had never seen Gere look so frustrated. She wanted to reach out and smooth the frown from his brow, but she knew she had no right. "She'll never agree to marry me without her parents' approval."

She paced up and down the tiny porch he'd added on to his log cabin, her mouth pursed in thought. "She might agree if we surprise her with it. I won't tell her where we're going. Once we arrive, between the two of us, we can probably convince her. I can't believe the Garrisons will back out of the agreement even if there's no marriage."

Gere asked softly, "And what if you're wrong, Aimee? What if they refuse to ally the businesses after Sigrid and I are wed? You know how much Ragnar wants to convert to steam. What if the deal is abrogated because of you?"

Aimee flinched. "Gere, what am I to do? Surely you realize I can never bind myself forever to a man like Captain Garrison. Can't you see how unsuited we are? Am I to condemn myself to unhappiness just so my father can further his ambitions?"

"Why are you so convinced you'd be unhappy? Garrison seems a strong man who would make a good husband."

Aimee looked at him, worried. "That's the problem. He's too strong to let me go my own way. We'd be at each others' throats the entire time."

Gere seemed on the verge of arguing, then he sighed. "Very well, what will you do after Sigrid and I marry? It's you Garrison really wants, and what's to keep you free after our wedding?"

Aimee looked lost for a moment, then she tilted her head. "Have you ever known anyone to make me do something I was totally opposed to?"

Gere's mouth twitched wryly. "No. But you've never known a man like Luke Garrison, either. He's no boy to be put off by sweet evasions." Aimee flushed and turned away, and Gere knew his words had hit home. Whether Aimee knew it or not, she needed Luke Garrison. He would tempt her out of herself; tempt her into a relationship she didn't even know she longed for. Gere had seen the half-scared, half-fascinated look on her face as she stared at him.

"Aimee, why do you dislike Captain Garrison so?" he probed. Aimee gave a small start, but again evaded that question.

He touched her shoulder gently. "He's greatly attracted to you, you know. It would be very easy to make him fall in love with you, if you'd open up and let him see the caring, wonderful person you are behind this proud little face." Gere forced her mutinous chin even higher until she boldly met his eyes.

"But I don't want him to love me," she said, flinching from

his grasp. "All I want is to be left alone. Is that asking so much?"

Gere's smile disconcerted her. It was a strange smile with a world of masculine meaning behind it. "Yes, it's asking too much of a man like Luke Garrison. You've challenged him, he's accepted, and now you've no choice but to give in or to fight."

With a frustrated groan, Aimee whirled away. Men! Gere seemed so sympathetic toward Garrison. She looked at him reproachfully. "Why are you saying this? *He* challenged *me*. I admit I was a little rude to him, but he deserved it. From our first meeting, he's acted like he owns me. Am I supposed to be grateful his lofty eye has landed on me?"

Gere sat down in the carved rocker he had made himself and went back to the whittling Aimee had interrupted. He studied the figurine of a Laplander in his hands before speaking. "I've never known you to be so dishonest with yourself, Aimee. If you truly found him distasteful, he'd leave you alone. But he's an experienced man and he senses your attraction to him. You challenge him by refusing to admit it, by trying to escape as much from yourself as from him. Since he's strongly drawn to you, how can he do less than try to make you acknowledge it?"

For the second time in two days, Aimee lost her temper. She pounded a balled fist against the porch railing and wailed, "I'm not attracted to him, I'm not! And he doesn't care about me. All he wants is to humble me. If he won my submission he'd lose interest."

Gere's head snapped up. He'd found the real problem. He was considering how best to probe deeper when she turned on him like a cornered tigress.

"You're as bad as he is," she hissed. "Is that all men can think of? Owning, possessing, subduing. What of me? Don't my feelings matter? And you, do you really care what Sigrid thinks? Or do you just want a lovely wife to see to your needs and obey your commands—'*Ja*, Gere, whatever you say, Gere'?"

Gere's worried expression froze. He rose to his full, imposing height. "You've no right to speak of Sigrid so," he snapped. "Of course I care about her. If I only wanted someone to see to my needs, I'd take a mistress or a maid." He flung the carving and his knife into the rocker and stepped up to Aimee.

Gere grasped her arm and pulled her close to him, so she couldn't whirl away and close him out. "You're a coward, Aimee. You have so much love to give to the right man, too much sweetness to waste, but you hoard it greedily rather than take the chance of being hurt. Have you ever considered that your behavior might have hurt Captain Garrison?"

At her sniff of disbelief, Gere released her arm in disgust. "No, I guess not. Well, consider this: feelings stifled too long can be buried forever. Independence is wonderful as long as it doesn't smother your softer feelings. Love, emotion, caring—that's where happiness lies. Remain independent, Aimee. Luke respects you for that. But if you go on the way you are, you'll find your freedom very lonely in your dotage."

Aimee bit her lip, but she couldn't dam the tears that flooded her eyes. How could he attack her so? "That's not fair, and you know it, Gere. I care very deeply about many things. In fact, it's because I care so deeply that I hesitate to give my trust easily. Is that so wrong?"

Gere sighed and softened at the hurt in her face. "No, Aimee, it isn't. I just want you to be happy because I love you like my own dear sister." Gere shrugged ruefully. "I guess I'm short-tempered because I'm tired of trying to win your father's approval." They smiled at one another in understanding.

It was Aimee's turn to lecture Gere. "You know how pig-headed my father is. Sometimes you have to bash him over the head just to get his attention. I think you're too polite to him. If you let him walk all over you, he'll do exactly that. You should stand up to him like I do. Earn his respect, and he'll give it."

Gere looked thoughtful. "Perhaps you're right, Aimee. God knows I've tried everything else."

He stepped up to pull Aimee gently into his arms. "Dear one, how wise you are for one so young. Why can't you reflect some of that wisdom in your own life?"

Aimee shrugged wryly. "I am doing exactly that. I know without a doubt that I must be wary of Luke Garrison."

Gere took her hands and shook them gently. "You're as stubborn as Luke is. Do you realize what a battle you have on your hands?"

Gere was amazed to see a twinkle in her eye as she agreed blandly, "Yes, I do. Why, do you think I'll lose?" she challenged, lifting an eyebrow.

Gere didn't smile as she intended. He tightened his grip and said seriously, "Yes, Aimee, I think you'll lose if you reject Luke's suit without careful consideration. Whether you realize it or not, he's your perfect match. Won't you at least be polite and give him a chance?"

Aimee sighed, exasperated. "Not you too, Gere. Very well, I will be polite to Captain Garrison. In fact, I'm on my way to see him now."

At his pleased look, she added hastily, "To see about the foal he told me about, that's all. I'm truly not attracted to him."

Gere smiled when her eyes darted away from his glance. Very well, little one. Don't admit the truth, even to yourself. If I know anything of Luke Garrison, he'll face you with it soon enough, he thought.

Aloud, he said, "Thank you, Aimee, for helping me and Sigrid. Now, if you think you can convince Sigrid, I'll be waiting for you at five o'clock two days from now." The parting between them was amiable as ever, but Aimee had much to brood about during the short trip to Bergen.

She almost turned around to head back home, but with a toss of her head, she urged her little pony in the direction of the wharf. She had to prove to Gere that she was not attracted to Garrison. More important, it was time to face Captain Luke Garrison, wealthy heir to one of the world's largest shipping enterprises, because she must prove it to herself.

Luke was playing cards with Potter and several other crewmen when one of the "black gang," a coal pusher named Sims, came to tell him he had a visitor. "A right bonnie lass," the shy Scotsman added.

Luke glanced up eagerly. He threw in his cards and pocketed his winnings, ignoring Potter's vociferous protests.

"Cap'n, that's the third time in a row you've quit in the middle of the game. And damn if you don't leave with more than you had when you started." Potter shook his head in disgust.

The chief steward, Johnson, joked with him. "That's why he owns this ship and you're just the engineer. He knows how to quit when he's ahead." Potter shot him a scalding look and dealt the next hand.

Luke hurried to the grand saloon. He was disconcerted at the surge of emotion he felt when he spotted Aimee, but his confusion was hidden under an easy smile. "Thank you for coming. Where would you like to begin our tour?"

Aimee's heart raced as she glanced over his handsome features. Gere's words howled in her ears like banshees warning of calamity, and she was barely aware of her own response. "You know best."

Luke staggered back as if stunned. He put his hands to his cheeks in shock. "Those are words I never expected to hear from you," he teased.

Aimee turned crimson. Then she laughed, really laughed, and Luke joined in. She curtsied. "I deserved that, I admit. Well, sir, lead on. And of course I want to see the foal you told me about."

Luke's eyes traveled over her so intimately that Aimee's smile died. She clenched her hands to avoid squirming under the gaze she felt physically. Calm, I will be calm, he means nothing to me, she repeated over and over in a litany.

When his eyes finally landed on her face, she couldn't control a gasp. He stared at her mouth with . . . such a look of hunger, she felt stunned. Then he nodded. His lashes lowered like black fans, and the moment was gone.

When he looked at her again, he displayed nothing but mannerly acceptance. "I would greatly appreciate your help. But first, shall we have our tour?"

Aimee nodded just as politely. She dutifully admired the grandeur of the staterooms, the dainty ladies' boudoir and she even nodded in approval at the neatness of the storerooms. But inside, she was barely conscious of how she reacted. It seemed two people were battling for control of her heart and mind. Her senses had never felt so alive, so acute to another's presence. When he pointed out a particularly fine carved lintel, her eyes glanced at it, then fixed on the large, competent hand that pointed to the ornamented doorway.

When he brushed against her accidentally, she flinched, her arm burning where he touched it. She became impatient with her own contrary reactions. What was this strange hold he had on her? What devil's lures did he cast to tempt her away from her very will? Alarmed, she shifted and longed to escape his enervating influence.

Luke sensed her growing reserve. He wanted to groan with

frustration. He had never tried to use his position to manipulate or impress, and he was disgusted to realize that he'd broken his own unwritten vow. He had hoped seeing the *Mercury* would help her realize how much she had to gain by their marriage. Instead, she was retreating from him.

By the time they reached the hold where the horses were kept, both were stiff with tension. Luke wondered grimly what she'd do if he ordered the *Mercury* to sail and kept her captive. Aimee's skin prickled with danger at the look in his eyes. She turned to the foal, weak-kneed but relieved at the diversion.

The tiny horse slumped on its side, brown sides heaving as it slept heavily. Heedless of the dirty straw that clung to her skirt hem, Aimee knelt beside it. She touched the pulse in the animal's neck and frowned.

"What have you been trying to feed him?"

With an effort, Luke forced his attention away from her to the foal. "Milk mixed with a little grain." He gestured to a crude bottle standing on a stall shelf.

Aimee glared at it. No wonder the poor baby wouldn't eat. A large jar had been fitted with an old rubber glove with one of the fingers cut away to form a makeshift nipple.

She took the bottle down and sniffed it. Sour. She turned an accusing glare on Luke, then thrust the jar under his nose. "Smell. Would you drink this?"

Luke almost gagged. His brows creased in a look that boded ill for the person who had been given the task of tending the foal. "I'm sorry, I should have paid more attention to the poor little beast."

Aimee turned up the sleeves of her crisp white blouse. "Have someone prepare a bowl of milk mixed with one-fourth cream. Add a little honey and heat it to lukewarm. Then bring a sponge and some towels."

Luke's mouth trembled in a stifled smile, for she reminded him irresistibly of Hedda at that moment. She issued her commands with the confidence of a drill instructor. Nodding, he turned to do her bidding, his smile breaking into a grin. He couldn't wait to watch the sparks fly when she met Hedda.

When Luke returned with the items she had requested, he found Aimee cradling the foal's head in her lap. Her face was soft, tender and so lovely as she stroked its velvety muzzle that Luke longed to throw the bowl and towels to the ground, snatch her into his arms and demand she look at him the same way; all he could do was approach and feel ridiculous at his jealousy.

The straw crunched under his advance. Aimee looked up. Luke watched helplessly as her expression froze into another guarded mask. She gestured him over. He knelt beside her, torn between resentment and admiration. She tore the sponge to an angled point, then dipped it in the bowl and held it to the foal's mouth.

At first the tiny horse shifted away, refusing to drink, but Aimee repeated the motion patiently, again and again, until, frustrated, the foal licked at the milk dribbling down its muzzle. The pink tongue lapped with increasing enthusiasm at each drop, and soon, when Aimee held the soaked sponge to the foal's mouth, it sucked eagerly.

Aimee closed her eyes in relief. A strange need to see Luke's reaction made her open them and focus them on his face. Her mouth parted in a soft gasp under the emotional impact of that stare. He was kneeling so close she could feel the warmth of his taut, hard thigh next to her, but this time she did not feel threatened. His expression was so admiring she felt warmed, and, for a moment, she dared believe he really cared about her.

Luke was mesmerized by her happy, broad smile. For this instant in time, there were no barriers between them. They were not adversaries, nor even man and woman; they were friends united in a common cause, each triumphant at achieving a common goal.

"Well done, *kjaer*. You have my deepest thanks," he said. Luke's smile faltered as he noticed her withdrawal. Her eyes lowered to the foal again, and she didn't lift them until the bowl was empty.

His careless endearment sent reality crashing down. She must never forget he was an experienced man who knew every seductive ploy ever written. She berated herself for the pleasure she had felt as she basked briefly in his approval. But even anger could not stifle her awareness of him. She felt his warmth, the flexing of powerful muscles, and the fresh scent of the sandalwood soap he used.

As she soaked the sponge with milk a last time, her nerves screamed with the need to escape before . . . Before what? Before she was forced to concede how attractive he was? Aimee almost bit through her lip as she admitted that Gere was right. Different as he was, arrogant as he was, infuriating as he was, she was drawn as she'd never been drawn to a man before.

The reluctant admission made her feel not one whit more charitable toward Luke, however. In a way, she was even angrier, for he had defeated her resolve to remain unaffected by him. If she had searched Norway from Christiana to the Arctic Circle and back again, she could hardly have selected a more unsuitable man for her. Even if he wanted more than to crush her rebellious spirit, their natures clashed too much to blend into a harmonious union.

So, when Luke helped her to her feet and brushed the straw away from her skirt, she stood rigid and unresponsive. But Luke had had a tantalizing glimpse of how it could be between them, and he was not willing to let her hide from him again without a fight.

He attacked point-blank. "All right, Aimee, let's have it. What have I done now to return you to that haughty stance?"

Aimee felt relief at the assault. Here, at least, was familiar territory she knew how to defend. Her eyes widened in genuine disbelief. "You accuse me of being haughty? *You,* Sir Luke of Arrogance?"

Luke's brows lowered in a brooding frown that seemed to confirm her charge. "Suppose I admit you're right. I can be arrogant. But so can you. In my opinion, we make quite a pair. Neither one of us would become too bloated because we'd take pleasure in pricking the other's bubble. We should suit admirably, don't you agree? Shall we set the date for our wedding?"

It took all Aimee's self-control to avoid shrinking from him. He would never leave her alone. Now that she knew her own weakness for him, it was more important than ever to keep him at bay. But, for Sigrid's sake, she must keep him guessing for at least two more days.

She laced her voice with huskiness. "Perhaps. When I've had time to accustom myself to the idea."

Luke had been trying to goad her and he was unprepared for her capitulation. It had come much too easily. His eyes narrowed to suspicious slits. "How long do you need?"

"Shall we say two days? I'll give you my answer then."

His every sense now alerted, Luke knew she was planning something. But what? He searched her blank face to no avail. He offered his arm. "Very well, Aimee. I will call on you in the morning two days hence for your answer."

She cast him a swift look of alarm as she put her fingers very lightly on his sleeve. "Ah, yes, the morning . . . ," she said breathlessly.

Luke peered at her head as though he would delve inside and read her every thought. He nodded. "And I will appoint someone else to attend the foal, mixing its milk as you suggested."

When they reached the main deck, Luke escorted her to a cabin so she could wash up, then he led her to the shore boat and lifted her lightly into it. His hands lingered on her waist, and for an instant, his breath caressed her hot cheeks. He kissed her mouth lightly, giving her no time to back away.

Her mouth tingled. She blurted, *"Adjø,* Captain Garrison. If you follow my instructions, I feel sure the foal will be fine."

Luke caught sight of Gere's gleaming blond hair in the bright sunshine. He frowned when Gere emerged from behind a box and put a finger to his lips. He gestured at Aimee. Luke smiled at Aimee absently.

"I'll see you soon, my dear. Take care."

The shore boat was winched down to the sea, so Aimee never observed Gere stepping up to Luke. Nor did she hear Gere's urgent, "I must speak with you, Luke."

Her eyes unaccountably seemed watery today. It was only the emotional scene with the foal, she admonished herself. But the memory she carried away in a heart that ached was of a tall, black-haired man who made anything seem possible. It was an effort to remind herself he was also a devil tempting her to surrender the values she'd formed over her brief lifetime, and pledge herself to him.

Aimee was depressed when she returned home, and, for the first time, she doubted her own wisdom. What if Gere were right? What if her refusal to wed offended the Garrisons so that they backed out of the business deal? How could she bear to hurt her parents yet again because of her own stubbornness?

She had not been pleased to discover that she was greatly attracted to Luke. More loudly than ever, her mind screamed of danger. Luke had threatened her when she hadn't cared about him; if she allowed his physical appeal to deepen into an emotional one, she would be giving him a weapon to hold against her. She would be entirely dependent on someone else—someone probably untrustworthy over time—for her most basic happiness.

Yet she couldn't bear the thought that, in order to save herself, she must sacrifice her father. He was a proud man and he would be humiliated if his well-known plans fell through. And what if Sigrid refused to marry Gere? What then? Aimee retreated to her room, flopped on the bed and buried her face in her arms.

Gere's response to her suggestion had seemed strange. Almost as though he played for time, humored her instead of agreeing to the stealthy wedding she considered the best way to save Sigrid. But what else was there to do? Wed him yourself, came the answer. Aimee leaped up and strolled restlessly to the window, her rationality soaring and overcoming her with every step. It's the most sensible solution. Sigrid will be free to marry Gere, *Far* will get his capital, and you . . . you will be wed to a man who fascinates you more with each meeting.

Aimee shook her head desperately and looked out at the forest, the rich fields and the fenced orchards. In the distance, snow-capped mountains called to her with love of this rugged country. She didn't want to leave Norway, or her family. Yet . . . she had always longed to travel. As the wife of a shipping magnate, she could travel all she wanted. Surrender, make everyone happy, her logical half urged. But her independent side balked. Yes, make everyone happy but yourself. Condemn yourself to a tumultuous marriage. Luke Garrison will never allow you a mind of your own, decisions of your own, unless they fuse with his. *No!* Best solution or not, she couldn't yoke herself to a man who would never be satisfied until he occupied her every thought.

Aimee was on the verge of tears when a knock sounded at the door. "Come in," she said dully.

She wasn't surprised when her father entered. He came over to her and put an arm about her shoulder. He had said nothing further yet about Luke Garrison, but she had known it was just a matter of time. He seemed to believe that the moment was now, not realizing how right—for him—he was. He had found her in a moment of weakness. She gamely tried to shore up her flagging determination. Smiling to hide her turmoil, she turned to face him.

"Aimee, I think you know why I've come. Shall we sit next to the window?" He tugged her down on the window seat, sat next to her and held her hand. "Child, before I say anything else, I want you to know how much I love you. Surely you know I would never try to force you to wed a man who would mistreat you?"

Aimee nodded, her heart pounding. No, *Far,* don't. I can't bear any more, she longed to plead, but she bit her tongue to hold back her words. She was afraid to listen, but she owed her father too much to deny him that much.

"I've had a long talk with Luke, and I truly believe you'll each grow to care for one another. I know you don't see it now, but he's perfect for you. Can't you put aside this unreasonable fear and wed him? It's the only way to save the situation. Sigrid will be free to marry Gere, and the Garrisons will finance my conversion to steam."

"And me, *Far?* What will happen to me?" Aimee cried.

Ragnar's mouth set sternly. "And you, *datter,* will become part of one of the wealthiest, most influential families in America. You talk as if you'd be condemned to hell, Aimee, when you'd win a life of privilege most women would envy."

Aimee was hurt at the impatience in his voice. Even now, he didn't understand. "But I care nothing for that! I'd lose what is most important to me: my family and my right to make my own decisions."

Ragnar sighed. He looked down and stroked the back of her hand, frowning, then he stared bleakly into her eyes. "I won't force you to marry Garrison, Aimee. I understand why you're afraid, but I think you're being unreasonable. Do you think you can spend the rest of your life avoiding romantic ties?"

Ragnar rose and went to the door, where he turned to face his daughter. The mixture of pain and love in his eyes hit Aimee like a cold wave. "Please think very carefully about your decision. I won't force you to wed him, despite all my hopes and dreams, but I plead with you to be wise. And I would point out that, if the Garrisons insist, Sigrid will wed Garrison even if you won't."

Ragnar closed the door softly as he exited, but the noise sounded like a death knell in Aimee's ears. She had never felt so miserable, so low, in all her life. She felt as desperate as a cornered rat, and, at this moment, she felt just about as noble. Dear God, what was she to do?

Aimee stayed in her room that night, staring out the window. She didn't go down to supper, and even when Sigrid entered the room, she didn't move.

Aimee didn't see the exasperated look on her sister's face,
nor did she realize Gere had just left. Sigrid's mind was as
receptive to Aimee's moods as ever, and her anger at
Aimee's plans to manipulate her into marriage faded. She
had intended to confront her sister, but Ragnar had urged
her to wait and leave Aimee to him and Captain Garrison.
Reluctantly, Sigrid had agreed. And now, Aimee's face was
so bleak she moved instinctively to comfort her.

"Aimee, please tell me what's troubling you. Are you still
afraid *Mor og Far* will force you to wed Captain Garrison?"

Mutely, Aimee shook her head. She grasped Sigrid's arms
with sudden urgency. "Force *me,* no. But what of you,
Sigrid? What if Captain Garrison refused to go back without
a bride?"

Sigrid pulled away. She whispered, "Let us hope it does
not come to that. Captain Garrison doesn't want me, he
wants you."

Sigrid asked gently, "Why do you find him so distasteful,
Aimee? I find him very handsome and charming. Just think
what a challenge it would be to hold a man like that."

Aimee's smile was mocking. "Ah, not you too, Sigrid.
Please don't you try to convince me too." And, with sudden
fierceness, she added, "I won't be dictated to. If he was less
of a man, perhaps I could put aside my reservations. Don't
you understand? It's all a game to him. If he ever won my
regard he'd toss it away like a frayed ribbon and seek a shiny
new trophy. I know who I am, Sigrid. And that person could
never be happy with him. He'll not accept less than total
dominance of my every thought and I'll give no one that
degree of power over me."

Sigrid shrugged, at a loss how to argue with such certainty.
"Very well, Aimee. You, of all people, should know your
own mind. But I remind you that *Far og Mor* will probably
never be able to convert to steam without the Garrisons'
help. If neither of us weds Luke, and our parents one day lose
their business, we'll be to blame. I can't face that possibility.
It will tear me apart to give up Gere, but what else can I do?
What happiness would I have with him if it was built on the
ruin of my parents' lives?" Her eyes were as bleak as
Aimee's. Ignoring her sister then, she prepared for bed.

Once again, Aimee was left with only her disturbing
thoughts for company. And it continued into the next day.

Ragnar barely glanced at her when she told him she was going for a ride into the hills. But her haven offered no solace, this time, for she couldn't flee from her own conscience. Even if Sigrid agreed to marry Gere, which Aimee doubted, now, where did that leave her parents? Surely the Garrisons would have strong doubts about merging their business with a man who couldn't even control his own daughter?

Aimee stared blindly at the picturesque perfection of the fjord gleaming in the sun. A mere few days ago, she'd sat in this very spot and longed for a chance to prove her maturity and deep love for her father. Fate had granted her that chance, and she was too afraid to take it. Would she hate herself for the rest of her life if she didn't surrender?

The next morning, Aimee's head was dizzy from two sleepless nights, but she dressed carefully, as if for battle. When Sigrid came to tell her Ragnar wanted her in the parlor, she was almost relieved. They had to settle this before she went mad. She would either have to put her parents' fate in God's hands and hope the Garrisons would release them from the marriage stipulation, or she would have to fuse her fate with a man she found extremely threatening.

Such were the choices facing her when she entered the parlor. She wasn't surprised to find Luke Garrison there already, standing next to her father. Hands clasped behind his back, head erect with determination, he loomed like a warrior general come to demand terms for her surrender.

Ragnar shook his head at her once she was seated. "Aimee, I'm disappointed in you. Gere warned us of your plans. I must say he's smarter than I thought. Did you really think Sigrid would agree to such a charade? What gives you the right to make such decisions for her?"

Aimee clenched her fists. Suddenly, she was furious. "I was only trying to save her from unhappiness. Was that wrong? I never believed the Garrisons would be so angry they'd refuse to lend you the money you need."

Luke inserted dryly, "You can believe it. I did my best to convince my parents this marriage was unnecessary, but they're set on the idea." He strode forward to glare at her bent head. "Do you think you're the only one who didn't want to wed? They almost had to blackmail me into agreeing to marry someone I hadn't even met." Aimee was too upset to catch the significance of the past tense, but Ragnar looked at Luke sharply.

Aimee's stomach lurched at this confirmation of her worst fears. She could no longer escape, not if she wanted to save both her father and Sigrid. Groaning, she buried her face in her hands.

Ragnar shot Luke a warning look, then he crouched in front of Aimee to pull her hands away and cradle her face in his hands. "Aimee," he coaxed, "please consider carefully. What will you do if you don't wed Luke? You refuse to encourage any of our young men. Do you intend to spend the rest of your days alone?"

Aimee shivered. She was so confused. She no longer knew what was right for her. She loved her father. Perhaps she should trust him once more, believe that he was right, that she and Luke could be happy. Her eyes were huge with uncertainty as she stared at Ragnar.

He smiled at her so tenderly that tears welled up, and her throat tightened. He brushed back a curl of her hair and finally made the one argument she couldn't resist. "Aimee, Luke has made me realize how unfair I've been to you. Selfishly, I've wanted to keep you my little girl. I didn't want to lose you, but I see now that I already have. My little girl is no more. She's a young woman, with a woman's concerns, a woman's feelings, a woman's strength. There isn't anything you can't do, nothing you can't face. I want you to know that, whatever your decision, I'm proud of you."

While Aimee was still quivering under the emotional impact of the words she'd always longed to hear, Luke dropped to his knees on her other side and clasped her hands. Ragnar rose and moved away to give them privacy.

Gently, Luke caught Aimee's elbows and drew her forward. He bent his head and spoke softly, "Aimee, I swear I'll be as patient and gentle as any man can be, if you'll only marry me. I'll woo you as slowly as you like after we're wed, but now there's no time. I must leave soon and I want you with me. Isn't it time you quit running from yourself and admit what there is between us? My heart pounds for you, can't you feel it?"

Luke forced her slender hand over his heart, and the heavy throbbing seemed in rhythm with her own. "We're perfect for each other, sweet Aimee. I know it. And somewhere, deep inside, I think you know it too. Let us give this feeling a chance to grow. Please?"

Luke's silky voice soothed Aimee's taut nerves. She stared up into eyes whose soft black universe enticed her into uncharted but enthralling regions that stretched to infinity. He challenged her to explore, to delve with him into the vast mystery of what man could offer woman.

Ragnar watched, holding his breath as Luke mesmerized his daughter.

Luke's eyes never wavered from Aimee's as he literally tried to will her to agree. She was meant for him. Why couldn't she see it? He never let himself consider that her will to resist might match his need to win. This woman was more than a challenge; she was an obsession, and he wouldn't rest until he filled every thought in her head as completely as he longed to fill her body.

Taking a deep breath, Aimee forced herself to respond rationally. "We're not suited, Luke. Would you let me go my own way, do as I see fit, no matter what?" At his doubtful look, she added, "I am happy as I am, but you and your family would try to change me, force me into a role . . . Can't you see it wouldn't work?" Her voice was soft and passionate as she tried to convince him, and she watched with a sinking heart as he shook his head.

His smile was just as earnest. "I don't want to change you, Aimee. I like you as you are. It can work. We'll make it work."

"And your parents? They would feel the same?"

Luke looked down, then squared his shoulders. "Once they get to know you, I'm sure they'll accept you as you are. I'll stand beside you all the way." Luke's heart hammered with nervousness as he awaited her reply. He knew he intended to win her acceptance if he had to send the *Mercury* on without him.

Aimee looked from Luke, so handsome and appealing as the sun caught his lush lashes and shining black hair, to her father, his brown eyes both anxious and proud, and she knew she could fight no longer. She went limp. Bowing her head, she whispered, "You win. I will wed you."

Luke's face lit up with joy. He opened his mouth to praise her, but Ragnar motioned him to be silent. Luke clamped down his jaw, patted her hand and rose.

"Thank you, Aimee. I'll be sure you don't regret this decision. I'll leave the arrangements to your parents, but I have the license, and I'd like us to wed as soon as possible." He frowned when Aimee nodded, but still refused to look at him.

Ragnar escorted him to the door. "She'll be fine, Luke, don't worry about her. She's tired and bewildered, but she'll be at the church for the wedding, don't fear." The two men shook hands and smiled at one another triumphantly.

"I feel twenty feet tall, Ragnar. Thank you for your help. I know I never could have convinced her without you."

"Thank you, in turn. You said exactly the right things to her." Ragnar's smile faded as he clasped Luke's shoulder to warn. "Just see you take care of her and prove her decision wise. If that child is hurt, business or no business, you'll answer to me."

"I'll protect her with my life," Luke vowed.

While the men were congratulating themselves in the hall, Aimee trembled in the study alone and hid her face behind interlocked hands. She desperately sought to escape the memory of Luke's face. This man, this dark foreigner who had alarmed her from their first meeting, would soon be her husband. She despaired at the knowledge that she could never escape him. She stiffened as it occurred to her that she didn't *want* to escape him. She *wanted* to wed Luke Garrison, would have done so even if Sigrid hadn't been in danger.

Her mind, already confused, shied from this final revelation. Her only defense was the blessed numbness of shock. She straightened her back and composed her hands. Very well. She would be bound to Luke Garrison, and she would do her best to make him a good wife. However, she would also try to protect herself. Physically, she'd be at his side, but emotionally, she would remain in her own universe. He'd won her submission to his will, but she would never submit her heart and mind to him, no matter how attractive he was.

This unwavering resolve was little tested in the two hectic days that followed. Aimee spent the time in a blur. She was relieved that she didn't have to face Luke, for he stayed away preparing for their departure, Ragnar explained.

Aimee felt so devoid of feeling she barely comprehended Ingrid's relief and Sigrid's joy. Even when she met Gere's gentle, approving look, she felt no anger at his betrayal.

So, when her wedding day arrived, Aimee was, at first, calm. The day seemed to mirror her mood, for it was cloudy and sullen. With its ominous stillness, the sky seemed to promise a tremendous storm.

Aimee moved obediently as Ingrid dressed her in the simple silk dress hastily sewn by Bergen's most able seamstress. It was white and bordered at the low neckline and long puffed sleeves with silver-veined lace. The skirt was full, hemmed with a tiny frill of matching lace.

Sigrid arranged her hair in a complex series of braids interwoven with white roses. Aimee wore no veil, but the traditional silver diadem, lavishly carved and decorated with tiny bells, crowned her beautiful hair. Aimee barely heard her mother's gasp of delight at the results. She didn't see Sigrid's proud gleam. Even the moisture in Ragnar's eyes failed to move her.

Like a lovely Galatea awaiting Pygmalion's touch, Aimee sat in the splendid carriage, borrowed for the occasion. She didn't say a word. Only an occasional blink indicated she was a woman instead of a beautiful statue. Ragnar frowned, worried at her unnatural calm. He tried to engage her in conversation, but she either didn't hear him, or wouldn't reply. By the time they reached the church, Ragnar was frantic. He was tempted to call off the wedding, but when he helped Aimee from the carriage, she suddenly shuddered back to life.

This would be the last time she attended the church she had always loved. She examined its uniquely Norwegian architecture as if she'd never seen it before. Peaked, wood-shingled roofs piled atop one another like pointed hats. A cross topped each peak. The structure was crowned with an ornate tower and the stylized figure of a dragon, a legacy of Norway's Viking forbears. Trembling, Aimee put her hand on her father's arm and stared as the heavy, carved door yawned open.

And there, formidable in his formal black attire, stood her devil, waiting to claim her. Aimee longed to flee but inexorably her father led her forward. When Luke took her hand, his palm seemed to burn her. She didn't hear the murmurs of the guests at the lovely picture she made. After one peek, she refused to look at Luke, so she didn't see his appreciative, tender gleam. Aimee's eyes were so blurred with panic she barely even saw Father Erichsen, stately in his black robes and white ruff.

The ceremony began. As Father Erichsen's voice echoed in the chapel, outside the threatening storm finally broke. The guests had to strain to hear as rain beat hard against the windows. The pitter patter quickly increased to a thumping that sounded to Aimee like the thunder of doom. Her knees shook so much she could hardly stand.·

Several times the priest had to prompt her, but Luke made his responses in a calm, steady voice. She's mine, she's mine, he longed to shout to the rafters, but he felt the terror in his trembling bride, and he knew it was no time to show triumph.

The wind rose to a howl. Lightning flickered almost continually as Father Erichsen began his final blessing, and thunder resounded ever nearer. With the priest's last words the elements unleashed their fury in a gust of wind and rain so violent that, as Luke bent his head to plant a brief kiss on Aimee's lips, the church door flew open. He hugged her close to protect her from the rain that gushed in, but Aimee barely felt the cold gale, for she was already a block of ice from head to toe.

As Luke drew her face into the broad chest that seemed both heaven and hell, her stiff lips moved in a whisper that came from her soul. "Dear God, help me. What have I done?"

Chapter Five

THE LINGSTROM DINING room was packed with Bergen's wealthiest families. Some were curious, some were ambitious, a few were envious; without exception, they all wished Aimee well. They came to give their blessing to her sensible decision to wed Luke Garrison. They had not approved of her wild ways of late, and they were delighted she'd taken her proper role and furthered Ragnar's enterprise—and Norway's—in the process. They had known and loved Aimee since she was an impish little girl, and *menn og koner* alike were eager to meet the young man who had coaxed her into marriage. They also wanted to make themselves known to the heir of the Garrison empire.

Several of the young Norwegian men were motivated by something even more basic: envy. What was it about this American that interested Aimee as they never had? They were not as wealthy, true, but they knew Aimee had never been interested in wealth. Sven and Olaf had told them of the American's arrogance. They couldn't believe Aimee, untamed and independent as a rebel, had truly wed Luke Garrison, self-assured and demanding. Even physically, the two were strikingly different. He was tall, dark, strong; she was small, blond, delicate.

Thus, as the guests filed past the newlyweds to offer their congratulations, Aimee and Luke were closely scrutinized. Aimee tried to accept the hugs and handshakes in the spirit in which they were given, but underneath her gaiety, she despaired. When an old friend of her mother's hugged her, all she could manage in response was a fixed smile.

"Aimee, we're so happy for you," the little woman gushed, putting her plump cheek to Aimee's. The woman looked up at Luke admiringly. "She's a lucky young woman, you handsome fellow, but you are a lucky man."

Luke smiled and pulled Aimee closer. "I'm well aware of that. Now, if I can only convince her . . ." The woman's eyes widened but she was forced to proceed by the force of others behind her. Aimee flushed and tried to move away from Luke, but he held her fixed to his side. His fingers tightened more as Sven and Olaf moved to congratulate them.

Sven stammered, "Aimee, w-we wish you every h-happiness." Blushing, he bent down and kissed her cheek. Aimee kissed him back, ignoring Luke's scowl. Sven moved on, his mouth quivering. Aimee felt two feet tall at his expression. She shouldn't have encouraged him by promising to consider attending the festival with him. Wouldn't have, if she'd known what she'd be coerced into less than a week later. . . .

Olaf was of sterner mettle. He bowed over Aimee's hand. "Frøken Lingstrom," he began formally. He flushed as he realized his error and started over, "fru Garrison, it has been a privilege knowing you, and your presence will be sorely missed. I hope you find happiness in America."

Aimee's eyes burned at his unaccustomed stiffness. "Olaf," she said huskily, "I'll always remember you and Sven, too. I'll miss all the fun we had skating, climbing and sailing. If you and Sven are ever in America, you must come to see me. Isn't that right, Luke?" Her voice sharpened as she glanced at her silent husband.

His smile was perfunctory. "Certainly. We'll be living in New York. Washington Square. Ask at the docks. Anyone will be able to tell you where the Garrisons live."

Olaf stiffened at the subtle intimidation and turned to move on, but Aimee flinched away from Luke and grasped the young man's shoulders to plant a kiss squarely on his mouth. "*Adjø*, Olaf. You be happy, too." Olaf hugged her, then he marched on.

Aimee glared at Luke, but he was already greeting another guest, having dismissed Olaf from his mind. Was this the way it was to be between them? She couldn't even be friendly without being reminded that she wore the Garrison stamp? She had known Olaf and Sven since she was a child, and Luke had no reason to be rude to them. The admiring glances cast on Luke from the young girls, his easy replies, made her anger soar. He could flirt all he wanted, but she was not allowed to be courteous? Aimee glared at the emerald and diamond ring sparkling with every movement of her hand.

As the line of people dwindled, Aimee's anger increased. She had been a fool to give in. This dark raider had purloined her hand, her contentment and her freedom, and he offered nothing but material comforts and his name in return. There he towered, arrogant, wealthy, self-confident. He had probably never known a moment of misery or self-doubt in his life. He held her arm so possessively she felt like the prize he had labored long to win and now displayed as proof of his prowess. Aimee chanced one glittering look at his happy face, then snapped her head around and set her mechanical smile back on.

Fury washed through her in a tidal wave that carried all before it: misery, uncertainty and good intentions. She forgot she had promised herself she'd try to be a good wife; she forgot her parents had gone to great expense and trouble to make this day a happy memory for her. She was governed only by a primitive urge to humble this man as he had humbled her. Before the day was out, he'd regret forcing her into this unholy alliance, she vowed.

Luke chose this moment to catch his bride's hand. She flinched, and, frowning, he rubbed her icy fingers. He bent to whisper, "Sweet, if you'd rather forego this celebration, we can go directly to my ship." She shot him a glance of such panic and rage that his euphoria burst like a pricked balloon.

She made no attempt to disguise her bitterness when she muttered, "No, I would rather stay. I can't disappoint my parents after they've expended such money and effort to make this celebration." She nodded at the next guest in line.

Luke glanced up and saw Ragnar watching them worriedly. Ragnar signaled toward the parlor. Luke inclined his head, mouthing "Later." And he turned back to find Aimee greeting the last person in line with the most warmth she had shown all day. Too much warmth.

Luke glowered when Gere, his eyes twinkling, tugged Aimee to his breast and kissed her. Really, he was tired of having his wife ogled and fondled by all these audacious young men. Luke was outraged when Aimee encircled Gere's neck and stood on tiptoe to return the embrace. Gere cleared his throat and pulled her away. Luke moved to separate them, but Aimee flashed him a defiant look, clutched Gere's forearm and led him to the banquet table to fill a plate.

A wave of humiliation flooded Luke's bronzed face. He clenched his jaw to control the need to pry Aimee away from Gere and carry her off, over his shoulder if need be, to make it plain she belonged to him. He was unaware of the curious glances sent his way as, narrow-eyed, he watched Aimee flirt with Gere.

Aimee's heart leaped when she noted Luke's expression, but she turned away, her chin tilted higher. Damn him, and damn him for his triumph. Aimee knew she was causing a stir, that her parents and their friends watched her warily, as if they waited for her to do something outrageous. Well, far be it from her to disappoint them. She plopped several cream cakes defiantly on her plate and scanned the dishes for something that would make her stomach churn even more.

The table almost creaked under the banquet's sumptuous plenty. Ragnar hadn't counted the cost on this day of celebration. He had purchased such exotic imports as fresh oranges, French champagne and Russian caviar. Marthe had outdone herself in her preparation of sweet breads, cream cakes and decorated butter cookies. Meats included smoked salmon, beef with remoulade and glazed ham. After popping one of the cream cakes in Gere's mouth, Aimee wiped a napkin teasingly over his lips, watching Luke from the corner of her eye.

Luke strode forward at the sight. He'd see how handsome the Norwegian looked with two black rings around his blue eyes. Before he had taken three steps, Luke found his way blocked by a firm, but gentle Sigrid.

He reached out to push her aside, but she caught his arm. "You'll be doing exactly what Aimee wants if you cause a scene," she whispered. "Can't you see the way she's looking at you?"

Luke's rage receded a bit when he caught Aimee's secretive glance as she leaned against Gere. She ran a finger down his shirt. For the first time, Luke also saw the uneasy, embarrassed expression on Gere's face as he, too, looked their way.

Sigrid murmured, "She's acting outrageous because she's

angry and frightened. Right now she wants to show you, my parents and their friends that she won't be dictated to any longer. The best thing you can do is to ignore her, or, better still," with a teasing smile Sigrid leaned into him to run a finger down his silk vest, "join in her competition."

Luke relaxed and smiled into Sigrid's face. "I shall be delighted to participate in this game, sweet sister. Ah, perhaps I made the wrong choice. My mother was right. You will make a perfect wife."

Sigrid laughed huskily and fluttered her eyelashes at him as they neared the table. She caressed his bicep, and only Luke could hear the sarcasm laced into her voice when she whispered, "Indeed, Luke? You'd tyrannize me and I'd bore you within a month. We both know that."

Luke shrugged. He popped a cream cake in Sigrid's mouth and duplicated Aimee's gesture when he wiped the cream away. "Perhaps. But at least I wouldn't want to strangle you. We'd have a quiet marriage and you wouldn't take delight in tormenting me."

Sigrid swallowed and leaned forward to feed Luke a cake. "Aimee doesn't deliberately torment you, Luke. She's trying to protect herself, not hurt you."

Gere was whispering a similar concern to Aimee. "Don't you think this has gone far enough, Aimee? Luke will think you're trying to taunt him."

Through gritted teeth, Aimee smiled. "But I am. He'll wish he'd married a witch or a Valkyrie, anyone but me, before I'm finished with him."

Gere pried her hand from his arm and straightened. "Well, I'll no longer help you. You're being very foolish. . . ." She was looking beyond him and something in her eyes made him turn. He gasped when Sigrid wiped Luke's mouth as slowly and sensually as Aimee had wiped his.

He whirled back around. Did Sigrid believe he was really flirting with Aimee? Surely she knew him well enough by now to realize he was trying to soothe Aimee's fury. How dare she condemn him unheard? How dare she set out to humiliate him in front of their friends? His hurt soaring at what he perceived as Sigrid's mistrust, he joined wholeheartedly into Aimee's lesson of humility.

The guests were treated to the most shockingly entertaining wedding feast they had ever attended. The proper matrons were appalled, their husbands amused, their children delighted as the two couples tried to surpass each other in outrageousness.

When Gere played with a tendril of Aimee's hair, Luke kissed the top of Sigrid's head; when Aimee clasped Gere's arm closely to her side, Sigrid put her own arm around Luke's waist; when Luke tenderly smoothed one of Sigrid's eyebrows, Gere ran a bold finger along Aimee's mouth.

The townspeople watched the contest, their eyes bouncing between the couples. However, the indiscretion they half hoped for, half dreaded, never occurred. Neither couple became licentious, though they certainly behaved strangely for a newly wedded pair and an almost engaged pair.

Ragnar intervened, his face red with anger. He descended on Luke and hissed, "I expected such behavior from Aimee, but not from you. Shame on you! Go to your bride and escort her to the table so we can cut the torte and quiet the scandal you're all creating."

For the first time, Luke noticed the whispers, the curious looks. He was amused rather than embarrassed. No wonder Aimee rebelled against these gossiping old tabbies! As he looked at the ring of avid faces, his admiration for Aimee grew, for, despite his exasperation, he was proud of her spirit. Luke felt an urge to whisk her away and really give them something to talk about, but he restrained himself. It would not do to humiliate his new in-laws. From long experience, he set out to quiet the talk.

He met the eyes of several staring men until they shifted and looked away. He glowered at a group of whispering young men until they hushed, then he bowed to one thin, disapproving lady and smiled so roguishly she relaxed and smiled back. When the guests were once again concentrating on the food on their plates, Luke winked at Sigrid.

"Thanks for your help, Sigrid, but it's time I took my bride in hand." He strolled up to Aimee and grabbed her from behind in a bear hug.

"Nice try, pet. Unfortunately, your little escapade has embarrassed no one but yourself. You've had your fun. Now it's my turn."

Aimee stiffened. Under his raillery lay an undertone of iron. She vibrated with renewed fury at his arrogance, but Luke gave her no opportunity to voice the words she longed to hurl at him. Ruthlessly, he dragged her over to the small table where the cake and champagne had been set up.

"You can rant and rave all you want to, later, but for now, you've humiliated your parents enough. We will taste the wine together, we will calmly cut the cake. Understood?" When Aimee's eyes widened with shock, he added, "Unless you'd rather leave? That's my preference, actually. I'm eager to begin our union, aren't you?"

His brows creased so deeply on his last sentence that Aimee couldn't miss his double meaning. Her face colored a fiery red. Ingrid had tried to talk to her last night, but Aimee had been too upset to pay attention to her revelations, despite her curiosity. All she remembered was something about how a man and woman were constructed to fit closely together during the act of procreation.

Something in Luke's face told her sex was far more devastating than a mere coupling of bodies. His eyes were black as pitch, smoking with desire, his nostrils flared. She dazedly looked around for something to distract him.

She grabbed a glass of champagne and, her hand shaking, held it to his lips. "Drink," she ordered fiercely.

Luke complied, but his eyes never wavered from hers. When she lowered the glass, his tongue slowly, sensually rimmed his lips to lick away the residue. Aimee shivered. She ran a hand over her forehead, wondering why she felt so peculiar. Surely it wasn't possible to be both hot and cold at the same time?

Luke held the glass to her. He stared so intently at her mouth as she drank that her giddiness increased. He lowered the glass and ducked his head to kiss away a drop of champagne from the bottom of her lower lip.

"Hmm, delicious," he whispered in her ear. She gulped at the hoarse note in his voice. When he flicked his tongue along her lobe, she jumped and tried to back away, but he secured her to him with a gentle arm.

"No, Aimee, you can escape me no longer. You're mine, now and always."

Their eyes locked in the strange communion that had bound them together from the beginning. They were unaware of what a lovely couple they made as each tried to outstare the other. They only knew the potent rush of blood through their veins, and the heady sweetness of warm, wine-scented breath. Aimee felt soft and dainty, but very right, in Luke's arms; Luke towered over Aimee, indomitable as a rock wall, but just as protective.

Luke pleaded, "Aimee, don't keep running away from me. Let today be a happy memory, as it was meant to be. Respond to me as a bride should."

Aimee muttered, "I've given up my freedom and promised my loyalty. Isn't that enough?"

Luke answered simply, "No, it will never be enough. I won't rest until you mean those words we spoke today with your heart, mind and soul."

Aimee averted her head, defeated. He was direct, she had to give him that. The lines were drawn, the challenge issued. Dear God, they were but married today, and already he wanted total surrender. She felt so confused, so uncertain of his feelings and her own that she allowed anger to block every thought. He would be patient, would he? If this was his idea of patience, she would show him her idea of loyalty! Her eyes settled on the torte, narrowed, opened widely, guilelessly. She turned back to Luke.

"Now is not the time to discuss this. We've a cake to cut."

Reluctantly, Luke released her. "Very well. But later . . ."

Aimee quivered, but the grim resolve in his voice only fanned her own. She handed Luke the long silver knife, put her hand over his and helped him cut a tiny piece of the two-tiered torte.

Luke held the cake to her mouth. She took a nibble, wiped the corner of her lips and smiled sweetly. "Your turn," she cried.

As she intended, Luke watched her mouth, so he didn't see her pick up the small top tier until it was too late. "Enjoy this, darling. You've earned it!"

Luke could hardly flinch as she flung the cake directly in his face. He grunted in surprise as the sticky mess trickled down his expensive suit and into his shirt collar. The guests gasped collectively; Ingrid buried her mortified face in her hands; Ragnar groaned; Sigrid clenched Gere's hand and Gere hid a smile. Utter silence prevailed as everyone waited to see how Luke would retaliate.

He glared at his giggling bride. Charcoal eyes seared through the frosting on his face, but the effect on Aimee was not as he intended. Far from intimidating her, his appearance made her laugh harder. She folded over, holding her sides as she shook with mirth.

"That should sweeten your temper a little," she gasped.

Luke made a grab for her, but he was half blinded by frosting and missed as she hopped away. "It's your own fiendish temper you'd best sweeten, minx," he growled. Wiping his eyes, he pursued her purposefully, but again, Ragnar intervened.

He handed Luke a towel. He glared at his daughter, who was licking her fingers like a contented cat. "I'll speak to you later, miss. For now, it's best you leave before you ruin my good name forever. Our friends are going to think there's insanity in our family."

"Certainly, *Far,* I'll be delighted to leave," she responded pertly. She turned as if to obey, then darted up to run an insulting finger around Luke's sticky lips.

She jumped back again before he could do more than stiffen. She lifted her finger to her mouth and licked the frosting delicately away. Staring into Luke's angry eyes, she taunted, "Hmm . . . de-li-ciousss . . ." Then, hips swaying jauntily, she exited the room, a genuine smile on her face for the first time in three days.

Luke's mouth twitched. She reminded him more than ever of a mischievous fairy as she sashayed out of the room. He certainly had to award this round to the stubborn little imp. Luke's smile stretched into a grin, then widened until chuckles shook his white-spattered chest. Ah, what a girl! They might end up killing each other, but whatever happened, he would *never* be bored.

The guests gasped in disbelief as Luke Garrison, his expensive suit ruined by the wedding cake his bride of an hour had tossed at him, threw back his black head and roared with laughter.

Ragnar sighed. This banquet would indeed be talked about for months, but not for the reasons he'd hoped. He'd believed Luke was strong enough to handle his willful daughter, but now he wondered. What other man would laugh at such an embarrassing incident? "Luke, you can wear one of my jackets if you wish to change," he offered wearily.

Luke's chuckles faded. Eyes glowing with enjoyment and anticipation, he demurred. "No, I'll wait until I return to my ship, thank you. If you've no objection, I'll collect Aimee and we'll be going. It's time we were alone."

Ragnar frowned at the odd note in Luke's voice. "Let Ingrid and me see the guests to the door, then meet me in the parlor. There's something I must discuss with you first."

Luke nodded and exited, bowing to the guests as he did so. Their returning smiles were stiff. Luke could see he had astonished them, but he shrugged inwardly. He didn't care what they thought, but he was concerned about Ragnar's tension. What was wrong?

Luke was uncomfortable in the soaked clothing and behaved irritably. "Yes? What is it?" he barked when Ragnar joined him in the parlor. Ragnar shifted from foot to foot, and Luke frowned at his unusual nervousness. Luke took the second damp towel Ragnar handed him and wiped the rest of the mess away.

"It's Aimee," Ragnar began. "Ingrid tried to tell her yesterday the, er, details of conjugal obligations, but she doesn't think Aimee was listening. Aimee is very innocent: I just wanted you to know."

Luke stiffened. "I'm aware of Aimee's skittishness, but she's my wife now and I'll handle her as I see fit."

Ragnar looked so worried and miserable that Luke sighed. "For God's sake, man, I would never do anything to harm Aimee. But why the devil hasn't her mother explained the facts of life to her?"

Ragnar smiled sheepishly. "It never seemed . . . necessary. We wanted to protect our daughters from the harsher side of life. They should learn about such things only after marriage."

Luke strode forward to clasp Ragnar's shoulder, but remembered his sticky hand and settled for smiling ruefully. "I'll give her all the care I'm capable of. I admire Aimee's spirit greatly, and I would never do anything to stifle it."

Reassured, Ragnar clasped Luke's hand despite its condition. "Thank you, Luke. My daughter will respond to you eventually, I'm sure of it."

"If you don't mind, it's time we left. Shall you fetch Aimee, or should I?"

"I'll get her, but are you certain you don't want to bathe first? You must be quite uncomfortable."

Luke shook his head, that mysterious smile tugging his mouth again. "No, I've washed the worst away. The rest can wait."

Shrugging, Ragnar hurried up the stairs to his daughter's room. He found Sigrid and Ingrid chastising an imperturbable Aimee.

"He deserved it," she replied to their reproaches, her

expression cool. She remained unmoved even when their lecture turned into a scolding.

Ragnar rubbed his forehead, exasperated. He feared his spirited daughter had much to learn about Luke, but it was too late for regrets. It would do no good to add his condemnation, and he didn't want their farewell to end with an argument. "Aimee, Luke is ready to leave. Are your bags packed?"

Aimee bit her lip and her head drooped. "Yes, I guess I'm as ready as I'll ever be."

Everyone was silent for a moment, then Sigrid tugged Aimee into her arms. "Aimee, I'll miss you terribly. I know you're angry, but please, please, give Luke a chance. He's a wonderful man, a strong man, and he'll care for you and support you if you'll quit fighting him."

Aimee could manage only a nod in response. Ingrid, tears in her eyes, embraced her daughter next. "*Datter,* forgive me for the times I've been less than patient with you. I love you very much and I'm sure that one day, you'll be as happy in your new life as Hedda is in hers. And please, try to act like a lady."

For once, the admonition didn't anger Aimee. She hugged her mother back and turned to her father, her throat aching.

His strong arms shook when he reached out to cup her chin. He met her eyes, moisture swimming in his own. "*Kjaer,* I know what a sacrifice you've made for this family, and we are forever in your debt. Someday, I hope you'll feel this difficult decision was the happiest choice you've ever made. Be patient with Luke. Give him your loyalty and soon, I feel certain, your marriage will be ecstatically happy."

He cushioned her against his broad chest because he couldn't bear to see the tears trickling down her face. "And always, remember how much I love you, how proud I am of you. It's like cutting off my arm to let you go," he rumbled, "but your place lies with your husband, and it's time you found happiness in your own way. I have all the faith in the world that you'll face everything life gives you with courage and honesty, and that you'll make the best of whatever happens."

Aimee clung to him, choking, "Oh *Far,* I will miss you so." He patted her shoulder soothingly, and she forced herself to pull away. There was a painful silence as Aimee tried to imprint these three dear faces on her mind. She wiped her tears away and took a deep breath. Crying would accomplish nothing, and she wanted their farewell to end on a happy note.

She checked her tears and tilted her chin in the look they all loved. "I'll do my best to make you proud of me," she promised quietly. "I make no pretense I'm happy to be leaving, or that I love Luke, but I will try to make this marriage work. Who knows? Maybe one day you'll all visit me in America and be amazed at my refinement. I'll be the queen of New York society." She fluttered her hand through the air. "And I'll dazzle you with my dignity and consequence." She lifted her skirts to mince across the room.

Everyone laughed, and the tension eased. Ragnar gave her a final hug, so exuberant he almost cracked Aimee's ribs. The love and pride in his expression nearly set her to crying again, but he shook his head and wagged a finger. "Enough tears, now. A dignified matron never loses her composure, remember."

Aimee hesitated, then blurted, "*Far,* please let Sigrid marry Gere. He's perfect for her, can't you see that?"

Ragnar sighed, and it was plain he was still not convinced. "I confess my opinion of the young man has risen in the past few days. I must say he wasn't intimidated by Luke, as many a lad would have been. If only he had a more stable position. . . ."

Sigrid exclaimed indignantly, "You started the same way, *Far!*"

Ragnar's response was dry. "That's precisely why I hesitate. I'd like your life to be easier than your mother's and mine." He held up a hand when Aimee tried to protest.

"Enough, child. I will promise to welcome the young man into my home. If he can convince me he can provide for Sigrid and be good to her, I will withdraw objection to his suit."

Aimee sighed in relief. At least something good had come out of this marriage. She smiled in gratitude at Ragnar. "Thank you, *Far.*"

Aimee hugged Sigrid a last time and whispered, "I expect to receive an announcement of your wedding very soon."

Sigrid murmured, her voice filled with sadness, "You'll be the first to know. Aimee, how can I ever thank you for everything?"

Aimee pulled away before she started crying again. "Nonsense. I'll never be able to repay you for all the joy you've given me over the years."

They looked at one another, putting on brave façades to spare the other. Ragnar stepped up, cleared his throat and extended his arm to Aimee. "Madame, your carriage awaits."

Aimee took a deep breath, locked her arm into his and strolled down the stairs, her step much lighter than her heart. A subdued Ingrid and Sigrid followed.

They found Gere and Luke talking in the parlor. Luke came forward to meet them. Aimee watched him warily, expecting anger to blaze, but his smile was instead filled with understanding. "Have you made your good-byes, sweetheart?"

She nodded.

Luke took her hand. "Well, let's be off, then. I have business in Stockholm soon, and I'd like to show you a little of the city first."

Aimee's false calm didn't fool Gere. He kissed her cheek and gave her a mock punch to the chin. "Courage, little tiger, and you'll have all New York as enamored of you as we are. Here's a present for you, but don't open it until tomorrow." He stepped back after she put the small parcel in her reticule. There was no more reason to delay, so Luke coaxed her to the door.

The others followed, watching as Luke untied Polaris. "You're welcome to take the carriage, Luke," Ragnar protested.

"No, send it on with the wedding presents and Aimee's baggage. Polaris will be faster." Reins in one hand, Luke shook hands with Ragnar and Gere, tapped Sigrid's white cheek and smiled at Ingrid.

He caught Aimee's tiny waist and boosted her onto the stallion. He mounted behind her and waved at his assembled in-laws. "Thank you for a lovely wedding, everyone. Please don't worry about Aimee. We'll have our arguments, I'm sure, but I'll do my best to make her happy." Compassionately, Luke paused to give Aimee a chance for a lingering good-bye.

Her heart tight with pain, Aimee looked at the four most important people in her life. Ragnar and Ingrid held hands, Gere's arm encircled Sigrid's waist; each, by their expressions of love and encouragement, gave her the strength to bottle her misery. Aimee knew there was only one thing left to do. Her smile was bold and jaunty, and, if it wavered a little, no one remarked on it. When Luke kneed Polaris into a slow walk, Aimee turned her head to watch her family disappear into the distance.

"Write often, *datter*. Remember, you'll be in our hearts and thoughts constantly," Ragnar called. "And see you visit us soon, mind."

Aimee and Luke waved. Luke urged Polaris into a trot, they rounded a bend, and Aimee's last glimpse was of her father, waving bravely. She closed her eyes to stem the rush of tears, cradling his image in her heart.

Luke pulled Aimee against him in silent comfort, but he knew he could offer little solace. To distract her, he asked questions about the sights they passed. "What kind of orchard is that, Aimee?" And, "What is the name of that lake, Aimee?" She responded dully, at first, but when they neared Bergen, she seemed more alert.

"Is there anything you want to see before we sail?" Luke queried. Aimee shook her downbent head, and Luke sighed. A gleam appeared in his eyes.

He drawled, "Good. I'm ready to get out of these filthy clothes. And, like the good wife I know you're going to be, you'll help me, won't you, my dear?"

As he had known she would, Aimee stiffened. She tried to pull away, reddening as she realized his sticky vest was soiling her new blue linen traveling costume.

Luke grinned as she surreptitiously leaned forward. He pulled her back to him and teased, "Perhaps we'll stick together—for life. Wouldn't that be an intriguing situation?"

Aimee whirled angrily. "That's just the kind of remark I'd expect you to make. Haven't you any compassion? Must you taunt me now?" Luke's sweet smile silenced her.

"But you feel a little better now, do you not?"

Aimee realized anger had chased away much of her pain. She spun back around. Damn him, why must he be so understanding? It was easier to dislike him when he was his usual arrogant self. Nevertheless, she felt less miserable when they reached the dock.

Luke nodded to the two crewmen who manned his shore boat. He dismounted and held his arms up to Aimee.

He watched her hesitate, bite her lip, then, with an exasperated little sound in her throat, reach out to him. He set her gently down on the pier, mouth quirking as she grimaced and pulled at the back of her dress.

"Not too comfortable, is it, dearest?"

She froze, dropped her hand and met his teasing eyes. "I'll survive," she retorted.

Luke unsaddled Polaris and led him into the boat's special stall. The walls were padded to protect the valuable horseflesh Luke carried from time to time. Luke tossed the saddle in the corner of the boat and held out his hand to assist Aimee up the small gangplank.

Aimee ignored the gesture and turned for one last look at Bergen. She bit her lip, telling herself she would cry no more. She'd always wanted adventure, hadn't she? Well, she'd be getting a surfeit of it. It wasn't as if she'd never come back to Norway again.

The bravado didn't work, and her mouth shook as she took one last look at her beloved home. Home. That word had a foreign ring to her; for her, home now lay far across the sea in a land she had never visited and could never love as she loved Norway. She would visit Bergen again, but she would be exactly that—a visitor. This knowledge gave a special poignancy to her farewell as she paid homage to the old city.

Her eyes drank in the crenellated fortress, the tower, the Tyskekirken, the exchange, the customs house, trying to memorize the familiar scene. A comforting hand descended on her shoulder, but Aimee flinched away. Using her sleeve, she wiped the tears from her eyes, sniffed, and strode up the gangplank. During the short trip to the *Mercury,* she composed herself, her back held erect, but she didn't look at the harbor again.

Luke saw the grim set of her mouth and sighed. Now he would be blamed for taking her from her home. Indeed, he felt a twinge of guilt, for she had been coerced into leaving. But she'll never regret it, he defended to his conscience. Slumping against the seat, he rubbed his tired back. This day had been almost as tense for him as for Aimee. Then, recalling what he had planned for his audacious little witch when they reached his stateroom, he smiled. Vitality flowed through his limbs again. He whistled tunelessly, watching his bride out of the corner of his eye.

Once aboard, Luke ordered his crewmen to return for her luggage. Aimee was looking about and didn't hear his other, more ominous order: "Bring supper to my cabin in an hour, then see that we're not disturbed." Nor did she notice the curious looks the deckhands sent her way.

Luke hustled her below before she had a chance to more than glance at the broad promenade lined with a row of deck chairs. The wide corridor they traversed was thickly carpeted, stateroom doors leading off on each side. Luke opened the door at the fore end, extended his hand and bowed.

"Madam, after you." His smile was so boyish and charming that Aimee relented and smiled back.

She took but one step into the cabin before halting in amazement. She stared about, wide-eyed. She had seen the other staterooms, but even their luxury had not prepared her for this. The cabin was huge, decorated in blues and greens. The entire left side served as both study and living area. A wide, intricately inlaid desk under a large porthole was flanked by two carved, cabriole-legged chairs covered with plush light blue velvet. Blue velvet curtains framed the portholes. The carpet underfoot was a light green and several couches artistically placed to accent one another were all upholstered in blue. Scattered beige silk chairs were used for contrast. The tables and bedroom suite were of the Chippendale style. A tranquil atmosphere had been achieved with these colors of the sky and of the sea.

The bed riveted her attention the longest. Never had she seen one so magnificent. It was a tester bed crowned with a delicate, elaborately carved pagodalike structure. The bed hangings were blue silk, embroidered with a sea motif of variegated sea horses, fish, and cavorting dolphins.

Swallowing, Aimee stared at that bed. Its peaked crown reminded her vaguely of Norway's stave churches, and surely the whole structure was almost as vast. Aimee's heart pounded at the realization that she was supposed to sleep there with Luke. Her brow crinkled as she tried to remember what her mother had said men and women did in bed, and she jumped when Luke cleared his throat.

"This royal magnificence was my father's idea. Sometimes it makes me damned uncomfortable, but he's right that it's best to display your wealth when you're making business deals." Luke turned away and went to a recessed, curtained alcove.

It must have been the chamber's powder room, for the sound of splashing waters as someone freshened up reached her ears. Aimee was too engrossed in exploring her surroundings to wonder long where her spouse had gone. She roamed about the chamber, fingering an ornament here, smoothing a plush chairback there. Preoccupied, she didn't notice when Luke entered the main cabin again.

Luke was in no mood to be ignored. Watching her through narrowed eyes, he began removing his clothes. He expected Aimee to bolt. Instead, she ambled over to the bed and caressed the hangings. She so obviously enjoyed the silky texture that Luke's own hands paused on the last button of his shirt. A shiver ran through him as he watched her stroke gently, dreamily, and he would have been less than a man if he hadn't wondered what that dainty hand would feel like on his own flesh.

Aimee turned to go to the porthole adjacent to the bed. She found her way blocked by Luke, but it was Luke as she had never seen him. She froze where she stood, her eyes glued to his broad chest. His shirt was open to the waist, allowing what seemed an endless expanse of bronzed, hair-covered muscle to gleam in the sun-filled cabin. He had already removed his shoes and socks, and, as she watched, he undid the last button of his shirt, took it off and tossed it over a chair.

The muscles in his wide chest rippled as he began to move. When she belatedly realized that he was advancing on her, she squeaked and tried to bolt, but she was too late. He took her shoulders in his hands, tracing her collarbones with his thumbs. Aimee's huge eyes went from one flexing bicep to the other, and her heartbeat accelerated until she could barely hear his gruff drawl.

"Well, sweet wife, what do you think of our cabin?"

Aimee inhaled and forced herself to brave his eyes. It took all her willpower not to recoil under that deep stare, but something primal told her this was no time to show fear. "It's beautiful. I'm very impressed. I never realized it was possible to travel anywhere so luxuriously."

"More and more steamers are being designed with comfort in mind. For instance, did you know my bathtub is built-in and has both hot and cold fresh running water?"

She felt the strange tingling sensation ripple through her again, spreading from the rough thumbs massaging her collarbones. She longed to jerk away, but his wolfish gleam told her he hoped she'd do exactly that.

Mentally, she consigned him to the devil, but aloud, she said, "No, I didn't know. How very . . . convenient." She tried to squirm away from his hold without appearing alarmed, but his fingers tightened.

"Yes, indeed, it is most convenient. Come, let me show you." He took her hand to lead her toward the alcove.

It was impossible to hide her panic any longer. "No! I, er, would prefer to explore the rest of the cabin first."

"There's time enough for that later. I thought, like a loyal wife, you might want to assist in my bath. After all, it's your fault I'm such a mess." When she dug in her heels and refused to move, Luke swooped her up in his arms without missing a stride.

Contact with that hard, hair-roughened chest sent the last of Aimee's composure flying. "No, Luke, put me down! I don't want to help with your bath. You've no right . . ."

He interrupted smoothly, "Do you already forget the words we spoke today? I have every right over you now. You belong to me, body and soul."

When they entered the bathing alcove, he set her on her feet. He tried to pull her into his arms, but she fought in earnest now, legs kicking, nails scratching. "Let me go! I don't belong to you! I belong to no one but myself. You'll never own me, never!"

Luke subdued her effortlessly. He trapped her wrists behind her back with one hand, then insinuated an iron-hard thigh between her legs to immobilize her. With his other hand he cupped her chin. "Someday, you'll be glad you belong to me. Someday, I'll be your whole existence." He knew he shouldn't threaten her any longer, but he was too frustrated by her obstinance. The soft thrashing of her body only aroused him. He forgot the need for patience.

She looked at him with such fierce, outraged pride, her mouth open to spit defiance, that he couldn't resist silencing her in the age-old way. He lowered his mouth hotly over hers. His head spun as he drank in her soft, alarmed gasp. She stiffened in his arms, trying to close her lips, but his tongue pleaded for entrance. He dipped inside her honey-sweet mouth, avid as a bee after nectar.

As he shuddered with longing and urged her head back over his arm in a passionate embrace, he had no way of knowing he was having a far greater effect on her than he realized. That urgent, warm mouth consuming hers made her quiver with strange feelings she had never known: fear of his male need, fascination, pride that such a man desired her. He held her tightly, tenderly, and feminine instinct told her he'd never hurt her. She almost succumbed to the urge to kiss him back, but memory of that bed, waiting like a warden in the next room to punish the prisoner if she misbehaved, overpowered her softer feelings.

She began to struggle, so desperately, he let her go. Confused, breathless, she backed away. Casting him a furious look, she jerked a small towel from the rack next to the marble lavatory, put it into the bath water and scrubbed her face and mouth. Lowering the towel, she marshaled her forces, but the look in Luke's eyes warned her.

He watched her broodingly before he whirled away to grab a bar of soap and drop it into the pale green marble tub. However, Aimee caught that flash of vulnerability before he turned away. Could her wariness actually hurt this self-confident, masterful man?

"Very well, madam, go. I've never forced my attentions on a woman in my life, and I'm not about to start now, wife or no. Leave me in peace." Ignoring her, he began unbuttoning his close-fitting trousers.

Aimee's eyes widened, but she fought against her fear. He was her husband now, and their life would be unbearable if she flinched away from him at the slightest touch. She still didn't understand what the intimacies of marriage involved, but she knew normal marriages required far closer contact than a mere kiss. How could she adjust herself to those intimacies if she couldn't even accustom herself to the sight of her husband?

Luke looked up at a soft sound, then he angrily balled up his breeches and threw them against the wall. She scurried away like a frightened little mouse afraid of the big, bad cat. He'd never realized she was such a coward. Luke stepped into the tub and lay back, too distracted to enjoy the soothing warmth against his skin. He stared at the ornate faucet, but he saw only Aimee's panic-stricken eyes and felt only the trembling of her body as she tried to escape him.

He was too lost in thought to notice another soft sound, and he didn't see his wife enter the alcove until she grabbed the towel she had moistened. He glanced up. His eyes widened. She had removed her short jacket, untied her blouse and rolled up her sleeves above the elbow. Her unruly hair was, as usual, escaping the confines of its braids, and her cheeks were flushed either with embarrassment or heat. Straight white teeth clamped against her bottom lip. She advanced slowly, shyly, then dropped to her knees beside him.

"Hand me the soap, please, and I'll scrub your back," she whispered, eyes averted. She hadn't looked at him since she entered, and she was still quivering, but Luke was no longer offended.

A warm feeling spread through him. Wary she might be, but a coward? Never. Silently, he handed her the soap and leaned forward. At first, the feeling of the towel rubbing his back was soothing, but soon the touch of her breasts, brushing him accidentally as she leaned to reach his far shoulder and arm, and the gentle caress of her breath on his neck began to have their natural effect.

When the towel dipped low on his spine, he choked, "Enough. I can manage the rest. Thank you for the help." He held out his hand for the towel, keeping his eyes down and his hips under the water, expecting her to leave. But when he chanced a glance, he was stunned to see her sitting, chin propped on knees, watching him. From her position on the carpet she couldn't see into the tub, and he relaxed a little. Her eyes watched his every movement as he rubbed the soap into his chest. He was delighted at the fascination she made no attempt to disguise.

"Isn't it uncomfortable to be covered with so much hair?" she asked, head cocked with interest.

The towel paused. "No, not at all. Does it bother you?"

She frowned, giving the matter serious thought. "No, I don't think so. If you rub against me, it feels strange, but just looking at you, it seems . . . right."

The towel resumed an erratic course as the hand guiding it shook at this revealing response. Could it be she was physically attracted to him and was too innocent to realize it?

"Have you never seen an unclothed man before, Aimee?" he asked cautiously.

"Only Gere. Once, during the summer, when he was building the porch to his cabin. He doesn't look like you, though. His chest is smooth, and not nearly so brown."

"And how did you feel when you watched him? Did he make you feel 'strange'?"

She hesitated. "No . . . I thought him attractive, but he

didn't make me feel hot and cold at once, like you do."

Luke clamped down on his elation at this answer. He forced himself to calmly raise one leg to begin soaping it. "I see. Do you have any idea why I make you feel that way?"

"No, I don't. Perhaps I'm ailing, for I've only noticed the feeling quite recently."

Luke rinsed his leg, then turned to look at her, absent-mindedly soaping his other thigh. "I don't think you're sick, Aimee. Unless I'm sick, too, because that's precisely the way you make me feel." He watched her eyes widen in surprise, then shift to fix on his long, muscled leg. His voice deepened and grew rough. "What we feel is perfectly normal, sweet. It's the desire of a woman for a man, and a man for a woman."

Aimee straightened carefully, some of her fear returning. His eyes were darkening in that look that made her feel disoriented. Could he be right? Did she desire him? She admired him as a man, she found him very handsome, but she wasn't at all certain she would ever desire him, as Sigrid desired Gere. Why, he couldn't even kiss her without making her tremble.

Her eyes wandered over him again, and he was, indeed, physically appealing. She watched him rinse his leg, and she felt a sudden urge to look into the tub and discover for herself if his lower half was as sleek and muscular as his torso. When she finally met his pleased, knowing eyes, the truth almost blinded her.

Fool! She shrieked to herself. She was no longer frightened of him. She hadn't been since the second time he'd kissed her. Yes, she still trembled at his passion—but not with fear. To the contrary, she'd enjoyed that hungry mouth on hers. This admission had such implications for her that she sat immobile, even when Luke braced himself as if to rise. However, he merely leaned over the tub to rim her mouth with a wet finger.

"I'm delighted you find me attractive, darling. I thought it would take weeks before you'd admit it." When she remained frozen, her eyes glassy, he leaned back into the tub. His tone softened further. "Don't fear, little one. I'll go slowly, as I promised. We'll do nothing you don't want to do." His husky voice turned mocking. "Now, unless you want to embarrass us both, you'd best leave so I can get out of the bath."

Aimee shuddered back to life. She sprang to her feet, her head bobbing with the speed. She ran out of the alcove, her ears burning as Luke's deep chuckles followed in her tracks.

When Luke entered the cabin, he found his wife sitting on a dainty, armless chair, ankles primly crossed as she read the latest Ibsen play. She glanced up at him. Her eyes skittered over his tall figure, robed in ruby velvet, then returned to her book.

Pleased with himself, Luke went to his chest and removed his brush. He had heard a knock while he was drying off, but he began to brush his black riot of hair as he strolled over to an array of boxes and trunks to survey them. When another knock sounded, Aimee jumped. Luke, as if on cue, casually called, "Come in."

Potter entered carrying a covered tray. He barely glanced at Luke. He was too busy staring at Aimee to notice the small table blocking his path. Luke dropped his brush and whisked the table away.

Potter turned, saw what had happened, and reddened. "Sorry, Cap'n. Where shall I put your supper tray?"

Luke nodded at the long table in front of one of the sofas. "There. Thank you, Potter. Tell Jimmy I'm not to be disturbed for the rest of the evening. Sail for Stockholm on the morning tide."

"Aye, sir. Will there be anything else?" He stared so intently at Aimee that Luke laughed.

"All right, you old sea dog. I had intended to officially introduce my wife tomorrow, but I suppose you can be the first to meet her." Luke went to Aimee's chair and pulled her to her feet. "Darling, this is Potter, our chief engineer."

Aimee nodded shyly. *"God aften."*

Potter bowed. "The pleasure is mine, ma'am."

When Aimee looked blank, Luke interpreted, adding, "I must start teaching you English right away. The proper response would be, 'How do you do.'"

Aimee opened her mouth to correct him, but an inspiration struck her. It could be very convenient indeed to have him believe she didn't speak English. They had been conversing in Norwegian because Luke had mastered the language and wished to employ it. But now she saw she needed every advantage since she had so foolishly revealed her attraction to him. She repeated his words hesitantly, as if they were foreign to her.

Potter bowed again and backed away, this time knocking over a small plant stand. Luckily it was bare of a plant at the moment, and he caught it before it hit the ground. Luke sighed, shaking his head. Potter's clumsiness was the crew's favorite joke. He shot Luke a sheepish look, carefully set the stand straight, then retreated.

When he was gone, Luke turned to Aimee and gestured to the sofa. "Shall we eat, my dear?"

Aimee sat in the far corner. She took the plate he handed her, and found her appetite unpiqued by the simple meal of roasted chicken, rice and green beans. Luke ate heartily, watching her push the food around her plate.

He knew why she was moody—she was alarmed at her response to him. Her attraction relieved him, for now it was just a matter of time before she returned his caresses. Conversely, it was more imperative now than ever that he proceed warily. Her defenses were alerted, and she would fight this feeling to the bitter end, of that he was certain.

Thus, after the brief meal, Luke went to her trunk, removed a plain cotton nightdress and handed it to her. "Come, sweet, I know you must be exhausted. Prepare yourself for bed. I have some work to do, and I won't disturb you." He walked to his desk, retrieved some papers and sat in a chair with its back to her, a lantern at his side.

Aimee retreated to the alcove and put on the nightgown, her head whirling with tiredness and confusion. She returned to the cabin. She knew she should be frightened, on her guard, as she climbed into the big bed, but she was too tired. The down mattress closed around her like comforting arms, and she fell asleep before she had time to worry whether Luke intended to join her.

And so they passed their wedding night. Luke worked late, until his eyes hurt from reading; his bride slumbered deeply, dreamlessly in the vast bed, alone. When Luke was tired enough for sleep, he removed a blanket and pillow from a linen chest and spread them on a couch. He prepared to remove his robe, but his noble intentions couldn't prevent one last, longing look at his bride.

She slumbered so sweetly. He would have felt a violator had he asserted his rights. She seemed such an innocent angel, despite the womanly wisdom she displayed in her frequent fireworks. He went to the bed, his eyes more tender than he knew as he watched the gentle rise and fall of her chest. He leaned down to caress her cheek with his fingers. He planted a delicate kiss on her parted mouth and hastened away before his impulses urged him to seek more earthly pleasures. Then, shaking his head, Luke removed his robe and tried to compose his long length comfortably on the narrow settee. He squirmed for over an hour before he found a position that allowed him some rest. His last hazy thought before sleep claimed him was that this was a damned odd way for a man to spend his wedding night.

Chapter Six

AIMEE DREAMED OF big, rough hands caressing her, soothing her fears away. She buried her fingers in black, black hair soft as thistledown. A warm body claimed her, rocking her into soporific contentment. Gradually, the gentle swaying awakened her. She stretched and yawned. Why did she feel so good this morning? She drowsily opened her eyes and turned to say good morning to Sigrid. Instead of her sister's blond head across her bedroom, she saw Luke's wide, bare, hairy chest across the cabin.

Aimee started and jerked to a sitting position. Her cheeks flushed as she realized who it was she'd dreamed of, what hands had tempted her to pleasure, what bronzed torso she'd longed to lie against. Warily, she watched Luke, but she relaxed when she realized he was asleep over there, his face sweet and defenseless as a boy's. The strange glow incited by the dream burned hotter as she looked at the man who was her husband. Husband. The word gave her a strange thrill that both alarmed and enticed her. She eased out of bed and tiptoed to Luke's side.

Her eyes absorbed his handsome face with an instinctive feminine enjoyment she no longer struggled against. She had every right to look at him, she told herself. His lashes were thick and curled; his mouth, a beautiful curve that, even in sleep, looked determined. For once his vibrant maleness was unthreatening, and, boldly, she examined the clean lines of his body.

111

Each steady breath accented the strength of his chest. Curiously, she looked at his flat brown nipples, so small in comparison to her own pink ones. The blanket was caught under his hips, revealing one long, perfectly shaped leg. His muscular thigh tapered to a taut calf and strong ankle. Finally, her heart pounding with mingled embarrassment and excitement, she looked at the mysterious area barely shielded by the blanket, her hands clenching with the longing to touch him.

Suddenly, he shifted. The blanket fell aside, revealing all his male glory. Aimee gasped and reddened at her temerity, but she couldn't draw her eyes away from the powerful body so very different from her own. His chest hair was sparse and silky compared to the abundant thatch at his loins. When Aimee trembled at what that hair surrounded, she told herself she was afraid. Still, she was unable to tear her eyes away even when his relaxed maleness awakened, becoming thick and hard. Aimee's skin prickled with awareness. Slowly, she lifted her eyes. Her flush deepened almost to purple under the hot caress of his stare. He was not only awake, he was every inch the preening male, pleased at her obvious curiosity. She wanted to sink into the sea at his rakish smile.

"All you see is yours, sweetheart. Feel free to look as long as you like, or to touch anywhere you please."

Appalled, Aimee escaped to her trunk and tossed clothes about until she found a plain dress of olive green. She fled to the alcove, but she couldn't evade his voice.

"Now that I've bared all, so to speak, isn't it your turn? Let there be no secrets between us." He chuckled to himself when the only sound was the hurried rustle of clothing. He rose and crept forward.

Aimee's arms were raised in the act of pulling on her chemise when he walked into the alcove. He got a glimpse of pert, uptilted breasts crowned with rosy peaks before she jerked the garment to her waist. She had already pulled on her drawers, but the sheer cotton was little protection from his raiding stare.

He was still nude, and the intimacy of the moment was too much for her. She clenched her fists. "Married we may be, but I insist on privacy when I dress. Please leave me." She turned around to pull on her first petticoat, ears straining to hear him leave. There was no sound but his ragged breathing.

She felt his eyes burn into her back, and, frustrated, she

whirled around. Her nose brushed his chest, for he had stepped up to her while her back was turned. He caught her hands and forced them to his chest.

"Don't ask the impossible of me. I can't leave you, not after you've awakened me so pleasantly. Come, a little experimentation can do you no harm. Think of me as a strange animal you're free to examine. I won't move a muscle."

Aimee's throat was dry with fear and another, more alarming emotion as her hands curled into the soft, warm mat of hair that covered hard, warm flesh underneath. She hesitated, but yearning got the best of her. She stroked his pectoral muscles, amazed at the strength she felt under her exploring hands. She sneaked a look at him. He was calmly gazing down at her. Emboldened, she moved her hands to his breasts, felt the nipples, then followed the line of hair down his chest to his belly. Her hands faltered when he jerked.

Her eyes flew to his face. She wondered at the sheen of sweat on his forehead. Why was he perspiring? It wasn't hot. He made a funny little noise in his throat and backed away from her.

"That's enough of a lesson for today. Finish dressing, quickly, please." He beat a hasty retreat before her eyes fell from his face to the one part of him he could not control. He ached with need. He feared if he stayed another moment, he'd be unable to control his desire to explore with his hands what his eyes had so briefly seen.

Luke jerked on his own clothes, so flustered he was hardly aware he'd dressed in his usual captain's uniform. It wasn't until he went to comb his hair that he remembered he'd intended to dress casually since there were no passengers on board.

Ruefully, he muttered to his flushed reflection, "Lusty Luke, huh? You poor fool, if anyone knew the mere touch of that seductive imp's hands made you lose control, they'd laugh you out of New York."

Still, he had to admit that to awaken that morning under his beloved's assessing gaze was enough to make any man lose control. He would have to be more careful in the future. Aimee was responding better than he had hoped, but if he went too quickly he could ruin everything.

Thus, when Aimee emerged from the alcove, she found Luke casually seated atop the desk, swinging one navytrousered leg back and forth under the kneehole. He straightened.

"You look lovely, Aimee. But why do you always wear your hair in braids? I confess I'd like to see it down, at least in the privacy of our cabin."

"It's too long and it gets in the way, so I keep it braided," she said in Norwegian. Each averted their eyes as they tried to avoid thoughts of what had occurred between them this morning. Both, for vastly different reasons, were determined to proceed more warily.

Luke nodded. "I see. Well, it's very attractive, no matter how you wear it. Would you like to meet my crew? I know they're eager to meet you. I thought we might breakfast with them in the mess."

Aimee sighed with relief that they wouldn't have to be alone any longer. "That sounds wonderful. I am starved."

"We'll go to the bridge first. I want to check on our progress."

Luke opened the door, bowed, then escorted her down the companionway to the main deck. They climbed more stairs to the bridge. The wheelhouse was the highest point on the ship, with the exception of the crow's nest. Almost the entire upper half of the structure was glassed in to allow those on the bridge the widest view possible.

Luke ushered her into the wheelhouse. Aimee, fascinated, looked around. She'd sailed on her father's vessels, but her father's finest ship was a simple affair compared to this. A small desk sat against the wall, bearing a large black book which Aimee assumed to be the log. Several cases containing maps, drawing instruments and nautical charts had been built into the bulkhead. Aimee was astonished to note that the wheel was much smaller than the wheel on any of her father's ships. She noted not one, but two compasses, each flanking a side of the helm. They were both made of shiny copper, balanced on pivots, and appeared larger, more complex, than any she had seen before.

A slight, brown-haired man standing at the helm turned and smiled when they stepped into the cabin. Luke led Aimee up to him. The man turned the wheel over to a junior officer who had been reading a chart on a tilting drawing desk.

"Jimmy, this is Mrs. Garrison, my wife. Aimee, this is

Jimmy Vaughn, my first mate and friend. He speaks Norwegian, so if you need anything and I'm not available, tell him."

Aimee nodded. *"Morn."*

"It's a pleasure to meet you. *Velkommen,* madam," he said in her language, his grasp a touch smoother than Luke's. "I bid you a hearty welcome to the finest steamer ever built, the *Mercury.*" Jimmy's grin was broad and infectious, and Aimee's shy smile widened in return.

"I've never seen a mate prouder of his vessel. I think Jimmy would personally tuck the *Mercury* in at night if he could find a blanket big enough," Luke said dryly.

Jimmy grimaced at Luke. "Listen to him. And he, with his shiny brass buttons about to bust from the strain of his puffed out chest." Jimmy bowed gallantly to Aimee. "But he's more reason than ever to be proud, now. May I be the first to wish you both congratulations?"

Luke smiled down into Aimee's flushed face, encircling her waist with a brawny arm. "You may, Jimmy, you may. I do feel a lucky man this morning."

He glanced at his beloved.

Smiling black eyes encouraged her to trust him, to share with him a marriage of more than name. Inexplicably, belonging no longer seemed such a terrible thing. For the first time, she hoped they could reach an accord. Could she not remain free, her own person, and still be his wife?

Hardly aware of it, she leaned against Luke's arm naturally, without reserve. The quiet joy in his smile, the pride in the way he held her was as intoxicating to her as a narcotic, numbing her anger and resentment. For the first time, she seriously pondered why he had chosen her. She no longer believed he had married her solely to subdue her will. He was too complex and intelligent a man to tie himself to a woman for that reason alone.

He'd had nothing to gain from choosing her over Sigrid. To the contrary, the choice had complicated his life. He not only had to quiet his bride's rebellion, he had to appease his parents' anger. So why had he done it? Before she had time to puzzle long over the question, Luke released her and turned to Jimmy.

"Could you summon all hands who aren't on duty to the mess so I can introduce Aimee? I'll show her around the bridge while you do so."

Jimmy nodded and hastened to do his captain's bidding.

Aimee followed Luke about the bridge, listening as he explained each instrument. "No doubt you know about the compasses. These are probably very similar to those on your father's ships except that we have two, as a safety measure. They're also corrected more for deviation, since the *Mercury* is an iron vessel." He led her over to another instrument mounted on a movable stand. "This is the azimuth compass, which compensates for magnetic variation from true north on the open sea so as to give us a more accurate heading. We move it as needed, sight objects on or above the horizon through these vertical bars, then read the bearing through the small magnifying glass. I keep the chronometer in my cabin so it won't be polarized by the compasses."

Luke went to one of the cases and removed a sextant. "I'll take our latitude after we breakfast. Do you have any questions?"

"Yes, why is the wheel so small? I would have thought a vessel of this size would have required an enormous wheel."

Luke was pleased at her acuity. "It would be impossible to steer manually a ship of the tonnage of the *Mercury*. That's one of the advantages of steam; an engine controlled by the wheel actually moves the rudder. It's quite easy to steer. Would you like to try it?"

Before Aimee could protest, Luke urged her over to the wheel, requesting that the young officer step aside. Aimee gripped the wheel, her palms sweating. When the compass quivered in protest, Luke put his hands over hers. "All you need is a little practice, sweet. You're doing fine." His voice grew soft, husky with a meaning that had little to do with sailing.

She shivered with the desire to turn into his arms, but her feelings were too new, too powerful, and she didn't trust them or herself. She was relieved when Jimmy returned.

Luke released her and let the mate take back the wheel. The other officer was already poring over the charts once more.

"Shall we go to breakfast, sweetheart?" Luke asked.

Aimee rested her hand on his forearm and went with him down the stairs, below the main deck and first-class cabins. When they entered the mess, over two-score men rose in greeting, men of every size, shape and age, but of similar expression: curious, approving and welcoming.

Luke conducted her around, introducing her to each crew member. Only a couple of the names stuck in her mind —Potter, the engineer, and Sims, one of the coal pushers. When Sims shyly bobbed his head, wringing his hat in his hands, Aimee smiled at him warmly, trying to put him at ease. He peeked up at her, reddened and shifted from foot to foot. Briefly, Aimee regretted her pretense that she couldn't speak English, so she could communicate some soothing words. Instead she let Luke lead her to the head of the table.

She sat at his right. As she looked at him, her defenses went up again at his air of total command. Did nothing ever upset his supreme self-confidence? Why couldn't he be more like Sims? She could handle him, cherish him. He would never threaten her emotional freedom. She poked at her hearty breakfast of eggs, bread and smoked ham, resenting Luke even more when she realized he would grow less menacing with each passing day.

For a while, all was silent as the men ate hungrily. Aimee nibbled at her food, controlling a flinch when Luke teased his men.

"There's no need to act like schoolboys nervous of the teacher. At ease. My wife doesn't understand English, so carry on as you normally would."

Rumbling voices gradually filled the silence. Aimee's cheeks burned as she caught snatches of conversation that obviously referred to her. "Pretty, sweet little thing. The captain will have no problems with her." And, "What a strange match! The captain will eat her for breakfast!"

Aimee peeped at Luke to see if he'd caught the murmured comments not intended to be heard. From the smile playing about his lips, she assumed he had. All doubt was erased when he leaned close to whisper, "My men think you're a fragile little flower without a thorn upon you. I wonder how they'd react if they'd attended our reception yesterday?"

Aimee glared at him and hissed back, "I wonder how they'd react if they knew how you coerced me into this marriage?"

Luke answered dryly, "With utter astonishment, no doubt."

He returned to his breakfast, but Aimee throbbed at the underlying meaning of his words: any other girl would consider him a prize. His conceit infuriated her, but as she returned to her eavesdropping, she realized he had good reason for it.

"Aye, the sound of breaking hearts will echo over the Hudson when we reach New York. How many women do you suppose the captain has loved and left?"

"A score or more, I don't doubt. To think, all those beautiful heiresses couldn't snare him, and here he is shackled to a bit of a thing who looks as if a strong wind would blow her away." The boatswain shook his head sagely. "Just goes to show that the more we have, the more we're burdened with responsibility. I heard he married to please his family."

"Mrs. Garrison should be pleased, right enough. She'll turn this little gal inside out and put her back together again until she won't know herself."

Aimee shoved back her plate and leaped to her feet. "If you'll excuse me, Luke, I have some chores to do in the cabin," she muttered, still maintaining the Norwegian. She bobbed a quick curtsy to the staring men, and hurried away, ignoring Luke's surprised expression.

What the devil had gotten into her? Luke rose and smiled at the ring of curious faces. "Excuse my wife, men. I'm afraid we both have a lot of adjustments to make." With a wave indicating they should go about their business, Luke followed her. His crew buzzed more loudly than ever.

Luke looked for Aimee in their cabin and was not surprised to find her gone. She'd used an excuse to escape. After taking his daily latitudinal reading with Jimmy, he took his sextant back to the bridge and began a systematic search for Aimee. He prowled for her in the boudoir, the grand saloon and even the smoking salon, finally finding her leaning against the promenade deck rail. Her eyes were closed, her face turned into the wind.

He put his hands on her shoulders and probed gently, "Why did you run away? Did one of my men do something to upset you?"

Her face veiling her confused emotions, she eyed him. "No, I just felt . . . stifled. I wanted to be alone. I'm fine now." As if to prove it, she pulled away and flung her arms out at the passing scenery.

"Have you ever seen anything so beautiful? It's been years since I've been this far down the coast. I wish we had more time. This is the best season to see the fjords." She pointed. "Look, see the lighthouse? We're nearing Stavanger, which lies on a small peninsula past the Boknfjord."

Luke turned to look, and indeed, the scenery was lovely. The coastline varied between rocky, barren mountain walls and flat lush land teeming with vegetation. They were passing the Boknfjord, and Luke glimpsed blue-gray islands. They looked mysterious in the misty air and dotted the bay's water like hump-backed whales. Farther on, the ship passed a flat peninsula, tumultuous waves crashing on the sandy shore. The upper reaches were neatly cultivated, and bordered by a purple fringe of heather. In the distance, more blue mountains towered as massive symbols to Norway's rugged beauty.

When Aimee finally turned to catch Luke's reaction, she was surprised to find him gone. Biting her lip, she propped her arms against the rail. Why was she upset to learn about all the women Luke had known? No man as handsome and wealthy as he could reach his age without experience. She had all the more reason to be wary of him. How would she ever know, inexperienced as she was, whether he cared about her? How would she know that he loved Aimee the person, not the fact that he'd won her submission as his wife? I'm not jealous, she told herself. I don't care how many women he's known.

But her eyes were blind to the passing scenery as she pictured Luke embracing a beautiful, experienced brunette. Her eyes burned, her throat hurt at the mere idea of his turning from her to another. She was still vague on the details of intimacy, but common sense told her she had no hope of holding him unless she allowed him to approach her more closely. Again, a thrill ran over her skin at the thought. Luke suddenly appeared at her side again.

"I decided we had time enough for a brief detour."

Aimee's turmoil subsided as she smiled her gratitude. "Thank you, Luke. That was kind."

Luke tried to pull her back against his chest, but she stiffened. His hands sagged to his sides. "I wanted to give you another look at the fjords. Besides, I, too, would like to see them," he muttered, turning his head away.

He propped his elbows against the brass rail. Aimee did the same, and for a while, they were silent as the steamer plunged through the choppy waves. When they entered the mouth of the fjord, Luke stared around with awe. He had thought Norway's coastline the most beautiful he'd ever seen, but his earlier glimpses had not prepared him for this close-up view.

"This is the Lysefjord," Aimee said softly, reverently. "It's considered one of the area's most beautiful fjords for its towering mountains."

Indeed, mountains hovered on all sides, and they rose so high, Luke had to crane his head and squint to catch their sky-piercing peaks. Ice glittered in some of the deepest crannies, but dwarf birch and juniper had managed to flourish on the lower slopes. Flowers defied the chilly air, blue gentians and rose-colored azaleas bobbing their heads gayly in concert. Stately white saxifrages adorned even the most inaccessible fjord clefts.

One of the mountains had a queer rock formation. "That's called *Praekestolen,* the pulpit," Aimee explained, "because of the way the rock projects over the water." The more deeply they entered the fjord, the grander the scenery became, the mountains rising steeply out of the water to shadow over their dwarfed craft.

The *Mercury* seemed a crude nineteenth century intruder intent on marring the masterpiece it had taken Nature centuries to shape. The steamer sliced ruthlessly through the mirrorlike surface of the water, obliterating the beauty reflected back. The mountains muffled all sound except for the churning of the steamer's engines and the occasional screech of a bird.

"Look," Aimee pointed.

Luke saw the reddish hide of a large deer. The buck looked scornfully down at them, his head autocratic as a monarch's. A set of antlers Luke thought must span at least fifteen points crowned his head. The buck snorted, then pranced away.

"You're right, old boy. This is your world, not ours," Luke saluted him softly.

Aimee looked at him with such surprise that Luke explained, "Somehow, I feel an intruder. Such beauty humbles me. But it's a good feeling. It makes me realize yet again that, omnipotent as we think we are, we're but one part of everything that makes this world such a wonderful place to live. And too often, I fear, we're the worst part that spoils the whole for everything else."

Aimee's intent to distance herself from him was shaken

under the impact of his words. Her eyes softened, became luminous with admiration as, yet again, she realized her new husband was the only person she'd ever met who shared her concern for nature. Reserve had no place in this meeting of two minds, and, spontaneously, Aimee put her hand on Luke's arm. "Oh Luke, I'm so glad you're so empathetic. I thought I'd never meet a man who could see what I can."

Luke pulled her gently to him, his throat a bit tight. These natural gestures from her were so rare, so precious; he savored each one. He cleared his throat. "I meant every word. Back home, I've argued about the need for caution with our resources until I'm blue in the face. That's one reason I'm so glad engines are becoming more efficient; one day, we could run short of coal even as we've lost so many of our forests. Slowly, I think more people are coming to realize that the mythical cornucopia is exactly that—a myth. We must learn to be more careful with what we have. In fact, did you know last year our Congress established what we call a national park in a place called Yellowstone? The people will serve as custodians, and there will be no development or denuding of its forests."

Luke and Aimee sat down in deck chairs, immersed in discussion so deep they didn't notice when they exited the fjord and resumed the course toward Stockholm. All the rest of the day, into the night, they exchanged opinions on the environment. These discussions led naturally into politics, and Luke was surprised to find Aimee so knowledgeable.

"Where did you learn so much of world affairs, Aimee?"

"Through books, mostly. Gere travels a lot, and he would almost always bring me a book, or sometimes a newspaper. Father has always maintained a library, though I'm the only one who has ever exploited it. I know most about Scandinavian affairs, of course."

Luke shifted uneasily. She had made her scorn for Swedes quite apparent. "Are you aware that we'll be going to the court of Oscar II?" His sense of foreboding increased when her eyes narrowed.

"No, I was not. Am I expected to attend with you?"

"I'd prefer it if you did. What use is it to have a lovely wife if I can't show her off?"

Aimee flushed with pleasure, but she sighed. "You may regret it if you take me with you. I would try to hold my tongue, but Swedes are arrogant, and I resent their stranglehold on my country. If the King or his courtiers criticize Norway . . ."

Luke teased, "And you, of course, would not dare criticize Sweden."

Aimee met his eyes, smiled impishly and struck a demure pose. "I? Of course not!" She looked down at her folded hands, but slanted a sidewise gaze at him that did not match her pose.

When he burst out laughing, she added seriously, "Truly, I would try to hold my tongue. I realize I could jeopardize your business negotiations by being too blunt."

They had just finished a late, leisurely supper and were seated on the long settee in their stateroom. Luke took Aimee's hand, deciding it was time to press his suit. He rubbed each of her fingers, murmuring, "Sweet, I'm mystified as to why you seem so innocent of your own power. Don't you realize how lovely you are?"

When she stared at him uncomprehendingly, he gave her hand a warm squeeze. "I'm not in the habit of forcing women to wed me. I came to Bergen resolved to allying myself with a girl I knew nothing of, and I was determined to honor the family commitment. Yet one look at you and everything else flew out of my head. At every meeting, you delight me more. It was you I wanted, not Sigrid. So I did everything I could to win you, and I'll make no apologies for it. I intend to make you happy, if you'll let me."

When Aimee refused to look at him, Luke gently cupped her chin and lifted her head so they could lock eyes. "You're the only thing that's yet to make me forget a commitment. You're the only woman I've ever kissed who can make me lose control. Doesn't that tell you something?"

Aimee longed to believe him. Yes, she admitted, maybe he found her appealing, but even she knew physical attraction and love were not the same thing. When she was close to him, it didn't seem to matter why he wanted her. But what would happen after he'd satisfied his desire, and yes, she admitted, her own? She pulled her head away and leaped to her feet. "I thought you were trying to bend my will to yours because I'd spurned you."

Luke reddened. He rose, his tone as unflinching as his eyes. "Yes, your coldness angered me at your mother's luncheon, but it only added impetus to my urge to win you. It was your strength, your intelligence that drew me, for it is so at odds with your delicate appearance. I know now I would have wanted you instead of Sigrid no matter what your reaction had been." Luke stepped forward to clasp her elbows and pull her gently to him. "I always thought women were boringly predictable, but you're a mystery to me, Aimee. I know you're attracted to me. I also know you're fighting it. Why?"

Aimee's heart thudded against her ribs. Oh God, how was she to resist him? Didn't he understand that the very potency of his appeal, the depth of his desire made her wary? He was a man who felt things as deeply as she. If she answered his needs, they would consume each other in an inferno of passion that would burn away all barriers. She would be stripped of any defense against him, unutterably his in name, body, mind, and heart. Thus, though she trembled in longing, she said nothing.

Luke searched her eyes, trying to understand her deep emotions. His breathing quickened. His husky voice took on a tone of urgency. "Please believe me when I say you attract me as no woman ever has. Physically, mentally, emotionally, I think you're beautiful. All I ask is that you remember I will never do anything to hurt you. Unleash your feelings, respond to me as I can see you want to. Give our marriage a chance."

Part of Aimee longed to run and hide, but another part yearned to yield to him. She battled with herself, wondering why, oh why, fate tied her to this man. She was not experienced enough to resist his wiles. Even now, knowing he was determined to invade her body, soul and mind until her very thoughts were not her own, she was still trapped inside the sensual web he wove. Hapless as a fly, the more she struggled to escape his silken net, the more tightly it bound her.

He stroked her back soothingly, languorously, sending panic to surge through her at his very gentleness. She had been able to fight his arrogance and attempts at domination; this gentle seduction was far more lethal. How was she to resist him when she found him more attractive by the hour? The rapport he had with his men, the respect they obviously held for him, his knowledge about world affairs and his concern for the environment, all blended with his potent physical charms to form an explosive recipe she could no longer resist. When he lowered his mouth to hers, her lips parted in helpless anticipation.

Her reward was a kiss that shook her to her core. His mouth sipped at hers so sweetly, drinking in the taste of her, that she was lost. The hard body curved around hers was both comfort and torment as his lips pleaded for response. Aimee's will collapsed in the unequal struggle between body and mind. She gave him the reply he longed for—passion, delicious, eager and natural. She curled her arms about his neck and stood on tiptoe to crush her awakening body against his.

He groaned against her mouth, intoxicated by the wine of her response. Slowly, he deepened the tenor of their embrace. He caught her head in his hands, moving it in conjunction with his own until their mouths slanted together, melded in a kiss more deeply arousing than any he had ever known. His heart thundered against her breast, his tongue explored her mouth in an invasion his manhood longed to imitate. And when her tongue responded hesitantly, then boldly to explore his own mouth, his teetering control collapsed.

He lifted her into his arms and carried her to the bed, his mouth still devouring hers. He eased her down and nibbled at her arched throat while his feverish hands worked in her hair. When her locks were free, billowing about her shoulders like a flaxen cloud, he went to work on her dress. However, in order to remove it, he had to lift his mouth away from the pounding hollow in her neck.

Aimee's heart drummed so loudly she could hear nothing else, but her sight was not impaired. She saw Luke leaning over her, his face flushed, his eyes blazing with desire, and she wondered vaguely if she looked the same. The thought snapped her out of her passionate daze. She felt her dress fall open to the waist and moved to close it, but Luke's hands pushed hers aside to begin unlacing her petticoat. She opened her mouth to demand her release, but he took her breath away with another soul-shaking kiss.

This time, however, she fought the weakness invading her. Her head moved restlessly from side to side, but his relentless mouth followed, seeking her lips with blind urgency. Her petticoat gapped. He hurried to untie her chemise, cupping the prizes in his eager hands. She felt that intimate touch for the first time in her life, and she froze at the strange sensation as Luke's trembling fingers caressed her. She was too stunned to move even when he leaned away to see what his hands savored so hungrily.

Breathless, she stared at him. His face was stamped with passion, his eyes half-closed as he explored her delicate white flesh. With a harsh moan, he lowered his head over her breast. She arched with shock at the first touch of his lips, and it gave her the strength to push him aside.

"No!" she choked. "Leave me be!"

Luke was unprepared for her resistance. He fell away from her to the edge of the bed. Aimee nudged him farther away with her foot, desperate to escape all contact.

It was enough of a kick to send him over the edge to the floor. An ominous silence followed his thudding fall, then his black head appeared above the mattress to beam a different kind of passion at her. His pants slowed to an even rhythm. He ran an agitated hand through his hair, then froze her with a stare as frigid as a black Arctic night.

"Of all your faults, I never would have believed you were a tease. Hasn't anyone ever told you it's dangerous to respond so passionately to a man only to change your mind midway?"

Aimee shook her head mulishly, her face rosy, her eyes sparkling. She looked so lovely in her silky tumble of hair, her breasts bobbing temptingly at him, her mouth red with his kisses, he couldn't control his urge to lash out at her, to hurt her as deeply as she'd hurt him.

"There's a woman in you clamoring to get out, but you're bound and determined to hold her prisoner, aren't you? Well, so be it. I have no need for a cold little hypocrite who doesn't know her own mind. No doubt I'll find women aplenty in Stockholm who know how to be feminine." Luke subdued the guilt he felt at her stricken look and went to the chest to remove his blanket and pillow. Without another word, he removed his clothes. He ignored Aimee as he reclined on the cramped settee across the cabin. He turned away from her, feigning sleep, so he didn't see the tears trickling down her cheeks.

Aimee pulled off her mussed gown, too distressed to brush and braid her hair as she did every night. She crawled under the covers of the large bed in her petticoat and curled up into a ball. The trickle of tears grew into a torrent. It was clear to her that she was afraid not only of losing her independence, but of being too inexperienced for him. With all those beautiful women he had known, how could she, who didn't even understand the marital act, satisfy him?

But if he found her unattractive, why had he kissed her so passionately? Were all his words earlier this evening false? Her tears dried as she realized she had rejected Luke at a time that seemed . . . uncomfortable for him. Perhaps he hadn't meant to be so cruel? She tried to imagine how she would have felt if she'd been kissing him and he'd shoved her away. Pain pierced her at the very thought, but, oddly, she was comforted. Indeed, he'd probably been justified in lashing out at her.

Another thought brought even greater comfort. No matter what he might say, he had chosen her over Sigrid. If he found her as truly fetching as he claimed, their marriage had a chance. Before she could decide whether this conclusion was comforting or terrifying, she fell asleep, Luke's name on her lips.

Aimee's first sight the next morning was Luke's face, bending over her as he kissed her cheek. Her mouth quivered into an uncertain smile as he sat down on the edge of the bed and played with a long, tangled tendril of her hair. He looked uncertain too, and her shyness faded.

"I was a bounder last night, Aimee, and I'd like to apologize," he said gruffly. He flashed a look at her, then returned to his intent appraisal of her hair. He smoothed back the tumbled mass from her forehead. "My pride was hurt, I suppose. I so enjoyed our embrace that it was an unpleasant shock to discover you didn't feel the same."

Aimee stared at her fingers worrying at the expensive coverlet, so she didn't see him watching her tensely, as if hopeful she would deny his statement. Her voice was apologetic. "I'm more to blame than you. I didn't understand how . . . intimate you'd want to become when I first kissed you. A man has never . . ." Face scarlet, she averted her head.

Luke rumbled, "A man has never touched you as I did?" She shook her head, too shy to look at him.

Luke heaved a silent sigh of relief. He had been afraid, once his anger cooled, that he'd frightened her into irreversible disgust. However, maidenly modesty he could deal with. All he needed was patience, understanding and control; propinquity would do the rest. This morning was as good a time as any to begin. . . .

"Aimee, what we did last night is perfectly normal. Intimacy between a man and woman is richer, more satisfying, if allowed to grow slowly. I was too hasty."

His hands paused in her hair. He took a deep breath. "Will you allow me to look at you? You must become accustomed to my eyes and touch if we are to trust one another."

Aimee's eyes widened. She longed to decline, but she forced herself to consider his suggestion. How would she ever become experienced if she couldn't even bear for him to look at her? She met his steady black eyes and knew, somehow, that she could trust him. He knew she was not ready for intimacy, and he would force nothing upon her. For once, he didn't demand; for once, she squelched pride and independence under the even stronger need to please him. She bent her head and nodded a shy assent.

She sat still while he folded back the covers to the end of the bed. She jerked her head to the side when he put gentle hands to the top button on her petticoat, but he balked. "Sweet," he murmured, an undercurrent of gentleness in his voice. "This little exercise will be pointless if you pretend I'm not here."

How had she ever thought his eyes cold or threatening? If so, they were now warm and comforting as hot, steaming coffee on an icy winter morning. She kept her eyes locked on his face as he unfastened the first button, then the next, and the next, until the sleeves of her slip pooled around her shoulders. He opened the chemise, his touch gentle against her silkiness. The soft fabric slipped down as well, leaving the gentle slope of her shoulders exposed, her bosom precariously covered by the material that had not yet fallen to her waist.

He paused, and patiently stroked the pearly planes and curves of her shoulders, collarbones and neck. She sat quietly, her eyes glued to his features. How soft his face was. No arrogance in it now, only the deep enjoyment of a man who touched something precious and fragile.

His soothing hands nudged the cloth lower. Chemise and

petticoat fell to her waist, leaving her small, perfect breasts exposed to the sun-filled cabin, bare to his eyes and his hands. Still she watched him, thrilling at the way his shoulders lifted in one quick, uncontrolled suck of air. And this time, when he touched her, the action was not soothing. Her lips parted in a soft moan that called an echo from his throat when his hands filled themselves with warm, womanly flesh.

He cupped her tenderly and savored the moment in the brilliant sunlight, his hands treasuring the feel of her, his eyes enjoying the look of her face. Her lips were parted as she gave quick, rapid pants; her cheeks were as rosy as the tips of the flesh he covered; her eyes were wide with amazement at the feelings coursing from his hands to her body. He felt his manhood throbbing, thrusting urgently against his breeches, and he knew he'd pushed his control to the limit. He couldn't resist one taste of the luscious flesh that was as tempting as forbidden fruit. He bent, resting his black head against her bosom briefly before he turned to nuzzle each breast. He savored her thudding heartbeat, the tightening of her nipples in the warm prison of his mouth. Closing his eyes in sheer agony, he pulled away.

He didn't see the shattered look on her face as she realized she wanted him to go further, sweep aside her defenses and make her his. Was this what desire was? This curling, writhing warmth in the pit of her womb, the apex of her legs that begged for . . . something. She barely noticed when he pulled her clothes back up and fastened them with shaking hands.

"That's enough of a lesson for today," he said practically, hoping she didn't notice the huskiness in his voice. "But there's one thing I need to know—did I do anything you found distasteful?"

Aimee opened dilated eyes to him. The warmth in his inquiring look almost undid her composure, but she sat erect, fluffed her pillow and sank into it as she carefully framed her thoughts. "No, not distasteful. Perhaps alarming would be a better word. I don't like feeling so helpless."

Luke rose and went to his chest to remove his hairbrush. He went back to the bed, sat down and propped her between his legs. He drew the brush through her hair, smoothing out the tangles.

"There's something you apparently haven't realized. Tell

me, Aimee, did I seem strong and in control when I touched you?"

Remembering the trembling of his hands, the soft look on his face, Aimee realized he'd been as vulnerable as she. The thought was a revelation. Her voice was laced with wonder. "No, I guess not."

Luke kissed the top of her head. "I suggest you keep that in mind, next time you're alarmed by how I make you feel. You see, you make me every bit as helpless. Perhaps more so, for I understand the power of passion. You don't." But you will, sweet, he told himself, you will.

Luke drew the brush through her hair a final time, stroked the silky cascade tenderly, then grabbed fistfuls of hair on each side of her head and turned her to face him. Green eyes locked with black ones in a search for greater understanding of the other's complexities. Each knew it was a turning point for them. From this moment on, their relationship would either flower into fulfillment, or wither into a brown husk that held nothing but the dry rattle of duty.

Luke released her from the grip of his hands and eyes and went to brush his own hair. He was dressed in black breeches and boots; his shirt was red silk. The flamboyant costume suited him, made him seem more of a dark tempter than ever. But this devil used charm rather than aggression in his temptations. Whimsically, Aimee wondered which was more dangerous. . . .

Luke put his brush down and winked at her in the mirror. "I've neglected my duties enough. I must relieve poor Jimmy. Do you think you can entertain yourself until dinner? You can stay in the cabin and ring the bell if you need anything. If you'd rather see more of the ship, I can have someone show you around."

"For now, I'll stay in the cabin. I want to have a bath in that delightfully sinful bathtub." She smiled wryly.

Luke swallowed and backed to the door, his eyes glued to the rosy fullness of her lips. "That's my cue to leave. Have a good day, sweetheart."

Luke made his way to the bridge by instinct, for his head and his eyes were still clouded with emotion. A reserved Aimee was distracting enough, but a shyly responsive Aimee was enough to send him over the edge. How was he to control his increasing urge to make her his?

Aimee flung out her arms and spun in place. How wonderful she felt! Humming, she went to unpack fresh clothes. She came across the package Gere had given her. She unwrapped it. Her happy smile quivered, and her body tingled with poignancy. Gere had painstakingly carved a likeness of her family into wood. Ragnar stood, feet apart, head erect in a pose Aimee immediately recognized. One hand was nestled on Ingrid's shoulder, another on Sigrid's. Ingrid had turned her head to watch her husband lovingly; Sigrid stared into the distance, her face sweet and dreamy. Tears gathered in Aimee's eyes. She kissed her finger and touched each wooden face, then she set the statue on the dresser and returned to her bath. She felt comforted by the likeness of Gere's rendering.

The remainder of the brief voyage to Stockholm was a frustrating interval for Luke, and a happy time for Aimee. They increasingly found that, despite their different natures and backgrounds, they had much in common. Both enjoyed literature, nature, good food and the theater; each was impatient of society's silly protocol and sillier restrictions. Luke admired Gere's carving and they had fun opening the wedding gifts.

This mental empathy led gradually to a physical one that Luke found far more upsetting than Aimee. Each evening, after dinner, Luke led Aimee to the bed, kissed her cheek and turned away to his cold, hard settee with only a mournful look. And, when he took her on a detailed tour of the steamer, to point out the *Mercury's* best features, it seemed natural to take her hand. He clasped her arm as he escorted her up and down stairs; he put his arm protectively around her waist as he led her through the engine room. And when they lunched alone in their stateroom, they sat closely side by side. Luke felt scorched where their knees and shoulders met.

Aimee became accustomed to his touch. She enjoyed, even sought, the light physical intimacy they shared. Luke was disconcerted by her new responsiveness. It was what he'd longed for, striven for, but his triumph was bittersweet. She was still not ready for the fullness of passion, and he was long past the stage where he was even remotely content with these chaste embraces.

Such was the situation when they reached Stockholm. The

sun was shining when they sailed past the first islands, making
the sandy shores sparkle like gems; other isles were forested
by birch, pine and oak which served as sturdy windbreaks
against the brisk Baltic air. The sheer number of islands was
amazing. They varied in size from tiny islets to the massive
bulk of Gotland, which they had earlier passed.

Luke and Aimee stood at the rail, watching the passing
scenery. When they struck inland, between the islands, Luke
explained, "Stockholm is built on a dozen islands on the
shores of Lake Malaren, where it spills into the Baltic. It's
sometimes called the 'Venice of the North' because of its
beautiful bridges and waterways."

The topography changed between peninsulas, wooded
cliffs and forests as they approached the city. Everywhere,
there was water and lush vegetation, but Aimee sniffed,
unimpressed. The bland scenery couldn't compare to the
beauty of Norway's fjords.

Smiling inwardly, Luke decided a tour of the city would
change her mind. She couldn't fail to be charmed by what
must surely be one of the most beautiful cities in the world.

Indeed, when they docked, even Aimee had to admire
Stockholm's festive air: colorful small and large boats drifted
in their berths, workmen sang, shoppers strolled, frolicking
children occasionally shrieked with laughter. "Will we tour
the city?" she asked, looking about curiously.

"Yes, we'll check into a hotel today, and we'll have time
for a tour. We'll be here at least for several days, and I
thought you might enjoy getting off the *Mercury*. As for
tonight, would you like to have dinner in town?"

Aimee nodded eagerly, then caught herself. She shrugged,
"Whatever you'd prefer."

"I'd rather sup outside the hotel this first night. And
tomorrow, I thought you might like to see a seamstress. Your
new social life will require more dresses."

Aimee flushed. So he had noticed her meager wardrobe.
She opened her mouth to refuse, then shut it as she realized
that she would embarrass them both if she went to court
dressed in one of her simple skirts and blouses. "Very well.
You are right. I will need them. Should I change into
something more formal for this evening?"

Luke appraised her plain maroon dress, smiled and extended his arm. "Mrs. Garrison, I am proud to be your

escort. Shall we go? Stockholm awaits to dazzle you."

Aimee put her hand on his arm and followed him to the shore boat, repeating her new title to herself. How strange it sounded! Still, as Luke clasped her waist in his hands to lift her into the boat, the thought struck her that it was a name she was rapidly growing accustomed to.

Chapter Seven

THEY BEGAN THEIR tour at Gustav Adolf's Torg, a spacious square in the oldest part of the city. Flowers of every color and variety bordered the square. Their scent seductively tempted Aimee to relax and enjoy her honeymoon as any bride would. The brisk breeze played with her braids. The sun beamed down on her, chasing wariness away. To the devil with prejudice and maidenly fears, she decided. This was a day meant for enjoyment, and enjoy it she would.

Luke watched her inhale the air and look appreciatively about her. She was a sensual woman who didn't know it yet, he reflected. He clenched his hands to suppress an impulse to run his hands over her lissome form and force her to the same burning conclusion. Instead, he took a deep breath and pointed to a long granite bridge leading off the square. "This bridge leads to the City Between the Bridges, where the Royal Palace is located. Time allowing, we'll see it as well, but I wanted you to see this statue of one of Sweden's greatest kings." Luke pointed to the square's core where a magnificent statue of a man in full regalia sat atop a prancing stallion.

Luke continued, "This commemorates Gustavus II Adolphus, King of Sweden . . ."

Aimee read aloud from the plaque: "King from 1611 to 1632, he led Sweden to victory against Denmark, Poland and Russia during the Thirty Years' War. He later died on the battlefield when he led his troops against Germany to save

Protestants from Roman Catholic domination."

Miffed by the glowing words, she whirled to exit from the square and asked blandly, "What else would you like to show me?" She slanted him a teasing look.

She shrieked when Luke spun her into his arms and swung her around. "I'll show you how to display proper respect for your lord and master . . .," he growled. Despite the stern words, his eyes twinkled with merry pride at her grasp of history. He leaned even nearer to whisper, "And then I'll show you how I reward obedience. . . ."

Aimee shivered when he nibbled her ear lobe. She pushed against him and backed a couple of paces away, her hands framing her flushed cheeks. "You'll get us arrested for indecency. People simply do not embrace in public in Scandinavian countries," she scolded breathlessly. She was too busy trying to compose herself to see Luke's smile swell.

"Then I guess it's a good thing no one can read my thoughts, hmm?" When her flush deepened, he took mercy on her confusion.

"Come. Enough loitering," he said briskly. He took her hand and led her north out of the square. They arrived at the busy shopping district of Drottninggatan. Shops of all kinds lined each side of the narrow street: tailors, weavers, dressmakers, jewelers, milliners, shoe shops, silversmiths. Aimee stared into the windows she passed, dazzled by the array of goods. She hated to admit it, but neither Bergen nor even Christiana could boast such a cosmopolitan assortment of wares.

She stopped dead in the middle of the sidewalk, her eye caught by the strangest dress she'd ever seen. It was daintily frilled at bust, neck, sleeves and hem. Even more intriguing, it was not as full as the crinolines still considered the height of fashion in Norway. The green taffeta was pulled tight at the hips into an odd protuberance at the back from which cascaded a short, frilled train.

Luke smiled at her amazement. "It's called a bustle and is considered a must for every fashionable woman. See how it emphasizes the figure? You'll own a wardrobe full of such dresses by this time tomorrow night."

Aimee looked at him, distressed. "I'd look ridiculous in that. I think I'd have to walk spradle-legged to balance my bottom." She reddened as she realized what she'd said.

Luke roared, attracting curious looks from passers-by. Her embarrassment deepened. Chuckling, he took her arm to escort her down the street. "Your bottom seems in balance to me—most distractingly so, I might add." He lifted his eyebrows and leered over his shoulder at her hips.

In an effort to distract him, Aimee blurted, "Where are we going?"

"The dinner hour is approaching. It usually begins around two here in Stockholm, and I, for one, am starved. I know of a little restaurant around the corner that has tables in a courtyard where we can enjoy the scenery and the sunlight, if it's to your liking."

Aimee was delighted with the open-air café. After entering through the cloakroom, they emerged into a dining area furnished with fewer than a dozen small, rough-hewn tables covered with blue-checked cloths. Ruffled blue curtains framed the windows and scenes of Swedish wildlife decorated the walls. This cheerful chamber was empty. They found the diners in the adjoining courtyard outside savoring the short Swedish summer.

A pink-cheeked *flicka* wearing a white, frilly bib apron over her dress escorted them to a small, wrought-iron table. She took their order of *pytt-i-panna*, meat and potato hash with fried egg, and pea soup, served them with sweetened herring and acquavit, then curtsied and retreated.

In the corner of the courtyard, musicians tuned their instruments to begin an impromptu concert. Soon they burst into a rollicking Danish song about a doleful suitor pursuing a flighty maid. Several women strummed the guitars and bowed the fiddles as two men blew loudly and less than tunefully on their horns. The lead was a portly, graying violinist who coaxed the others to play with such enthusiasm, the diners were soon clapping their hands in unison.

Luke smiled when Aimee joined in, eyes shining, cheeks flushed as usual. She beamed in return, sending his eyes flying back to the band to hide the effect she had on him. He wished he could cast a spell on her and keep this vibrant, glowing girl forever beside him. He glanced around and noticed that he wasn't the only one appreciating her. Proprietarily, he edged nearer to her and sent a narrow-eyed look at Aimee's admirer until the young Swede turned away.

When the music ended after several more songs, Luke

took her hand and teased, "Another minute and you'd embarrass me by dancing on the table. What do you think of Stockholm now?"

Aimee was too happy with the beautiful day, with Luke's friendly smile, and even, oddly, with her marriage, to take offense. She admitted, "I could learn to like it, I'm sure." Her eyes strayed back to the band. "Oh look! He's going to perform alone." She nibbled at her food when it was placed in front of her, her eyes glued on the portly man. Luke's eyes were glued on her.

The old gentleman bowed in thanks for the coins and notes flung their way, then he held up a hand to silence the audience while the guitarist collected money. "Ladies and gentlemen, we conclude our performance with a good-humored look at the various nationalities that visit and live in our fair city. We challenge you to identify each group."

Aimee shoved her plate back to prop her elbows on the table. She took an absent-minded sip of her acquavit, coughed and hastily set the glass back down. Eyes watering, she looked gratefully at Luke when he held a water glass to her lips. After she had sipped, he lowered the glass and wiped her mouth, slowly, sensually. Only a brassy introduction from the horns tore their stare apart.

The rotund little man mussed his hair, opened his coat and let his eyes cross slightly as he staggered across the patio. "A Norwegian!" crowed one of the diners. Aimee sent him an angry look. Norwegians were probably somewhat more abstemious than Swedes.

Luke patted her shoulder and whispered, "Look what he's doing now. I think he's a Frenchman, don't you?"

The merry fellow was clasping his hands, sighing and smiling wistfully, eyes ardent. Aimee nodded. Luke shouted, "A Frenchman!"

The performer bowed to their table. "Very good, sir. See how you like my next impression." Smiling mischievously, he took great, arrogant strides across the grass, chin haughty as he looked down his nose at them. Then, grandly, he sniffed and seemed about to pull his handkerchief out of his pocket, only to blow his nose rudely on his sleeve. Luke reddened as he caught the reference. Aimee giggled, anger forgotten, and caroled, "An American!"

The fellow beamed at her, winked slyly at Luke and began his last impression. He scowled, brows beetling over his nose that twitched as though assailed by evil odors. He held his breath, puffing his cheeks out until his face was red with disapproval. The diners called out, "A Dane!" and "A Spaniard!"

Aimee frowned in concentration, watching as the impressionist grinned witlessly, removed an imaginary snuff box from his pocket and took a dainty pinch to sniff it up his nose. Aimee and Luke laughed. Their eyes met as they called simultaneously, "An Englishman!"

The performer applauded them. He plucked a white rose from a bush behind him and handed the blossom to Aimee with a deep bow. "This rose is a poor rival for your grace and wit, madam," he intoned gravely.

Aimee blushed and took the flower, nodding her head in thanks. Luke slipped the violin player a large note and shook the man's hand. Briskly, the band gathered up its instruments and departed, leaving the diners in a gay mood—none more than Luke and Aimee.

She teased, "I found his impression very appropriate in your case. He reminded me of you when he strode across the courtyard. You look just like him when you stalk up and down the bridge, king of all you survey."

Luke pretended to be offended. He straightened haughtily. "And I suppose next you'll accuse me of using my coat for a handkerchief."

Aimee almost ruined her charade by laughing, but instead peered at the sleeve of his handsome brown linen jacket. "Indeed. Isn't that a stain I see on your sleeve?"

When her nose wrinkled in distaste, Luke sneaked a glance at his sleeve before he caught himself. She sent a merry peal of laughter into the air at his gullibility.

Luke stilled his twitching lips and mocked, "And what of you? Poor fellow was too impressed with your 'grace and wit' to notice your thorns. And I have the bruised pride to prove it."

Aimee retorted, "Your pride can stand a little bruising."

Luke picked up the rose and stroked his face, then he leaned down to rub their cheeks against one another as if to compare the texture. He pulled away only far enough to whisper, "But he was right, you know. This flower is a poor rival to you in every way. And you're worth a thousand bruises if that's what it will take for me to pluck you."

Aimee swallowed and tried to lean away, but he held her

trapped against his arm and her chair. She croaked, "Remember what happens to a plucked rose? It withers and dies, all beauty and life destroyed."

Luke stroked the flower against her cheek, his eyes fixed on her mouth. "Haven't you ever put a bud in sugar water and watched it send out new shoots? You can then transplant it and watch this one tiny little flower grow into a mighty bush that offers joy, comfort and sustenance to many different life forms. If left to wither on the bush, it will die alone, unappreciated by any but the chance passer-by, unable to experience the fruitfulness of procreation."

His sexual innuendo was accompanied by the disturbing, incessant, gentle stroke of the flower on her cheek. Her head was filled by the rose's heady scent, and as her senses throbbed, she absorbed the look and feel of him. For a dangerous moment, she let his black eyes burn coal-like to her very core and tempt her into forbidden realms of pleasure. His spell was so powerful she wavered in her chair and leaned helplessly toward him.

Only the *flicka*'s return saved her. She shattered the intimacy when she asked if they required anything else. Luke scowled and threw the rose on the table.

"No," he snapped. To atone for his gruffness, he smiled, paid for the meal and left the girl a generous tip. When they were alone again, he stroked a beguiling finger over Aimee's mouth, but she had rearmed herself and met his bold stare calmly.

"Safe for the moment, little flower. Hide while you can. But we both know the time is coming when you'll burst into full bloom. And then I, and only I, will be there to pluck you."

Courteously, as if he hadn't just threatened her with seduction, he pulled back her chair, took her arm and escorted her from the café. For the remainder of the evening, they strolled about Stockholm, admiring the many parks, the bridges, and waters hosting ducks and Dalecarlian boatmen. When the Northern twilight finally descended, they walked to the Hotel du Suede. The magnificent granite edifice dominated its section of Drottninggatan like an aristocrat scornful of the smaller, more modest buildings encircling it.

Aimee had said little since dinner, and Luke allowed her to retreat—for the moment. He pointed out features of interest, answered her few questions and acted as tour guide and protector, nothing more. The Machiavelli who had enchanted her in the café was brisk and businesslike when he registered them at the hotel.

Aimee looked around the luxurious lobby. Tan marble pillars rose grandly from the highly polished floor, and murals of boating and shepherding scenes covered the walls. An enormous round couch circled a magnificent, cascading fountain in the center of the lobby. It and the accompanying chairs and lounges were covered in rich gold brocade.

Aimee started when Luke took her arm. He gestured to a bellhop who was carrying two small trunks. "Jimmy had a few of our things delivered, as I asked. I've booked a room. Shall we go up?"

They climbed the curving granite staircase to a room on the second floor. Luke tipped the bellhop and went to check the view at the window. The street looked charming in the lingering twilight. Rows of street lamps flickered like fireflies, winking off adjacent windows. Luke pulled the heavy velvet drapes shut.

He turned to find Aimee staring at the fourposter, her eyes dilated with strong emotion. He wasn't sure she knew herself whether she was afraid or fascinated, but he moved to reassure her.

He caught her arms gently. "You've nothing to be afraid of, sweetheart. I'll sleep on the couch, as usual. I want nothing you don't want to give me."

Aimee relaxed, asking hesitantly, "Then why did you threaten me in the café?"

Luke winced. "I didn't intend for you to take my desire for you as a threat. Don't you know it's a compliment when a man wants to be intimate with a woman?" He turned away to riffle through his trunk. He pulled out his robe and slammed the lid shut.

Aimee watched him go to the pitcher by the bed, splash water into the bowl, remove his jacket, vest and shirt and sluice down his face and torso. His movements were agitated. She was distressed as she realized she had hurt him. The sensible restrictions she'd placed on herself had grown stifling.

As she watched the lantern light play on his flexing muscles, she knew with sudden clarity that she could not resist him much longer. Indeed, how could any woman? Back arched, hair a lustrous blue-black in the lamplight, he was Man, Man as God had intended when he blew life into dust eons ago. And she knew with the feminine certainty she was just beginning to listen to that she was as drawn to him as Eve must have been to Adam, after being formed from his rib.

Without thought, without fear, she went to him and put her hand on his damp shoulder. "I'm sorry, Luke. It's not you I fear so much as . . . what comes after. Please be patient with me. Perhaps if I understood more of what you want of me, I'd be less wary. . . ." Her voice trailed off into embarrassment.

Luke stiffened at her touch, feeling the tingles race through his body even at that slight contact. He roughly dried his face and chest, dropped the towel on the stand and turned to take her hand and lead her to the couch.

His voice resonated with feeling. "Thank you, darling. You don't know how much it means to me that you're coming to trust me." He played with her fingers, locking them with his, smoothing each one in a sensual caress. "As for what I want of you . . . Hasn't anyone ever explained to you how a man and woman . . . show their devotion?"

Scarlet-cheeked, Aimee mumbled, "My mother tried to, but I'm afraid I was preoccupied and paid little attention. I have seen animals mating. I assume men and women mate in a similar manner?"

"Only in the most basic sense. When men and women join, it can be the most fulfilling, enjoyable act either will ever perform, in both a physical and, if they're lucky, in an emotional way. There is much beauty and tenderness involved, as well as passion."

He was so matter-of-fact that Aimee's embarrassment eased. She asked curiously, "And what exactly do they do?"

Luke, experienced man of the world, was chagrined to feel himself reddening. What a position to find himself in! It was surely a supreme irony to have to explain the mechanics of love-making to the one innocent, exasperating girl he desired above all others. He felt a rush of anger at Ragnar for keeping Aimee so sheltered for years. Now her own husband had to explain the basics of physical love, couched in terms that would not tip off his own seductive ploys.

He searched for the most enticing way to explain the

earthy facts. "It usually starts with kissing, first on the mouth, then on other parts of the body. . . ."

"As you kissed me the other day?"

"Yes, but often in an even more intimate way."

Her eyes widened in amazement. "Even more intimately than you kissed me? At my, my . . ." She looked away and crossed her hands over her tingling bosom.

Luke shifted uncomfortably. "There are other, more . . . sensitive parts of the body that are very receptive to the touch."

She wouldn't let him avoid the issue. "Where?" she asked bluntly.

Luke took a deep breath and rushed, "On the legs and, er, at their joining."

Aimee looked so astonished he hastily added, "But that intimacy is rarely performed during the first, er, encounter. After a period of kissing and touching, the man is ready, and, if he is a skillful lover, the woman is ready too."

"Ready? How so?"

Luke cleared his throat. "Ah, only when a man is excited can he complete the act."

"Why?"

Luke wiped a hand along his sweating brow, wildly searching for a delicate way to express the blunt truth. "When a man becomes aroused, certain parts of his body become . . . larger, even as a woman swells and becomes moist. Only when each partner is ready, can full pleasure be enjoyed by both."

"Ready for what?"

Luke let her go to drum his hands on the back of the couch. "Don't you know anything?" he burst out, frustrated. When she looked hurt, he heaved a sigh and propped his chin on his hand. He was making a mess of this. He pulled gently on a braid until she looked at him.

"Sweetheart, surely you're aware of the basic difference between a man and woman?" Aimee bit her lip and nodded shyly.

"Well, it's this difference that makes it possible to join. A man is . . . long and hard and a woman is . . . deep and soft. Do you understand?"

Aimee frowned. She nodded slowly. "I think so. Do you mean a man places himself inside the woman?"

He slumped with relief. "That's it exactly. This . . . filling gives pleasure to both, and at the peak of this pleasure, the man releases a fluid into the woman, that, at certain times of the month, can make her pregnant."

He was stunned to find himself nearly panting from discomfort and his brow again laced with sweat. He wiped it again.

When Luke looked at Aimee, he was appalled to find her staring at the crotch of his pants. This intimate conversation had begun to have an effect on him. Instinctively, he moved to shield himself with his hands, but he froze as he realized it was no time to act like an embarrassed schoolboy. He sat stone still, watching as Aimee's eyes went from his pants to her lap.

She put a wondering hand to herself, then she looked at him and shook her head. "No, it wouldn't work," she said with utter certainty. "You wouldn't fit."

She looked so disgusted, like a student who has been misled by a trusted teacher, that Luke chuckled. He put his hands on her shoulders and bussed her mouth. Playfully, he shoved her down on the couch and leaned over her.

"If you insist, sweetheart, I can show you I'm right." He tickled her ribs until she giggled helplessly, then he pulled her to her feet and drew her into his arms.

Black eyes delved into her green ones as he murmured, "It's not only possible, Aimee, it's inevitable. You will belong to me. The time will come when you'll yearn for me as much as I yearn for you." His eyes lowered to her mouth. His head bent lower, lower, but he snapped back and retreated to a safe distance.

"No, I dare not kiss you now. But someday, my wife, someday I won't hold back and you'll learn the truth of everything I've told you."

Luke went to her trunk, removed a modest nightgown and handed it to her. He took a pillow and blanket from the bed and made up the couch. Feeling more awkward then he had in years, he shouldered into his robe and removed his breeches from underneath, then folded them onto a chair. Then he lay down and blew his bride a kiss, his manner far more sanguine than his emotions.

"Good night, darling. Sleep well, for we've a busy day tomorrow."

He turned on his side away from her. Aimee stood where she was for several minutes, her thoughts whirling. She blew out the lantern and put on the nightgown. The experience he described sounded intriguing, frightening, and the ultimate in intimacy. Again she felt herself, wondering how she could ever accommodate that part of a man. Surely such a joining would be painful? Yet women did it all the time, many with apparent pleasure. She had seen her own mother flushed and eager to retire after Ragnar had kissed her, so surely women relished intimacy as much as men.

Then she remembered how enraptured, how helpless Luke made her feel when he embraced her. If what he had done to her was only the prelude to intimacy, she would surely be mindless by the time he was finished. She would be in the very position she had vowed no male would ever put her: helpless to control her emotions, utterly dependent for her well-being on a man who lived his life by his own rules and would expect his wife to do likewise.

Even for Luke, could she surrender so completely? She had never dreamed she would find a man so alluring. And perhaps Sigrid had been right. There were rewards for the woman as well as for the man in belonging. Belonging . . . Aimee visualized lying in Luke's arms, his mouth consuming hers, his body taking possession as he had described. And she quivered—but in fear or excitement? No matter how long she lay staring at the ceiling, torn between yearning and fear, she couldn't answer that question.

Aimee awakened to the smell of coffee and the sound of whistling. Luke brought coffee and pastries to the bed on a tray when she stirred. He kissed her cheek and moved away, as if he knew she was feeling wary this morning.

"Eat up, darling. The morning is getting away from us, and I have a stop to make before we can begin our shopping. Do you know who Alfred Nobel is?"

Aimee nodded, mouth full. She swallowed and said, "He's well-known through all of Scandinavia. He invented that new, safe explosive. . . . What is it called?"

"Dynamite. My father met him when Alfred was in America trying to get a patent for his earlier blasting oil. When Alfred turned over his patent to New York shareholders to promote his products in America, my father invested in the company, the United States Blasting Oil Co. However, shady business dealings of the other shareholders and insolvency led my father to withdraw. Another company was begun in California, and finally, after months of negotiation, the two companies have agreed to merge into one, the Atlantic Giant Powder Company. My father has been assured this company will be much better managed, and he's agreed to invest. I'm taking the final papers to Alfred, who is here on business. He recently moved from Hamburg to Paris, though he spends a great deal of his time traveling."

Luke had been dressing as he spoke and when he turned from brushing his hair, he was distracted to find Aimee standing at the window brushing her own hair. The morning sunlight silhouetted her curves, arresting him. He had to drag his eyes to her face when she turned and spoke.

"I'll be delighted to meet him. He is one Swede I have always respected. I have a cousin who was employed by him, and he describes him as generous, considerate and brilliant, if reserved."

"You'll soon see for yourself. I want to have a haircut, but I should be back soon." He backed out the door, his eyes still locked on her, leaving Aimee confused at his odd behavior.

By chance she turned in the direction of the mirror. She blushed as she realized what he'd been staring at. She might as well be naked! She spun away from the window and hopped into her clothes, trying to put the look on his face out of her mind. But no matter how primly she wound her braids or how high she buttoned the collar of her beige dress, she could not douse the warmth that made her cheeks flush and her skin tingle. She patted her hair when she was finished and stared at herself in the mirror.

She grimaced at her own wide-eyed look. At least now she knew she wasn't sick. Perhaps an illness would be safer, she told herself whimsically. At least then she'd have a chance of recovering. Constant company with Luke promised only a worsening of this ailment.

"You've got to get a grip on yourself, my girl. You'll never survive this marriage if a simple look from him sends your temperature soaring."

She moved about, straightening the room, still muttering to herself. She started when Luke returned. They stared at one another warily.

"Your hair looks nice," Aimee offered.

Luke nodded in thanks. "You look nice, also. Shall we go?"

With a stiff formality that said much about their inner turmoil, Luke and Aimee descended to the street. It was bustling with early morning shoppers. Luke hailed an open carriage and assisted Aimee inside, giving the driver their direction. They sat in silence for a while, but soon the shining sun, the mild, fragrant breeze and the busy scene, well-dressed pedestrians, elegant carriages of every description guided courteously through the streets by cheerful drivers, relaxed them. Every other block, it seemed, they passed a handsome monument, old church or pretty park ornamented with neat flower beds and benches. As they traveled into the newer part of the city, they passed modern offices and townhouses, many steep-roofed and three-storied in the French style.

They pulled up in front of one such townhouse. Luke helped Aimee down and asked the driver to return in an hour. He escorted her up the stone steps and knocked on the door. A manservant answered.

"I'd like to see Alfred Nobel, please," Luke requested.

"Who may I say is calling?"

"Mr. and Mrs. Luke Garrison."

The man opened the door and ushered them into a parlor. Aimee looked about. The furniture was of good quality, but plain. The house was certainly a surprise, considering Nobel's reputed wealth.

Luke saw her puzzlement. "This is probably a rented house. Alfred has purchased a small mansion in Paris that is, I understand, quite elegant. He visits Stockholm only rarely."

The door opened and Aimee turned in curiosity as a small man who looked to be in his early forties entered the room. He was elegantly but quietly dressed in black broadcloth. His frock coat was a bit fuller and longer than Luke's and his black tie narrower. His hair and full beard were dark brown. His blue eyes were wide with interest.

"It's good to see you, Luke. But I wasn't aware you had married."

Luke smiled down at Aimee. "We've been married less than a week and are, in fact, on our wedding trip."

Nobel looked appalled. "And you've dragged your bride here to see an ugly old man when there are beautiful sights for you to visit?"

The scientist, as if to redeem a bad situation, bowed stiffly to Aimee. "Mrs. Garrison, welcome to Stockholm. And I promise I won't keep your husband long." He smiled, but somehow the courtesy increased his reserved, melancholy air.

Aimee was intrigued that this brilliant, wealthy inventor, who surely had much to be arrogant about, yet seemed so self-deprecating. "Thank you, sir. I am happy to meet such a famous industrialist—who is, may I add, neither old nor ugly."

Nobel flushed and waved them into chairs. "That's kind, but I am not famous by choice, I assure you. I would gladly trade my fame for the chance to work in peace without the restrictions of small minds. Sometimes I feel I live in a fish bowl, and a moving fish bowl at that."

He looked inquiringly at Luke. "Now, I assume you're here to deliver the papers?"

Luke nodded and removed a thick sheaf of papers from his inner coat pocket. "Yes, the agreement was drawn up as negotiated and awaits only your signature."

Nobel took the papers and set them on the table beside him. "I'll take them to my barrister and send the signed copies to your hotel. Where are you staying?"

"The Hotel du Suede. But why don't you bring them yourself? We would enjoy having dinner with you."

"No, no, I wouldn't dream of interfering. . . ."

Aimee hated to interrupt, but felt obliged to anyway. "It would be no interference, truly. I would so like to discuss your discoveries."

Nobel looked startled. "Are you interested in science, madam?"

Aimee blushed at the 'madam,' and nodded shyly. Luke's smile at his wife was gently approving. "I believe my wife is interested in most things, Alfred. Tell me, how are your sales of dynamite?"

"Very good. They've nearly doubled in the past five years. Last year we sold 1,350 tons, and expect to sell even more this year."

Luke whistled. "That's good to hear. So the new company

should do quite well, then."

"It is to be hoped that is the case. Unless the shareholders are more interested in bilking the company than helping it produce." Nobel's brows lowered in contempt.

Luke sighed. "I know you were treated ill last time you were in America, Alfred, but I hope the experience doesn't prejudice you against my country forever. Not all its businessmen are dishonest."

"I'm aware of that. I have great respect for you and your father, but I nevertheless have no interest in visiting America again." His tone lightened. "Now, may I offer you refreshment?"

Luke shook his head and drew Aimee to her feet. "No, we have many more errands to run, and we need to get started. May we expect you for dinner then, in a couple of days?"

Nobel hesitated. Aimee encouraged him. "Please, sir, it would please me greatly."

Nobel seemed uncomfortable, but he looked at her pretty, pleading face and nodded. His smile was peculiarly sparkling. "Very well, madam, if you insist, I'll meet you both in the dining room at four in two days."

As Nobel escorted them to the door, Aimee sensed that he was glad they were leaving. He courteously bade them good-bye, but his eyes were already far away, as if he were lost again in his experiments.

"What an interesting man. But what happened to make him so disgusted with your country?"

Luke assisted Aimee into the waiting carriage, then ordered the driver to go to the shops on Regeringsgatan before replying. "Unfortunately the shareholders were more interested in getting the rights to his inventions and exploiting them for their own purposes than in carrying out their part of the agreement. I'm afraid Alfred's quarter of a million dollars in shares in the company turned out to be worthless paper. Not only that, but various forms of his blasting oil began appearing in competition. They sold under different names, but they were only slightly modified from his invention. Yes, he's every right to be bitter."

When they reached the shopping district, Luke paid the driver and lifted Aimee to the ground. "Enough about business. The rest of this day belongs to you, my lady. I am your humble servant." Luke put his palms together and bowed, but his roguish wink was anything but humble.

Aimee laughed and grabbed him by his lapel to tug him down the street. "That's just what I've always wanted to hear. You'll do exactly as I say today, won't you?"

Luke cast her an enigmatic smile of his own. "Certainly, ma'am, with one minor stipulation. The day is yours, if the night is mine." When Aimee stopped dead in the middle of the sidewalk, Luke tut-tutted. "What? Change your mind?"

Aimee looked at him uncertainly. Luke shook his head, laughing at her. "Now who's gullible? I'm only teasing, sweet. Come on, this looks like a good place to start." He took her arm and pulled her into an elegant little shop, so she didn't see the frustrated look in his eyes as he forced himself to patience.

A small, graceful blond came to greet them. "I am Elga, the owner. May I help you?"

Luke gently nudged Aimee forward. "Please. My wife needs an entire wardrobe, from undergarments to capes. She'll need quite an assortment immediately. Do you have anything made up in her size?"

Elga walked around Aimee, eyes narrowed. She nodded slowly. "Yes, I believe so. Some of the dresses may need shortening, but madam has quite a good figure." She looked surprised when Aimee blushed under Luke's gaze. Elga's eyes lit up. "Ah, you are newlyweds, are you not?"

When Luke nodded, she clapped her hands in delight. "Wonderful! I shall assist you myself, and when we are finished, your bride will look as elegant and lovely as a bride should." She gestured Luke to a chair and whisked Aimee into a curtained alcove.

Luke's nostrils flared as he heard the tantalizing rustle of clothing. When Aimee squealed, "Really madame, must you take everything?" Luke shifted restlessly. He tried to keep his eyes glued forward, examining the bolts of fabric, periodicals, mannequins and racks of dresses cluttering the small room, but against his will, his eyes strayed back to the intriguing sway of the curtain.

Elga emerged to go through several drawers in a wardrobe that towered against the wall. She called an assistant and gave several orders. She removed a lacy corset and filmy undergarments, nodded at Luke and returned to the alcove. Luke leaned forward when she opened the curtain, but he could see nothing. He sat back and whistled nervously to drown out the sound of Aimee's protests.

"I don't want to wear this thing. I won't be able to breathe!"

"Nonsense. See how it emphasizes your waist? You won't look good in a bustle unless you wear one."

"I don't care if I look good in a bustle. Now unlace me before I faint!"

Elga swooped open the curtain, her mouth pursed in disapproval, and beckoned to Luke. Luke pointed at himself and mouthed "Me?"

She nodded, foot tapping. Luke lumbered to his feet, his heart racing. He followed her into the alcove. He froze at the sight of his bride. Aimee jerked angrily at the back of the white lace corset, her bosom threatening to burst from its flimsy confinement. Luke's eyes swept over her hungrily.

She was wearing white lisle stockings and frilly garters that emphasized the curves of her legs. Her brief drawers and chemise were of a fabric so exquisite they were semi-transparent. And that damnable corset emphasized her waist and made her small breasts seem so temptingly full that he had to stuff his hands into his pockets to deny his urge to cup them. And, as if his rising passion needed a boost, her loose hair rippled over her shoulders, past her hips like a flirtatious golden sail.

At that moment, she looked up. She gasped and turned a fiery red as she tried to shield her bosom with her hands. She was so much the picture of the outraged virgin that Luke's sense of humor was pricked, despite his pounding heart. He gave a low-rumbling chuckle, then stepped up to caress her warm cheek.

"Don't be embarrassed, sweet. I'm seeing nothing a bridegroom isn't entitled to see. Do you know how lovely you are?" He turned her to face the mirror and pulled her back against him. Aimee glanced at herself, but her eyes were drawn to Luke's far more interesting reflection. Neither of them were aware that the proprietess watched them in bewilderment.

Luke gently moved her hands out to her sides. "Look, Aimee, can't you see what I see? Skin of white satin, tiny waist, slim legs and beautiful hair. You would make any man turn feverish, and I am no different."

Aimee swallowed, her heart racing. She longed to believe he found her as attractive as he claimed, but when she looked in the mirror, she didn't see the slim, delectable shape Luke saw. She saw the pale young girl she'd known all her life, a little fuller figured perhaps, but hardly voluptuous. Was this vibrant male truly lured by the girl who leaned against him in stark, white contrast to his dark power? She searched his eyes, seeking the truth. The desire for her there was so plain even her innocence could penetrate the thin skin shielding it. Weak with a like longing, she sagged against him.

Elga cleared her throat uneasily. "Tell her, sir, that she must wear the corset if she wants to look nice in her clothes."

"My wife is free to do as she likes. Aimee, if you don't want to wear the corset, don't. Your waist is small enough already."

Aimee laughed nervously and slipped away from him. "Perhaps I can try it for a day or two. After I become accustomed to it, it may not bother me." She was barely aware of what she was saying, so intent was she on getting rid of him. "Now please, go, so we can finish. I'm getting hungry and would like to eat soon."

Luke obeyed only after one last, sweeping appraisal. For several hours, Aimee tried on clothes. Day dresses, evening dresses, walking dresses, negligees, undergarments, outergarments of paletot jackets and capuchin capes. Luke even insisted they buy a fur-lined cape. "It's probably cheaper here than it would be in New York, and our winters are quite cold," he stated over her objections. So Aimee found herself the owner of a black velvet, hooded cape lined in ermine. Ermine tails bordered the front closure. Her huge muff held a jet pin from which swung two small tails.

Luke assisted her in selecting various designs from Godey's Lady's Book; together, they chose the fabrics and the trims. And when she finally appeared decked out in a lavender walking costume bordered by alternating rows of plum and cream braid, and a gored skirt over a cream lace underskirt, he rose in delight. His eyes sparkled at her bustle which he noticed was accented by an enormous plum bow.

"You look delicious as a plum pudding." He walked around her, rubbing his chin in consideration. "Still, I'd like to see you walk. I need to be ready to catch you if your bottom over-balances."

Aimee flushed. "Ssh! She might hear you. She already thinks we're strange. Don't make it worse."

Luke paid the curious Elga, ordered the balance of Aimee's clothes delivered to the *Mercury* and escorted his modish wife out of the shop. He tottered under his load of boxes. Aimee looked forward to lunch, but Luke insisted that they finish their shopping first—she still needed shoes, gloves and hats. Aimee groaned. Her feet already ached. Shopping had never been a favorite pasttime. However, Luke ignored her protests, loaded their packages into a hired carriage, then dragged her into a millinery shop. By the time they were finally ready for lunch, Aimee was wearing a small lavender hat with cream and purple feathers and new walking boots. She collapsed into her chair and cast a jaundiced eye at Luke, who seemed as vigorous as ever, and in fact, quite pleased with himself.

"What are you so happy about?" she asked tiredly.

"I'm just thinking what a good impression you'll make when we go to court tomorrow."

Aimee stiffened. "So soon?"

"Yes, I'm negotiating with Count Ingmar Christiansen for our line to transport his timber. Swedish export of timber has accelerated greatly in recent years as lumber has become scarcer in Britain and America. The Count is a member of the First Chamber, which is similar to Britain's House of Lords, and he suggested going to court to meet the King. There are good business connections by the by." He winked. "We'll conclude our business there."

Despite her hunger, Aimee picked at her food when it arrived. She dreaded this state visit. She wasn't sure she was sophisticated enough for court. Most Swedes considered Norwegians boorish and uncivilized, and she had no wish to foster the impression. Even more daunting, what if she ruined Luke's business deal by an outburst? Aimee felt as fiercely loyal to Norway, home or not, as ever. She wasn't sure she could control her temper when faced with the very people who refused to grant Norwegian independence.

Nevertheless, by the time they prepared for bed that evening, Aimee's chin was stubbornly high again. She would not be intimidated. She would do her best to make Luke proud, but if she caused a scene, then so be it. It was time Swedes learned Norwegians had every reason to want freedom. Comforted, Aimee fell asleep. Her dreams gave no warning that, before the week was out, she would be embroiled in a scene caused not by herself, but by her smooth, confident husband.

Chapter Eight

By the time Aimee was dressed for their afternoon audience with the King, she was in a combative mood. Hands on hips, she glared at her mirrored image, deciding she looked as ridiculous as she felt. She hated the corset, she hated the high-heeled satin shoes pinching her toes, and she hated the elaborate delicacy of her new hairstyle. The hotel had summoned a hairdresser at Luke's request, but Aimee didn't like the elegant, upswept style the woman had fashioned. As a further irritant, when Aimee turned her head, the profusion of ringlets dangling down her back tickled her bare skin. The dark pink silk flowers set atop her head as a coronet looked gaudy and artificial to her.

Even the stunning pink silk gown, adorned at hem and train with more dark pink flowers, no longer seemed as appealing as it had in the shop. Sighing, she turned away from the mirror, admitting it was not her appearance she resented as much as the need to make an impression on influential people she heartily disliked. Under the circumstances, she had no choice, but that didn't mean she had to like dressing up like a doll and acting just as wooden.

When Luke entered, she turned to shower him with admiration. He wore a black broadcloth cutaway coat that emphasized his broad shoulders and slim waist, a starched, snowy-white shirt and close-fitting pin-striped gray trousers. He wore a high black silk hat and carried a cane. He doffed his hat and made her a sweeping bow.

153

"Madame, your beauty astounds me. Can this be my wild little nymph of the woods?" When she sent him a haughty glare for his teasing, he twinkled, "Ah, I see it is. Not even the fine feathers can hide that stubborn look."

When she remained poker-faced, his whimsy faded into seriousness. "What is it, Aimee?"

She hesitated, then blurted, "I really don't want to go, Luke. Can't you go without me?"

Luke shook his head. He put a gentle but firm hand on her shoulder. "No, sweet, it's time you put this prejudice aside. Oscar II is no monster. In fact, if what I hear is true, he could well be one of Sweden's kindest, most intellectual rulers. Did you know he writes poetry?"

For the first time he saw a spark of interest in her eyes. "No. But I daresay it's atrocious."

"His subjects don't seem to think so. I heard that one of his poems, sent in anonymously, won a literary prize. And surely you know that making a good impression today is vital to our line's future interests."

Aimee's mutinous look faded at his use of the collective. How good that "our" sounded. She had the family honor to uphold. Looking into his earnest eyes, she felt all else of secondary importance. She couldn't disappoint him.

"You win, Luke. I promise I'll do my best to hold my tongue and play the brainless female." She looked so disgusted at the mere idea that Luke chuckled and pulled her into his arms.

"I don't think you could appear brainless no matter how hard you tried. Don't strain yourself, sweet. Just be polite and act naturally, and the King will be charmed."

Aimee followed him meekly down the stairs, warmed by his praise. They took a boat to Drottningholm Castle, the main summer residence of the royal family. When they arrived, they paused to admire the grandeur of the palace set out like a centerpiece on a sumptuous table. The elegant French style of architecture impressed Aimee, reminding her vaguely of pictures of old chateaux she'd seen in books. On one side, the palace windows looked out over Lake Malaren, on the other, a sweeping vista of the royal park. An avenue of small trees bordered the drive to the front gate, and the grounds were studded with neat hedges, flower beds and ornate statuary. A magnificent fountain cascaded merrily into a marble basin set at the top of the drive.

As they approached the steps, a stately old gentleman met them. He bowed, introducing himself as the Court Chamberlain. Luke bowed in return, relating their names.

"The King is expecting you," the man said formally. "Please come with me."

They followed obediently, listening as he explained some of the history of the palace. "It was built in the middle 1600s by Queen Hedvig Eleonara, according to plans by our great architects, a father and son team called the Tessins. As you'll see, it holds many art works."

They entered the Great Vestibule. Aimee stared at the lofty antechamber with its ornate stonework and gilded cornices. A grand stairway ascended to the upper gallery, the massive marble balustrades and granite steps so imposing that she stared in amazement. When her eye caught the blue and yellow of the Swedish flag and the coat of arms, her enthusiasm was quelled. The Chamberlain escorted them to the state chamber, then left them alone. Despite herself, she was impressed by the priceless Gobelin tapestries, lifelike busts and plush rococco furniture.

Just in time, she remembered Luke's instructions uttered earlier that day. "Curtsy very low and bow your head, and never sit in the King's presence unless invited to." Though it made her mouth flinch in distaste, she matched Luke's deep bow with a graceful curtsy.

The King waved them forward, and she followed Luke reluctantly. "Come, sign our visitors' book, Mr. Garrison," Oscar invited genially. Luke did so, leaving Aimee to squirm under the appreciative stare of her monarch.

"Welcome to Stockholm, Mrs. Garrison. What do you think of the fairest city in all Scandinavia?"

Aimee bit her tongue on the retort she longed to make. "It is indeed fair," she compromised. Loyalty made her add, "I, however, prefer Bergen."

The King's eyes narrowed at her response. "I see. Are you Norwegian?"

Aimee curtsied in assent. "Yes, Sire. That doesn't keep me from appreciating beauty, however." She looked around the chamber appreciatively.

Luke sighed in relief at her diplomatic response and looked at the King. Oscar eyed Aimee shrewdly, waving away the courtiers hovering over him. "Leave, please. I wish to have a private audience with Mr. and Mrs. Garrison." The courtiers trailed out of the chamber, peering back at Aimee.

Aimee met the King's gaze steadily, even when he rose to his feet and towered above her. Oscar the Second was almost as tall as Luke. He was a young, handsome man of regal bearing and splendid physique. His brown hair shone with health. He wore it short and combed back from his cerebral forehead. His intelligent eyes twinkled when he stepped so close she had to crane her neck to see his face.

"And tell me, what does this pretty Norwegian girl think of her King?"

Luke held his breath. Aimee glanced away, hesitating, then she boldly met Oscar's eyes. "I think you are both handsome and earnest in your wish for the good of your people."

Oscar rubbed his chin, as if gauging her sincerity. He said blandly, "I suspect there is more to your opinion, but you are too canny to voice it."

Aimee didn't deny it, and he turned away from her to stride up and down in reflection. "My loftiest goal as a monarch is to see Norway and Sweden united, two great countries working as brothers. Did you know I chose for my motto, '*Brødrafolkens Val*'?"

Aimee was not surprised that he wished to promote "welfare of the brother nations," but she knew that could never come to pass. Norway would accept union only on an equal footing, and Sweden would never grant it. Despite her feelings, she knew better than to voice her thoughts.

Oscar strode up to her again, demanding, "Tell me why Norwegians are so stubbornly opposed to union with Sweden."

Aimee glanced at Luke. His eyes pleaded with her to be discreet. She sighed, marshaling her thoughts. "Sire, every nation and every people is unique in its history. Sweden has been more fortunate than Norway. It is less isolated, has more arable land and natural wealth. We Norwegians are proud of our accomplishments, paltry as they may seem to you, but we also know that, on an equal footing, we would have little chance in competition with Sweden. If our two countries unite, we could lose the one thing we have kept through centuries of domination: pride in our heritage. We would gradually be consumed by Swedish ways; we would eat Swedish food, adopt Swedish customs and ranks, even speak Swedish, denied again the privilege of speaking our own language." Her soft voice faded away, but the impact of her words lingered in the large, airy room.

Luke was moved by Aimee's eloquent but reasoned defense of her country, and he looked at her with pride. He had known she was mature for her age, but he had never expected such wisdom from a young, sheltered girl, even one such as Aimee. He couldn't quell admiration. Straight and tall she stood, so small she should have been dominated by the bulk of her King, yet somehow she seemed to match him in stature. He felt more possessive than ever. He shifted uncomfortably and dragged his gaze away from her and looked at Oscar.

Oscar seemed both moved and troubled at her words. He took a couple of quick, agitated strides away from her, then he whirled and nodded. "You make a strong case for your country. I, too, would resent losing all that makes me proud to be Swedish. However, I hope you will try to understand that we have no wish to dominate Norway. We want to share our blessings with it and strengthen both our countries into one great nation and people."

Aimee bowed her head, curtseying deeply. "I understand, Sire. Thank you for asking my opinion."

Oscar took her hand and raised her up, kissing the back of it. He eyed her so roguishly she reddened. "Ah, ambassadors come and go, but a woman is a woman the world over." He glanced slyly at Luke. "Mr. Garrison, did you know you had married such a charming woman?"

"Indeed, Sire, she charmed me from the first." He put his arm around Aimee and smiled down at her, his eyes telling her gently of his approval.

The King gestured for them to seat themselves on chairs near his. "Now, Ingmar informs me you and your father own a large shipping line in America. I was allowed to hope for a naval career when I was a boy. Who would have dreamed I, as a third son, would ever ascend to the throne? I think above everything, I miss the freedom of the seas."

Aimee listened as they talked. She watched Oscar gesture, his face animated, as he and Luke traded sea stories. She watched his mien grow wistful, then become resolute as he recalled himself to his duties. Could it be he genuinely regretted the burden of his royal crown? He was not the tyrant she had always visualized, but a good, responsible man who wanted the best for his kingdom and his subjects. The idea was radical to one who had been raised resenting Swedish dominance, but, when Oscar drew her into the discussion, Aimee was convinced she was right. No megalomaniac would probe a subject's feelings about the state of relations between Norway and Sweden, and truly listen, engrossed.

Aimee was so relaxed that she lost all wariness and answered naturally when he asked her opinion of his desire to purchase new iron warships for the navy. "I think it a wise choice, Sire. I am sure my husband would agree that steam is where the future lies. Indeed, he may even be able to handle the transaction for you. He has many connections in America, and I'm sure you know that some of the finest shipyards in the world are there."

Luke felt a thrill of pleasure at her deft maneuvering. It was becoming clearer to him all the time what an asset she was. This marriage would have many more rewards than fulfillment of desire. He smiled, anticipating more than ever her meeting with his parents.

Luke wasn't the only one impressed by her business sense. Oscar arched a surprised eyebrow, looking from Aimee to Luke, then back again. "I've seldom been propositioned more ably." When Aimee blushed, he added blandly, "Or by a prettier businessman." Aimee couldn't meet his or Luke's sparkling eyes.

Luke inserted, "I know several yards that have built American warships our navy has had success with. I would be honored to be your representative, Sire."

Oscar smiled noncommitally. "Nothing is settled yet, but I will keep you in mind, Mr. Garrison." He rose, signaling that the interview was at an end. Luke bowed; Aimee curtsied.

Oscar took her hand and said gravely, "It has been a pleasure speaking with you, Mrs. Garrison. Thank you for your honesty. It's something a King hears all too little of."

Aimee's admiration for him increased. This man was King in more than name. He had an honest desire to hear all opinions, whether they differed from his own or not. "I meant no offense, Sire."

The King smiled, charmed, then walked them to the door. "Thank you for coming. I will instruct my Court Chamberlain to attend you and invite you to tomorrow night's ball. Can you attend?"

Luke answered, "We would be honored, Sire." Aimee and

Luke made their final bow and exited.

Luke looked around, then hugged Aimee so fiercely that she gasped. "You missed your calling, Aimee. You should have been a diplomat. And you were worried you wouldn't be able to hold your tongue."

When his grip eased, Aimee leaned back in the circle of his arms. "I found him charming, Luke, and no monster, as you said. It was easy to be pleasant to him, though my father would be appalled to hear me say it." She grimaced wryly. He led her to the staircase, one hand at her back.

She was almost at the bottom when she stumbled. Luke made an instinctive move to catch her, but he missed. He could only watch as she landed in the strong arms of a young man just beginning his ascent.

Aimee looked up into glittering brown eyes. He was a tall, rangy fellow with dark blond hair falling over a high fore-head, and he had a full, sensual mouth that seemed to stay parted. Those bold dark eyes appraised her a little too intimately for her liking. He had the air of a man who knew the world and his own place in it and was satisfied with both. Aimee was both drawn to and repelled by his rakish charm. He was dressed in the height of fashion, his lithe physique accented by a tight blue waistcoat and tan breeches.

Gazing deeply into her eyes, he teased, "I have ever wanted to rescue a fair maiden in distress. Prithee, fair maiden, are thee fleeing from a dragon?"

Aimee squirmed out of his arms, uncomfortable at his bold embrace. She glanced over her shoulder and saw Luke approaching them, his nostrils flared as if he would blow fire at any moment. He looked . . . could he be jealous? Aimee was so enchanted by the possibility that she was tempted to test it.

So she replied pertly, "Indeed, sir, he cometh hence. Save me, I implore thee." A wicked gleam in her eyes, she whisked her skirts around to hide behind the stranger's broad shoulders.

Luke's eyes narrowed at her flirtatious manner. He growled, "Sir, stand out of the way. My wife needs no protection but my own."

The stranger looked surprised. He cast a reproachful glance over his shoulder at Aimee. When Luke reached out to shove him aside, however, he backed off, one arm out to shield Aimee. Luke saw the calculating look in his eyes, and his anger increased when the man smiled tauntingly.

"Now don't get angry. Your charming wife was merely responding to my teasing. Would you rather she had fallen and bruised her pretty face?"

Aimee watched the confrontation raptly. Her eyes went from Luke, to the stranger, and back again. This thrill of power at being able to goad Luke was both new and enticing. Head cocked, she decided she liked seeing the confident Luke for once at a disadvantage.

She should have known better. In two strides, the more powerfully built Luke shoved the blond aside and grasped Aimee by the elbow. "My 'charming wife' may yet bruise more than her 'pretty face' if she isn't careful." He glared meaningfully down at her and stroked her bustle.

Aimee jumped away, eyeing her husband carefully. Was he truly enraged?

The stranger meanwhile studied them, trying to assess the degree of tension between them. Perhaps the pretty Norwegian bitch would not be averse to a little dalliance? He eyed Luke's broad shoulders and decided now was not the time to find out. He cleared his throat, then bowed deeply. "Ah, fair maiden, it appears the dragon has first claim on thee. But methinks thy beauty will soothe the savage beast, so I will bid thee a fond, regretful farewell." He swept off an imaginary plumed hat, winked, and started his ascent again.

Peeping at Luke from the corner of her eye, Aimee called, "Farewell, kind sir. Until we meet again." Luke dragged her out of the vestibule before she had time to hear his response.

Teeth gritted, he snarled, "You defy me at every turn. How dare you flirt so shamelessly with a stranger on the steps of the palace. You spurn your husband and encourage a rake. I thought better of you, Aimee!"

Aimee wrenched her arm free and spun to face him, her fury soaring again at his arrogance. He didn't own her. She could be polite to whomever she pleased. He hadn't objected when the King teased her. "So divorce me," she spat, arms crossing her bosom.

Luke closed his eyes and took a deep breath. When he opened them again, the red gleam in their anthracite depths was gone. "I will never do that, no matter what you might do. Mine you are, and mine you stay. The sooner you accept that, the better it will be for both of us." It was his turn to smirk with satisfaction when she gasped in outrage. He grasped her arms and jerked her against his chest to drawl, "And consider yourself warned: if you again try to goad me as you have today, you may not like the consequences." He stared at her mouth so hotly that her lips tingled.

A discreet cough interrupted them. They started and turned to see the Court Chamberlain shifting uneasily from foot to foot. "Excuse the interruption, but His Majesty requested that I invite you to the ball His Majesty is hosting tomorrow evening." He tendered a vellum envelope. "A smorgasbord will be followed by dancing. May I tell him you'll attend?"

Luke took the envelope and replied smoothly, "Indeed you may. Thank him for the invitation." The man nodded and hastened away, a disapproving look stamped on his face.

Luke escorted Aimee down the steps and led her around the palace to the rear. He signaled her to sit down on a bench overlooking the lake. "Stay here, out of mischief. I'm meeting Count Christiansen to discuss business."

Aimee fumed as she watched him join a tall man with a broad, kind face who had apparently been waiting for them next to a statue. The two men moved to another bench and sat, engrossed in conversation.

Aimee sighed and propped her chin on her hand. He was just like her father. It would never occur to the Almighty Male that she had a brain in her head and might even be able to contribute to their business conversation. Despite his earlier words of praise, he wanted to keep her sheltered in her woman's world, just as her father had.

Aimee watched them broodingly for what seemed hours, then she jumped to her feet and strolled to the water. She longed to remove her shoes and stockings and wade in the shallows, but did not dare. She strolled up and down the shore, enjoying the boats in the distance, the swooping birds and the blue of Lake Malaren. She lifted her face into the sun and took deep breaths of the flower-scented air. The soft lapping of the waves soothed her nerves. She closed her eyes and let her thoughts drift unchecked. Immediately her mind was filled with the image of a tall, raven-headed figure with mesmerizing black eyes that enraged, moved and enchanted her all at once. Her cheeks flushed when she dreamed of a hard male mouth taking hers, consuming her fears and filling her with mindless passion. She started guiltily when a voice behind her intruded.

"Where is thy dragon, fair maid? Hast thee vanquished him?" The tall Swede popped from behind a birch, his hands comically to his cheeks in pretended wonder. In the bright sunlight, he didn't appear as attractive as he had in the palace. His blond hair seemed thin and straight after Luke's abundant waves; his tall figure seemed lanky compared to Luke's muscular grace.

Aimee wondered briefly why he had followed her, but she was glad of the distraction. "I fear not, gallant knight. He is but occupied." She motioned toward Luke. "Canst thou save me from him?"

The Swede looked at Luke, whose animated gesturing underscored his air of power and determination. With a mock shudder, the blond mourned, "Ah, I fear my puny strength would be of no avail against him." He straightened martially. "But for thee, fair maiden, I dare all." He turned as if to confront Luke.

Horrified, Aimee grabbed his arm. "No, no, I was just teasing. . . ." She trailed off when he raised a wicked eyebrow. He had had no intention of confronting Luke. She scolded, "It was very ungallant of you to frighten me so."

The Swede leaned over to whisper, "You make a man forget gallantry." His eyes ran over her covetously, even greedily.

Aimee stepped back a pace, disconcerted. She had heard much in Norway about the wickedness of Sweden's nobles, and she knew nothing of this man, after all. She was about to return to her solitary bench when he caught her arm.

"Forgive me, madam. It is not my custom to be so forward with a stranger. I regret any offense I may have given. This is a dull, proper court at the best of times, and you responded so smoothly, as if reciting well-learnt passages from a play, I couldn't resist. . . . Still, that's no excuse."

His eyes were grave, steady on hers, but his hand stroked her arm, and his words of apology somehow rang false. He didn't regret his actions one whit, instinct told her. What on earth was the matter with her? She'd never been attracted to rakes, as this man obviously was. So why had she encouraged him? When she longed with sudden poignancy for Luke's touch, she knew she had her answer. She didn't care a farthing for this Swede. It was Luke she wanted, and, if she could plumb his feelings by flirting with this Swede, she was not above using her feminine wiles. All that, despite her brave words to the contrary.

Aimee's cheeks burned with shame as a harsh voice interrupted, "Aimee, I told you to stay put!" She started and turned, unaware how guilty she looked as the Swede's hand dropped from her arm, or of their shattered air of intimacy.

Luke advanced, scowling. The Swede swallowed his genuine fear, but the situation was saved when the man at Luke's side stepped in. "Rolf, what are you doing here? When did you arrive from France?" The count heartily bussed the young man on both cheeks, turning him to face Aimee and Luke.

It was difficult to say whose astonishment was greater when the count added, "This is my only son, Rolf. He is an attaché to our ambassador in France. Rolf, I'm pleased to introduce you to Luke Garrison." He smiled at Aimee. "And this charming lady must be Aimee. I am delighted to make your acquaintance, Mrs. Garrison."

Aimee smiled hesitantly in return, still embarrassed.

Rolf bowed perfunctorily to Luke, his eyes absorbing the flush in Aimee's cheeks. Count Ingmar had arrived too late to catch Rolf's comments, so he was puzzled when Luke nodded stiffly, his manner barely civil.

Only his considerable self-control allowed Luke to back away without further comment. This timber deal was important to the merger with Ragnar. It would mark the Garrisons' first major transport agreement with a Scandinavian company, and it was critical to the future of the new line. Thus, he forced himself to nod and respond. "Pleased, I'm sure. Come, Aimee, we must be going. I'm sure Rolf will understand that we want to be alone. . . ." He shot a barbed look at the Swede as he spoke.

Rolf raised an eyebrow at this hands-off warning. He waved as Luke led Aimee away and called, "We will continue our conversation at a later date . . ." He paused and added insolently, "*Cherie.*"

Luke's determined strides paused, then continued faster, for he didn't trust himself to stay another moment. The arrogant little popinjay! When they were out of earshot he snarled, "What the hell was that all about?"

Aimee maintained a stony silence, angered anew at his arrogance.

Luke shook her arm. "Answer me, dammit!"

She jerked her arm away. "Don't curse at me! And it's

none of your concern. Nothing improper happened." She reddened under Luke's narrow appraisal but continued. "At least he treats me like an equal instead of a witless doll."

Luke pulled her into a leafy arbor of trees and heavy underbrush and shoved her back against a birch. No one could see them unless stumbling into this forested oasis on palace grounds. "Are you chafing at my gentle handling, sweet? That's easily enough remedied. If you want to feel like a woman, I'll be delighted to assist. . . ." His angry mouth descended over hers.

She just had time to wonder if her dreams had called to him in some strange way before all thought ceased. He cupped the back of her head with one hand and ran the other up her side until he reached a breast. Gently he kneaded it, teasing, probing, until she moaned into his mouth. He swallowed the betraying little sound, savored it, and rewarded her with a gentle wooing of her mouth that made her sag against him. Her hands crept around his neck and buried themselves in his thick hair. She couldn't get close enough to him, couldn't taste enough of him. She opened her mouth to his searching tongue, returning the sexual jousts with eager little stabs of her own. He quivered, nibbled her ear, trailed his tongue in a flaming path down the side of her neck, then returned to her mouth to kiss her even more deeply.

All sensation faded but the sweet taste of his lips and the feel of strong muscles flexing against her. Even when she felt a coolness at her breast, she didn't understand why until his mouth forayed and marched a trail of kisses down the white flesh of her exposed bosom. When his lips closed over her and she could feel him tonguing her, she understood what had happened, but she was so enraptured she didn't care. It never occurred to her that anyone might hazard upon them.

Luke, however, knew the scandal that would quake if they were discovered. His nerves shrieked in protest when he pulled away, but he could hardly throw her to the ground and take her there, as he yearned to. He crushed her to him for one last, passionate kiss, letting her feel against her belly what she did to him. She started but responded eagerly, and he moaned in actual pain as he thrust himself away from her.

Chest heaving, he watched her slowly come back to awareness. Her coronet was askew. Her hair tumbled over one breast, a rosy nipple peeking up at him provocatively. Desire scorched him as she licked her lips and pushed her hair behind her back. When she realized what he was looking at, she gasped and fumbled with her clothing.

His burning appraisal made her clumsy, especially when he drawled, "I trust you now believe I see you as a woman?"

Her clothes in order again, she stifled her longing to throw herself back into his arms and tilted her chin at him. "I admit you made me want you, but wanting is not enough in a marriage. How do you know I respect you any more than you respect me?"

Luke gritted his teeth and pushed her ahead of him out of the bower. "If you don't now, little girl, you will. You can count on that."

The brief steamer journey back to Stockholm seemed interminable to Aimee. When they stomped into their hotel room, each retreated to an opposite corner, Luke to read, Aimee to change her clothes behind a screen. When she emerged, she was garbed in one of her old blue skirts and a simple blouse. He raised an eyebrow at this defiant gesture, but he didn't comment.

Aimee stalked up and down, picking up ornaments only to bang them down so hard they tinkled. She nosed through her trunk, scattering items over the edge, then shoved them back into the trunk, slamming the lid. She drummed her fingers on the highboy. When Luke still ignored her, she snapped, "Well, you can stay if you like, but I'm going to dinner."

She hadn't taken two steps before Luke clasped her about the waist and escorted her to the door. "Excellent idea, sweet wife. Perhaps a little sustenance will sweeten your ill humor."

"My ill humor? You arrogant oaf, you think . . ." Her words became garbled behind his hand when he covered her mouth.

"Tsk, tsk, sweet wife, we can't quarrel. We're newlyweds and must enjoy our honeymoon bliss."

When he uncovered her mouth, she sputtered, ignoring the strange looks they received in the lobby, "The only bliss you want is your will uncrossed, 'Yes, Luke. No, Luke.' Well, you needn't expect that from me. You'll be rotting in your grave before you'll see it happen."

Luke picked her up and plopped her into a hired carriage. He got in beside her and ordered the driver to take them to an open-air café. He chided, "You're becoming tedious, dear wife. You know, I really can't have your defiance upsetting my stomach. Need I remind you of a very effective way I've found to block that shrew's tongue?" He tapped the corner of his mouth for emphasis.

Only then did she back down. She leaned against the squabs of the carriage and clamped her mouth shut. He was the most infuriating man! He had her in a constant turmoil, torn between fury at his arrogance and admiration for his strength.

At the café, when their meal arrived, she devoted herself to it, ignoring Luke's attempts at conversation. Gradually, however, his determined conviviality and the seductive scents wafting on the air relaxed her. She looked about.

The café he'd selected nestled off a canal. A charming little bridge inlaid with lacy ironwork spanned the water. A Dalecarlian boatman sang a melodious evening song as he poled his craft down the canal. It was late afternoon, and the sun bronzed the creamy stone buildings hovering around the embankments. The light breeze caused the riot of flowers rooted there to ripple, and two lovers hunched side by side, their heads pressed together in intimate conversation.

It was a scene created for romance. Aimee was too attracted to the infuriating devil opposite her to be immune to its charm. The strong Swedish punch she'd imbibed earlier was having its effect. She didn't notice when he wrinkled his nose at the ever-present schnapps, then, with a reckless look on his face, ordered ale.

They dawdled over their meal, and by the time they finished, Stockholm was bathed in the lovely summer twilight that would linger for hours. Aimee watched as the sun painted the clouds a fiery red, orange, gold and pink. Her head swirled in lazy contentment, and her irritation at Luke had long since faded. She had, after all, deliberately goaded him, so she wasn't blameless. When he took her hand, she was content to have it nestle in his.

"In a better mood, sweetheart?"

She nodded, her eyes still dreamily watching the sky, and it seemed natural to share her thoughts with him.

"Luke, isn't it strange how things we've taken for granted all our lives can be turned topsy-turvy in a few short weeks?"

"Do you mean your opinion of the King?" His heart beat a little faster, thundering in hope that she referred to their marriage.

Aimee hesitated. She longed to be honest with him, but she was still wary of the things he made her feel. Yes, she had been wrong about the King. But she'd been even more mistaken about him, and her own feelings for him. She was no longer angry for the way he stole her away from Norway. He had snatched her out of her safe, familiar world and set her in an exciting, challenging place where she was forced to face the unfamiliar. She was actually savoring the weeks ahead of her. She had much to learn, but, in the quietness of this moment, even America and her in-laws no longer loomed menacingly. Luke had opened up whole new vistas before her that she was eager to explore. And she knew, no matter how their relationship ended, that she was a better, stronger person for it.

When she finally answered, her voice was so low he had to strain to catch her words. "Yes, I was wrong about the King, but I was also wrong about you. You made me angry at first, so angry all I could think about was besting you. But I realize now you've done me a service. I could never have been truly happy in Norway. There were too many things I wanted to do and see. Staying rooted would have prevented my satisfying my curiosity. You've helped me outgrow my preconceived notions. I find I don't know as much as I thought, but, in an odd way, I'm glad. I've so much to learn, I look forward to life's lessons now in a way I never have before. And I've you to thank for that."

Luke looked away to hide his relief. He cleared his throat. "That's the nicest thing you've ever said to me, sweet, but you underestimate yourself. I haven't helped you gain anything you didn't already have inside," he said. "Why do you think I've been fascinated with you from the beginning?"

Luke stared at her, longing again to possess her. He'd never thrilled to a woman's touch, or humor, or even anger as he did to hers. Every quality fascinated him. He wondered if she realized how much she'd taught him. He doubted it. That sweet face possessed no knowledge of her power over him. A pleasure-pain pierced him as he realized Aimee was not like other women. She would not be content with half a role in his life. Unless he was willing to give her everything —loyalty, respect, fidelity, and most of all love—he would never win her. Vaguely, Luke realized he felt no distaste at the knowledge. Soon, there were things about himself he would have to face. But for now, he wanted to savor their intimacy.

His black eyes were compelling, his touch gentle, and, at

last, Aimee admitted she would never be free of him. She still wasn't ready to give him her total trust, but no matter what happened between them, he had won a place in her memory that no man would ever be able to match, even her father. She returned his warm hand clasp.

"Come, let us toast each other." Luke lifted his glass and she followed suit. They clicked them together as he added, "To us, our marriage, and our happiness." They upended the tumblers and drank. Luke was so exhilarated he ordered another round. By the time they left, he had downed more tankards of ale than he realized. He extended his hand.

"Shall we walk?"

They rose a trifle unsteadily. Luke swung her hand as they meandered down the street. When they came to a silver-smith's shop still open, Luke urged Aimee inside. They went from counter to counter, admiring his splendid artistry. The little man eyed their weaving progress warily. When Luke leaned against a case, it scraped against the floor and trembled. The owner scurried forward.

"May I help you, sir?" He tried to ease the case back to its proper position, huffing, when he noticed Luke still leaning his weight on it. He cleared his throat. "Er, if you wouldn't mind, sir, I'd like to move the case."

Luke nodded genially. "Certainly. Where?"

The owner gestured, and Luke kindly decided to assist the little man, who looked none too strong. He shoved the case in the direction indicated. A gurgling noise caught his attention. He looked at the owner's red face, wondering why the man gasped for breath.

Aimee blinked, realized what had happened and hurried forward to help. She shoved Luke out of the way and inched the case back. Luke staggered against another case, slamming it against the opposite wall with an ominous crash.

The beautiful jewelry scattered inside, bracelets, rings, necklaces crashing together to land in a tangled heap. When the owner regained his breath, he brushed past Luke, muttering to himself.

Aimee looked at Luke's offended expression and giggled. He beamed back at her, blinking against the light. She had never seen him so lovably clumsy. He reminded her of an awkward teenager who hadn't grown into his hands and feet.

The owner snapped, "If madam doesn't want anything,

may I suggest you take your friend and leave before he demolishes my shop?"

Luke looked around, trying to figure out who was being talked about. Aimee laughed weakly and tried to pull him out of the shop. Luke refused to budge.

"What did we come in here for?" He frowned, trying to remember. His face lit up. "I know, I want to buy you a present."

He advanced unsteadily on the little man, who jumped and cowered against the wall. Luke looked puzzled by this odd behavior, then shrugged. "Come, come, fellow, no need to be afraid. Just want to see your finest jewelry."

Watching him warily, the silversmith sidled up to a case, opened it, and pulled out several pieces. He spread them out on a black velvet board. "I just finished this ensemble last week. It's one of my best. Would you care to try it on?"

He looked at Aimee as he spoke, but Luke thought he was talking to him. His eyes crossed slightly in confusion, but he shrugged and picked up the bracelet to clasp it around his wrist. Perhaps Aimee could best judge its appearance if worn by another. Luke struggled with the dainty clasp, unaware that Aimee and the proprietor watched him with gaping mouths.

The owner snatched the bracelet away, cheeks flushed with outrage. "*No*! If you care to wear jewelry, sir, you must select something more . . . manly. Now I have a beautiful ring over here . . ." Aimee tried to stifle her laughter by clamping a hand over her mouth as a benumbed Luke stumbled to another case.

To the owner's amazement, he insisted on trying on every ring, every stickpin and fob. When Luke brought a particularly fine ring close to his eye, it bumped his mouth instead. The little man jumped, expecting this mad customer to pop the ring into his mouth. He slumped with relief as Luke set the ring back down, and sweated profusely when Aimee finally pried Luke away.

Before she could urge him out of the shop, a pretty music box caught his eye. He picked it up, wound the key and watched the tiny, gilded fairy twirl in time to the leitmotif from the "Pastoral Symphony."

He looked from it to Aimee and chortled, "See how much you look like her? Come, dance with me, sweet fairy."

Before Aimee could protest, he dragged her to the middle of the shop and tried to imitate the graceful whirling. His feet shuffled, his arms weaved in the air, and he looked so pleased with himself, Aimee had to laugh. He gestured for her to join him. She hesitated, but grinned and decided she could hardly do worse. She executed a dainty pirouette that resembled the fairy's grace more than she knew.

Out of the corner of her eye, she saw the owner's face color with fury. He zipped from side to side to shadow Luke's path and salvage his precious objects should Luke fall into a case. The music was winding down, and Aimee took pity on the shop owner by keeping Luke from rewinding the box.

"We should be going. I think he'll be glad to see the back of us," she whispered.

Luke tried to focus on the silversmith, but his head was spinning, and when he stepped forward to make his purchases, his feet ignored his command to stop. He stepped squarely on the silversmith's foot.

He yelped and tried to shove Luke away. "You're crushing my foot!"

Luke apologized and moved to the side, stepping on the owner's other foot in the process. The man hobbled away to a safe distance, then turned to glare at Luke.

Luke shrugged. "Excuse me, I can't imagine how that happened. I'm usually quite dexterous." He drawled the word and looked so puzzled at his pronounciation, he left a gap the proprietor quickly stepped into to fill.

"Would you do me a favor?" he asked in a surly tone. Aimee and Luke looked surprised and nodded. The shop owner looked Luke squarely in the eye and snapped, "Take your business to my competitor across the street!"

Luke looked abashed. He pulled out his purse to make amends, but his action failed to appease the little man. After the owner had wrapped the music box and the filigreed set of jewelry, Aimee dug her hand into Luke's sleeve and dragged him out the shop door, making a mental note never to come near it again. She glanced over her shoulder, Luke still murmuring incomprehensible apologies. She had to hide a smile when the proprietor mopped his brow with his handkerchief and hastily locked the door behind them.

Aimee carried the package in one arm and guided Luke with the other. She had to steer him around the other pedestrians, for Luke, who despised wearing jewelry, was obsessed about his new ring. He would twist it around on his finger and scrutinize each new angle. Aimee had to let him go to hail a carriage. He tottered, and it was only with the driver's assistance that she muscled him inside.

She hooked arms to hold him upright. She colored when he burst into a bawdy sailor tune, leaving a trail of turned heads in their coach path. He smiled so sweetly when she tried to hush him that she gave up. She snuggled against him, enchanted by this new, vulnerable Luke. An old bromide said liquor revealed one's true nature. If so, then she had much to learn about her new husband. Underneath that unyielding masculinity lurked a very human person.

One of the bellmen helped her wrestle him to their room. She tipped the man handsomely, ignored his ribald wink and turned to glare at Luke when he plopped face down on the bed.

"Luke, you can't sleep like that. Come, at least take off your jacket." She shook his shoulder. "Luke!" Only a gentle snoring answered her.

Grunting and straining, she managed to turn him over. She removed his jacket and boots, covered him with the sheet and put on her nightgown. She was turning away to the couch when she looked down at his peaceful face. He was still smiling slightly, as if his dreams were pleasant, and, unable to help herself, she kissed the crooked smile. Sighing deeply, he put his arm around her and pulled her down beside him. Aimee stiffened, but he made no threatening moves. There was something soothing about his leashed strength. His warm breath stirred her hair like a seductive breeze. She yawned, deciding she'd let him hold her, just a little while, since he was asleep and unaware. That was her last thought before she, too, fell into pleasant slumber.

Aimee was the first to awaken the next morning. When she tried to stretch, she was dismayed to find herself intimately entrapped. Luke's arm was around her waist, one long leg pinned hers to the mattress, and his head lay on her shoulder. When he didn't stir, her shock faded and she relaxed, enjoying the feel of his closeness. A deep, quiet contentment flooded through her. It brought her hand up to stroke the black head on her breast. She vaguely realized she should be wary of the tenderness washing over her as naturally as the tide, but, for the moment, she was too happy to question herself.

It was a good thirty minutes before Luke stirred. He rolled over and plopped his head on the pillow next to hers. He groaned and fluttered his lashes open. He stared into her soft eyes, blinked, and looked again, as if he couldn't believe his eyes. When she didn't disappear, he groaned simply, "Aimee, sweet darling," and rolled on top of her to take her lips.

Aimee's vow to allow herself but one kiss was quickly broken. His warm mouth tugged so gently, so sweetly, like the lover of her dreams, that even when he cupped her face between his palms to deepen the contact, she didn't struggle. She followed blindly where he led, slanting her mouth under his, opening at his eager urging, consumed and consuming until even their passionate dueling of tongues crescendoed.

He released her face to roll her on top of him. His hands had free access to the silken skin under her nightdress. At first she made no protest when he raised the gown to the small of her back, for the rough feel of his hands on her body set her ablaze. He caressed her from the sensitive hollow behind her knee to the middle of her back, circling, teasing until she quivered with that strange weakness that was becoming familiar to her. Even when he kneaded and cupped her buttocks she didn't protest, for all the while, his mouth drank hungrily from hers, sapping her will.

However, when he lifted one leg between hers to urge them apart, she stiffened. And when that mesmerizing hand probed her softest place—a place no one had ever touched before—she gasped and jerked away. He made a grab for her, but his reflexes were slow, and she leaped to her feet. Her eyes were dilated, her hair a tangled skein of silk around her shocked face. The liquid warmth oozing between her legs confused her as much as the thrill of pleasure she'd felt at the intimate touch of his hand. She was even more disconcerted by her longing to feel that touch again. She sensed if she went near him, nothing would save her, so she kept a safe distance.

Luke propped himself on his elbows, grimacing when his temples pounded in protest. He soothed, "Aimee, don't be afraid. Come back to bed. I won't hurt you, I promise. I just want to touch you, and you must want me to, or surely you wouldn't have stayed here."

Aimee turned away from his pleading eyes. She gritted her teeth and told herself this mad pulsing in her body was rage and fear, but her reflection in the window told another story.

Weakly, she grabbed the first dress she came to and retreated to the screen.

Luke leaned back against the pillows and closed his eyes in defeat. Would it ever be so? She tantalized him, then pulled away as soon as he became intimate. He had been as patient as he knew how to be; he'd wooed her, flirted with her, charmed her, to no avail. Never had he expended so much effort to win a woman, and never had he so little to show for it. And she, his own wife. He felt like laughing in bitter rage, except his head was filled with a splitting headache.

His pride was further outraged when he realized he'd made a fool of himself again. Over lunch, he asked her what had happened last night. She told him, wondering at his wince as she recounted events. He scowled at the ring on his hand, jerked it off, and gave it to their waiter as a tip.

"If I ever again order ale, don't hesitate. Knock me over the head and have me carried out," he ordered glumly as they left.

Aimee was puzzled at this strange request, but she smiled and agreed, "Certainly. It will be a pleasure." She met his glare with innocent eyes.

She treated him to frozen courtesy for the rest of the day. She spurned his touch, even the most innocent attempt to help her down the stairs. Her instincts clamored an alarm, warning her to put some distance between them or she would become irrevocably his. She was too enraptured by his kisses, too drawn to his strength to survive the intimacy he nurtured. If she surrendered, would she become even more dependent on him than she was?

Aimee stared out the window, trying to explore her own feelings. Would it be so bad to lose part of herself to Luke? He would never deliberately hurt her. But neither did he love her. Well, why do you want his love? she asked herself. This was a marriage of convenience, and she wanted nothing but to go her own way. If he loved her, he could never allow that. If she loved him, she wouldn't want to. Aimee shied away from the awareness that, with every day she wanted less to escape Luke and more to take him in her arms and treasure him as he deserved. Aimee was so distressed at the feelings she was just beginning to understand that she began to get ready for the ball hours ahead of time.

Luke, in his turn, was both enraged and hurt at her retreat from him. He had hoped, prayed they were forging a bond that would lead to a normal, healthy marriage. He brooded into his tea, wondering why he longed for the relationship he'd spurned for so many years. He hadn't questioned his own motives in marrying Aimee. She was spirited, lovely and very much a woman. He desired her and he had to marry. At the time, it had been reason enough. And now? He was haunted by an aching desire coiled in his gut like a great, ravenous snake. He had expected her to fall into his arms before now. That she hadn't, hurt more than his pride, he vaguely realized, but he, too, shoved the disturbing feelings away, finding them as alarming as Aimee.

Luke paced up and down in black tails, tie and top hat, with a lustrous white silk vest across his chest. If he paused, he invariably heard the tantalizing rustle of clothing, so he kept himself busy by pacing back and forth. He wore a path into the thick carpet. Aimee's coolness had not dampened his ardor, as she had intended. To the contrary, he felt as determined as a rutting stallion who had scented a mare. If he had to chase her until she dropped, he would. And then? a tormenting voice asked. Scowling, he crushed the thought.

When she emerged, Aimee retreated a step from the Luke who turned to appraise her. He reminded her more than ever of a seductive devil, a warlock who would win her, foul or fair. The rich but somber attire had never made him seem more darkly attractive, more menacing to her peace of mind. Though he doused the fire in his eyes when she backed away, her skin felt singed where his eyes had landed. And since she was wearing the most revealing dress she had ever dared, she flamed all over.

She, too, was wearing black, but there was nothing somber about her attire. Her black lace overskirt was cinched on each side with black velvet bows; a garden of beaded silver flowers covered the front of the lacy underskirt. More silver buds sparkled at the tiny puff sleeves. Her bustle was layered by cascading lace. Beads sparkled at the bottom of each tier. A seductive flounce of black lace bordered her heart-shaped decolletage. With every movement, the lace swayed, allowing tantalizing glimpses of cleavage. As a final touch, she wore the silver jewelry. The filigreed tiara sat regally over her upswept curls. Bangles tinkled over her black evening gloves and a heavy pendant, carved in a lacy, stylized egret, seemed suspended in flight on her creamy bosom.

After the first shock, Luke's eyes narrowed in disapproval.

"You can't wear that! It's much too revealing. Change immediately."

Aimee, who had privately decided the same thing, now perversely disagreed. "You're the one who insisted I buy this. It would look lovely against my fair skin and hair, you said. Besides, it's the only ball gown I have until the other clothes arrive. Now, if you'd rather I didn't attend . . ." She plopped down into a chair, crossed her arms and stared through her seething husband.

He clenched his hands. "Dammit, you know I didn't see you try it on." He turned away to rip off his hat and slap it against his thigh in frustration. "Oh, very well, come along." He hauled her out of the chair to her feet. "But you stay close to my side, and if you feel the urge to flirt with that foppish Swede, I suggest you remember this. . . ."

He crushed her in his arms and fastened his mouth on hers. He kissed her with all the pent-up passion inside him, his lips hotly demanding, his tongue delving into the sweet cavern of her mouth. She couldn't miss the sexual symbolism. When he set her away, they were flushed and breathless. Without another word, he put his hat back on, took her arm and escorted her out the door.

They turned heads as they entered the ballroom, even among that glittering throng. There were other women more beautiful, other men more handsome, but none so vibrant. They struck a chord of contrast: Aimee was delicate and blond, Luke tall and dark. Despite the fact that the midnight attire emphasized his power and highlighted her fragility, somehow, the two of them matched. When their names were announced, Luke took her arm.

She flinched, and looked into his eyes. More than one person would carry away the memory of the glance they exchanged. It was as if they were meant for one another, alike in spirit, pride and intelligence—if they would only quit a pointless tug-of-war. His look warned he would be master; her toss of the head defied him more loudly than words. So the contretemps that occurred later that evening surprised only the less insightful.

Count Christiansen strode up to them, his expression lit with delight. "Luke, I didn't know you would be here. How fortunate, for my manager completed the figures you were asking about only today. I have them in a satchel in one of the antechambers. If you'll come with me . . ."

Luke started to follow him, but he froze when he saw Rolf bowing over Aimee's hand. He gritted his teeth as the Swede stooped overlong. Finally Rolf straightened.

"Mrs. Garrison, you are ravishing!" Rolf kissed her fingers in the French style, ignoring Luke's glower.

Luke encircled Aimee's bare shoulders with a protective arm. She could do little more than blush. "You've made your admiration quite apparent, Christiansen. Now take it somewhere else." Luke turned to the count. "If you don't mind, Ingmar, we'll talk later. My wife and I are both famished."

Ingmar nodded. He glanced worriedly over his shoulder at his narrow-eyed son. "Certainly, Luke. And please, excuse my son. I've scolded him for being too forward, but I'm afraid he's used to the freer habits of the French court. He doesn't mean to do more than flirt. . . ."

Luke brushed the apology aside. "No need to explain, Ingmar. He's an adult and must answer for his own actions." Luke looked over Aimee's head to Rolf, who was still watching them, and deliberately raised his voice. "I know how to protect what is mine." He turned away from Rolf with an insulting air of dismissal.

The Swede's eyes smouldered with fury as he watched Luke saunter away. This uncouth American would regret his arrogance, he vowed. Then he turned to ply his charms on a passing young girl.

Luke slammed smoked fish, cheese, salads and breads on two plates. Aimee peeped over her shoulder at Rolf, turning quickly back around when she saw him staring at them. She watched the pile on the plates grow until it tottered.

She put a restraining hand on Luke's wrist, starting when he jerked away as if burned. Exasperated, she drew a deep breath, unaware his eyes dropped to watch her ruffle bounce. "How many people are you planning to feed?" she asked tartly.

Luke glanced down at the plates, realized what he'd done and rolled his eyes in disgust. He popped a bite of bread in her mouth when she opened it. "Maybe I'm trying to fatten you up so you'll appeal to no one but me," he suggested.

She choked and glared at him when he clapped her on the back. Recovered, she hissed, "You're the one who needs fattening up." When he looked puzzled, she tapped his temple and added sweetly, "There seems to be a lamentable lack of meat up here." She dumped most of the contents on her plate into his and stalked off to watch the orchestra tune up.

Luke clenched the plate so tightly his knuckles whitened, then he trailed after her. He had deserved that one, he decided, so he'd let it pass. They were both too full to eat much of the smorgasbord supper. The food helped relax them, though each drank very sparingly of the wine. By the time the tables were cleared away, the ballroom was hushed with an air of expectancy. Aimee found herself craning her neck along with everyone else as they awaited the arrival of the King and Queen.

Horns trumpeted their arrival. A chamberlain held open the door, and King Oscar II and his consort, Queen Sophia, entered. They were an attractive couple, both tall, handsome and regal. Oscar's blue coat glittered with medallions and ribbons; Sophia wore a purple silk gown with one of the longest trains Aimee had ever seen.

They nodded graciously as they walked up the reception line, greeting some men and women personally. When Aimee curtseyed low, Oscar twinkled. "Ah, the Norwegian rebel! Will you honor me with a dance, Mrs. Garrison?" Aimee gulped, hesitated, then nodded, for she could hardly refuse such an honor. Sophia smiled at her worried expression.

She bent to whisper, "Don't worry, he won't step on your toes. Despite his height, he's quite graceful." They passed on before Aimee gathered up enough courage to explain that she was worried about treading on *his* toes.

While Oscar and Sophia launched a waltz, Luke watched Aimee shift nervously. "What is it, sweetheart?"

Aimee shook her head, but he drew her to an antechamber and demanded, "Out with it. Do you still dislike Oscar, is that it? You don't want to dance with him?"

Aimee walked up and down, agitated. "No, no, I don't hate him anymore. But I haven't danced much. What if I trip him? I would die of humiliation!" She rubbed her leg, unthinkingly.

Luke lowered his eyes to hide his sympathy. For one so brave and independent, she could still harbor strange fears. He stepped up to take her hand and grasp her waist in the classic waltz position. "There's only one way to find out, isn't there? Experiment on me first." And he whirled her away in time to the Strauss music that was all the rage.

His touch was light but firm, his lead easy to follow. When she faltered, he encouraged, "Don't struggle against the music. Let it flow through you. You've too much rhythm not to feel it. Why do you think I liken you to a fairy? You're every bit as graceful." And every bit as hard to capture, he added to himself, but his admiring smile into her eyes never wavered.

Gradually, his confidence in her became instilled. She relaxed and paid less attention to her steps and more to the sheer pleasure of dancing with him. When he laughed and twirled her faster, she had no problem keeping up. The music ended with an exuberant flourish and Luke spun her off her feet in a circle. They collapsed onto a sofa, laughing.

Aimee leaned her head to the side to thank him. "What a fool I am. I wouldn't worry if it was anyone but the King. Swedes tend to look down on Norwegians as boorish, and I couldn't bear it if I stepped on him. With your able tutoring, I know I'll do fine."

Luke took her hand, turned her glove down and kissed her wrist, trailing a warm path to her elbow. "Indeed, you will. But only one dance with him, mind. The rest belong to me," he whispered against the crook of her arm.

When he straightened and looked at her, Aimee's eyes dropped to his mouth, parted a little with swift breaths. Oh God, he had such a beautiful mouth. She teetered toward him. She was about to fall into his arms when a voice interrupted.

"Oh! Excuse me, I don't mean to intrude." Rolf looked slyly from one to the other. "But the King is looking for you, Mrs. Garrison. He wants to honor you with the second waltz."

Luke glared at Rolf, then he sighed and helped Aimee to her feet. "We'll be right there," he snapped.

Rolf bared his teeth in a false smile and retreated. Luke led Aimee back to the floor and turned her over to the King. He watched them waltz away, turning when Ingmar touched his arm. "Shall we conclude our business, now?" Luke hesitated. He didn't see Rolf in the crowd, so he decided it was safe to leave. He followed Ingmar.

Aimee bit her lip as she concentrated on her steps. Oscar smiled at her furrowed brow. "I promise I won't tell anyone if you step on my foot," he whispered. Aimee jumped, lost her step and did exactly that. She flushed with mortification.

Oscar sternly controlled his impulse to laugh for he could see it would only make her feel worse. "You're light as air, child, so quit worrying. I'll tease you no more, I promise."

Aimee sighed and relaxed a little. They danced in silence for a moment, then Aimee's curiosity got the best of her. "How do you bear always being on display?"

Oscar stiffened slightly. His eyes grew cool, but he could see she was genuine, not looking for gossipy tidbits. Her head was cocked to one side, and she reminded him of his youngest son when he asked a mischievous question. He answered candidly, "Sometimes it is very difficult. But the rewards can be great. For instance, when I can use my power to right a wrong, help the poor or pardon an innocent man."

Aimee nodded solemnly. "Yes, I can see that that would be rewarding." Her gaze lingered, then she lowered her lashes, as if abashed. "Sire, I want you to know I regret the tension between our countries. If my bluntness gave offense at our first meeting, I apologize."

Her monarch shook his head. "Not at all. I asked your opinion, remember?" He lifted a teasing eyebrow. "Does the little rebel find the tyrant a just man, after all?"

Aimee nodded. "Yes, I'm sorry I ever thought otherwise. You deserve better."

Oscar looked pleased, but wistful. "And I infer I can't change your mind about Norwegian independence." It was not a question.

Aimee hesitated, but he had asked for honesty, so she gave it. "No, Sire. And I doubt very much if you'll change very many other Norwegian minds, either." The music stopped, so Oscar released her. He bowed deeply in response to her curtsy.

"Thank you for your honesty, Mrs. Garrison. I respect your strength of character. Many people tell me what they think I want to hear rather than their true thoughts. I find it one of the most exasperating things about ruling. I hope, however, you'll respect me when I tell you, your opinion and your countrymen's opinions notwithstanding, I will do all in my power to prove you both wrong."

Oscar escorted her off the floor with a light hand at the small of her back. He bowed to his next partner and led the flustered woman to the floor.

Aimee was looking around for Luke when Rolf approached and asked her to dance. Aimee hesitated, Luke's

warning ringing in her ears. But she couldn't spot his
handsome dark face in the crowd. With Rolf waiting impatiently, she accepted.

Aimee didn't notice, at first, that Rolf held her too tightly.
He kept up a witty stream of anecdotes about various guests.
Aimee laughed, but she looked at him through clear eyes
when she realized his jokes were somewhat cruel. A voice
whispered inside her, "Luke would never be so unkind at
another's expense."

She was exasperated she couldn't be away from Luke for
five minutes without thinking of him. Dancing had warmed
her, so she assented when Rolf invited her out to the park.
They strolled among the statues, Rolf relating the history of
each one. When they came to the fountain, he bade her lean
over so he could see her reflection.

He affected surprise when he saw two images staring at him
in confusion. "I just wanted to see if you are a witch," he
explained. "Apparently not, for I can see your image, and
they say witches cast no reflection." He took her arm, pulled
her away from the fountain and whispered, "But witch or no,
you've beguiled me, and I must taste those luscious lips."

Aimee recoiled and tried to turn away, but she was too
late. He wrapped her in his arms and fastened his lips over
hers expertly, his fragrance and taste faintly disgusting. She
didn't struggle at first, because she wanted to see if she could
respond to another man. Nothing but distaste filled her
senses. She was about to push away when an enraged roar
shattered the twilight peace. Rolf was jerked violently away.

Aimee gasped at seeing Luke holding the Swede in a
powerful lock. The light cast eerie shadows across his face;
his teeth gleamed in fury. She didn't blame Rolf for backing
away, but Luke blocked his path.

Cornered, Rolf fought with the ferocity of a rat. He threw
the first punch. Luke's head jerked back, then recovering, he
slammed his own fist into Rolf's jaw. Rolf countered with a
vicious kick to the groin. Luke leaped aside just in time and
the blow struck his thigh. He stumbled, and Rolf took the
opportunity to flee back toward the brightly lit ballroom.
Luke's longer strides caught him easily before he reached it.

"You slimy worm, you'll never touch my wife again," he
growled. He slammed a fist into the Swede's mouth. Rolf
howled and landed a solid blow to Luke's midsection. Luke
barely paused. He slammed another fist into Rolf's eye, then

launched a punch on the chin that knocked him flat. Luke stood over the Swede, shaking with rage, but, when Rolf cowered, Luke turned away in disgust.

Aimee had run after them as quickly as she could, and swallowed her fear when Luke turned on her next. His eyes glittered with rage, his hands flexed as though he ached to get them about her throat. Before he had time to say a word, she caught a movement behind his head.

"Look out, Luke!" she screamed.

Rolf's blow with a tree limb struck Luke's shoulder when he pivoted at Aimee's cry instead of hitting his head. Goaded beyond his limits, Luke strategically aimed a punch into the Swede's belly, knocking him back to the ballroom door. Aimee glanced uneasily at the windows. She wanted to slink into the park when she realized they were being observed by a growing crowd of people. She opened her mouth to plead with Luke to stop, but she was too late.

"Next time you want to flirt with another man's wife, remember this," Luke raged. He smashed one last powerful blow against Rolf's chin that knocked him through the doors into the shocked crowd. Chest heaving, Luke tried to get a grip on himself. When his fury had cleared, he realized what a scene they'd created. He sent Aimee a dark look that made her tremble, then he dusted off and straightened his clothes as best he could. He gripped her elbow and marched her into the ballroom. He stepped over Rolf as if he were a pile of refuse and hustled Aimee toward the door, staring down the buzzing crowd whose expressions varied from shock to disapproval to admiration. Rolf was not generally liked.

Before they could reach the doors, however, Ingmar blocked their path, glaring at Luke. "The idea! What did my son do to deserve such a beating?"

The damage was done, Luke decided. The only way to lay the blame where it properly rested was to tell the truth. "He accosted my wife," Luke said baldly. Gasps and angry murmurs came from the crowd.

Ingmar paled. He turned on Rolf when he staggered to his feet. "Is this true, Rolf?"

Rolf sneered, "I kissed the little witch, yes. Accosted her, no. You can't accost someone who doesn't struggle."

This time all eyes flew to Aimee. She blushed with outrage, but kept her head. "I was about to slap your face when my husband did the job for me." She gave him a withering look.

"And much more effectively, I might add."

It was Rolf's turn to flush with fury, especially when his father ordered, "Leave. We'll discuss this later."

Rolf sent one last nasty look at Luke and Aimee before he obeyed. Luke watched him go, then he turned and said quietly, "If you want to abrogate our agreement, I understand, Ingmar."

Ingmar sighed, hesitated, then slowly shook his head. "No, Luke, I guess I can't blame you. I'm afraid my son is something of a rake. With time, he'll mature."

Luke couldn't encourage him in that hope, but he nodded and moved to escort Aimee to the door. This time their path was blocked by an even more powerful figure. Aimee tried to hold the gaze of her King, but her eyes dropped under his disappointed stare.

Oscar's mouth was tight with disapproval. "I never once recall a brawl at my court, and I am not pleased with the precedent you have set, Mr. Garrison. I hope you'll understand if I say you're not welcome here again, sir." He looked at Aimee, his eyes reproachful. "Or you, madam." He waved a hand and indicated they walk ahead of him.

He escorted them to their boat, shocking them by shaking Luke's hand. "I'm sorry to have to be so harsh, Mr. Garrison, but monarchs are creatures of duty. Rolf, too, will be banished for a time. It would create a scandal if I acted differently." He swept an appreciative glance over Aimee, then added, "Just between you and me, I understand your feelings."

He stepped back so they could board their hired boat. As they passed, he whispered beyond the boatman's hearing, "My subjects won't be surprised if I relent. Shall we say in a year or so?"

He looked Aimee full in the face. "For we all know, do we not, that I am a just man?" He smiled when she looked at him gratefully. He waved as they pulled away.

Aimee slumped against the seat, her emotions exhausted. She felt Luke's eyes on her, but she was afraid to whirl around. She expected him to burst into a tirade at any moment, but he maintained a stony silence that, in the end, was a much more effective punishment.

By the time they reached the dock nearest the hotel, she was almost shaking with tension, especially when she looked at Luke as he helped her to the quay. His eyes were as black as a snake's, and they scared her just as much. His continuing silence even when they reached the hotel unnerved her further. He clasped her arm and trooped her up the stairs, yanking the door open until it banged against the wall, and slammed it harder. Slowly, with deliberate movements, he locked the door and turned to face her. She had seen him furious before, but this anger sent her heart plummeting to her shoes. Underlying the boiling rage was a sorrow that was far more troublesome than rage. How much longer could she deny him, and, increasingly, herself?

Chapter Nine

IN THE QUIET solemnity of their room, sad green eyes locked with black ones. The intimacy of the bed behind them, still cluttered with their robes, drew the tension tauter between them. The air was charged with emotions too long denied and needs too long stifled. Even the street below was quiet. No sound penetrated the room that should have been their bridal suite except the frantic beating of hearts struggling to bear the pain of regret.

Tears clogged Aimee's throat as, for the first time, she watched Luke struggle with words. She had never meant to upset him, or hurt him, and she had done both. Dear God, she would never forgive herself if her pride, her willful determination to rebel against his possessiveness, had ruined all chance of happiness between them.

Aimee watched Luke advance, too miserable to be afraid, even when he stepped so close she could feel him shaking with rage. She flinched when he reached for her shoulders. The black fury in his eyes faded at her reaction, but that other, more troubling feeling grew until she wanted him to scream at her, slap her, do anything but lock disgusted eyes on her. His hands fell to his sides. He turned away as if he couldn't bear the sight of her. He leaned against the window, palms flat on the sill and forehead against the glass.

His voice was hoarse with restraint when he muttered, "Tell me, sweet wife, is it only me you spurn? Is it only my touch you scorn? Why else would you betray me with another man on our honeymoon?"

Tears glistened in Aimee's eyes as she watched him struggle for control. She despised herself for being a coward. If she hadn't been determined to distance herself from Luke, none of this would have happened. . . . She held out a beseeching hand, but he remained unmoved. Her hand drooped back to her side. "I guess I deserve that, Luke. But you misunderstood the situation entirely. . . ."

He whirled to face her. "Misunderstood? What is there to misunderstand about my virginal, pure little wife lying quietly in the arms of another man as he kisses her passionately?"

Aimee closed her eyes, sick at the scene he described. For the first time, she understood how it must have looked to him. When she opened her eyes and saw his pained face, her tears spilled down her cheekbones. Oh God, she had to right the wrong she had done him, no matter what the cost. She had put that look in his eyes. Her longing to erase it surged with such force that caution was swept away. Her heart bade her run to him, and for once, she gladly obeyed.

She put her arms around his waist and buried her face in his chest. "Luke, Luke I'm so sorry. I never meant to hurt you. I was going to push him away and slap him, I swear it. I never intended for it to go so far. . . ."

Luke gently held her away from him. His mouth quivered when he demanded, "Why did you go with him? You knew I didn't want you near him. Above all, how could you let him kiss you? How *could* you give so freely to a stranger the embraces I have to steal like a thief?"

Aimee hesitated, biting her lip. Her contrary, independent half reminded her, you go to bed at night thinking of him. You rise, eager to face the day because you know he will be there. If he knows how weak he makes you, he'll press you even harder until you yield all: your body, your heart, your every thought. But her gentle half argued as persuasively, you've hurt him, you must make amends. Humble yourself, you deserve it.

She was tempted to obey, tempted to lower the last barrier of pride between them, to give him the same tenderness he lavished on her. The gold in her eyes brightened, shimmering with the promise of a Viking's hoard lost in the mists of antiquity.

Luke's heart pounded as she struggled for words. He

sensed she was about to make a revelation that would profoundly influence their future. They stared at one another, black eyes yearning, gold eyes confused. Aimee opened her mouth, closed it, swallowed, opened it again, then, groaning in frustration, she turned away. She folded her arms against the highboy and buried her face in them. She couldn't do it. She was too afraid to give him power over her when he only promised her physical loyalty.

Luke's shoulders slumped; the light went out of his eyes. Feeling old and tired, he dragged his aching body to the chair across from the bed. He collapsed into it to speak the words she must want to hear, the words he'd never thought to say.

They were issued quietly, those words, spoken in a monotone, no portentous rumble to trumpet their impact on their marriage. "You win, Aimee. I'll pursue you no longer. What happens now is up to you. If you want to come with me to America, fine; if you want to return to your family, fine. Whatever you decide, I will accept. We've done our duty, so I guess our families can't complain if we separate. I won't try to hold you any longer when I so obviously make you unhappy."

Aimee lifted her head, aware of nothing at first but his bitter monotone. When the sounds fell into meaningful sentences, her heart leaped to her throat. He was letting her go? She moved around to face him, unable to believe her ears.

He was sitting as she had never seen him, elbows on his knees, head buried in his hands, broad shoulders slumped. Her heart fell back in place, heavy. She had disgusted him. He wanted her out of his life. She had regained the freedom he'd snatched away, but where was her jubilation? She put the back of her hand against her mouth to stifle a moan of pain. She visualized the home that had once been all to her. Instead of the lush green mountains, she saw a wasteland, barren and arid because it was empty of him.

Her eyes widened with shock as the truth hit home. She had struggled to deny Luke—and herself—the strange new urgings of her body not because she was afraid of giving him too much, but because she was afraid of winning too little of him. She had become his even before their marriage. She had *wanted* to marry Luke, would have married him even if Sigrid and her father had not been in danger.

She searched her feelings and found no resentment toward

him for his power over her, found instead an odd sense of rightness, of peace. As Sigrid said, it seemed natural to belong to him, comforting to know that he would protect her physical well being if necessary. After all, had he not risked an important business agreement to protect her?

And what had she given him in return? Her loyalty, her attempts to help in his business, and her trust, but little else. She withheld what he wanted most because she was afraid to make that final concession until . . . Until what? Her eyes perused his slumped form and still found in it the very embodiment of the man she had always dreamed about. Quite simply, she wanted him. She wanted the feel of those strong shoulders in her hands, the long length of him pressing down on her, making her his. So why did she still hesitate?

Aimee frowned in concentration, searching her own feelings as never before, and again, the truth hit her with staggering force. She denied them both because he was already so important to her that she wanted their first time together to be more than a bonding of the flesh. She wanted to be as important to him as he was to her. She wanted him to belong to her, as she belonged to him. Aimee knew only one word to describe what she wanted of him—love. It was a word she had never thought to use in connection with a man, but then she had never dreamed she'd meet a man of Gere's patience and her father's strength.

She silently tested the word on her tongue and found it sweet. This enjoyment of her need for another person was a radical departure for one who prided herself on her independence. Aimee's head whirled in confusion. She wondered if she loved Luke. She waited for her usual alarm to ring. But it didn't sound off. Instead, a beatific glow spread through her every pore. Aimee shook her head slightly, confused at her own feelings. But she was certain of one thing: the woman who won Luke's devotion would be blessed. And she longed to be that woman.

Without a thought for her pride, without an instant's hesitation, she rushed to him and fell to her knees beside him. "Oh Luke, we're both such fools. Where is the man who vowed to take us both through hell rather than let me go?"

Luke laughed harshly. "I've already tried that! I'd say we're pretty close to that now, wouldn't you?"

Aimee gently drew his hands away from his face and forced him to look at her. He held his breath when glittering gold eyes greeted him. "No, I can think of worse hells. Being without you, for example."

Luke searched her eyes, as if afraid to believe the riches promised there, then he groaned and pulled her into his arms. "Aimee, Aimee, don't say such things to me unless you mean them. You shouldn't taunt a starving man with a banquet. . . ." He cradled her on his lap, his hands trembling as he pulled the tiara out of her hair and undid the pins until the stormy silver waves flowed about her shoulders.

She put a finger against his lips. "Hush, let me finish before I lose my courage." His hands became still. His eyes were riveted to her face. She took a deep breath and blurted, "I went outside with Rolf for two reasons only: to see if I could respond to him as I do to you and to make you jealous."

His hands clenched in her hair. He growled, "You certainly succeeded in making me jealous. But why would you need to test your reactions to another man?"

Aimee thrilled secretly at his gruff jealousy. "Think, darling. Why would I need to make the comparison if you weren't disturbing me terribly?"

Luke was so diverted at the endearment he almost missed her words. His eyes narrowed when he caught her point. "Are you telling me you deliberately let another man kiss you because you are so attracted to me? That's a woman's logic for you."

Aimee smiled at his male disgust. "Nevertheless, it's true. And you know something else?" She pulled his head down until she could whisper in his ear, "I felt absolutely nothing but distaste. I wished he were taller, stronger, dark instead of fair, and arrogant as the devil. . . ."

Luke's arms tightened around her convulsively. He buried his face in her hair and sent up a fervent little prayer of thanks. He rocked her gently back and forth, cradling her to his heart. Where she belonged. His eyes darkened when the thought popped into his head, but he resolutely silenced the warning bell ringing in his mind. Nothing would intrude on this luxurious moment. Aimee had come to him of her own accord. She didn't want to leave him. She had not betrayed him. These facts made everything else seem unimportant. Just having her close, holding her in his arms, knowing she would one day be his, satisfied him enough.

It seemed enough, that is, until Aimee locked her arms about his neck, pulled his head down and planted her mouth fully on his lips. He stiffened with mingled shock and delight. Her lips were inexperienced, but so soft and sweet that his head whirled with longing. He answered the first kiss she had voluntarily given him with the gentleness he knew she needed rather than with the passion his body bade him express. His patience was sorely tested when Aimee made an impatient little sound, cupped his cheeks and slanted his face to deepen the kiss. She nibbled the corner of his mouth and licked the spot she'd bitten. When he gasped in pleasure, she flicked her tongue over his with the teasing little jabs he had taught her, inciting, thrilling, making him yearn for more.

Luke turned her in his arms to bring her more fully against him, his hands tracing the fine lines of her bared back and shoulders. Aimee snuggled against him, settling her buttocks over his aching groin, testing his control to the limit.

Luke tore his mouth away and set her from him. She blinked at him in surprise, pouting, "Why did you do that? I was enjoying our embrace. Weren't you?"

Her dress had fallen off one shoulder, baring it and the top of one creamy breast. With her hair tumbling down her back, her mouth moist and red from his kisses, she had never appeared more seductive. Perhaps it was time he tested her. He walked up, caught her buttocks and pulled her hard against him. He savored her shocked gasp and rosy confusion as he let her feel how much he had enjoyed their embrace.

He bent down to whisper in her ear, "I am ravenous for you, sweet. Are you ready yet to give me what I want?"

Aimee met his smoky eyes and hesitated. She had been so enthralled she hadn't given a thought to what came after their kiss. She longed to give in, to end this conflict between them and answer the needs calling to her from the hard male body pressed against her own.

As if he sensed he was influencing her decision, Luke stepped back two paces and left her standing alone. This was to be her decision. He thought he'd explode with frustration if she denied him, but he knew he wanted more of Aimee than one night of relief, or even a lifetime of such nights. He wanted that stubborn little mind and heart of hers to long for him with equal passion. He could not force such feelings from her. He could only watch and hope. He watched her eyes drop to the crotch of his pants where he was still swollen with need of her. When she paled, he slumped in defeat and braced himself for her rejection.

Aimee folded her arms over her bosom to still its frantic pounding. Her eyes dropped to the floor in shyness as she stunned him with her reply. "Yes, Luke. I want to be yours."

Luke's head jerked up. The blood ran through his veins in a torrent, causing an actual ache in the part of him he longed to meld to her. He walked forward slowly, eyes on her downcast face, afraid he had heard her wrong. He put out a hand to her chin, then dropped it to his side in disappointment when he felt her tremble. "Aimee, look at me," he coaxed.

Aimee raised her eyes. They stared at one another. Now there were no barriers between them, no rancor, or even pride. They left their feelings bare for the other to see. Aimee saw a desire so strong she was awed by it, yet his ardor was tempered with tenderness.

He saw confusion, longing, and another emotion that acted like a brake on his runaway passion: fear. Luke's hands clenched in recognition that hungry though she was, she was still wary. Another time, perhaps, he could have been patient enough to coax her out of the natural maidenly modesty. But this moment was too rife with raw emotion to allow him the control he needed to initiate her. Grinding his teeth against a moan of pain, he forced himself to turn away.

"Now is not the time for us, Aimee. We're both too tired. It's late. I'm going to bed." His voice was harsher than he intended. He was too afraid to look at her again and test his strained control, so he didn't notice her stricken look.

Blindly, Aimee retreated to the screen in the corner. Her fingers, toes, even her cheeks felt numb as she forced herself to act normally, trying to soothe the stabbing pain. He didn't want her, after all. It had taken every ounce of will she possessed to set aside her remaining doubts and allow her body to control her mind. And her sacrifice had been for nothing. She paused, one foot in her pantalettes, one foot out. Could that be it? Luke had felt her fear. She sensed he wanted her free response as much as she wanted his love. He had no interest in a scared little virgin. He wanted a full-blown woman who could give a woman's response. Aimee's anguish receded as she pulled her nightgown over her head.

She looked at Luke thoughtfully when she rounded the screen. He was lying on his back on the couch, arms folded behind his head, glaring at the ceiling. When he felt her eyes, he turned to her and smiled. It was a stiff smile, a forced smile, but a smile nonetheless, and she slumped in relief as she realized he was not angry with her.

"Good night, sweet. Sleep well." Better than I, he thought sardonically. He turned on his side and tossed and turned the whole night.

Aimee, comforted, slept the peace of the innocent, unaware of the feelings she stirred in the man who lay nearby.

Aimee and Luke both pretended last night had never happened the next day, if for different reasons. Savoring each other's company helped them forget the increasing strain they felt in the privacy of their room.

They toured the "City Between the Bridges." They admired the Royal Palace, harboring the statuary of Swedish Kings, artwork and the charming little enclosed park. The Riddarhuset, House of the Nobility, impressed them with its ornate pediment, columns and grandiose grace. From there, they crossed the Riddarholm's Kanal by a quaint bridge and explored the ancient Riddarholm Church. A kindly priest revealed its history: it was founded in the thirteenth century by King Magnus Ladulas and was used as the mortuary for Sweden's kings since Gustavus Adolphus II. In the square outside the church they paused to admire Fogelberg's statue of Birger Jarl, the leader revered throughout Sweden as the founder of Stockholm.

Under the surface of their light banter, turbulent currents ran. When Luke touched Aimee's hand, or caught her waist to point out a fine painting, the contact was charged with emotion, disconcerting them both in different ways. Aimee felt vulnerable, threatened as much by her own feminine needs as by the flame of desire flickering in the back of Luke's eyes. It was increasingly difficult for Luke to restrain his urge to touch her. He chafed at the knowledge that last night she could have been his if he'd only had more control. With every moment that passed, will was depleted further. Passion was a heady draught, clouding his head with need of her.

He could see by the way she started when he touched her, by the evasive comments she made if he tried to steer the conversation into more intimate channels, that she was not ready yet to come to him, and his temper grew short. He was uneasily aware how important she had become to him—*too* important. When he'd found her kissing Rolf, the pain and betrayal pierced too deeply to be explained away as possessiveness, or even unfulfilled desire. This fervent need to make her his surged like a deep wellspring ever near the surface of his consciousness, but he shied away from seeking its source. He was, quite simply, afraid. He, who had always scorned women as weak, was fusing himself to a girl innocent of her power over him.

So, by the time they went downstairs to meet Alfred Nobel for dinner, Luke's stomach was churning with a painful mixture of emotions. He glared at Aimee as she greeted Nobel charmingly. She looked so cooly lovely in her gown of ice blue taffeta bordered with navy blue that he longed to shatter her ice and recover the warm, feminine creature he glimpsed when he held her in his arms.

Luke's emotions were too chaotic for him to participate in much conversation. He listened with half an ear as Nobel patiently explained the prelude to his discovery of dynamite.

"I knew almost from the beginning that a safer explosive than nitroglycerin must be found. Some of the stories I've heard about how it was transported make me shudder. Did you hear about the 1865 explosion in New York, Luke?"

Luke gave Nobel full attention for the first time. He replied dryly, "I could hardly fail to hear about it after the ruckus it caused."

Aimee's eyes widened and Luke detailed the newsy item. "A German traveler brought a box containing ten pounds of nitroglycerin to a hotel in New York and left it with the porter. He apparently intended to collect it later. According to the story I heard, the porter used it sometimes as a seat and sometimes as a footrest when he polished shoes. One day a waiter noticed a red vapor curling from the box. He warned the porter, and the porter carried it into the street." Luke paused to take a leisurely sip of wine. He wiped his mouth with his napkin, then thrust it back onto his lap.

Aimee squirmed, and when Luke still didn't finish the tale, she prodded him. "Well, are you going to leave me in suspense?"

Luke glanced at her, then leaned forward and drawled, "I just wanted to test your nerves to see if they are as strong as you expect mine to be, my dear."

Aimee flushed and played with her fork. Nobel looked puzzled as he glanced from her downcast face to Luke's sardonic grin. Luke shrugged and salvaged the intriguing story. "The porter left the box and returned to the hotel. A moment later it exploded. Doors and windows shattered, the fronts of the nearby buildings were seriously damaged, and the road had a new four foot hole sunken into it. Luckily no one was injured. I don't know for sure, but I would imagine the porter attended church that Sunday to give thanks to God."

He clapped. "There's the fable, my dear."

Aimee studied her plate, but her skin prickled when she felt Luke's sly grin and intense gaze on her. She turned back to Nobel. "So you knew a safer explosive was needed. . . ."

Nobel nodded when Luke unspun the tale, and now took up the reins. "Yes. I tried methyl alcohol first, but I soon realized a solid was needed to give it explosive but stable properties. I tried paper pulp, black gunpowder, brick dust, charcoal, clay, gypsum bars, and other substances. I tested various blends and decided *kieselguhr* was most promising. *Kieselguhr* is an infusorial earth that is greatly porous but chemically unreactive. We enclosed the solid explosive in cartridge paper and formed sticks. The process was neither dramatic nor accidental as sometimes claimed. I worked long hours in the laboratory, in a systematic way, to reach the most effective combination. I never found nitroglycerine spilled at the bottom of a crate and mixed with *kieselguhr* into a magical paste." Nobel sounded a little offended that anyone could propagate such a myth.

They ate in silence for a while. When the plates were taken away, Aimee became grave. "Mr. Nobel, have you ever worried that your explosives will be used for evil?"

Nobel stiffened. His bushy brows lowered to paint a sullen, brooding look on his face. "To date, they have done far more good. Have you any idea how many man hours of toil are saved by blasting out a canal or mine? Hours, my dear. And no doubt lives are saved from cave-ins or heat exhaustion." Nobel shoved his glass back to prop his elbows on the table. His eyes produced gentle blue flames as he leaned toward her. "Consider, Mrs. Garrison, what science has done for us. Someday, I believe we'll live in a world without toil, where mankind can turn his energies away from physical effort to mental problem-solving. Disease, hunger, poverty. They cause wars. If science can help us eradicate them, then perhaps, one day, wars will no longer exist."

Aimee's eyes softened with admiration. "Perhaps you're

right, sir. I hope and pray you are." They smiled at one another in accord.

After the post-dinner acquavit, Nobel rose and made the customary bow of thanks. "It's been a most charming evening, and I appreciate your letting me disturb your honeymoon."

He raised a brow at Luke's sour look and turned to Aimee. He bowed over her hand. "Mrs. Garrison, I have enjoyed our talk. You are unusually perceptive for such a young woman. I hope we have the opportunity to meet again."

Aimee curtseyed. "I hope the same, Mr. Nobel. I am honored to have met you and I wish you the best of luck in your enterprise and in your future experiments."

Nobel turned to Luke and held out his hand. "Give your father my regards. I think you'll find the papers in order. And tell him I hope this business venture is more successful than our last."

Luke shook his hand and walked with him to the hotel lobby. "I'll do that, Alfred. My father will do what he can to see that you're treated more honestly than last time. Thank you for taking time out of your busy schedule to dine with us."

They strolled together to Nobel's carriage. Nobel turned as if to climb in, then hesitated. "If you have occasion to come to Paris, I hope you'll visit me," he said, whirling on them. "I'll be happy to show you my personal laboratory, Mrs. Garrison."

Aimee flushed with pleasure. "That would be delightful, sir. I wish you a safe, speedy journey."

Nobel nodded. He eyed Luke's firm hand on Aimee's arm and mused to himself as he climbed in: "And I wish you both the same, in a physical and emotional sense." He spoke to the driver, waved, then was off.

Aimee puzzled over Nobel's studied glance. Finally she asked Luke, "What did he mean by that glance?"

Luke moved to stare out the window before he answered in a mocking voice. "I should think it's obvious. He's a very perceptive man, and he sensed all was not right between us. He's too reserved to comment directly, but very little gets past him."

Aimee reddened with mortification. Her eyes fell under Luke's blistering stare when he whirled on her. "Embarrassed, sweet wife?" he growled. "How do you expect to hide our problems from outsiders when you stiffen every time I touch you?"

Aimee's face pokered up. "Need I remind you it was *you* who didn't want *my* touch last night? I honestly don't know what to make of you. You claim deep desire for me, yet when I offer myself to you, you reject me."

Luke chuckled bitterly. "Of course, I should have known you'd misunderstand." He stepped up to thrust his face into her defiant one. "Woman, don't you realize my control was in tatters? I didn't reject you because I didn't want you; I rejected you because I wanted you *too much!*" He shouted the last words, then moved away to pace the room.

"What would you have done," he muttered to his feet, "if I'd whirled you on your back and taken you, then and there, fumbling my way through your clothing?"

Aimee blushed at his deliberate crudity. She shivered at the image he conjured up. He halted and pointed an accusing finger at her.

"See? You tremble at the mere thought. Well, if I had taken you last night, that's exactly what would have happened." He looked at her with dislike, as if scornful of her cowardice.

Aimee flushed even redder under his accusing stare, but not with embarrassment. "I might have known it was all my fault," she spat. She paced up and down, then she whirled on him, her anger just beginning to rise. She swept aside caution, refusing to be blamed either for cowardice or the tension between them. She fumbled with the buttons at her back and hissed, "I've had enough of this. Take me, then. It will be worth it if I don't have to put up with your glowering anymore. But don't expect me to be grateful to you in the morning for ruining something that should have been beautiful."

She snatched her dress off her shoulders so roughly that the delicate material tore. She stepped out of it and began on her petticoats, her challenging eyes goading him on. Even when his gaze raked over her body, she was too angry to care. Their eyes locked when Luke took one step toward her, another, another, until he reached out to run a gentle finger along the white vee of skin peeking above her camisole.

Fascinated, he watched her breathing quicken. He could see her pulse pounding in the hollow of her throat. He slipped a hand behind her neck and tilted her head back, hoping, yearning to see his passion mirrored there. His excited heartbeat slowed to disappointment when she met his eyes bravely but swallowed in fear. Memories of his sleepless night made her offer even more tempting. He eyed her hungrily, but he knew she was still not ready. He could lose her forever if he ripped through the delicate fabric of their relationship and satisfied his physical lusts.

He shook his head. "Keep your sacrifice. I want no martyrs in my bed. If you're not woman enough to give as a woman—and a *wife*—then don't flatter yourself. I don't want you anyway."

And with this blatant lie, Luke tore off his own clothes, shrugged into his robe and stretched out on his inhospitable settee. Aimee went through her usual evening ritual, her eyes on the head averted from her. So, she had been right. He wanted her willing and passionate, or not at all. When she climbed into bed and blew out the lantern, she lay on her side, her eyes open and staring out into the night. She firmly denied that the sick feeling in her throat was caused by disappointment. If he'd accepted her foolish challenge, she'd have run screaming from their room. Wouldn't she? Yes, she fiercely answered herself. But this time, she tossed and turned as much as Luke did.

Luke and Aimee were both glad to get back to the *Mercury*. Luke needed occupation to distract him from the scent, look and touch of Aimee, who hovered tantalizingly out of reach, like forbidden fruit. Aimee was relieved to have him occupied, but above all, she wanted to get this interminable trip over with. One more stop, then less than two weeks to America. She was no longer afraid of meeting Luke's family, and she was eager to see the vibrant new land of opportunity which had drawn so many Scandinavians.

On the first day back at sea, Luke ignored her. He didn't even take his meals with her. He appeared in their cabin but once, to change his dirty clothes after working in the engine room. Aimee started and shoved her book guiltily behind her back. He asked her to fetch him a towel. She did so, and when she returned, he took it with terse thanks and a hard look. After he left, she scurried to her book. It seemed undisturbed, but she knew if he'd read the title, he'd explode. He'd discover she had lied about not speaking English, and his fraying temper would doubtless snap.

The next day, he reverted to the old, easy charm, but she caught him watching her guardedly the way a hungry cat eyes a caged bird. She was a little surprised when he informed her Potter would be supping with them that evening, but she didn't protest. A third party would be a welcome diversion.

When Potter arrived, she was touched when he held out a slightly withered bouquet of summer flowers. His brown hair was slicked back and he wore a stiff, obviously new suit. She stifled a grin when he tiptoed around the sumptuous, delicate furniture, as if determined not to embarrass himself.

"Thank you for having me, ma'am," he said, shifting his feet nervously after he sat down.

Aimee was careful to look at Luke for a translation. She watched closely as he repeated the sentence. His voice was expressionless and he didn't look angry. She relaxed.

"Tell him we're pleased he could join us, and ask if he would like some sherry before dinner." Luke obeyed, and, when Potter assented, he rose to pour them each a glass.

They sipped in silence for a moment, then Luke became animated. "Potter, what do you and the other men think of my wife?"

Potter choked on the sherry and spit it back into his glass. He eyed Aimee uneasily, but she was staring into her drink with apparent unconcern.

Luke encouraged him. "My wife doesn't understand English, so you can speak freely."

Potter still hesitated. "But why do you want to know? It ain't seemly for me to pass judgment on your bride."

"I won't get angry, whatever you might say. I have my reasons for asking, believe me. Give me your honest opinion, please."

Potter looked at Aimee again. She still seemed relaxed, so he replied slowly, "We all think she's very pretty and sweet, but too . . . gentle to stand up to your ma." He gulped the remainder of his sherry, finishing it off.

Luke nodded. "I see. But you've never seen her in a temper, have you?"

Potter looked doubtful. "She looks so cool that butter wouldn't melt in her mouth. You mean she actually defies you? A little bit like her?"

He sounded so astounded that Luke smiled. "Indeed she does. In fact, I asked your opinion because I was hoping you could advise me on how best to train her into the proper, submissive role of a wife. I know you've been married three times, so you must have experience in these matters."

Potter's chest puffed out. "That I do, sir. And each of my wives has been more obedient than the last, God rest their souls."

Sure of himself now, Potter set his glass down and leaned toward Luke, ignoring Aimee. "Women need to be handled gently but firmly, you see. Never let them step out of their proper place, but always treat them kindly, and they'll reward you with obedience."

Luke cocked his head. "You mean rather as you would train a horse?" Out of the corner of his eye, he could see Aimee's hands balled into fists. He folded his arms across his chest and grinned.

Potter nodded. "That's it exactly, sir. Women remind me of horses, in a way. Beautiful, not too bright, but loyal to those who treat them well. If you bring them flowers and gee-gaws, tell them how pretty they are and such like, they'll be content as a filly in a stall full of hay."

Luke tapped his finger against his chin in thought. "But what if they still defy you even after you've treated them well, given them presents, and so on?"

Potter frowned severely. "That's when you must show a firm hand. You must never, *ever* let a woman get above herself, or she'll ruin your life and hers."

A knock sounded at the door. Aimee started. While Luke let the waiter in, Aimee retreated to the alcove to bathe her flushed face. When she came back out, her face was again expressionless, but Luke saw her jaw quivering as he seated her.

"Something wrong, dearest?" he asked blandly.

She was afraid if she opened her mouth she wouldn't be able to close it, so she shook her head mutely. After they had all been served with steak in green peppercorn sauce, peas and carrots and cheese soufflé, the waiter retreated and Potter resumed his lecture.

"These women who are now demanding the right to vote, for example. It's my opinion, they wouldn't be so unhappy if some man hadn't let them step out of their place. Imagine that Susan B. Anthony woman voting in deliberate defiance of the law! I tell you that if we give in to such creatures, the world will never be the same again."

Aimee's fork slammed down on her plate. She snatched up her napkin to wipe her face. She muttered something behind the fine damask.

Luke leaned toward her. "Did you say something, dearest? Speak up."

Aimee glared at him over the napkin, lowered it and took a deep breath. "No, no, I just choked, that's all."

"Is the food too ill-prepared? I can send it back," Luke offered solicitously. When Aimee shook her head, he turned back to Potter.

"You were saying . . ."

"Well, you see, sir, it's like this. God meant for man to be ruler of the earth. Woman is his helpmate. She bears the young and nurtures the home, but she's too fickle and weak-minded to understand the complexities of business. It's our duty as the stronger sex to keep them safe and content, and it's theirs to serve us, as the good Lord intended."

Luke almost burst out laughing when Aimee gurgled behind her napkin again. "But what do you do with a woman who won't keep her proper place, who believes herself as independent as a man?"

Potter scratched his head in puzzlement. "Well, if she doesn't do as she's told, you must discipline her, I guess."

When Luke frowned, Potter added hastily, "Not physically. Tighten the purse strings, forbid her to leave the house, things like that. I'd wager she'll step back in line then."

Aimee could stand no more. Snarling, she leaped to her feet, knocking the nearby soufflé squarely into Potter's lap. The thick, warm cheese oozed over his breeches. He yelped and leaped to his feet.

Aimee grabbed up a towel and flung it at Luke. "Apologize to him for me. Tell him I can't *imagine* what made me so clumsy. Maybe he's contagious." She retreated to the alcove and whisked the curtain closed.

When she came back out, Potter was gone, and Luke was calmly finishing his after-dinner brandy. Aimee flung herself into a chair opposite him, trying to control her urge to shriek like a fishwife.

Luke swirled his snifter and murmured thoughtfully, as if to himself, in English, "Now I wonder if I should take Potter's advice? A man should certainly be master in his own home, and it's time Aimee learned that. Still, what's the best way to subdue her? She doesn't seem impressed with pre-

sents or flowers. There must be another way to reach her."
His eyes narrowed in speculation. "She's admitted she enjoys
my touch. Hmmm . . . Perhaps I've been too patient. Could
it be she's waiting for me to make the first move?"

Luke's eyes raked her figure with insulting thoroughness.
"She certainly whets my appetite." He licked his lips so
sensually that Aimee's eyes dropped to his mouth before she
could stop herself. "What pleasure we could give one another. I'd be gentle. I'd kiss that Cupid's-bow mouth until she
was weak with desire. Then I'd bare those sweet breasts and
suckle them until they rose to my touch."

His eyes caressed her heaving bosom as he spoke, and
Aimee was embarrassed to feel her nipples rise. "I'd nibble
at that satiny skin until she quivered, then I'd kiss my way to
her navel, down each smooth thigh and up again until I came
to . . ."

Aimee surged to her feet. "Enough!" she cried in English.
She swayed dizzily for a moment, torn between anger and a
weak, hungry feeling that increased when he towered to his
feet above her.

"What? You mean you speak English after all?" Luke
affected surprise. "My dear, how quickly you learn."

Aimee recovered her senses at his mockery. "You mean
you deliberately taunted me, first with Potter, now with
your . . . by . . ."

"By describing exactly what I want to do to you? Yes. I
knew you wouldn't be able to sit still for such honesty, you
little coward. Why the hell did you pretend you don't speak
English? What could you possibly gain by it?"

Aimee's hands fluttered defiantly to her hips. "Time. And
I wanted to learn more about you. Was that so wrong?"

Luke sighed heavily. "No, it wasn't wrong. But did it ever
occur to you all you had to do was ask? I'll be happy to tell
you anything you want to know about me. I despise subterfuge of any kind. I hope you'll remember that in the future."

"And I despise arrogance of any kind. I hope *you'll*
remember *that* in the future. And I warn you, if you try to
take that idiot Potter's advice, you'll see exactly how miserable I can make you."

Luke glared at her, but Aimee glared right back. Luke
purred, "Actually, I think it quite a good idea to lock you in.
You'd see no one but me until you came to look forward to
my visits. Maybe you'd be a bit more agreeable, then."

Aimee's eyes narrowed in rage. "You crude boor. When will you learn you can't force me to do anything? Just try to lock me in. I dare you." She stabbed a warning finger at him. "But if you do, you'd better be wearing armor the next time you come in."

Luke looked politely disbelieving. "Are you threatening me?" He eyed her slight figure mockingly.

Aimee bristled. "Size has nothing to do with it. You've pushed me about as far as I'll be pushed. . . ."

Luke laughed in harsh amazement. "That's rich. *I've* pushed *you?*" He suddenly reached out and pulled her against him. "There's probably not another man within a thousand miles who would have been as patient with you as I have. You're my wife, but you've treated me to nothing but disdain since we first met, and I'm sick of it, do you hear?" He tightened his arms around her in warning.

She threw back her head to spit defiance, but he cut her off. "I've given you enough time. By your own admission, you enjoy my touch. There's only one way to settle your fears. It's time you learned you belong to me." He whirled her around to undo the buttons at the back of her dress, but she ducked under his hands and retreated behind the couch.

"That's your answer for everything. You're no different from any other man, after all. All you care about is satisfying your own base desires. My needs, hopes and happiness mean nothing to you." Her voice quivered as she expressed her deepest feelings.

Luke froze in his advance around the couch. "How can you say such a thing? I've done everything I know to make you happy. My God, girl, I'm not a saint. I don't know how much longer I can go on like this. . . ." His voice was so hoarse with emotion that Aimee lifted her head to look at him.

The pleading, longing look in his eyes nearly drew her to him. She took one hesitant step, then stopped and shook her head in desperation. "I can't, I'm sorry, I yearn for you, I admit it, but I want more than a night. Can you look me in the eye and tell me you love me, you'll never leave me, that I'm not just another woman to you?"

Luke replied steadily, "I can promise you're not just another woman to me. It's taken me all my life to find you, so why would I ever want to leave you? And do I love you?" Luke hesitated. For the first time in his life, he was fearful of his own emotions. He didn't want to love her; he was afraid to love her. He struggled so long with himself that Aimee finished the sentence for him.

"No, you don't." Aimee quivered in pain when she realized the truth. She lifted her chin. "Well, I never expected otherwise. Love is rarely involved in arranged marriages. But surely you can understand why I must know you better before we . . . before I . . ."

Luke rubbed the back of his neck in fatigue. "Yes, I can understand." He straightened and warned, "But I suggest you resign yourself. Before this voyage is over, you will belong to me in body as well as name. Now, if you'll excuse me, I have some things to attend to." He charged out of the cabin.

Aimee stood where he left her, eyes blind to her surroundings as his warning reverberated, "belong to me, belong to me." She clapped her hands over her ears to shut out the sound. Dear God, what was she to do? She sometimes thought if Luke were a lesser man, she could accept her plight. But every time she visualized that handsome face leaning over her, eyes black as night as he peered into her very soul, she panicked. If she could give him her body but not her heart, she would, if only to end this conflict between them. But she could not. She knew herself better, understood him too well to believe he could ever be satisfied with a soulless union. Even more terrifying, she knew she could never be satisfied with such a relationship either. The forces drawing them together were as natural and irresistible as the tides; if she submitted to her bodily longings, she would be swept away, as powerless as a child building a wall of sand against the encroaching tide.

Her independence, the bedrock of her nature, would be washed into a vast sea of uncertainty where her only anchor, her only haven, would be Luke. Despite her yearning for him, she couldn't bind herself to him without his love. So what in heaven's name was she to do? Go back to Norway? Try to get a job and live alone? Or take a chance that he would come to love her?

By the time they docked in London, Aimee had still not decided. Luke's restlessness and short temper made it imperative that she do something. This waiting was unfair to both of them. She toyed with the idea of running away, but she had no money and few skills, and, deep down, she knew she didn't want to leave Luke. His patience was almost exhausted. If she spoke to him, he snarled. His eyes followed her every movement, making her want to scream.

Aimee felt torn in half, so she was almost grateful when fate took a hand and tipped the scales of destiny. On the morning they docked, Aimee was standing near the wheel-house, shielded by the bulkhead, when she overheard Jimmy talking to Potter.

"Do you know what's wrong with the Captain, Potter? He's been vicious as a hungry grizzly for the past few days."

"I think he's having trouble with that little gal he married. She's a pretty little piece, but no woman's worth so much trouble. He probably wishes he'd told his parents to go to the devil and then not wed her."

Jimmy seemed surprised. "They seemed happy enough when they first boarded. What could be amiss?"

"I don't know. But it's my guess he's changed his mind about allying his business with her pa's. He was against it from the beginning, and now this little gal has deepened his regret. I'll be surprised if the Garrisons follow through on their part of the agreement." Potter laughed coarsely. "Once he tires of that pretty body, he'll probably leave her to his ma and enjoy his old life. Such a young gal hasn't a hope of holding him."

The voices retreated, so Aimee didn't catch Jimmy's reply, but she'd heard enough. She bit her lip to stem the tears. She swayed as pain knifed through her, but she took a deep breath and straightened. It was best she discover the truth now. Surely Luke's own men, who had seen years of service under him, knew his most intimate thoughts better than she. Despite her hopes to the contrary, her fears had proved right: she was too young, too innocent, or simply too independent to hold him. She was fiercely glad she'd left the marriage unconsummated. It was too high a price to pay for a brief, physical fling. She would not be used and cast aside by any man, not even Luke. Would he really do that to her? He said no. She longed to believe no, but she knew few of the rules in the seduction game.

In the pain of the moment, she even wondered if Potter was right about the Garrisons. Would they renege, refuse to lend her father the money he needed? She told herself she was wrong, that Luke would never betray, but her anguish forced her to accept the possibility. It was plain at last what she must do. And she must not delay while Luke was ashore arranging to have the timber unloaded.

She rushed to their cabin, packed the smallest portmanteau with bare essentials, leaving behind all but her old wardrobe and the silver jewelry. She refused to take the money Luke kept in his desk, and salvaged some kronor left from their stay in Stockholm. She'd find an exchange bank.

She sat down at the desk, ignored the tears falling from her eyes and penned a quick note to Luke. She propped it on the desk so he'd see it. She swept one last look over the cabin, trying to imprint its beauty on her mind, then bent to pick up the portmanteau, but Luke's robe folded carelessly over the couch back caught her eye.

She walked over to touch the soft material. Hands trembling, she lifted it to her face. His clean scent wafted into her nostrils, so reminiscent of him she could almost feel him beside her. Memories of him tormented her: Luke daring her to touch him, Luke dangerously tipsy as he weaved around the silversmith's shop. Luke kissing her passionately, opening a door to heaven or hell, she still didn't know which.

Now she never would. Aimee inhaled one last time, wiped her eyes on her sleeve, set down the robe and carefully smoothed it out. She picked up the sculpture of her family and dropped it into her case. She forced her lethargic feet to the door. "Good-bye, my darling," she whispered, somehow hoping he heard her, wherever he was.

When Luke arrived back at the *Mercury,* he oversaw the cargo unloading before hours later he returned to his stateroom. He was a little surprised to find Aimee gone, but he assumed she must be on deck. After fetching some papers from his desk, he turned to leave. The envelope sitting atop it caught his eye.

The handwriting was Aimee's. Urgently he tore it open. He froze. It read: "Dear Luke: This was a painful decision for me to make, but after considerable thought, I've concluded we're better off apart. I can't give you the total loyalty you want, and, indeed, deserve; you can't give me the love I need. I will always remember you fondly, and be grateful to you for your consideration, and I hope you will not think too ill of me. I will contact you when I've found a job. Don't worry about me. Please know I do this for both our sakes. And please, please, make sure your parents lend my father the money he needs. Forgive me, Aimee."

Luke sank to the top of his desk and read the letter over

again, trying to believe his eyes were deceiving him. Fearfully, he looked at the dresser. The sculpture was gone. He crushed the letter in his hand and flung it away. Pain hit him so hard he doubled over. Did she hate him so much she believed he wouldn't carry through on their business agreement? That she would flee alone to one of the most dangerous cities in the world rather than live with him?

Aimee, come back, he cried inside. I can't live without you. You're the only woman I will ever . . . love. It was such a little word, so easy to say now that she wasn't there to hear it. The confession was a hollow comfort, for it was made too late. He knew London too well to believe he would find her easily. If at all. He thrust the thought violently away and leaped to his feet to alert his men. Find her he would, if he had to tear London apart brick by brick. And when he did, she would regret this little adventure, the rest of her life. . . .

PART III

The day will not come when I'll forget you; for if I'm asleep, in my dreams I meet you. By night or by day the same you're near me; and when it is dark, I see you most clearly. I walk, and around me your form is fleeting. I hear you in my own heart's beating. Wherever my feet may take me, you are there with me like a shadow too.

—Aasmund Olafsson Vinje,
"The Day Will Not Come"

Chapter Ten

AIMEE WOULD ALWAYS remember that long walk down the gangplank as her most rigorous journey. Her muscles ached, her heart raced, her legs dragged until she landed on the huge wharf. She started as incoming steamers bleated long and loud, as if issuing a plaintive warning of disaster ahead. Birds wheeled above her head, their cries mocking her every step. Even the wind seemed to conspire against her, blowing full in her face as if to push her back up the plank.

Aimee faltered. She was torn between anguish at leaving Luke and despair at knowing he didn't love her. Potter's comments rang in her ears. Luke had never seemed to put great credence in Potter's opinions, but Aimee cringed from the mere suspicion that Luke could be bored with her or turn to another. And if he should betray her father . . .

You won't help your father by leaving, a gentle voice whispered. And you'll never win Luke's love by this cowardice. A prideful voice countered, if you stay, you'll fall so deeply in love with him you'll never dig your way out. It will hurt that he doesn't love you, but he'll become so vital to your existence that you'll accept whatever crumbs he throws your way and be thrilled. You'll be the weak, submissive woman you've always scorned. Leave now, while you still can.

The curious looks Luke's crew gave her, portmanteau clutched in her hand, galvanized her into action. In the midst of her confusion, the old instincts that had molded and strengthened her character defeated the new urgings. She took one hesitant step, and another, faster, until she was running, tears flooding her eyes. She hailed a hansom cab and scrambled inside, shivering with misery and shock. She bade the driver take her to the financial district so she could exchange her kronor.

The rush of tears strangely calmed her, and soon, the sounds, scents and sights bombarding her senses helped her regain control of herself. With her usual determination, she straightened her spine. The die was cast. There was nothing left to do but march on. Regrets would gain her nothing.

So Aimee turned her attention to sights so new, so strange, so intriguing, she was soon hanging out the window, gaping in amazement. Even Stockholm had not prepared her for London. Her head bobbed from side to side as she tried to adjust to the pandemonium around her. London was, quite simply, the most amazing city she had ever seen.

She had thought Stockholm large and crowded, but London was a din of people and noises, and contrasting colors. The crowd milled about its business through streets as narrow and dirty as any rabbit's warren. As her cab left the wharves, the scenery gradually improved. From hulking warehouses and rotting taverns, sailors in high boots and pea jackets strolling about with slatternly women or brawling with dock-workers, the streets became cleaner and broader.

Here solid middle-class workers scurried to and fro on errands: white-aproned bakers, top-hatted merchants, capped maids and porters. And everywhere she looked, it seemed, construction was in progress. Buildings were being torn down, others erected; streets were being broadened, sewage drains laid down.

The hodgepodge of vehicles crowding the streets was astonishing. Well-worn cabs, like hers, plied the road next to elegant carriages, footmen perched behind, and lone horse-men. The driver of a heavy dray, pulled by the largest horses she'd ever seen, shook an angry fist as a top-hatted dandy in a sporty curricle pulled in front of him. Most interesting to her practical mind were the large public omnibuses plodding steadily along their routes. Painted on their sides were their destinations.

Grim-faced passengers swayed on top. Aimee wondered if anyone in this odd city ever smiled. Aimee studied the faces of passers-by, and suddenly, she was more than miserable. She was afraid. All the tales she'd heard about the decadence and danger in London came back to haunt her.

By the time they reached Lombard street, symbol of London's money market, Aimee was trembling. When she stepped out of the cab, she looked so lost and bewildered that the driver, who had seen too much over the years to be overly compassionate, warned gruffly, "'Ere lyday, watch w'ere yer' goin'," and pulled her out of the path of the hurrying pedestrians.

However, when he demanded his fare and it wasn't immediately forthcoming, his brief sympathy fled. "Wot's the meanin' 'o this? Ye' can't pay me?" He grabbed her arm roughly.

She shrank away and stammered, "Y-Yes I can. Please wait and I'll exchange some currency and return."

He pulled his hat low over his eyes and scowled, "If ye' don't mind, I'll come wi' ye'." He hauled her inside the imposing bank and led her straight to a teller.

Aimee was dismayed at the few pounds she got in exchange for her kronor, but she swallowed her disappointment and paid the driver. He immediately went back into the street.

She hurried after him. "Please wait, I want to go to a hotel now."

He either didn't hear her, or ignored her, for he leapt into his carriage, clucked to the horse and went in search of another fare. One who knew the score, he muttered to himself. He sent a pitying look over his shoulder as he drove away, but whirled around at the dismay in her face. "That one'll be fox to the 'ounds fore' night comes," he sighed. But he didn't turn back.

Aimee lifted her head and strolled down the street, her portmanteau and reticule clutched closely to her side. She tried to step jauntily, but, judging from the strange looks cast her way, she was unsuccessful. She was beginning to realize the enormity of her action. In Stockholm, she might have been able to find a job and build a future for herself, but here, she was as defenseless as a lamb.

She stopped and leaned against a lamppost to wipe her brow, seriously considering going straight back to Luke. Even his dangerous influence over her emotions was preferable to these leering male passers-by. One gentleman in particular had been leering at her since she came out of the bank. From the corner of her eye, she saw he was still there.

Almost simultaneous with the thought came a vicious tug on her reticule. With a cry of dismay, Aimee started. A tiny street urchin in rags had grabbed her bag and made off down the streets. She could not get far in pursuit. Her heavy portmanteau dragged down her footsteps. She was shoved aside by the same man who had been scrutinizing her before. He outran the lad and tackled him. The pair scuffled, then the thief fell away to be pulled roughly to his feet and shoved over to Aimee. The thief, under coercion, handed her the reticule with a bow.

"Here's your bag, ma'am. I'll turn this little bugger over to the constable for you." He looked about, as if exasperated a "peeler" wasn't in sight at that very moment.

Aimee watched the boy. He was gaunt, with the sunken eyes and red hands of the hungry and poor. Her throat closed with compassion. If she'd been less desperate herself, she would have given him every pound she possessed.

"Let him go," she pleaded. She opened her reticule and took out a shilling. "Here, get yourself something to eat," she suggested. With a crafty look sent to his tackler, the boy grabbed the coin and scurried away.

The man looked disapprovingly at Aimee. "You can't let scum like that get away with such things, ma'am. That was most unwise."

Aimee nodded cooly. "Perhaps. Thank you for your intervention, sir. Now, if you'll excuse me . . ." She continued down the street.

The man called, "Wait, please. Don't I deserve a small reward for my help?"

Aimee turned back, embarrassed. When her hands went to her bag again, he hastily assured her, "No, that's not what I mean. I would welcome your company for dinner. In a public place, of course."

Aimee hesitated. He looked respectable enough. He was dressed fashionably in the tailed coat, walking stick, and fancy waistcoat of the dandy. His brown hair was brushed neatly back, his side whiskers were long but trimmed. His brown eyes were direct, but held a narrow, assessing look that disturbed her. Still, he was obviously comfortable in this huge metropolis, and he could probably advise her on how to find work. A public place should be safe enough. . . .

She nodded. "Thank you. I would welcome the company."

"Excellent! Now, I know the nicest hotel with a little supper room that makes superb roast beef. . . ."

Before Aimee knew it, she was whisked into his carriage. They traveled several blocks. He assisted her down and then into a multi-hued granite, respectable-looking hotel. They were escorted into an intimate supper room that was, to Aimee's consternation, set for two.

However, the gentleman soon put her at ease with relaxing chatter. "John Goodman is my name. I'm a barrister and I've lived in London all my life, so if you've questions about our great city, just ask. It's obvious you're new to London."

Aimee nodded shyly. "My name is Aimee . . . Lingstrom and I am new to London. I was wondering if you could advise me as to how I can find stable employment. I have experience in bookkeeping."

He took a thoughtful sip of wine and waited until the waiter had served them before replying. "I do happen to have a friend who's looking for someone to keep his accounts. Hasn't found anyone suitable yet. Would you like me to introduce you to him?" He smiled at her warmly, but Aimee was uneasy at the way his eyes roamed over her hair, her lips, her body.

She hesitated. Her instincts warned her to be wary of such amiability from a stranger. "I'm afraid I can supply no references. I just arrived in London today. . . ."

"That's no problem. A word from me will be enough reference for my friend. It's plain to see you're honest and intelligent. But of course, I can understand your hesitation. I can buy a *Times* for you if you'd prefer to seek on your own. . . ."

He sounded a bit miffed, and Aimee felt guilty at her mistrust. He was, after all, the only friendly face she'd yet found, and he'd given her no reason to be suspicious of him. Besides, it was imperative that she find employment soon.

She smiled in gratitude. "If you think your friend would consider me, I'd be happy to meet him, sir."

He beamed at her, relaxing back in his chair. "Excellent! I'll take you to him as soon as we've finished." He chattered while they ate, putting her at ease. She listened eagerly to his descriptions of the wonders of London.

"Now if you don't want to go to the usual tourist haunts like the Tower and Westminster, I suggest some wonderful new sights, like Albert Hall. It's a circular concert hall named in honor of Prince Albert. It seats literally thousands upon thousands of people in tier upon tier of boxes. Here, my dear, you're not drinking your wine. It's an excellent French vintage, quite worthy of your consideration, I assure you." Aimee obediently sipped as he talked.

"And perhaps you've heard about the Metropolitan, our underground railway system? The most amazing engineering feat man has ever devised, in my opinion. The St. Pancras station has to be seen to be believed, it is so immense. Of course, so many poor people were displaced, their homes torn down to make room for improvements. Still, that's progress, I suppose. . . ." He pressed another glass of wine on her.

By the time they left, Aimee's head was swimming just enough to soften her guard. Goodman kept up his chatter, pointing out sights of interest as they wound through London's best district. Aimee was awed by the grandeur of the houses they passed. Set back from the road, some of them sprawled almost half a block, their three and four stories towering imposingly above the street. Most were surrounded by high, ornamental fences and set within lush, well-kept grounds. The streets here were almost perfect. The carriage barely bounced as it rolled over the macadam.

When they stopped in front of one of the mansions, Aimee felt no hesitation in accepting Goodman's hand to descend. The creamy stone edifice he led her to was the essence of wealth and respectability. Georgian in style, it was fronted by ornate pillars and an ornamental porch. Each window had a stone ledge that matched the lavish quoins abutting the ends of the building.

Goodman rapped the lion's head doorknocker. The butler who opened it seemed surly, but respectable enough. He bowed when Goodman introduced Aimee.

"The master is out at present, but you may speak with Mrs. Tuttle. She engages all the staff." He led them into a sunny parlor on the second floor and asked them to wait. Aimee wondered at the stiffness in his manner, but she shrugged. Perhaps servants in London were all like this.

Aimee was shocked at the appearance of the woman who entered. She was the antithesis of Aimee's idea of a house-keeper. Indeed, her stiff skirts rustled as she moved, but not with starch. She wore supple emerald silk that whispered with her every movement. Her gown was cut low, but not so low that she wasn't respectable. She wore a discreet amount of cosmetics. Her bright red hair was pinned atop her head in a flirtatious crown, but it was her manner of conducting the interview that most surprised Aimee. She walked around Aimee, surveying her from all angles, as if her physical appearance were as important as her ciphering abilities.

Goodman bowed and said hastily, "This is Aimee. She is new to London, and, though without references and experience, she should fit the position perfectly, don't you think?"

Aimee frowned a little. His introduction glimmered with underlying meaning. . . . Mrs. Tuttle, however, seemed to understand him perfectly.

After one final look at Aimee, she nodded briskly. "Indeed, she should do nicely." She named a salary that sounded very generous. "When can you start, my dear?"

Aimee's eyes widened in bewilderment. "But don't you need to see a sample of my work? Perhaps you have some figures that need totalling?"

Mrs. Tuttle smiled slightly. "I've seen all I need to. Mr. Goodman has never failed us before in his recommendations."

When Aimee still hesitated, her smile faded. "Well?" she snapped. "Do you want the position or don't you?"

Aimee bit her lip, looking from Goodman to Mrs. Tuttle, to the quiet elegance of the room surrounding them. She told herself she was being foolish. Everything was as it seemed. Besides, she really had little choice.

She nodded. "Yes, I'll accept the position."

Goodman and Mrs. Tuttle both relaxed. Goodman walked forward to take her hand and kiss it. "I'm delighted we met, Aimee. Enjoy your new position." He bowed and went to the door, Mrs. Tuttle following. She saw the woman hand Goodman something, and wondered what it was.

Aimee strained to catch their low-voiced conversation, but only heard scattered snatches. "She's perfect . . . Begin tomorrow . . ." Mrs. Tuttle turned back to Aimee with a charming smile. She summoned a footman to take Aimee's bag upstairs, escorting Aimee to a pretty blue chamber.

"Rest for this evening, my dear. Your duties will be light. All we need to do tomorrow is to fit you for your, er, uniform."

Aimee turned from examining the feminine bedroom. "I have no objection to beginning immediately, ma'am. In fact,

I would prefer it. Is there nothing I can help with?"

Mrs. Tuttle shook her head. "You'll be busy aplenty soon enough," she said dryly. "I'll have a tray sent up for you. You'd best have an early night."

Mrs. Tuttle turned to leave, but Aimee halted her. "Ma'am, I forgot to ask. What is the name of my employer?"

Mrs. Tuttle hesitated, then replied blandly, "One of the wealthiest men in London, my dear. The Earl of Wimberly." She exited before Aimee could question her further.

Aimee repeated the name to herself. Her half-felt fears receded. It certainly sounded like an upstanding name. She picked up the periodical on the table by the bed and sat down to read, unaware that the name that sounded so respectable to her belonged to the most notorious womanizer in London.

Luke approached another dockworker, praying he would be the one who would remember the beautiful woman on the wharf strangely by herself. But this man was as surly and unhelpful as the rest. Luke sent an anguished look at the sinking sun. He wished he could hold time still, and keep the sun from setting. If he didn't find Aimee now, chances faded he would find her at all. Without protection, without money, she would be sucked into London's great cesspool of an underworld.

He knew she only had the kronor left from Stockholm and the silver jewelry, neither of which would go far when she tried to exchange them. She had even left her wedding ring. He had no illusions about her ability to fend for herself. Her innocence would clash against London's savvy masses and tempt every unsavory criminal within miles.

Frantically, he questioned another man, and another, and another, until dark descended and the first morning stars winked in the sky. His men finally had to pull him away as they returned from their own fruitless search.

Jimmy grabbed his arm. "It's no use, Luke. We're doing no good this way. We must go to the police."

Luke jerked free and descended on another man, who backed away, alarmed at the look on his face. Jimmy planted himself in front of Luke and took him by the shoulders.

"Luke, listen to me. We've tried this for hours. You know how busy the docks are. One slight girl getting into a cab isn't likely to be noticed by anyone. She could be anywhere. The police will know what to do." When Luke looked at him,

Jimmy had to turn his head away from his friend's raw pain.

"They'll be able to do nothing we can't do. Do you have any idea how many missing people they look for every week?" Luke's voice was hoarse with weariness and worry.

Jimmy forced him back aboard the *Mercury*. "Then we'll start again after a few hours' sleep. But killing yourself will do nothing for Aimee."

Luke balled his hand into a fist and slammed it against the bulkhead. He whirled on Jimmy. "How could she do this to me? I've treated her like glass, I would have cherished her to the end of my days. . . ." He choked and buried his face in his hands.

Jimmy urged him to his stateroom and rang for food. He gave the only comfort he could. "I don't know why, Luke. But I wager you'll find out for yourself soon enough. Because we'll find her if we keep looking. Perhaps we should try the hotels next. She may be safe and sound in one at this very moment."

Luke lifted his head to look at him, the old fighting spirit flickering in his eyes again. "Do you really think so, Jimmy?"

Despite his inward doubts, Jimmy said steadily, "I do. It's just a matter of time before you have her safe again."

But as he served Luke a light meal, Jimmy was careful to keep his eyes down. Luke knew him too well to miss the doubt.

Aimee got little sleep that night. Every time she closed her eyes, she saw Luke's face reproaching her. She buried her head in her pillow; she sat up, turned up the gas lamps and tried to read, but without avail. She could not blot out the memory of his touch, his voice, his face. She missed him so much she literally ached. She had put physical distance between them, yes, but he might as well be in the same room for all the control he exercised over her thoughts.

Had she done the right thing? Luke didn't love her, true, but if she was to be miserable, she might as well be miserable with him. She felt calmer then, and reflected how it had been wrong to doubt his honor, even for an instant. Luke would never betray her father, even in anger at her. Potter was wrong. So why had she fled?

Aimee stared blindly at the periodical. Deep in her heart, she had never believed Luke would betray her. She wondered if she had ever really believed Potter's claim that Luke would tire of her, then turn to another. Aimee remembered the passion in Luke's face as he vowed his undying interest in her. His anger and impatience stemmed from frustration, not lack of desire. But, coward that she was, she had used Potter's words as an excuse to flee. She needed escape not from Luke, but from herself. Another night with him and she would have yielded all. Cravenly, she had fled rather than admit she'd long ago lost the unequal struggle between heart and mind.

Curiously, as she finally faced the truth of her feelings for Luke, peace descended on her like a warm quilt. How foolish she had been! She could no more escape him than she could wrench out her own heart and still live. He had taken possession of her heart and had made it forever his own.

She loved him. It was as simple as that. She had struggled against him so long, so violently because, from the beginning, she had sensed his threat to her independence. Aimee waited for her usual panic at the thought of being totally dependent on another person. She smiled mistily when it didn't come. Instead, she was filled with such joy that she longed to sprout wings and fly to Luke without delay. So what if he didn't love her now? She would make him so happy, give him so much of herself that he soon would.

Aimee's euphoria faded as quickly as it had been born. What if she was too late? What if he was even more disgusted by her cowardice than she was? Perhaps he was even glad she was gone. He could now turn his attention to someone less obstinate, someone who would give him her heart and body without protest.

Aimee's mouth became set with determination. Well, if that's what he wanted, that's what he'd get. She could be as compliant and loving as any woman. At least, she hoped she could.

The mysteries of what happened between a man and woman in bed had never seemed more enticing. And more alarming. She wasn't afraid of giving herself to Luke. He had already shown his gentle side. She visualized those long brown hands caressing her and quivered with pleasure. But what if he found her lacking? His past was littered with experienced women. She had no idea how to shower on him the same pleasure he'd given her.

Aimee blew out the lamps and clambered back into bed, trying to quiet her douts. She had always been a quick learner. He had enjoyed their earlier embraces, after all. Besides, she suspected that the moment he touched her all her fears and doubts would drift away like wind-blown thistledown.

Comforted, she slept. She was awakened around dawn the next day by a returning carriage and a loud voice. She went to the window and saw a large man dressed in evening attire emerge from an elegant landau. He was supported by two footmen who shook their heads and looked uneasily around when he burst into bawdy song. The front door opened and closed, shutting off the sounds.

Aimee dressed thoughtfully. She longed to get back to Luke as soon as possible, but she had made a commitment here. Since her duties hadn't begun, perhaps Mrs. Tuttle would make no objection if she left.

Aimee set her hair up in a tight, neat bun, trying to look as prim as possible. She wore a plain green skirt and white blouse, unaware that the sober dress threw her wild vitality into higher relief. Taking a deep breath, she opened the door and went downstairs.

She looked around the spacious parquet-floored hall, wondering where to look for the housekeeper. She heard a door slam and looked up when footsteps descended the stairs. At first she thought her ears were deceiving her, for she could see no one; then her eyes lowered, and she glimpsed a small brown head belonging to someone descending the stairs.

Aimee smiled, relieved. Surely if a child lived here, this was a respectable household. She started forward. She froze when she got a good look at the figure.

The small brown head belonged not to a child, but to a dwarf. Aimee judged him to be less than four feet tall. He was dressed plainly, in black broadcloth vest, pants and jacket. Tiny boots covered his feet. But it was his face that held her attention. One of his eyes was crossed, his nose was bent, as if it had been broken, and several of his teeth were missing. Yet, ugly as his countenance was, there was something imposing in the regal way he held his body, as if he were a man used to command.

He stared at her just as long, looking stunned. Aimee wondered at the look on his face. One of . . . recognition. He barked in a voice that sounded too deep for his body, "Who the hell are you?"

Aimee flushed, embarrassed at staring. She curtsied. "I am

Aimee. Mrs. Tuttle hired me yesterday to keep his lordship's books."

The man's bushy eyebrows lowered. His face colored with anger, then he turned a hostile glower on her. He shouldered past her without another word.

Aimee stared after him, puzzled by his behavior. He had seemed ready to contradict her. She hastened after him. "Sir, please wait."

The little man strode on, but Aimee's longer stride allowed her to catch up with him. She grabbed his arm and pleaded, "Please, do you know where I might find Mrs. Tuttle?"

He stiffened at her touch, then paused. "I'm not privy to her movements. Find her yourself," he said harshly. He didn't look at her again, but pulled away and went out the front door.

Aimee sought Mrs. Tuttle, but couldn't find her. When she questioned the other servants, she found them as uncooperative. Aimee paced the hallway, her eyes burning as her thoughts flew to Luke like homing pigeons. She thought about packing her bag and leaving without another word, but the responsibility she'd learned at her father's knee made her stay. She wondered at the odd looks the servants kept giving her, but she shrugged and wandered into the library.

She looked about at the rows and rows of books. The heavy desk near the fireplace was bare, as if it were rarely used. The books lining the walls gleamed with oil, as if they had recently been cleaned of the dust accumulated from neglect. Aimee's wandering eyes paused, riveted by the portrait over the fireplace. Her heart beat faster, then she stepped up to examine it.

A slight woman dressed in a gold gown braced a handsome boy on her lap. She was seated by a lake, in a swing. The floppy hat she wore didn't quite hide her silver-blond hair. Her eyes were green, and they looked straight at Aimee. They beamed a mischievous, willful pride that mirrored the look in Aimee's eyes, had she but known it. Her face was rounder, softer, but her energy was oddly familiar.

Aimee was puzzling over this coincidence when the door opened. She turned to meet the eyes of a tall, dark-haired man of about forty years of age. He appraised her closely, his eyes going from her, to the portrait behind her head, back to her. He came forward and held out his hand, smiling.

"You must be Miss Lingstrom. I am Clarence Webb, his lordship's estate manager."

Aimee grasped his hand reluctantly. His smile was too smooth, his brown eyes too calculating, his dress too overdone for her taste. Immediately she distrusted him and withdrew her hand.

"Yes, sir. I was looking for Mrs. Tuttle, but perhaps you can help me instead. I've decided to return to my husband, so I won't be needing your position after all. . . ."

Webb frowned so blackly that her words trailed off. "You can't back out now. Your services are needed here. You've given a commitment, and I expect you to keep it."

Aimee stiffened at the command in his tone. "Since my duties have not even begun yet, surely there is no hurry. You can hire someone else. My husband doesn't know where I am, and he'll be worried."

Webb seemed to relax a little. "What you say is true. It's just that now is a devilishly inconvenient time. If you could stay just a day or two . . ."

Aimee bowed her head in thought. Luke wasn't scheduled to sail for two days. She should have time to work out a quick notice. She nodded shortly. "Very well. But I can only stay until tomorrow."

Webb smiled. "Excellent! You're invited to sup with his lordship tonight. Until then . . ." He bowed and turned to exit, but Aimee halted him.

"Can you tell me whose picture this is?" she asked, indicating the portrait over the mantle.

There was the barest of pauses before Webb replied. "It's Marie, his lordship's late wife. She and their son died in a boating accident a couple of years ago." He hurried out, as if afraid she would ask more questions.

Aimee sank into the chair by the window, her brow creased in thought. Something odd was brewing. She couldn't shake the suspicion that she'd been hired for more than her ciphering abilities. Indeed, if his lordship had an estate manager, wouldn't he be keeping the books?

Aimee was so deep in thought she didn't hear the door click open, but the soft sound of footsteps made her look up. The ugly little man strode to the desk and removed a ledger. He listened warily a moment, then opened the book and scanned a page. It was obvious he hadn't seen her, and just as obvious that he wanted no one to see him.

Aimee looked on steadily, more certain than ever that something was amiss. As if he felt her eyes, he glanced up. He stiffened, shoved the ledger back in the desk and slammed the drawer shut.

He strode forward with an arrogance that should have been ludicrous, but somehow wasn't. "All right, Miss Innocence, how much are you being paid for your services?"

Aimee frowned in bewilderment. She named her salary, but snapped back, "What business is it of yours?"

He stepped up to her chair and glared in her face. Their eyes were locked on a level when he scoffed, "And you really believe you're being paid that much for bookkeeping? You may pull the wool over his lordship's eyes, but mine are not blinded by drink. What do you and Webb have planned?"

Aimee's mouth parted in a soft gasp as her suspicions were confirmed by his words. She leaped to her feet. "Nothing. Oh please, tell me what's going on. I accepted nothing but the position of bookkeeper, I swear."

He searched her alarmed features. His hard brown eyes softened. "Then you have my deepest sympathy. Webb has his hooks into you, and if I know him, he'll not discard you until you've served his purpose."

"But what can he possibly want with me?"

"To use you to keep the earl buried in his maudlin grief so he can bleed him dry."

Aimee was sickened and stunned by the man's words. She sank back into her chair, appalled at how easily she'd been duped. Then fury came to her aid, stiffening her spine. She surged to her feet again.

"How despicable! I shall go to the police at once."

"And tell them what? He's been clever. He's done nothing illegal as yet, at least, nothing I can discover. I can find no discrepancy in the books, hard as I try."

"Why don't you just tell the earl what Webb is doing?"

The little man sighed. "I've tried. He won't believe me. And, frankly, I'm not sure he'd care even if he did. All he wants to do is drink and womanize himself into a stupor until he's no longer haunted by his dead wife." An undercurrent of pain colored his voice, and when he looked at the portrait, his eyes were bleak.

Aimee asked softly, "And who are you? She obviously

meant a great deal to you as well."

He cleared his throat. "My name is Pete Newcombe," he said harshly. "I'm just one of many who loved her. I'm doing what little I can to help the earl recover from his grief. She wouldn't have wanted him to act this way, but so far I haven't been able to make him understand. She literally picked me up out of the gutter and gave me a home after I was injured in the circus. I worked there as a . . . kind of . . . freak. I was her groom first, her friend second, and, at the end . . ."

His voice trailed away, but Aimee could fill in the words he left unsaid. He loved her not as a friend, but as a man. Aimee's eyes were drawn to the portrait, misting with sympathy for such a vibrant life cut short, leaving so many to grieve. She was unaware that Pete's eyes were now on her face.

Aimee sniffled and wiped her eyes. She turned to find Pete watching her steadily. His intense gaze puzzled her. "Pete, I can help a little by leaving. At least then Webb won't be able to use me in his scheme."

Pete shook his head. "It's not that simple. Haven't you noticed that you've never been alone since you awakened?"

Aimee's eyes drifted. She had thought it odd that wherever she went, a footman, or maid, or the butler, was always near. A chill ran over her. "Do you mean I'll be forced to remain?"

He looked away from her ashen face, his own features pained. "Aye. That's exactly what I mean."

Aimee was still absorbing the implications when the door opened and Mrs. Tuttle entered. She eyed Pete with suspicion. "You've duties to perform. Now get to them!" she snapped.

Pete didn't move a muscle. He eyed her with hauteur. The woman backed down under his steely stare. "Excuse me, *sir*, won't you please leave us? I have things to discuss with our new employee."

Pete dismissed her with a glance and smiled encouragingly at Aimee. Then with great dignity he walked out.

Aimee longed to accuse the woman of perfidy, but she knew her smartest course was to bide her time. If they knew she was privy to their plans, they'd change their strategy, dangerously so. So, when Mrs. Tuttle asked her to follow so she could be fitted with her gown, Aimee nodded in apparent unconcern.

In her bedroom upstairs, a dressmaker awaited. Aimee swallowed down nausea as she saw the garment the woman held. It was a gold silk gown styled exactly like the one in the portrait. She pretended ignorance and allowed herself to be fitted.

Both women nodded in satisfaction when Aimee turned to face them. "Perfect!" approved Mrs. Tuttle.

The gown did indeed suit her, clinging to her slim form with loving detail. It had long, tight sleeves and full skirts that rustled with her every movement. The sleeves and neckline were bordered with fine, creamy lace. The heart-shaped bodice was almost indecent, cut lower than the gown in the portrait, but when she tried to pull it up, Mrs. Tuttle shoved her hands away.

"Leave it. Remove it so we can have it ready for tonight."

Aimee did so gladly, her skin crawling with distaste at their cruelty. There had to be a way to stop them. She must find Pete. Accordingly, when Mrs. Tuttle turned to her after the seamstress left, she yawned.

"Excuse me. I didn't sleep well last night. Would you object if I lay down for a brief nap?"

Aimee caught the woman's small sigh of relief. "Of course. Dinner is not until eight. I'll come about seven to help you get ready."

Aimee gritted her teeth and forced herself to nod agreeably. "That will be fine."

The minute the woman was gone, Aimee rushed to the door and listened. When the footsteps receded, she opened the door a crack and seeing the corridor empty, slipped into the hallway. She passed a room with a door slightly ajar. She shrank against the wall when she recognized Webb's voice, trying to steady her breathing.

"Are you certain she suspects nothing? What was Pete talking to her about in the library?"

Mrs. Tuttle answered, "I don't know, but she made no complaint when we fitted her with the gown. Surely he's not foolish enough to share his suspicions with her. He has no proof anyway."

Webb's voice quivered with fury and hatred. "I'd put nothing past that deformed little bastard. Always watching me, condemning me."

"Can't you convince Winston to get rid of him? Sometime

when he's in his cups, plant a few suspicions . . ."

"I've already tried that. It's one of the few times he refuses to listen to me. Said his wife trusted him with her life and he'd do the same. No, if we get rid of him, we'll have to do it another way."

Aimee heard footsteps coming. She missed the rest of the conversation as she ducked into an unused room. After what seemed an age, she finally heard Mrs. Tuttle and Webb go downstairs.

She followed as quietly as she could, poking her head around the corner to examine the hallway below. For once it was empty. Her heart leaped to her throat as she realized now was her chance. If she was to make it back to Luke, she must leave now. She didn't dare return for her clothes. She felt a pang at leaving the carving and silver jewelry, but escape was more imperative.

She flew down the stairs and tried the door, but, to her horror, it was locked. She heard someone coming, so she fled into the library. She hid behind the door, her palms sweating as it opened. She slumped with relief when she saw Pete.

She hissed his name. He started, turning to face her. "Here you are. I looked for you in your room. I think I can get you out of the house now, if you'll follow me. Most of the servants are at luncheon, and the others think you're in bed."

Aimee realized it was his steps she'd heard upstairs. Her heart seemed to grow within her chest at the thought of seeing Luke again. But, as she took a step toward Pete, the portrait over the fireplace caught her eye. Those haunting green eyes seemed to plead with her not to leave; they pleaded for Aimee to help Pete save her husband.

Aimee struggled fiercely between her conscience and her need to see Luke, but then she sighed, defeated by those entreating green eyes. She could survive another day without Luke. What Webb was trying to do was indescribably ugly, and she'd never forgive herself if the earl lost everything to that scoundrel.

Webb's ugly words rang in her ears. Before she left, she had to help Pete. He was a gallant man, who put his own life at risk to help both her and the earl. She couldn't leave him to face those villains alone.

She turned to Pete resolutely. "I'm not ready to leave yet. I'm in no immediate danger, but you are. I overheard Webb talking to Mrs. Tuttle. They both hate you and will stop at nothing to get rid of you." Aimee ignored his stunned expression. He'd suspected the worst of Webb, but he had never expected this woman to decline freedom and safety. She went to the desk to remove the ledger.

Pete's surprised look turned into a scowl. He strode forward. "I'm well aware of their plans, but I don't need your protection. Now no arguments. You'd best escape while you can."

Aimee sensed his wounded pride, and she hastened to reassure him. "I don't doubt your abilities. You've held those awful people at bay this long. But won't you let me help? As long as they belive me malleable, I'll have a chance of warning the earl. Maybe I can even collect proof of their guilt. I've had some experience with accounts. Won't you at least let me peruse them? They've tried to use me to ruin an unhappy man. Willing or not, I'm involved."

Pete started to shake his head, but he was defeated by the courageous, stubborn look in those clear green eyes. Instead of voicing his doubts, he found himself snapping, "Oh, very well! Just like a woman, having to interfere in everything . . ." Still grumbling, he came forward to assist her.

He stood beside her, waiting for her to open the ledger, but Aimee bit her lip, hesitating. She didn't think she was in real danger, but if something should happen to her, Luke must know. She couldn't tell him where she was yet, for he'd rashly appear to drag her back to the *Mercury*. But, it would be wise to tell Pete who she was now, just in case.

She sat down at the desk and folded her hands on the ledger. "Pete, my name is really not Lingstrom. It's Garrison. My husband is Luke Garrison. He's on his steamer, the *Mercury*, berthed in the old wharves. I want you to know, just in case. . . ."

Their eyes met grimly. Pete nodded. "I understand. I'm familiar with the name. Why the devil such a man is letting his wife run around London unprotected is more than I can figure."

He waited for her to elaborate, but she just smiled and opened the ledger. She didn't see his half-anxious, half-admiring look as he studied her bent head. He stepped close, his nose twitching at the fresh scent of her perfume.

"Why did you leave your husband?" he persisted.

Aimee looked up at him. His ugly little face was sympathetic, ready to accept the emotions raging within her. Aimee opened her mouth to evade him, but somehow the truth came tumbling out. She told him the whole story, deleting only the intimate details. She spoke of her hasty marriage, her confusion, her disgust with her cowardice, her fear that Luke wouldn't want her now.

Pete patted her shoulder. "Oh, he'll want you all right. I've not a doubt of that. Do you love him?"

Aimee's eyes softened to greenish gold moss. "I'll love him until the day I die," she said softly, her face so radiant that Pete looked away.

He heaved a sigh, hoping Aimee's choice made more sense than Marie's had. Briefly as he had known her, he felt protective of this small, vibrant girl. She reminded him of Marie only in the physical sense. Aimee's personality was stronger, more determined, but just as appealing. He wondered if a man who had known only wealth and privilege appreciated what he had. Pete's mouth tightened. Aimee placed no blame on Luke Garrison, who obviously didn't know how to treasure a real woman.

"He's a lucky man," he said, summing up his feelings, then he bent over Aimee's shoulder to watch her work.

Aimee straightened in her chair, her emotions calmer now that she had given voice to them. She looked at the man next to her, wondering at the hardships mapped into his battered features. He had overcome a disability far worse than her bad leg with a courage and moral fiber that humbled her and made her even more determined to help him. Without thinking, she kissed his cheek, totally unaware of the effect her soft lips had on him.

"Thank you for listening." When she met his eyes, her admiration for him was clear to see.

Pete turned a fiery red, dropping his gaze back to the ledger. He clenched his hands. Aimee turned to the ledger as he composed himself. For over an hour, they stared at the neat columns of figures, adding them, cross-checking them, and adding them again. Nothing seemed amiss. Pete cursed and prepared to slam the ledger shut.

"There's nothing. If he's embezzling yet, he's doing it very cleverly."

Aimee stayed his hand, her eyes firing into a brilliant gold. She had an idea. Pete looked at the delicate hand covering his, to her face. His own eyes darkened.

This time Aimee surveyed the columns again more pointedly. Then it hit her. The figures had been slipped cleverly, small amounts listed in each expense column as miscellaneous. All the columns tallied at the bottom, but there was no explanation for those mysterious "miscellaneous" expenses. They combined to create a hefty total. Aimee speculated that, somewhere in London, there was an account in Webb's name that equaled the money missing here. She had turned to tell Pete of her discovery when the door slammed back on its hinges.

Webb stormed in, his eyes narrowing to pinpoints of light when he saw Aimee. "Your rest was very brief, my dear." He didn't give Aimee a chance to reply, striding up to Pete to hiss, "You slimy little bastard, how dare you go through my accounts? This is the last straw. Leave, or I'll have the constable after you."

Pete scoffed at the threat. "For what? Trying to save the earl from your greed?" Webb gestured to the two brawny footmen outside to come in.

Aimee's heart lurched. Hers and Pete's only hope was to brazen it out. She frowned, as if puzzled, and asked, "But what is amiss? I just wanted to take my first look at the accounts. Pete merely showed me where the ledger was kept."

Webb snorted. "You just couldn't wait to get to work, right?"

Aimee nodded firmly. "Indeed. I intended to take a nap, but I couldn't sleep. I want to leave the books straight for the next person. That's why you asked me to stay, isn't it?" Her innocent expression could not quite hide her disgusted anger.

He smiled slyly. "You'll earn your pay, all right. Beginning tonight." He shoved her roughly to the door, ordering one of the footmen to usher her to her room. A guard was to be posted. Aimee struggled, but had not a chance against the footman's strength.

An ugly look on his face, Webb turned on Pete, gesturing for the other servant to grab him. Pete stood motionless until the last moment, then he ducked neatly between the approaching man's legs, and hooked an ankle as he came out the other side. The man crashed to the floor. Pete swung to the door, only to find his way blocked by Webb.

When the other servant tried to force Aimee out the door, she balked, and waited for events to unfold. She was elated when Pete displayed a jeering grin, then folded his compact body together and somersaulted through the window, his feet hitting the walk at a run.

Aimee hurried up the stairs willingly now, eager to see if Pete got away. She ran to the window in time to see him make a thumb's-up gesture in her direction and melt into the crowd. By the time Webb and the footman scrambled out the front door, he was gone.

Aimee was in ecstasy until she realized she was well and truly alone. She nibbled her fingernail—a bad habit—trying to decide what to do. She thrust her finger away. She knew Pete would be back—but could she afford to wait? She hadn't had a chance to tell him of her discovery. She wondered if Webb was suspicious, but dismissed the idea. If he knew what she had discovered, he'd kill her instead of lock her in her room.

Aimee looked out her window to assess her chances of escape by that avenue. But a sheer drop to the ground made her stomach reel. She had no option but to wait, and hope that Pete could find Luke from the few directions she'd given him. She leaned against the window, trembling with mingled fear and anticipation. Aimee whispered his name, repeated it, amazed as her fears faded because of it. Nothing could happen to her now that Luke was coming to take her back. There were too many things she had to tell him, too much love she had to give him. God would not be so cruel as to take her from Luke now.

Aimee was so comforted that even the thought of his inevitable anger no longer troubled her. She stood in the bright sunlight, her face basking in the sun. She was warmed by the glow emanating from within herself, as well as by the light of the sun.

But just then the door clicked open and an angry person strode in.

Pete glanced at his watch, cursed and ran faster. How the hell could he have been so stupid as to leave without his purse? He'd tried to barter his watch for the fare to the docks, but his dishevelled clothing and the blood on his face from broken window glass had discouraged the frightened cabbie. He had driven on, ignoring Pete's plea to wait.

Pete leaned against a lamppost, his chest heaving. He saw a bobbie up ahead and almost hailed him, but then restrained the impulse. It was his word against Webb's at the moment, and his past experience with the police indicated they would believe a respectable estate manager of one of London's largest fortunes, not a battered dwarf rescued from a circus. They would probably regard Aimee with equal suspicion. Webb would paint her as a whore who had left her husband for the earl.

No, it was best Aimee not be involved with the police at all. Pete waited until the bobbie rounded a corner, then he ran on, praying Aimee would be safe until he could return with Garrison. If subconsciously he worried that maybe even Aimee's husband wouldn't believe him, he couldn't pause long enough to let it sink in.

The day was wearing on, and the longer Aimee was trapped inside the townhouse, the greater were her chances of not seeing tomorrow's sunrise.

When Mrs. Tuttle came to help her dress, Aimee ignored the woman's suspicious glare. She obeyed the stiff commands barked to her as quietly as possible. She even stifled her fury when the woman styled her hair after Marie's. Aimee held on to her temper, knowing time was her only friend at the moment.

"Ma'am, why was I locked in? And why did Mr. Webb object to my looking at his accounts?"

Mrs. Tuttle appraised her sharply, relaxing a little when Aimee's eyes remained clear and calm as a Midlands pond. "The little man you were speaking with is dangerous. You were locked in for your own protection. And Mr. Webb objected only to his snooping, not to your starting work."

Aimee yearned to laugh in the woman's face, but instead she nodded thoughtfully. "I see. But what has this man done?"

Mrs. Tuttle clasped a diamond necklace around Aimee's neck and added a matching bracelet before answering. "He is a thief and a blackmailer, but we haven't been able to convince the earl of his unsavory nature."

Aimee burned inside. How dare they foist their own crime onto Pete? But she managed a creditable imitation of horror. She shivered. "I thought there was something sinister about him." Inwardly she shriveled at the lie, but Mrs. Tuttle misunderstood her shiver. She rewarded her with an approving smile.

The woman's fierce suspicion had been lulled by the time she escorted Aimee down the stairs. "You will dine with the earl. Be kind to him. He's a lonely man."

Webb was seated at one end of the table, and the earl was slumped at the other when she entered the dining room. Aimee obeyed Webb's gesture to sit down beside the earl, though she longed to fly out at him, unveiling his villainous treason.

Webb cleared his throat. "Winston, there's someone I want you to meet."

Aimee watched the bent brown head lift slowly. Her throat tightened at his haggard look. She sat motionless as glazed blue eyes peered into hers, looked away, then flew back to her face. The earl squinted, as if afraid to believe his eyes. His features were regular, and he must once have been a very handsome man, but the ravages of drink had left their mark.

"Marie," he whispered, reaching out a trembling hand to touch her cheek.

When he felt the warm reality of flesh, he groaned and rose unsteadily, then pulled Aimee out of her chair into his arms.

Aimee took the opportunity to whisper desperately, "No, your lordship. My name is Aimee! You're being duped by . . ." but his hungry mouth silenced her frantic explanation. Aimee gently tried to pry herself free, but, even drunk, Winston was much stronger. Her tender heart ached at the longing, the need he communicated to her. It was a need that brought to mind the face of another. She lay placidly in his arms, allowing him the brief comfort of her body.

Webb finally pulled her away. The earl blinked, swaying, and reached for her again, but Webb soothed, "Not now, Winston. Marie has to prepare for bed. You'll see her again later."

Aimee glared at Webb and whirled to warn the earl. "He's lying! He's trying to—" But Webb dragged her from the room before she could complete her sentence. He shoved her up the stairs. Mrs. Tuttle waited in her bedroom, unaware of the near disaster below. She was holding green lace in her hands.

Aimee now knew the plan, and found all pretense impossible. Just as they had planned. "You disgust me, both of you. How can you be so heartless?"

Webb laughed nastily. "That spineless jellyfish deserves what he gets. He's no use for his own wealth. Give him a bottle of gin and an alley to wallow in, and he'll be just as happy."

Aimee backed away, fighting down nausea. She looked about for a weapon, something, anything to foil them, but Webb cornered her and wrapped his hands around her throat.

"You'll do what we tell you or I'll make a gift of you to the dogs in the alleyway. No one will know better. We'll dress you in rags, and the dogs will so mutilate you, you'll be no longer recognizable. They'll bury you in the pauper's cemetery. Do you get my meaning?" When she grew even paler, he smiled with satisfaction and said, "Yes, I see you do. Now, you'll wear this gown and spend the night with his bloody lordship. If you perform well, in the morning, you'll go free. Which is it to be?" His hands tightened slightly about her throat, digging the diamonds into her skin.

Aimee met his eyes boldly, ignoring the frightened pounding of her heart. "What if I go to the police?"

Webb interjected, "So? It will be your—a foreigner's— word against mine. And never have we so misstepped that an illegality could be found. In fact, everything's quite legal, my little Norwegian whore. . . ." Aimee flinched, deciding the man was mad. His eyes glimmered with it. "In the morning, the earl will be so grateful to me for finding his precious Marie he'll reward me with full power of attorney. He'll go on a long trip I've been urging."

"Do you really think he'll believe I'm Marie?" Aimee asked, trying to upset his smugness.

"All cats are gray in the dark," the man sneered. "The earl will remember what he wants to remember. Then, after one night of ecstasy"—his voice mocked the beauty of the word—"when you disappear, he'll drink himself to death even more rapidly, with my blessing."

He jerked the lovely nightgown out of Mrs. Tuttle's hands and threw it at her. "Dress. Now. Or I will do it for you."

When his eyes ran over her, Aimee felt as if she'd been caressed by a snake. She shivered in disgust. "At least allow me the courtesy of privacy."

Webb bowed mockingly. "Certainly milady. But let me warn you, if you whisper anything but sweet nothings into his lordship's ear, you'll regret it. You won't see the light of morning." When she seemed to slump in despair, he cooed, "Five minutes." He and Mrs. Tuttle exited.

The minute they were gone, Aimee straightened. She muttered expletives she'd heard on the *Mercury*, too angry to care that she didn't know what they meant. Aimee vowed Webb's threats would not frighten her. She had to think, map out her plan of action. Somehow she had to survive the night until Luke saved her, and she had to survive it unviolated by the earl. Yet if she didn't let the earl violate her, Webb would kill her with his bare hands. He would probably do it anyway, even if she complied. How could he let her wander the city free, knowing she knew his secret? He was too unscrupulous to allow that. Aimee had reached an impasse.

Needing to vent her fury, she tore the beautiful necklace off and threw it against the wall. Instead of the solid thunk she expected to hear, there was the distinctive shattering of glass. Aimee bent to examine the damage, her eyes widening when she fingered the splinters: the jewelry was fake. Like Webb.

When the earl had glanced at the necklace, the light of recognition kindled his eyes. He would never have given his beloved Marie glass for diamonds, so that left only one explanation. Webb had stolen the real jewels and substituted the copy.

Her disgust for Webb grew.

Aimee used a towel to sweep the mess under the bed. She flung off her clothes with feverish haste. Now she had two concrete pieces of evidence. If the jewels should be found by the police in Webb's room . . .

She jerked the gown over her head, wondering what was taking Pete and Luke so long. She needed their help *now*. Aimee pulled the negligee over the gown, her hands icy with nervousness and worry. If Luke should burst in on her with the earl, would he listen to her explanation or turn away in disgust? Aimee dismissed the thought almost before it was born. Somehow she knew he would believe her, trust her, even as she trusted him.

"Luke, dear love, come soon. I need you," she whispered.
Love. The word tasted so good on her lips, and it filled the
secret chambers of her heart. She turned to face the door as it
opened, fortified by the smiling face in her mind.

At the precise moment she so tenderly called up Luke's
image, he stared into his brandy with a rancor that bordered
on hatred, seeing the face that had haunted his every minute
for two days. His harsh whisper, "Aimee," was a bitter
sound, for indeed in this moment he hated her. She made his
heart ache cruelly. He had never known such agony in his
life. If this was love, he wanted no part of it.

For two days they had searched, and they hadn't turned up
a single clue to locate her. The police were little help, for they
could only retrace the steps Luke and his men had already
taken. They questioned dockworkers and cab drivers who
frequented the area.

One surly fellow had finally admitted to taking her to
Lombard Street, but he'd left her on the sidewalk after she
came out of the bank. Jimmy had to pull Luke away when
Luke tried to throttle the man. They questioned every hotel
in the area, but not one reported a guest fitting Aimee's
description. It never occurred to them to check the supper
rooms. . . .

The Garrison ship was scheduled to sail in two days, and if
Luke didn't find her before then, he'd have to send the
Mercury on without them. Luke would have to stay, looking,
alone. For the first time in his life, he barely thought about
his duties. Even his responsibilities as captain and the
Garrison heir became meaningless under the force of his
despair, worsened with each passing hour. Hope was dying a
slow, tortured death, draining his spirit of the will to go on.

Luke stared at his great bed, that bed where he had once
had dreams of possessing her, leading her into delight after
delight, ecstasy engulfing them until neither knew where
their pleasure began or ended. Now, he had to face the
thought that he might never see her again. Never see her
tongue on her lips after feasting on a rich dessert; never see
her defy him, head flung high with pride; never win one of
those sweet, trusting smiles he worked so hard for. Never
hold her and lavish on her all the loving tenderness she made

him feel—to his own amazement—in her presence. Oh God, make her come back to me, he prayed. I love her, I need her, don't take her from me. . . .

He slumped his head, afraid he prayed for naught. Elusive, darting fairy of his dreams, she had flitted into his life, turned his world upside down and flitted out again, leaving a chasm with only her ghost. Suddenly he couldn't bear the pain.

His pain was so agonizing that he had to call up rage to blunt it. He hated her for his vulnerability. He hated her for opening up a door of happiness, giving him someone to share himself with at last, then slamming the door in his face and condemning him to this soul-scorching loneliness.

"To you, sweet Aimee," he toasted drunkenly. "May you feel all the misery you've caused me, wherever you are."

His words echoed in the vast stateroom like a reproach. Despising his impotence, he flung the glass of brandy at the bed, and stained the expensive spread. The sorrow he'd held at bay became too much for him. He buried his face in his hands and wept.

"Forgive me, Aimee, I don't mean it. Come back to me, love, please, come back . . . ," he whispered achingly into his hands.

His tortured emotions wore him out. The sleep that had eluded him for two days finally came. He slumped against his chair, too exhausted to waken even when his head sagged against the chair arm. It was dark when Jimmy entered and shook him.

Luke groaned and heaved himself to a sitting position, rubbing the side of his stiff neck. He focused bleary eyes on Jimmy's excited face, blinked, then came to full alertness.

"You've had word?" he snapped, his heart surging back to life.

Jimmy led a strange-looking man forward. The man was a dwarf. "This is Pete. He says he knows where Aimee is, Luke." Jimmy's voice rang with hope. Luke slumped back in his chair, relieved. He offered a silent, fervent prayer. Then he opened his eyes and looked at his savior.

He rose, realized how difficult it was for him to see Pete's face, and hastily sat back down. He gritted his teeth, clasped the arms of his chair and forced himself to calm down, despite his growing worry at the man's bedraggled appearance. He looked as if he'd been in a fight.

"Won't you be seated, sir?" Luke indicated a chair.

Pete pulled himself up and sat, his legs dangling from the chair. He stared boldly, assessingly, at Luke. Luke waited, and when Pete remained silent, Luke leaned forward and clasped his hands so tightly, the knuckles turned white. "Well? What do you know of my wife? If it's money you're waiting for, I'll reward you handsomely. Lead me to her."

Pete looked offended. "I'm here to take you to her for her sake, not for any reward. . . ."

Luke cut him off by surging to his feet. "Well let's go, then. Where is she? Is she in danger?" Luke hustled the little man out the door.

The man cast him a cautious look. "I don't think I can explain it all now. . . ." He studied Luke as if to assess the depth of his anger at Aimee.

Jimmy took a step after them. He paused, went to a chest and removed a pistol, thrusting it at Luke when he caught up with them. Luke took it without a word, not even breaking stride, and ordered Jimmy to stay and look after the ship. Jimmy hurried off, shouting that he would find Potter and some others to go with him.

Pete had to run at full speed to keep up with Luke's long-legged, impatient strides. When they reached the main deck, Pete suddenly stopped. Luke whirled on him with a growl, but Pete crossed his arms and stared defiantly into Luke's angry face.

"I will not take a step or tell you a thing until I know you will not lay a hand on her. I don't know why she left you, but I know enough of her to believe she must have had a good reason. If I take you to her, you have to give me your word of honor that you won't hurt her."

Luke glared at Pete. The knifelike stare that had intimidated many powerful men glanced off Pete's steely eyes without effect. Luke's jaw clenched, but he nodded shortly.

"You have my word I will not beat her. Though she deserves to have her little bottom tanned until she can't sit down for a week. . . ." Pete pretended not to hear. He boldly preceded Luke down the gangplank.

Luke's temper mounted. His emotions had veered from utter despair to giddy hope in the last few minutes, and now this brash little man was deliberately trying to goad him for unfathomable reasons. Luke couldn't take time to find out

Pete's motives. He clamped down on his anger and followed the man, knowing he was the only link to Aimee. They rushed down the street and around a corner, looking for a cab. The men Jimmy had sent arrived seconds too late to see where they had gone.

"Where is she, then?" Luke forced his tone to civility.

Pete spat into the dirt. "Somewhere she shouldn't be—and wouldn't be if you'd loved her. Hail that cab."

Luke's jaw clenched, but he obeyed. After Pete was settled on the carriage seat, he snarled, "Well, are you going to tell me where she is now, or waste more time and put Aimee in more danger?"

Pete met Luke's fiery stare coolly. He bit off the address to the cabby, tipped his hat over his face and sank back in his seat, intent on keeping to himself for the moment.

Luke watched him closely. What a strange man. And how the hell did Aimee end up with such a fervent, unlikely champion? Pete was obviously smitten with Aimee, for Luke recognized the same jealousy in the dwarf that had tortured him. What had Aimee done to encourage him? Luke's temper was frayed almost to the snapping point when Pete lifted his head and peered up at him.

He seemed ready to speak. Words spun from his mouth as he regaled Luke with what had happened to Aimee since she entered the sumptuous, expensive house. Luke paled more with each word. When Pete finished, he was so horrified at the danger Aimee was in that it took him a moment to gather his wits.

He burst out, "You fool, why did you leave her? What's to prevent this Webb from killing her?" Pete's calm response took a moment to penetrate his raging fear.

"Simple greed. She's too valuable to him, at least until she's served her purpose. I'd wager we have until the morning. That is . . ."

For the first time, Pete seemed uncomfortable. Luke's eyes narrowed. He sensed why Pete hesitated, and despite his violent repulsion, he voiced his fear.

"Webb won't . . . take her, will he?" he asked hoarsely.

Pete shook his head. Luke slumped with relief, only to stiffen again in fear when Pete added, "But he might well give her to the earl."

There was no sound between them but the clip-clopping of

horse's hooves and the click of a well-oiled gun as Luke rotated the chamber of his pistol to be sure it was loaded.

Aimee stood in the darkness, trying to prop up her courage as the door was shut and locked behind her. "Marie?" came a husky voice from the bed.

Aimee took a deep breath and said, "Sir, please listen. I'm not your wife. I only look like her. Webb is using me to control you, to steal from you." She waited, praying he would believe her. Their lives depended on it.

The voice that answered sounded so forlorn that Aimee's eyes burned with tears. "I don't care. I'd give all I possess for the chance of holding Marie in my arms again."

Aimee groped by the bed, sighing with relief when she touched the lantern. She turned it up and sat down beside the earl.

Aimee had forgotten her seductive attire, and the lust it might ignite. She didn't question why she was so determined to help. Was it Marie's haunting portrait, her admiration of Pete, her pity for the earl, or her need to prove she could fend for herself that made her so determined to foil Webb? Aimee didn't pause to discover the answer; she knew only that she must keep this man from self-destruction.

The Earl of Wimberly sat up in bed. His shoulders were broad and furred with dark hair against the pale sheets. He eyed her slim form, the flame of the lantern reflecting his passion. Aimee remembered then her own alluring attire.

Aimee looked down and gasped, drawing the negligee more tightly about her, but the spidery lace provided scant cover over the sheer silk beneath. Her hand shook a little as she forced icy fingers around Winston's chin, raising it until he looked at her face instead of her body.

"Look at me. Am I your Marie?"

He searched her eyes, reading the sweetness, the sympathy there. His head slumped forward on his chest. "No. I'm sober enough to know you're obviously not here willingly, much as I'd love to pretend otherwise. You have my leave to go."

Aimee stayed where she was, eyeing his bent head. He shifted away, snapping, "Go! Don't pity me. Just leave me in peace."

Aimee shook her head gently. "You'll never be in peace as

long as you behave like this. Marie would not have wanted grief to kill you. Hasn't it occurred to you that she'd be devastated at your behavior?"

His head snapped up in shock, and it was obvious he'd been too full of self-pity to consider this. Aimee continued more forcefully, "Pete was almost killed today trying to help you. If you don't snap out of this condition, Webb will not only take your fortune, he'll kill Pete to keep him silent." She kept to herself her suspicion Webb would very likely blot her out as well. "Do you want that?"

He paled, looking a little sick at the picture she painted. "No, of course not!" He rubbed his forehead, muttering, "God, I need a drink." This time, when he looked at Aimee, anger rather than lust burned in his eyes. "Marie loved Pete like a brother. Did Webb really try to kill him?"

"He would have, if Pete hadn't gotten away. I've discovered evidence that Webb is already embezzling funds and stealing your wife's jewels. He also threatened me if I didn't cooperate. . . ." They were too intent on their conversation to notice the stealthy footsteps at the door.

They started when the door flew open. Webb filled the gap, his face twisted with anger and greed. Aimee looked at the pistol in his hand and swallowed, this time consumed by fear.

She felt the earl inching his hand to the drawer beside his bed and blurted, "Your game is over. The earl knows the truth and will be on his guard now. You might as well give up."

Webb cocked the pistol and warned, "Winston, if you make another move toward that gun you keep beside your bed, I'll kill you and tell the police this little slut did it because you discovered her stealing from you."

Winston fell back against the pillows, releasing a sob. Aimee decided his frustration made him healthier than he'd been in months since it burned some of the drink from his system. She'd accomplished something, at least. She'd stoked his sense of reality: he had a firmer grasp on it. But had the truth come to him too late? For both of them?

Webb mocked them. "I guess I'll have to cut my losses. I've a tidy little sum laid by already. Too bad my plans went awry, but serves me right for being so soft-hearted. Should have killed Pete months ago, then this little bitch never would have figured out what was going on. . . ."

Winston interrupted harshly, "You degenerate. The mere sight of you sickens me. You'll never get away with this. I'll hound you over England, the continent, to hell itself. . . ."

"To hell is right. Because that's where you'll be before the night is over. Everyone knows how you drink. Accidentally spilled a bottle and set yourself afire. Such a tragedy it will be." Webb's laugh was vile. The glimmer of insanity Aimee had glimpsed before seemed stronger.

Suddenly, she knew their only hope was to act.

Webb was too busy enjoying his taunts to notice Aimee's darting movement. She jerked up the Chinese vase beside the bed and flung it at Webb's head. He ducked, but not quickly enough. It glanced off his temple, sending him to his knees long enough for Aimee to leap up and grab his gun away. The earl bounded out of bed, his own pistol clutched in his hand. If the situation had not been dire, it would have been ludicrous—the earl stood unsteadily on his feet in nothing but his drawers.

Webb struggled to his feet, whitening as he found both weapons trained on his heart.

Aimee and the earl exchanged a jubilant grin. The earl opened his mouth. A clamor from downstairs diverted his attention briefly, but long enough for Webb to snatch the gun from his hand. He shoved it in the earl's ribs.

"Drop the gun, or he dies," Webb hissed between his teeth.

Aimee hesitated. He apparently didn't believe she had gumption enough to fire. He was a full arm's length away from the earl, his body rimmed by the light behind him. Aimee dropped her head as if in defeat, then she quickly pulled the trigger. She'd never shot a gun before, but she reasoned that she was too close to miss. Webb looked stunned at the red tide staining his shoulder. The pistol dropped out of his numb hand to the floor. Aimee kept the gun leveled on him, not trusting him even now.

This was the sight that met Luke's eyes when he burst into the room. He blinked, unable to believe it was Aimee, attired in a revealing negligee, standing with a smoking gun on a wounded man. In a daze, he shoved his gun into the belt of his pants.

Aimee stiffened as she sensed his presence. She turned her head. Her face lit up with a glow so radiant that the little man at Luke's side winced. Aimee flung the gun away.

Meanwhile the earl had whipped on a robe and now grabbed Webb roughly. Winston ignored his erstwhile manager's cry of pain as he forced the wounded man past Pete and down the stairs.

Pete muttered, "I'll fetch the police." He retreated, shutting the door softly behind him.

Aimee was oblivious to everything but Luke. She rushed to him and threw her arms around his neck, laughing, crying, apologizing.

Luke caught her and squeezed her fiercely. He ran his hands over her, afraid to believe he had her safe at last. But she didn't disappear like the ghost that had haunted him for the last two days. He sighed, resting his chin on her shining curls, too relieved for his anger to flare. The questions and reproaches could come later. Right now he only wanted to savor the feel of her in his arms.

They were silent, letting their desperate coiled clutch of arms and hands express their feelings. Silence prevailed in the sumptuous bedchamber. There was no ticking clock, no breath of wind, no creak of floorboard to disturb their utter concentration on each other.

Aimee moved away at last, wanting to get the chastising over with. She peeked up at Luke, then bowed her head and waited meekly for his tirade.

His voice was hoarse when he asked, "Aimee, have you been harmed?"

She shook her head. He heaved a great sigh of relief and reached out to take her back in his arms. When he saw the way his hands trembled, he drew them back in disgust.

"Aimee, right now I'm too relieved to demand explanations. I only have one question to ask, and I expect an honest answer."

She flung her head back to look at him, flushing when his eyes dropped to her body, then landed gently on her face. "Do you want to come back with me? Not because of duty, fear or remorse, but because you *want* to?"

Aimee didn't hesitate. She met his searching eyes directly, making no attempt to disguise her own feelings. "Yes, Luke, I want you."

A shudder shook his tall frame, but this time his hand was steady when he held it out. "Come, then."

For once the command in his voice, his eyes, his very stance, didn't anger her. She welcomed it. He had shown by his actions today that his commitment matched her own.

She took his hand and followed him out of the room into the corridor. To her, the future seemed ablaze with promise. The hallway seemed brilliant, though only a few lanterns lit it. Luke paused long enough to wrap his jacket around her before leading her down the stairs.

Luke would have hustled Aimee straight to the cab, but Aimee pulled free and looked around. "Where is Pete? He brought you here, didn't he? I must tell him good-bye."

Luke snapped, "No, we're leaving *now*, before you decide to run away from me again. That little man would be only too happy to help you."

Aimee looked at him, some of her happiness fading. "Don't be ridiculous. He put himself in danger to protect me. I must go thank him." She ignored Luke's glower and went in search of Pete.

She found him in the library with the earl. She pulled Luke's jacket close about her, but it couldn't shield the pretty length of her legs. She flushed as she realized that both men were staring. She felt Luke at her back, but ignored him and murmured, "Pete, I wanted to let you know what I discovered." Quickly she explained about the diamonds and the books. She then turned to the earl. "His intent to kill you is sufficient to hold him, sir, but I thought you both should know. Are the police on the way?"

His eyes on the floor, Pete nodded. Aimee frowned, wondering what was wrong with him.

Winston glanced curiously at Luke's poised figure, then turned to her. "You have my deepest gratitude, Mrs. Garrison. Pete has explained the situation to me. Mrs. Tuttle and Webb are locked in the pantry until the constable arrives. The servants are there to make sure. Those two will get their due, I promise. I'm sorry you were ever involved. If there's any way I can repay you . . ."

"Take command of your life again. That's all. It's what Marie would want."

Winston's eyes clouded, then shifted to the beautiful woman in the portrait above the fireplace. Grief glimmered in his eyes, then faded. He sighed softly and agreed, "I believe you're right." He dropped an arm about Pete's shoulders and added, "If I forget, I'll have this little man to remind me."

Aimee saw Pete wince. She slipped from Luke's impatient presence hovering nearby and bent to hug Pete, whispering for his ears alone, "Good-bye, great man. I'll never forget you. And I want you to know that's the way I'll always remember you—as one of the biggest men I've ever known in the only ways that count."

Pete hugged her back with great emotion. She kissed him fully on his quivering mouth. He cradled her face when she tried to pull away, and they shared a deep, intense look that made Luke clench his hands in impatience. Aimee's throat tightened at Pete's sad expression.

"I'll never forget you either, Aimee Garrison. Be happy with that . . . impatient . . . husband of yours."

Aimee smiled through her tears. "I will," she vowed. She straightened, waved and blindly walked from the townhouse to the curbside, Luke remaining behind. She was touched to find her bag strapped neatly on top of the cab. Pete must have had a servant fetch it for her. She was too eager to escape the driver's prying eyes to ask him to pass it down. She rushed inside the cab.

Luke shook the earl's hand, then Pete's. His smile was frozen as he offered a bundle of notes. "My thanks to you, Pete. I'd like to reward you for bringing me to Aimee."

Pete straightened, looking insulted. "The only reward I want is for Aimee to be taken care of and cherished as she deserves. Understand, Garrison?"

Luke stiffened with hauteur, but relaxed as he sensed Pete's genuine concern. "You have my promise on it. . . . Well, the best of luck to both of you." He hurried out to join Aimee in the cab.

She swallowed when she saw him. He was tense, his black eyes brooding. He struggled with his jealousy, but couldn't stifle a warning. "This is the last time you run from me into the arms of another man, wife. After tonight, you'll have no doubt whatsoever about where you belong. Understand?"

Aimee met his smoldering coal-black eyes boldly. She merely nodded. He raked a possessive stare over her body, then turned to appraise the London scenery, clenching his teeth. Fear and anger had become, with his relief, an overpowering need to know the deepest intimacy with her.

Had he seen the look on Aimee's face, his control would have been pushed beyond his limits. She watched him, her skin prickling, a strange liquidity invading her lower parts. She held a hand to her fluttering heart, the smile of Eve on her face as she decided that for once she welcomed her husband's arrogance, and lusty suggestions.

PART IV

Each happy hour thou hast secured will cost the like in grief. If many follow, still be sure the lending space is brief. There will soon come a sorrow time with sighs for every smile. The penalties are mounting fast at double rate the while . . . Too much of laughter gavest thou, tears requite it now.

—Bjørnstjerne Bjørnson, *Marie Stuart,* "Taylor's Song"

Chapter Eleven

It was dawn by the time they reached the docks. The sun peeked above the horizon, painting the clouds gold, just as their carriage jerked to a halt. Aimee stretched sensuously under the gentle finger-rays of the sun that massaged her white skin to the color of blushing rose petals.

Luke reached out to touch the exquisite buds peeking above the low-cut robe before he caught himself. With a frustrated groan, he jerked his hands back and shoved open the carriage door. Aimee smiled at the look on his face as he launched himself out of the carriage to pay the driver.

She stretched again, enjoying her new, heady power. Her strong, possessive darling was no more able to control his desire for her than she could control her love for him. It was a beginning, at least.

Aimee looked out the open window, admiring the crimson clouds arching over their heads in a warm canopy of hues. The soft morning breeze caressed her face as pleasurably as the silk on her bare skin. Aimee lifted her face to the wind and the sun. These earthy pleasures intensified her anticipation of the even more sensual delights to come.

When Luke reached inside for her impatiently, the seductive smile she wore sent bolts of desire through his aroused body like lightning. He froze, his heart leaping from the confines of his chest as he gazed at her subtle feminine wiles. Dear God, he had hungered for this womanly response. Did he dare believe the promise in her eyes? He had never felt so uncertain of himself with a woman. What was it about Aimee that inevitably knotted his composure so he became a stumbling, fumbling schoolboy?

He took refuge in anger. Glaring at her, daring her to protest, he tightened his coat around her possessively, then pulled off his shirt to wrap around her legs. When she nudged her face against his throat and kissed the pounding hollow, he paled and almost dropped her. Biting off a curse, he scooped her into his arms and stomped up the *Mercury's* gangplank.

The fall of lace and silk at her bare feet swayed enticingly as he walked, but his mean glare was enough to discourage most dockworkers from staring. When he reached the main deck, he yelled at his own men, "Well, what are you looking at? Get back to work!"

Even when Jimmy hurried down from the bridge, a delighted grin on his face, Luke's savage expression did not ease. "See that we're not disturbed, under any circumstances. Have the bag removed from the cab."

Aimee wondered vaguely why she was not afraid. Perhaps because the exaltation swelling within her left no room for cowardice? Twice now Luke had risked physical injury to protect her. She had seen the gun in his hand when he burst into the room; she had seen the fury in his face as his gaze swept in the scene. Aimee thought humorously that Webb should be grateful for a mere shoulder wound. Luke would have damaged him far more if given the chance.

No, the rage vibrating in him from some primitive core wasn't frightening because it was mirrored in her: the desire to become one with him, to combine his powerful passion with her own.

They could not hold back their desires any longer. They were bare of all but the primal needs of man for woman, woman for man. Aimee knew now that this moment had been inevitable from their first meeting. She had struggled against it. She had sensed it would leave her defenseless, stripped of the pride and independence that had sustained her through her childhood illness and recovery. But Luke had told her not to forget—he, too, was vulnerable. Vulnerable because of his feelings for her.

Aimee smiled against Luke's throat in jubilation. They could *trust* each other. Nothing on this earth had thrilled her as much as the thought of being with Luke did now. If loving meant losing a measure of independence, then so be it. With someone you could trust, the rewards were far greater than the loss. And no other man could make her tremble with the merest touch, could give her this feeling of absolute happiness. At last, she welcomed her driving, primal urge to join with this wonderful male being.

And so, when Luke almost trotted the last few steps to his stateroom and propped his shoulder against the bulkhead to brace Aimee's weight so he could open the door, a slim, eager little hand was there before him. Luke stiffened. Slowly, almost fearfully, he looked into her face for the first time since coming aboard. His furious heartbeat lurched, then pulsed faster as she smiled knowingly at him. He had never seen her look so . . . free, as if her vibrant spirit had broken away from her fetters.

Their eyes remained locked as Luke shoved open the door and kicked it shut. He deliberately brushed every slim inch of her down his body as he set her on her feet. Narrowly, he watched for the slightest twitch of fear, but, to his amazement, she linked her hands behind his neck and pressed against him.

He took a deep breath and clasped her waist beneath the jacket, almost afraid to touch her. He could not bear it if she evaporated under his touch like the phantom of his dreams. If he was only imagining this willingness from the woman who consumed his thoughts, he would go mad. But when he tightened his hands on her waist and crushed her to him, she buried her hands in his hair and fondled the thick, unruly waves.

Their eyes locked intimately. "Today, I want you and I will have you. Nothing on this earth will stop me," Luke warned her boldly, searching one last time for any hesitation in her, for he knew that this alone *would* stop him.

Aimee's lids lowered. When she looked up again, her golden eyes were large and unwavering. "I'm running from you no longer. I want you, too, and I will have you. Nothing on this earth will stop me."

His hands shaking, Luke pushed the jacket off her shoulders. It fell to the floor, leaving her clothed in green mist and sunlight. He stepped back to consume her with his eyes. He could savor her at last. She stood straight and proud, the dark mahogany door a perfect backdrop to her white and silvered beauty.

Aimee was, at last, certain of her own alluring powers. The

hunger in his look, his heaving chest, his trembling hands were signs of an attraction too potent to dismiss. Luke wanted her. He wanted *her,* as she was, slim, contrary, willful, proud. When his roaming eyes finally landed on her face, she smiled.

It was a simple gesture, but it was one Luke would treasure to the end of his days. It was the smile of a temptress—the smile of a woman who knows herself desired and enjoys the feeling. It was the smile of a wife—a rebellious bride who has at last found more joy in loving than in defying. And it was the smile of a lover—the smile a woman bestows on the man who ignites her own deepest passions.

Luke's eyes stung with tears. He was no longer jealous; he no longer even cared that she'd run away from him. If his weeks of frustration, even the last two days of agony had been the price he had to pay for the promise contained in this smile, then every moment had been worth it. Her name on his lips, he went to her.

He nuzzled her temple, cradling her in his arms. "Sweet darling, tell me I'm not dreaming. Tell me you'll let me take you at last. . . ." His mind went blank with panic when she drew away and slowly shook her head.

She ran a finger over his mouth and contradicted softly, "No, darling devil, you've misunderstood. I'm not letting you take me. . . ." When his hands convulsed on her waist, she drew his mouth down to hers and whispered into it, "I'm not giving myself to you. I'm *with* you. I long for you in every way possible. . . ."

He fastened his lips over hers. The kiss they shared contained the heat of the sun. No longer did Aimee hesitate to show her love with the fullness of her generous heart and sensuous body; no longer did Luke demand with the arrogance of one afraid of rejection. Aimee opened her lips under his, enjoying his moist mouth with all the passion she'd smothered for so long. Luke, sure now of her response, reined in his exploding ardor to give her the tenderness she would now desire.

He broke away and put her from him, his hands caressing her bare shoulders. He devoured her with his eyes, from head to toe, torn between impatience and the desire to savor this moment.

Aimee wondered at the almost pained look in his eyes as he lifted a lock of her hair and rubbed it against his cheek.

Aimee drew in a shaky breath, removed her hair from his clasp and stepped away.

Barely breathing, he watched the passion he had ignited flame hotter in her eyes as she shrugged out of the lace robe and let it fall to the floor. Her hands went to the tiny bows lacing the silk bodice of her gown closed. Her fingers slowly opened the soft fabric inch by inch.

A bead of sweat trickled down his temple, betraying the control he exerted over himself. His obvious desire and fascination as he watched her disrobe for him gave Aimee courage to finish what Luke had started.

Her eyes steady on his face, she untied each bow. The intensity of his gaze seemed to push the sheer gown to her waist. Her unbound hair glittered like pewter in the morning sunlight. She read his unspoken need and brushed her hair behind her shoulders. She stood erect and unafraid even when he reached out to touch her supple white flesh.

His touch barely brushed her skin, electrifying them both. Her rosy nipples tautened. Luke groaned and bent low over her to savor her arousal with his lips. He clasped her waist in his hands and held her still, his rough tongue gently stroking each peak.

Aimee stared over his head, her eyes wide with amazement at the feelings that coursed through her. He caught a nipple in his teeth and nipped gently.

Her knees started to buckle, but he propped her up with his hands and laughed shakily, "Not yet, darling. We're only just beginning. You must be strong if you're to last through what I have planned for you. . . ." He rose and tugged her upright.

Embarrassed now at her own passionate response, she tried to bow her head, but he would not allow it. He tipped her chin up. "Passion is nothing to be ashamed of, sweet wife. Before this night is over, you'll be as demanding as I, that I promise you." He stepped back, folded his arms over his chest and pleaded, "Finish this torture before I explode."

When Aimee's eyes dropped below his waist and widened, he added hastily, "I promise I'll discipline my unruly hands until you're ready for me to touch you."

He looked so doubtful of his willpower that Aimee laughed, her embarrassment gone. Taking a deep breath, she pulled the last tie at her waist. With a twist of her hips, she let the silk flutter to the floor. Bold though she longed to be, the intimacy of the moment was too poignant. She looked down, missing his indrawn breath.

Aimee waited, her heart pounding with shyness, with joy, with love. What if he found her too skinny? Self-consciously she shifted her left leg behind her right, trying to shield it. When she didn't speak or move, she finally found her courage and looked up at him. She quivered at what she saw in his face.

He ran his eyes down her body slowly, eyeing each soft inch of her with such relish that her embarrassment returned. The flush in her cheeks spread to her throat and down her bosom when his eyes paused on her left leg. She stepped back a step, only to find herself pinioned against the door by two strong hands. She was shocked when Luke fell to his knees before her. He blazed a trail of kisses down her left leg so passionate that her self-consciousness melted away. She buried her hands in his hair and let him kiss her, her head flung back against the door, her eyes moist with love for him. Even now, with an overwhelming physical need for her, he was empathetic to her feelings: he put her needs before his own. As he always had, Aimee realized with shock. Her tears increased.

He planted a last kiss on her ankle, rose, took a shaky breath, and forced himself to move away. He shook his head at her gently. "Don't ever be ashamed of yourself, Aimee. Your left leg is as beautiful as your right. I've never liked heavy women, and you are exactly . . . to my taste." He smacked his lips as if a culinary expert and she giggled. All embarrassment was gone. "I long to touch you all over, in every delicious nook and cranny. . . ." His tone no longer teasing, he ran his eyes over her delicate shoulders, tiny waist, curving hips and slim legs.

She watched his chest move up and down with his rapid breathing as his eyes lingered at her firm, pretty breasts. And when he looked lower at the feminine triangle, nothing else mattered but the need to admit him to her core.

She was so close now her scent filled his head; the warmth of her body seeped into him, draining his will. He was reaching out to grab her when she teased, "Now, don't you think it's time you satisfied my curiosity, too? That other time, I was too embarrassed to really look at you." Her hands went to his chest, gliding over the supple warmth of smooth skin and taut muscle. She cocked her head on one side and fingered his tiny nipple. Her hands traced the path of hair that arrowed down his chest beneath his pants. Her fingers hesitated, then boldly strayed to his bulging fly.

The absorbed, sensual look on her face enchanted him. She was truly awakened now, a woman in every sense of the word. Knowing he had incited this passionate curiosity acted like an aphrodisiac on him. He knew he had to slow them both down or lose all control.

He clamped his hands on her wrists, croaking, "Another time, darling, you can undress me. But right now, unless I'm very careful, our first encounter will end before it's barely begun." When she flushed, he led her gently to the bed. "Now, lie down and cover up before you drive me mad." He ripped off his clothes, throwing them where they willed. He climbed into the bed beside her and pulled the hangings closed.

The morning sun shone through them, bathing Aimee's ivory skin in soft blue light. Her hair tumbled about like sea-foam waves; her uncovered breasts beckoned. Her eyes, deep pools of mysterious green, were as bewitching as Circe's. Never had she been lovelier, more alluring in her power to hold him spellbound. His male urges trumpeted in his brain ith need, but he silenced them. He laid his head next to hers on the pillow and drowned in the depths of her eyes.

"Darling, I can't promise it won't hurt, at least this first time, but I can promise I'll give you such pleasure you'll barely remember the pain. Do you trust me, Aimee?"

Aimee gazed into the smoldering black eyes that were permanently etched in her thoughts, in her dreams. How she loved him! Didn't he know she'd suffer pain gladly for the joy of being in his arms? But her thoughts were too new, too precious. She would wait to share them with him when she had a better understanding of his own.

She lowered her lashes to hide her feelings. "Yes, Luke. I know you will never willingly hurt me."

With a fervent, "Thank God," he pulled her into his arms.

She gasped when she first felt the contact of bare body against bare body. He was so hard, so warm, so very *male* that she closed her eyes and let herself drift away on a cloud of enjoyment. At first, when he caressed her, she was relaxed under the gentle touch of his hands.

But when he tossed the covers back and explored every inch of her virgin territory, her breathing quickened. He ran his hands over her collarbones, down her sides to her waist, over her hipbones and down each leg to the ankle, learning her with a need so deep he felt he might never be satisfied, no matter how often he made love to this pretty woman.

Next he ran his hands up the front of her body, from her dainty feet, over her calves to the slim thighs. He hesitated at her pelvis when she gasped, reluctantly leaving that undiscovered interior to caress her tender breasts and bury his mouth in her throat. He kneaded her satiny skin gently, his mouth roving from the throbbing vein in her neck, to her shoulders, to the globes he held imprisoned.

This time, he gave his desires the freedom they cried for. He pressed her white flesh together and feasted on it, his tongue lapping at each nipple until she moaned. Then, when she was writhing with unarticulated need, he nibbled at the tips, sending great shudders through her awakening body.

She tossed her head from side to side, moaning his name over and over. She was too inexperienced to understand the iron restraint he used on his own tortured body. She only knew she had never felt more cherished, more wanted in her life. He made her tremble, he made her burn, he made her yearn for something she didn't understand. She felt empty, incomplete, an aching void in the part of her body that felt hot and strange.

Luke fanned her passion, his own heart pounding so hard his ears buzzed. He had never had to curb his impatience so as a vital part of the act of love.

He darted his tongue in a teasing path down from her breasts, to her soft stomach, stabbing into her navel. He kissed each smooth thigh, inching her legs apart to insert his hand and test her readiness. He stifled a groan at the heated moistness he felt there as she arched toward his probing hand. His chest heaving like a bellows, he paused to compose himself.

Aimee felt bereft at his absence. She opened her eyes, moaning, "Why did you stop? Have I displeased you?"

Luke answered by lowering his weight full on top of her. He enjoyed the way her eyes widened as much as he savored the knowledge that he was the first man to touch her so intimately. "Do you feel how much you please me, Mrs. Garrison?" He urged her legs farther apart and set himself against her, letting her grow accustomed to the feel of his firm silky virility. He watched her, searching for resistance, but, to his delight, she wrapped her arms around his waist and tried to pull him into her.

He laughed throatily, cupping her face in his hands to meet her eyes, desperate to see if she was as enraptured as he. She gazed back, the green depths misty with . . . His heart pounded faster. There was something more in them, some emotion even deeper than desire. Surely there was a great tenderness there that rivaled his own?

"Aimee," he groaned. He pushed her knees up and back, stroking her moist femininity with a teasing finger, tormenting himself with the delay. He could feel the passion soaring in his throbbing flesh, but he desperately fought it back. She had to be ready. He clasped himself, and tested her, savoring the look on her face when she jerked and cried out.

Aimee felt lost, stolen away from herself by a stranger who had lurked within her, waiting only for Luke's skillful touch to rule her, body, heart and will. This stranger had always been a part of her, needing only Luke's embrace to come to life, promising her wonderful things if she would only put aside all resistance. Aimee gladly obeyed its dictates. When Luke at last pushed her legs widely apart so he could lie between them, she adjusted herself to meet him. She gasped at the jolt of feeling that pleasured her when his hard warmth nudged against her.

Luke's longing and desire grew almost unbearably as he rotated erotically, heightening the pulsing in her body until she panted as heavily as he. Then, trembling with need, he used his hand to open the moist entrance to that mystic chamber. Despite his hardness and her softness, he was the vulnerable one at that moment. Never had he felt so humble, so lucky as he caught her waist in his hands and shoved gently. Her eyes flew open, a surprised, pained look in them. She tried to squirm away.

"No, darling, it will only hurt a moment, I promise. Be still. . . ." She subsided, her eyes trustingly on his pleasured face. He thrust his hands in her hair and pulled her head back, burying his mouth in hers at the same instant that he buried his manhood inside her. He swallowed that first, sweet cry and held himself still, deep inside her, letting her pliable flesh open to his hard warmth.

The pain gradually faded. Aimee lay quiet, enjoying the feel of him against her, in her. She felt no resentment at the invasion of his tongue, or at the deeper invasion of his maleness. His hard presence within her seemed natural, inevitable, something she had waited for all her life, for it produced a strange pulsing in the flesh that was answered all around it.

When he gently withdrew, and as gently pressed home again, she didn't shrink away even when the pain returned, for that exciting beat pulsed harder within her with every deep insertion of his manhood. Some age-old instinct told her how to please him in return. The next time his hips pushed slowly into hers, she hesitantly thrust back.

Voice slurred, he encouraged, "That's it, darling. Can you feel how much I want you? You're soft as velvet inside, sweet as honey. . . ." His sentence trailed off as ardor left room for nothing else, even rational thought. His hips moved faster when she rose to meet each eager plunge. He knew he wouldn't be able to hold out much longer. He wanted it to last, wanted to feel her cradling him forever, but the tight, moist clasp around him was too arousing to his starved senses.

He felt her opening, responding, and he tried to hold on, but it was impossible. "Aimee, forgive me," he groaned in self-reproach. He burrowed deeply into her tight warmth. The first man to bathe her with fulfillment . . .

Aimee's eyes opened wide as she felt that warm flow pulse into her and soothe her abraded flesh. It felt good, it felt right, but something was missing. . . . She bit her lip in frustration when he collapsed against her, his heart sledging against her ribs. The throbbing in her womanhood slowly faded, and she sighed at its passing. Luke buried his face in her shoulder, heaved a disgruntled sigh, and moved away.

Embarrassed, he averted his head, but then he forced himself to look into her disappointed face. "I'm sorry, Aimee. I have no excuse except that I wanted you so very badly. . . ." He trailed off, abashed.

She cocked her head in confusion. "You mean you stopped too quickly? It isn't always like this?"

"No." Luke shook his head adamantly. "If I had been able to last longer, you would have felt the same pleasure as I."

Aimee sighed with relief. "Well, we'll just have to do it again," she said practically.

A slow, delighted grin stretched Luke's mouth, but he shook his head. "It's too soon, my seductive wench. Aren't you sore?"

She felt herself. "Yes, but not terribly so. I daresay I'll be fine." She flung her head back to look at him. "I really enjoyed what you did to me, Luke, except there at the end when I felt so . . . frustrated. Is that the way you felt when I rejected you all those times?" At his gentle nod, she buried her face in his broad chest in apology. "I'm so sorry, I didn't know. . . ."

"That's all right, sweet. I deserved it after all I put you though." He stroked her hair.

They enjoyed holding each other for a time. When Luke stirred and asked why she had run away, Aimee rubbed her cheek against his chest hair, shaking her head at her own foolishness.

"Because I was too afraid to face the feelings you stirred in me," she said boldly. When he looked at her quickly, she smiled into his chest and added, "Before the day was out, I knew I'd made a mistake. I was miserable without you. I had already decided to come back to you when you found me."

Luke shuddered and caught her even closer. "I've never been so terrified in my life as when I heard that shot. . . . And then, when I saw you standing over Webb brandishing a pistol, I was torn between admiration and fury. You seemed to get along fine without me. I'm sorry I was so angry on the way back to the ship, but I was so afraid you didn't need me as much as I needed you. . . ."

Lifting her head, Aimee kissed his chin in apology. "I was never so glad to see anyone in my life as I was glad to see you. I was terrified, but more afraid that Webb would kill the earl and me if I dropped the gun. Thank God I didn't miss."

They closed their eyes in a mutual prayer of gratitude. For a while, they were silent, then Luke asked hesitantly, "What did you mean in your letter about my keeping my word to your father?"

Looking guilty, Aimee told him of the conversation she'd overheard. When he scowled, she blurted, "I didn't really believe Potter. Deep inside I knew you'd never betray a commitment. I just used Potter's words as an excuse to flee. Please forgive me?"

Luke's anger softened under the kisses she rained on him. He sighed, knowing he would forgive her anything when she behaved so tenderly. He cupped her face and kissed her deeply in wordless but explicit reply. Soon, the feel of her pliant flesh against him began to tell. He felt unsatisfied, restless. He would not be content until she cried out with joy in his arms. However, it was too soon. . . . He forced himself to pull away from her clinging hands. "Aimee, much as I'd like to give you your second lesson now, it must wait."

He was astonished to feel her hand caress his buttocks when he stood. He whirled, swallowing as her eyes traveled down his body. She eyed his wide, hair-roughened chest, his taut, flat belly, his long, powerful legs with womanly enjoyment. He felt himself harden still more under her fixed, fascinated stare. She rose to a sitting position, propped the pillow behind her shoulders and smiled sensually. She brushed her hair behind her shoulders and held out her arms to him. Her nipples peaked under his hot gaze.

"Come back to bed, darling. I'm the best judge of how sore I am. Right now, I'm troubled by something much worse than soreness." She dropped her eyes to his hips and purred, "And I can see you have the remedy for my ailment." She tossed the covers back invitingly.

He took two steps toward her before hesitating. "Aimee, love, you'd test a saint's willpower, but I don't want you to be sore in the morning. We'd best wait?" What he'd intended as a firm command sounded like a hopeful question, and he flushed when she laughed.

"You beast, you've done nothing but order me about since we met. Now it's my turn. *Come to bed!*" She beckoned imperiously.

Luke propped a knee on the bed and leaned over her, his eyes admiring, his arousal quite evident. "Somehow the imperious effect is a bit ruined, my sweet wife, with all that lovely white skin showing. Still, I can't think of a stronger inducement for me to meekly obey your every whim. . . ."

He leaped on top of her not at all meekly, shoved the covers aside and lustily whirled her about until she was lying atop him. He taunted, "Well, here I am. Now what do you intend to do with me?"

She smiled inwardly at his teasing, put her hand over her mouth and stifled a bored yawn. "I've decided I'm too tired and sore after all. Perhaps I'd rather rest."

He glared. His mouth twitched as she giggled. He smacked her lightly on the rump. "Wench, I'll teach you proper respect yet."

But when his hands urged her mouth over his, they coaxed her instead of forcing her. From the first touch of lips, their passion exploded. Luke yearned for full mutual satisfaction; Aimee ached to know the climax of these enticing new sensations.

She trailed her hands over Luke's body. He lay quietly and enjoyed her touch, the awed look in her eyes as she explored him at last.

Aimee was amazed at his strength. How different they were! Where she was soft, he was hard; where she was curved, he was angled. He was beautiful, she decided, as perfect as the statues she had seen. When she expressed this opinion to him, he roared with laughter.

"Beautiful, am I? What an insult! My father would be appalled."

She stubbornly shook her head, but he forestalled her argument by fastening her lips to his. He whispered, "But I'm pleased you find me attractive, for I find you more attractive than any woman I've ever known."

She responded with a long kiss, engulfed soon in an overwhelming wave of sensation. When Aimee kissed her way down Luke's stomach, he jerked and tightened his hands in her hair. When Luke stabbed his tongue along the aching length of her throat, she propped her head aside to give him freer access, her eyes half-closed in pleasure.

Passion soared between them, in them, as Luke urged Aimee on to greater response, and as Aimee, in turn, urged Luke to greater passion by her eager response. Luke invaded her mouth, nibbling, sucking, demanding, his hands conquering every hill and dale in her quivering body. He stroked her from waist to ankle, pausing behind the sensitive hollow behind her knee to tickle gently. He drew an index finger around the curve of each breast so lightly the touch was more torment than pleasure. He laughed shakily when she arched toward him and he obediently lowered his mouth over the throbbing tip. The moist, sweet tugging at her breast delighted her, frustrated her. She was eager to see if she could please him as much.

She shoved him back and planted herself over him, her eyes narrow and intent, gold flames consuming the green. She ran her fingernail over each of his flat breasts, nearer and nearer the nipple, but never quite touching, and only when he, too, was trembling, did she lower her mouth over him and suck gently.

And so they pleasured one another, in a give and take that

was the most enriching physical experience either had ever had. All of Luke's experience had not prepared him for the helpless ecstasy this sensuous girl gave him; all of Aimee's girlhood fears now seemed foolish in the face of this joy. And when Luke shoved her down and gently parted her legs, she gladly pushed them wide. Now, at last, she would find what had been denied her before. This powerful urge to join with him in every way possible would culminate in a feeling she sensed would surpass everything she'd ever known.

Simultaneously, she felt Luke's hard male strength ease slowly into her, stretching, filling, satisfying, arousing. The twinge of pain at his probing was cushioned by joy. He burrowed deeper into her, and when she felt him at her very core, he paused and tipped her head back to look at him. "You are my life, sweet Aimee. Nothing has meaning to me any longer if you aren't there. Don't ever leave me again. . . ."

Tears clouded her eyes. "I tried that and knew nothing but misery," she whispered. "I'll never leave you again unless you send me away."

A happiness such as he had never known gripped Luke. He felt light as a feather, tall as the sky. His woman, his only love, had committed herself to him at last. She might not love him yet, but she would. He would make her so happy she would have no choice. "Oh, my darling love, I adore you," he whispered in his heart.

But all he said to her was, "I'll never send you away. I'll bind you to me until you'll always want me as close as you are now." He took a deep breath, for control, and began a gentle pumping that rubbed against her feminine parts with nerve-tingling ecstasy. She revelled as each inch of his swollen heat explored the secret crevices of her body.

Soon she was moaning, panting, clutching at him with trembling fingers. "Luke, please," she begged, not knowing what she asked for, but, amazingly, he understood. He braced his hands on each side of her head and raised his hips a little until he was arching higher against her, rubbing against her throbbing self with urgency.

He closed his eyes, lost to everything but the feel, fragrance and taste of her. But never did he lose the sense of her presence, as he often did with other women. Even as his passion burst out of control and broke the bonds of restraint, he was vividly aware of Aimee. He heard every soft moan, delighted in the unpracticed but eager thrust of her hips, savored the trembling stroke of her hands over his back. And every time he buried himself within her, a joyous refrain clamored in his heart, "I love you, I love you. . . ."

Aimee's eyes flew open at the last. She wondered if she dreamed this incredible ecstasy. But no, there he was, this magnificent male who came to her with such gentle strength, such passionate intensity. What had she done to deserve such happiness? He was so skillful, so tender as he led her up sensation's mountain.

With a last, passionate thrust, Luke pushed them over the top. They quivered in unison as he bathed her throbbing womb with the nectar of his joy. She clenched his shoulders, dizzy as the world seemed to spin at her feet. Together, they cried out, blissfully alone on their mountaintop where nothing and no one intruded. They crested the summit and tumbled over the edge, whirling around and around, locked together, hearts pulsing in time. And when they gently landed on earth again, opened their eyes and found themselves anchored in place, they cried a little, in joy, in regret at the loss, in happiness that they could make it again when they wanted.

Aimee hugged Luke to her. "Thank you, my darling," she gasped. "I'm sorry I struggled against you so long."

Luke drew in a shaky breath and reluctantly withdrew. "Sweetheart, you've nothing to thank me for. You gave me far more than you received." His mouth formed a slow smile. "Besides, you're inexperienced. Imagine what awaits us with more practice."

When she blushed, he laughed and pulled her face into his shoulder. "I'll show you, but later. For now, I have something else to do."

Aimee felt deep relaxation as she watched him leap from bed and pour water into a bowl. He brought it and a cloth to her. His hips swayed even more arrogantly when he was nude, and, with his manhood still slightly hard, he was to her the most beautiful sight she'd ever beheld. She sighed in pleasure and wondered now why she'd struggled against him for so long. She grinned impishly. In truth, he faced her with an even more difficult problem. Now that she knew the pleasure he could give her, how would she keep her hands off him? When he sat down, she struggled into a sitting position and ran her hands down his broad chest, savoring the feel of his silky but springy hair.

Luke shook his head and lowered her on the bed. "Don't start something you can't finish. I'm too starved for you to resist you for long, and you must rest."

He soaked the cloth in the warm water, then applied the soothing fabric to the soft juncture that had so recently been joined to him. She started in pain even at the gentle stroking, and she realized she was indeed sore. He had taken her so out of herself she had been unaware of anything but him, even her own pain.

His tender ministrations were soothing, and when he set the cloth aside and pulled a gown over her head, she made no protest. She snuggled her cheek against his hand and yawned. "Thank you, Luke. I'll have a proper bath later. But now, all I want is sleep. . . ." She nodded off before she could complete the sentence, or eat the food Luke had set out for her.

Luke sat beside her, his eyes on her serene face. He stroked her hair, his throat tight with emotion. He'd never felt so content, so fulfilled, but a nagging worry bore into him. If he hadn't already admitted to himself that he loved her, the feelings she inspired when they joined would have erased all doubt.

No other woman had ever angered him so, pained him so, pleasured him so. And when she'd cried out at the climax of their union, he'd felt a joy that equalled the intensity of his own physical release. Now, in the quiet aftermath, the joy still lingered, but some emotion he dreaded to name intruded.

The last two days without her, culminating in this exquisite physical ecstasy, had taught him that, while Aimee could ignite greater joy than anyone else had, she could also inflict greater pain. He'd never been afraid of anything, even as a young man when he'd barely escaped a sinking ship in turbulent seas, or when as a man he'd braved death in a faulty boiler room. But this, this weakness, this bottomless well of emotion, this passionate love he couldn't control, made him helpless. He, who never did anything by half-measures, now loved with the full passion that ruled his manner of living.

He picked up Aimee's slim hand and kissed it tenderly, knowing he had sealed his fate. Her hand could reach out to him and lead him to a happy life, rich with love, or it could push him away and condemn him to despair. All at once, he rose and went to his desk. He returned to the bed and slipped Aimee's wedding ring back onto her finger.

He had never doubted his power over women before. This new pact was both humbling and dismaying. To him, Aimee was not like other women. He'd known that from their first meeting, and that difference had attracted him then as much as it scared him now. What if she turned from him to another? What if she was unhappy in America and grew to hate him for taking her away from all she loved? And most terrifying of all, what if she never grew to love him in return?

He took a deep breath and put her hand under the covers. He picked at the cheese and fruit, shoved it aside and clenched his hands. He'd never been afraid of anything, and he wasn't going to start now. Aimee would come to love him in time. He'd never failed to win what he valued. He'd strive to please her, laboring harder than he'd ever labored for anything. No matter what it took, he would make her love him.

"Sweet dreams, darling love. Rest. Tomorrow I'll woo you so ardently that you'll be as incapable of resisting as I'm unable to resist you." Worn out from pleasure and worry, Luke climbed into bed. They slept there together the rest of the day and through the quiet night.

It seemed a new world when Aimee opened her eyes the next morning. For a second she wondered why the cabin seemed so charged with energy and color, and noticed how the rays streaming through the portholes danced on the ring Luke must have slipped back on her finger in the night. It sparkled as if reflecting back her own happiness. Aimee smiled sleepily as she stared, inwardly hoarding precious memories of last night's shared rapture. She wondered where Luke was, and caressed his rumpled pillow.

How foolish she had been! She had fought long and hard to evade the most enriching experience of her life. She had always known she was a woman of intense passions, but Luke had nourished them to full bloom. From the very beginning, he had tapped her deepest emotions: anger, fear, joy, sadness, pride. With her body still sore from yesterday, she longed to explore with him the full range of joy.

Aimee savored the knowledge that she had satisfied Luke last night. Made him as happy and fulfilled as he had made her. The words he had whispered, the passionate glimmer in his eyes, the tremors that ran through his body when he threw back his head and cried out in joy. They were all signs of a man aroused and fulfilled ultimately. She had given him that satisfaction, despite her inexperience. She, and she alone.

She sat up, flung back her head and gave a yell of pure exhilaration. She tossed her head from side to side, enjoying the cascade of hair on her naked back, luxuriating in her own sensuality. She longed to see Luke. Anything seemed possible. It was just a matter of time, she told herself, before she won his heart. Surely their meeting of minds, their common interests, and now this physical union would seal their intimacy?

She leaped out of bed and raced to the porthole. Yes, they had put out to sea. So that's where Luke was! Aimee danced to her trunk, removed a bright red dress that was as cheery as she felt and hurried to the alcove for a quick bath. When she emerged from the cabin, she fairly waltzed down the companionway. She smiled gayly as she passed a group of women. When one stately old gentleman bowed to her, she bobbed an exuberant curtsy in return.

And when she opened the door to the wheelhouse, she glowed with such a fiery vitality that the officers straightened their ties and stared. Luke was bent over the log, his back to her, but he heard the rustle of her dress and whirled. He met Aimee's eyes, smiled and held out his arms. She flew into them with a little cry of joy.

Luke cradled her on his lap, too overjoyed at her obvious happiness to care that they were being watched. He leaned down to nibble her ear and whisper. "I can see you enjoyed our reunion as much as I, sweet wife. I'm glad. . . ."

She locked her hands behind his neck and leaned back into him. "I'm more athletic than I thought. My muscles are barely sore this morning," she whispered back.

His arms encircled her and he nestled his chin on the top of her head, his expression so soft that his men turned their heads away.

The remainder of their voyage was everything a honeymoon should be. When they were together, they relished the silky touch of skin as they clasped hands, or the sweet warmth of a bold kiss exchanged out of the view of the men. Luke would pull her into an empty corridor, or behind a canopy of sails to savor her feverish lips.

Aimee couldn't bear staying away from him, even for an hour. If he was on the bridge, she joined him; if he strolled about the decks to check on the well-being of the passengers, she strolled with him, her hand locked possessively around his arm. And everywhere they went, they created an aura of joy.

If they stayed for the nightly post-dinner carols, staged in the passenger lounge, their voices urged the other passengers on boisterously. And when they dined, they watched each other more often than they watched their plates. They paid hardly any attention to the cook's superb culinary skills and retreated quickly to their lovers' haven in their cabin.

Aimee had always been pretty, but now she blossomed to an exquisite, eye-stopping beauty. She smiled with equal impartiality at men and women, but if she didn't catch the admiration in the men's eyes, Luke did. And he worried. He sensed the delight she felt in her femininity. What if she worked her wiles on other men and enslaved them? For now, she probed and delighted in the sensual paradise he gave her, but what if boredom settled in and she turned her newly discovered charms to another?

He was well-aware of the irony lurking in his worst fantasies. In his other relationships, women had always eventually driven him off with their demands. Now, roles were reversed, and he was making the demands. What torment it was to have his lover enveloped in his arms, in his bed, but never totally his. No matter how often or how passionately he made love to her, he would never be satisfied until she spoke the words his heart longed to hear. He was delighted with her fascination with him, but he agonized over whether she would respond the same to any man.

So he brooded and allowed self-doubt to needle him. If she smiled a little too gayly at others, he wrapped his arm about her shoulders and ushered her away to an alcove where he kissed her fervently to remind her who treasured her most.

At first, Aimee delighted in his possessiveness, thinking it was rooted in deep caring. Each night, enraptured by each other's bodies, they tightened their bonds to each other.

Nothing would ever part them, Luke vowed as he consumed her lips in a deep kiss. I will never leave him again, she vowed, as she molded her curves to his hard body. And with every caress they shared, it became harder for them not to utter the words they needed to complete their joy.

Their last days at sea fled by before the harsh storms of everyday life once again intruded on them. The moment Aimee set foot in the strange new world she had heard so much about, her euphoria deflated and mundane worries unsettled her. Would the Garrisons accept her? Could she be happy in a world so far removed from Norway? Aimee had expected a big, bustling city, but even London had not prepared her for New York.

As they progressed through the Narrows and the Upper Bay to the family's Hudson River berth, Luke stood at the rail with her, engrossed in the magnificent view.

He said dreamily, "The Indians called this isle Manna-hata, isle of hills, place of surpassing beauty." He laughed at her doubtful look and teased, "When you get as used to city living as I am, this colorful, exciting place of contrasts will be as appealing to you as it is to me." He kissed her crinkled brow and excused himself to see to the disembarking passengers.

Aimee tried to remain excited when they finally disembarked, but the farther they traveled into the city, the deeper her foreboding grew. Her hands were clammy with fear at the prospect of meeting Luke's parents. The cauldron of humanity seething around them offered little comfort. Even without her other worries besetting her, the city itself was bewildering enough. It reminded her vaguely of London, but here hawkers seemed to cry out more loudly, more aggressively. The mix of people on the streets benumbed and intrigued her. The ragged poor mingled on the sidewalks with suited gentlemen and silk-garbed ladies.

And all of them bustled about even more aggressively than the English. Aimee shuddered as she saw a child fall among that melee, wondering if he'd been trampled. His mother whisked him up into her arms, however, and glared at the gentleman who bumped into her from behind. He glared right back, then they both continued on their way, each a nameless face in the streaming mass.

Aimee had never seen such an international mix in a city. As their carriage slowed to make way for a public vehicle, Aimee could count at least six different nationalities standing on a corner. By the time they turned onto a very broad, busy street, Aimee's eyes were dilated in astonishment. This chaotic place was to be her home? How would she ever adjust?

Luke sensed her trepidation and put his arm around her. "Come, sweet, it's not as frightening as it looks. We'll take a tour very soon, and you'll find the people every bit as nice as Norwegians. Perhaps nicer, in a way, for our ideas are freer. Anyone can become successful here, if they've the verve and drive to make a name for themselves. My father is living proof of that: he started with nothing." And when they made yet another turn, he gestured ahead. "Washington Square. Home." His voice rang out with a joy that Aimee did not share.

She could feel the city closing in around her, smothering her, and suddenly she longed for the rugged, clean mountains of Norway. The longing intensified when their carriage drew to a halt in front of a magnificent, red granite mansion crowned by a mansard roof. A high, black wrought-iron fence enclosed it, and the shrubs surrounding it were neatly trimmed, the flower-beds lush and colorful. It was a four-storied structure, of simple, flowing architecture. Dark brown marble pilasters graced each end of the house and smaller ones framed each side of the arched mahogany door.

Aimee bit her lip in worry. She was to be mistress of this . . . this . . . palace? She turned to share her fears with Luke, but the words died on her lips as she noticed his proud demeanor. A servant opened the door and unfolded the carriage steps. Luke stepped down and offered his hand.

Glancing from it to the mansion lurking behind him like a great beast, her eyes settled on Luke's handsome face. He smiled gently and whispered, "Welcome home, Mrs. Garrison. Come, you must meet my parents. They'll be as delighted with you as I, I promise."

Drawing in a shaky breath, she let him help her down, then they mounted the semicircular granite steps. Only Luke's firm hand on the small of her back emboldened her to enter the great yawning door.

A black-suited butler bowed in delight. "Mr. Luke! It's so good to have you home!"

A grand foyer staircase soaring to the upper stories caught Aimee's stunned eyes. She gazed over the cream and red marble floor, the priceless Chinese inlaid secretary flanked by two Louis XVI chairs. Inwardly, she winced. Outwardly, however, she lifted her chin and met the butler's surprised stare boldly.

"Thank you, Barton. This is my wife . . ." Before Luke

could complete the sentence, a door leading off the imposing vestibule burst open. A roar was followed by heavy footsteps.

"Is that you, boy? About time you got home."

At that moment, Aimee called on every courageous instinct of her Viking forbears. She braced her knees to keep them from trembling as a large man with a thick, unruly thatch of graying black hair entered the room. He was followed by a statuesque blond woman.

Luke winced when his father hugged him so tightly the air rushed from his lungs. He kissed Hedda's cheek and smiled, "It's good to be home. This—" he turned proudly to Aimee. "—is my wife . . ."

Again he was interrupted. Joshua pulled Aimee into his arms and gave her a hearty kiss on the cheek. "Well, of course it is. My dear, may I say how happy we are to meet you at last?"

As Aimee stared up into his admiring black eyes, so like Luke's, some of her trepidation eased. "Thank you, sir. I am happy to meet you as well," she answered evenly.

Hedda's manner was more reserved, but she, too, smiled in welcome. "I hope my rascal son has been good to you, my dear?" She watched in satisfaction as Luke put his arm around his bride and winked.

Aimee relaxed and smiled back at him, her eyes softly admiring. "Indeed he has."

Hedda and Joshua exchanged sceptical glances, then Hedda gestured to the stairs. "You probably want to freshen up, Sigrid. Let me show you to your room. . . ." When no one followed her, she paused on the bottom step and turned.

Luke's cheeks were flushed, Aimee's pale. Hedda's eyes narrowed shrewdly as she caught their reaction. She looked at Joshua. He shrugged and peered at his son.

Luke cleared his throat. "Ah, as I was about to say, this is my wife, Aimee. She is Sigrid's sister, as you know."

Hedda and Joshua stiffened. They turned as one to scrutinize her; she met their gazes coolly. The trio stared at one another, Joshua shocked, Hedda disapproving, Aimee proud, until the air was charged with emotion. The reactions confirmed Aimee's worst fears. Luke's parents would not accept her.

Suddenly, she decided she didn't care. Luke had selected her instead of Sigrid. They were married, and the Garrisons would just have to live with that fact. She lifted her head, and nodding to the butler who was directing the servants carrying in the couple's baggage, she signaled that she was ready to see her and Luke's chambers, by picking up one of her own hat boxes and moving toward the stairs.

But no one else moved.

Chapter Twelve

MORNING SUNLIGHT PIERCED the leaded panes facing the front door; dust motes danced in the bright rays. Luke shifted nervously as he watched the two women he loved most in the world face each other. Not a word was spoken, but the look Aimee and Hedda exchanged was an unveiled challenge.

Luke was wondering frantically how to ease the situation when Joshua strode forward to envelope Aimee's hand in his large brown ones. His deep voice rang out with quiet authority. "Aimee, daughter-in-law, we bid you welcome."

He turned his head to look at his wife. "Come, Hedda. Greet your new daughter," he commanded. The order was soft-spoken, but no less firm for its civility.

Hedda snapped her head around to glare at him. She looked regally offended for a moment, then she sighed and stepped down from the step. Sending a narrow-eyed look at her son, she nodded to Aimee. "I hope you will be happy here, child." Her voice was polite, but steely. Her disapproval was as obvious and unyielding as a stone wall.

Luke backed to the stairs, pulling Aimee along. "I'll take Aimee to our rooms. Did you get everything completed in time?"

Hedda nodded. "Yes, I'm quite pleased with the results. I hope you will be as well." She looked at Aimee as she spoke, as if daring her to find aught amiss.

Aimee demurred with quiet dignity. "I'm sure it will be fine." She wouldn't complain if spider webs clung to the ceiling and the bed hangings were in tatters.

As they mounted the stairs, they exchanged a wry glance when Joshua said, "After you get Aimee settled, Luke, come down to the study and tell us how your journey went."

Luke waved a hand, then led them up the curved staircase to the upper landing. Out of sight, he grimaced and mocked, "And tell us what the devil you mean by defying our wishes?" He cleared his throat uneasily.

Aimee stared. She'd never seen him nervous before. Obviously he respected his parents, if their approval meant so much to him. Why, then, had he selected her over Sigrid? He had known his parents would be angry at the switch in plans, but he had wanted Aimee enough to flout them. Could it be he felt more than desire for her after all? Aimee opened her mouth to question him, but he forestalled her by sweeping open a paneled door, inlaid with stained glass, at the end of the hallway.

He pushed Aimee inside, shut the door behind them and pretended to wipe his brow. "Whew!" he whistled through his teeth. "Is my hide still intact?"

Aimee barely heard him, so deep in thought that she didn't notice as Luke began to pace about their freshly decorated chambers. The decor was a subtle blend of luxurious gold and pale blue. The enormous ebony tester bed had bronze medallions embedded in each post. A large, oval porcelain plaque was set in the center of the headboard.

On closer appraisal, Luke realized that it depicted New York's harbor. The bed hangings were made of pale blue brocade, embroidered with gold silk leaves and flowers.

The other furnishings, highboys, armoires, dressing table and chairs, were also of ebony, carved in a leaf and flower rococo motif. The gold silk wallpaper was embellished with bluebirds; the blue satin curtains were traced with gold tassels. The adjoining sitting room had a magnificent marble fireplace as its focal point, with comfortable sofas and chairs grouped around it. The same color scheme was repeated, but this time in plush velvets.

Luke was touched that his mother had gone to such expense and trouble. When he turned to get Aimee's reaction, he found her blindly staring out the window, which he had pried open moments before. She jumped when he put a hand on her shoulder.

"What's troubling you, sweet?"

Aimee looked into his gentle eyes, searching for the love she longed more for with each passing day. She found nothing but husbandly concern, so she turned away and muttered, "I should think it's obvious. I don't enjoy being looked upon as a mongrel you've dragged in."

Luke sighed and turned her to face him. "Hedda is a strong-willed woman who hates to be crossed. She's angrier with me than with you. When she gets to know you, she'll care for you deeply."

Aimee was doubtful, but Hedda's reaction didn't rile her anyway. She closed her eyes and leaned against him, biting her lip to stifle the urge to tell him she didn't care if they accepted her. It was his love she longed for. His, and his alone.

Luke fondled her neck. "Don't worry, sweetheart. You are my wife, my helpmate, the woman I've waited a lifetime for, and I'll let nothing come between us, not even my parents." It was a vow that was to haunt him in the weeks to come.

Aimee threw her arms around him, hugging him fiercely. Her heart burst with love for him. She almost voiced her joyful emotion but he had yet to hint that he wanted more than her body. And until he longed for more, she was fearful of giving him that final power over her. So she stood in the secure clasp of his arms, tossed by contrary emotion: pleasure-pain, joy-sadness and hope-despair.

He might not love her yet, she told herself, but the pounding of his heart under her cheek, and the tremor in his voice gave witness to an emotion deeper than desire. Again, Aimee was struck by the inconsistency. Luke was not a person of half measures. He did everything with his whole heart. He had defied his parents, complicated his life, jeopardized an important business agreement, even conquered her own resistance to win her. Why would he go to such lengths for mere possessiveness, or even pride?

Aimee took a deep breath, pulled away and caught his shoulders to look him straight in the eye. "Luke, why did you marry me?"

Shutters appeared to her to slam across his eyes. He replied blandly, "Why, for the reasons I've already stated. I had to marry, and you attracted me as no woman had, so I wanted to be with you."

"And your attraction was so strong even your parents' reactions mattered not to you?"

Luke turned away to give himself time to frame a reply. What would she do, he wondered, if he told her the truth? That, almost from the very beginning, she had become so important to him that nothing else mattered, that he had barely considered the consequences of his single-minded determination to win her? He knew she was no more ready to hear those words than he was ready to speak them. There were too many unsettled factors between them, too many barriers yet to conquer before he could voice his love. He had never offered his heart to a woman before, and he wanted that momentous occasion to be a memory to cherish. For both of them.

He smiled wryly. He'd never considered himself a romantic, but he'd never met a woman powerful enough to evoke the romantic in him before. Aimee had taught him much about himself in the time he'd known her. Vaguely he wondered what other shocks she had in store for him. Blanking his face of all expression, he turned to face her.

"Let's just say I thought I could take their anger. And now is as good a time as any to begin. Are you hungry? I can inform the kitchen if you are. And I'll have the baggage brought up now."

Aimee shook her head, still watching him closely. Why was he trying to divert her? She sensed there was something he was not telling her, but she let the matter drop. He had enough to deal with at the moment. He had to quell his parents'—mother's—ire, as well as reacquaint himself with the family business downtown. She watched him straighten, as if bracing himself for the battle to come. She was both worried and thrilled that he cared enough to fight for her.

Suddenly, she had to touch him again. She stepped up and grasped his firm, muscular torso cloaked in semi-formal attire. "Best of luck, my darling. I'm sorry to be such a problem for you. . . ."

His mouth took her words as he fastened his lips over hers and drew on the sweet nectar. As always, the comforting embrace exploded into passion. Their hands wandered down the contours of their bodies, savoring, exploring, caressing. Their bodies rubbed intimately as they strove for closer contact; their mouths slanted together ardently. The embrace restored their spirits even as it sent their thoughts spinning to dizzy, pleasurable heights. They were breathless when they pulled apart.

Luke grinned rakishly. "You really know how to remind a man what he's fighting for, sweet. My parents won't have a chance against the ardor you inspire." He put his hands over his chest and heaved a soulful sigh.

Aimee fluttered coquettish eyelashes at him. "And what of the ardor you inspire? How will I compose myself until your return?" She put the back of her hand to her brow, the very picture of swooning womanhood.

Luke forked his feet to back away from temptation. "I will return anon, you shameless woman. You will have ample opportunity to relieve your ardor, that I promise you. . . ."

His eyes swept over her hungrily, and for a moment, she felt faint. He blew her a kiss and exited, leaving her standing in the middle of their room, cheeks flushed, eyes sparkling, worries allayed.

They both knew what he must do: pacify Hedda.

Luke's strides were firm and purposeful as he descended the steps. The glow left by her fragrance and light flirtation fortified him for the encounter to come. When he entered, through the carved library doorway, the atmosphere was chilly. He sprawled in a large chair across from his parents, who were engrossed in conversation. They halted to turn on him, serious looks on their creased brows.

Joshua growled, "For a man who didn't want to wed, you look mightily content. Or is that tomcat expression rooted in your glee at thwarting your parents?"

"I don't enjoy 'thwarting' you," Luke rasped. "But if you had met Sigrid and Aimee, side by side, you'd understand why my interest was incited by Aimee rather than the elder daughter."

Hedda frowned. "But Ingrid wrote that Sigrid is very beautiful. Quite voluptuous, in fact." She wrinkled her nose in disdain when both men eyed her. "Whereas Aimee is very slim."

Luke's slow smile stretched and his parents looked at one another in surprise.

"Yes, she is," he agreed. "But I meant their differences in character, not in looks. Sigrid is sweet as honey, but she would have bored me within a month, and you would have tyrannized her, Hedda."

Hedda looked insulted. "What a fiend you make me out to be, Luke. Am I too domineering, then?"

Luke chuckled. "Not to me, darling Hedda. I'd have you

no other way, but you must realize that you could be a bit . . . overwhelming to a young, inexperienced girl who wants to win your approval."

Hedda countered dryly, "Your bride did not appear at all overwhelmed."

"She was more nervous than she seemed, but you're right—she is not easily overwhelmed. After she settles in, I imagine you'll have quite a challenge on your hands." Luke made no attempt to disguise his anticipatory grin at the prospect.

Joshua demanded, "Am I correct in saying that you selected this girl over the other precisely *because* she's of sterner mettle?" Luke nodded. But when he looked away from Joshua's searching gaze, his father knew there was more.

Luke put his hands on his knees and leaned forward earnestly. "Don't you see, Father, that I would be unhappy with a woman I could dominate? You, of all people, should understand that."

Joshua's brows lowered at this clever thrust. His first wife had been no match for him. She was a lady who defied her parents to wed him, a rough seaman, then spent her remaining years regretting her choice. By the time she died Joshua was wealthy, but she was too unhappy and tired to care that she had proved her parents wrong. Joshua thought she was probably as relieved as he when she died of tuberculosis. Whereas Hedda had brought him nothing but delight from their first meeting, when, assigned to his Fulton Street office, she balked at his imperious commands. Joshua was pleased at Luke's sound logic. His remaining doubts dissolved.

"Very well, boy, you've convinced me. . . ." Both men looked at Hedda.

She worried at the lace on her sleeve, a sign of her unusual agitation. "And what of Ragnar and Ingrid? Did they approve of the switch?"

Luke nodded emphatically. "Yes, they decided, as I did, that Aimee was more suited to me than Sigrid. And what they did not tell you, Hedda, was that Sigrid was in love with another man. Had we married, we almost certainly would have been unhappy. . . ." His parents mulled over this new information, exchanging glances.

Luke added, "Besides, you're very wrong if you assume Aimee used her wiles to trick me into marrying her. It was quite the other way around, actually. I almost had to use blackmail to get her to marry me."

His eyes softened a moment. He didn't notice when his parents exchanged an arrested look.

"Perhaps this girl is what Luke has always needed," Joshua murmured to Hedda. "I've certainly never seen him so . . . taken before."

As she considered her son's transformed face, Hedda's resistence lowered. "I see," she said, dragging Luke's gaze back to her face. "Well, I confess I've my doubts about the girl, but if she pleases you, I'll reserve judgment. But I must say I've never seen such a stubborn expression on a woman. . . ."

Joshua drawled, "I have. And so have you. You see it every time you look in the mirror, dearest."

Hedda glared at him, but he merely chuckled to himself.

Luke smiled at the exchange. He suddenly realized he'd prefer the stormy partnership forged by his parents to any other kind. No submissive society wife for him. He wanted a woman who would stand up for her views, someone who could discuss business, yet someone womanly enough to turn passionate when the bedroom door was closed. Joshua, after a lifetime of searching, after an unhappy marriage, had at last found such a woman. Luke knew he was lucky to find Aimee while still young. Still, he'd had to labor much harder to win her. If he ever had won her . . . He brushed the thought violently aside and recounted his voyage in detail, including his meetings with Nobel, Oscar II, Christiansen and Ragnar.

He concluded, "So the business side of the voyage was a success as well. Have you heard from Ragnar yet? When does the first passenger ship sail?"

Joshua shrugged. "It's planned in a couple of weeks, but the steamer we purchased needed more refitting than we realized. He'll have a tough time making the date."

Luke's eyes hardened into agates. "And does our friend Jeremy know of the new line, yet?"

Joshua's smile turned nasty. "No, not yet. I'm leaving that pleasure to you. He'll most certainly be at the Fergusons' ball next week." Hedda shifted uncomfortably in her sumptuous leather chair, so Joshua smoothly changed the topic.

"Your sister is as much a handful as ever. She's shopping today, but when she returns, I hope you'll have a word with her. She's disappeared a few times since you've been gone, and she won't tell me to where. Maybe she'll reveal her interludes to you."

Luke looked doubtful. "I'll talk to her, of course, but you know I'm not her favorite person at the moment." He rose, kissed his mother's cheek and gripped his father's shoulder. "Now, if you'll excuse me, my bride is waiting for me upstairs. May I tell her she has your approval?"

Joshua nodded and sent a piercing look at Hedda. Her nod was less enthusiastic. "She has my qualified approval, provided she works hard at her new role."

Luke sighed at his mother's obdurate look. He almost felt sorry for her as he pictured her frustration when she discovered Aimee could not be dominated. Luke wasn't sure whether he felt worried or excited at the thought. But Hedda's reactions dimmed when he recalled Aimee's probing tongue, her exploring sensuous hands. His parents followed him to the door and looked surprised by his eager stride up the stairs.

Joshua grinned. "I don't think he's climbed those stairs so fast since we told him a puppy was waiting for him upstairs. I guess his bride has even more charms to offer. . . ."

Hedda sent him a shaming look and scolded, "You mustn't talk like that, Joshua."

Joshua kissed her tight mouth until it softened under his. Then he drew back to whisper in her ear. She relaxed and looked up at him with a most unstern expression. Luke would have been surprised to see the steel in her eyes suddenly melt. The two climbed the stairs, their hands clasped. Below, the butler began his final rounds before dinner.

Luke was delighted to find Aimee taking a bath. He entered quietly, shut and locked the door soundlessly and tiptoed to her. His eyes feasted on her soft white back and swanlike neck. The silver-gold curls piled atop her head hardly stirred when she leaned forward to soap her leg. He removed his own clothes and folded them over a chair, sneaking up behind her.

He roared, "What's the meaning of this? You should be waiting in the bed for your lord and master, not lazing about in the tub, you shameless hussy."

She jumped and whirled to face him, her indignant reply dying on her lips when he lifted her, sat down in the tub and set her on his lap. Aimee's heart began to race as she felt his muscles—and one in particular—straining against her.

She sighed in teasing remorse. "Oh, forgive me, husband." She tried to rise, but his arms tightened about her. He bent his head to nuzzle her neck.

"Too late, wife. I've decided I have you exactly where I want you." He shifted forward and drew her legs about his waist, setting his hardness intimately against her softness.

She gasped. The playful glint in her eyes was washed away by a brilliant tide of gold. "Surely it's not possible in this position," she protested breathlessly.

He cupped her buttocks and inched her forward, belying her words. "All things are possible to those who dare," he said unevenly. His eyes shut as he savored the encounter that warmed him, body and soul.

Aimee's own eyes closed as he rocked gently, barely creating ripples in the bath water but surging with amazing power in the secret depths of her body. She put her arms behind his waist and rested her cheek against him, a sound very like a purr stirring the hair on his chest.

Luke smiled with pleasure and paused, lifting away her squirming hips. "Is this the same little hellcat who spat and clawed every time I touched her?" he teased.

Aimee's lashes fluttered open. She stared into the black eyes sparkling down at her. Devil's eyes, she thought dreamily, but a tender devil who used compassion rather than force, charm rather than coercion. She'd never stood a chance against them from the first moment they caught her. Still, it wouldn't do for him to become *too* sure of her. . . .

Aimee drew back to tease the hair on his chest with a forefinger. She coiled and uncoiled the hair around her finger, then she leaned forward and blew on his nipple, a sultry smile creasing her face, as she fastened her mouth over him and sucked delicately. When he shuddered and tried to draw her hips over him again, she slipped away and stepped out of the tub. She languidly toweled her body, ignoring his scowl.

"Come back here, wench. As I recall, your ardor needed relieving. . . ."

Aimee pointedly looked down into the tub. "It seems you are even more in need of relief." She draped the wet towel over a chair near the tub and drew on her dressing gown, adding, "You seemed to delight so in teasing me that I wanted to delight you in return."

Hips swaying, she strolled to the nearby chest and sat atop it, crossing her legs to goad him. She seemed not to notice that her robe gapped open, revealing both legs fully.

Luke was both amused and exasperated when she fluttered her eyes at him, then looked quickly away. Served him right, he decided, to be saddled with such an impudent wench. But the emotions warming his soul bore no resemblance to regret.

Stifling a delighted smile, he ignored her and soaped himself. Slowly, he rubbed his gleaming, flexing chest, arms and legs, then rinsed as languidly as possible. By the time he stood and dried off, she was breathing unevenly, her eyes riveted below his waist.

He wrapped the towel around his neck and strode to the chest. She held her breath in anticipation, but he calmly moved her legs aside, opened a drawer and removed his brush. Standing so close he rested against her legs, he brushed his hair.

Aimee made a face at him and moved to jump down. "Beast. I might have known you'd rather alter the rules if you started losing the game. . . ." At once Aimee found herself pinned against the chest, her legs spread apart and her wrists held behind her.

"Is this playing the game more to your liking, milady?" he crooned, bending his head to nuzzle her robe open. He ran his lips over her revealed bosom, so lightly she barely felt them until he sucked each nipple, exactly as she had sucked him. Then he left them, aching and eager for more, while he ran his tongue between her breasts, down, down, to her soft belly, to the warm, damp triangle of curls. . . .

Aimee quivered and pulled at her hands. He released them, but she turned his smug smile into a groan when she cupped his straining length.

"Oh, Luke, I want you so," she choked. Very gently, she drew her hands up and down the turgid wand of flesh that performed such magic on her body.

Luke shuddered and spread his mouth over hers. Then, he whipped the towel from around his neck, slipped it under her hips to protect her bare bottom and took her there, on top of the chest, unable to wait long enough to get her to the bed. With one famished thrust he was inside her.

She was so eager to give and to take, in their passionate exchange, she wrung from him feelings he had never known. Sweet life to bless him so! Even had he been coherent, there weren't words eloquent enough to express his love for her.

Instead, he used this passionate duel to tell her with his body what he didn't dare speak. The stifled need made his desire all the more intense, for, in these brief moments, she was as close to him as it was possible to be.

Her moans matched his as he delved for her core, stretching for the essence that made her distinctively Aimee. And Aimee welcomed his deep, sliding invasion by clasping her legs around his waist and opening herself to him. She met his urgent lunge with an ardent thrust of her hips. She reveled in his passion. How wonderful it was to have him. If only . . .

Her emotional needs grew more intense even as her physical needs were so completely satisfied. When he sucked at the tender skin below her ear each time he burrowed himself within her, she bit her lip to hold back a cry of ecstasy.

Their hips moved faster as they strove to soar together above the earth and become beings without substance, without thought, beings of pure sensation. When Luke blessed her throbbing womb with his gentle shower, they seemed to merge into one incorporeal entity. They were formless, thoughtless, phantoms of a lover's dream, for surely such beauty was too fragile for earth's harsh realities. Sighing, gasping, crying, they opened their eyes as the mists receded and they found themselves separate again but with more tenderness for each other than ever before.

Aimee felt the towel against her skin; Luke heard the rapid thud of his heart; each smelled the scent of their mingled sweat. Both knew life's sensations would never be sweeter.

Aimee ran trembling hands over Luke's back, her face hidden against him to shield her emotion. Her legs were cramped, and, sighing in regret, she finally dropped them.

Luke cupped her face and made her gaze steadily into his eyes. His throat was tight with a poignant mixture of joy, love and fear. "Aimee, sweet darling, you make me so happy," he whispered. He kissed her brow. "Thank you, love."

Aimee bit her lip at the endearment. She closed her eyes to block the sight of his face. Beloved, was the word that came to mind, but even that term seemed inadequate in the face of their most exquisite encounter yet. The ecstasy they gave each other could not be explained as an experience of the body. It was emotional: it inhabited her very soul. It was minutes before she was composed enough to open her eyes.

She forced a light tone. "Thank *you*, Luke. Remind me to tease you again."

He laughed and hugged her before lifting her down. He swatted her rump. "We'll be late for dinner if we don't hurry, you distracting vixen. Come, you have my parents' approval, and they're eager to make your welcome more enthusiastic." He went to his trunk, which had been delivered while he was in the study, to remove a formal suit.

Aimee pulled on her underclothes thoughtfully. "I wonder what blackmail you had to use to turn Hedda around."

Luke shook his head ruefully. "You're amazingly perceptive, sweet. I regret to say you have her *qualified* approval, on condition you work very hard at preparing yourself for your new, exalted role." He grimaced as he mimicked Hedda's controlled tones.

Aimee gritted her teeth as she pulled her petticoat over her head. "You mean I'm to work very hard at obeying her every command."

Luke tied his narrow tie and turned to watch her wriggle into a green watered silk dress. A forest green velvet flounce bordered the low bodice and velvet-cuffed elbow-length puffed sleeves. A tiny row of velvet bows marched down the front of the skirt. An enormous matching velvet bow adorned her bustle. She tied a small bow around her hair and let it fall in natural waves down her back. As the finishing touch, she tied a narrow forest green velvet ribbon around her neck and attached her mother's cameo.

He brushed her struggling hands aside and fastened the row of hooks at her neck. "The first thing we have to do is engage a maid for you."

Aimee's mouth set. "I don't want a maid. I've never had one, and I see no reason to change."

Luke sighed and clamped his hands on her shoulders to draw her back against him. He met her eyes in the full-length cheval mirror. "Aimee, your life here will be very different from what you knew in Norway. As my wife, you must be well-dressed, and you will not be able to care for all the clothes you'll need. Please be reasonable and don't cause friction over such a minor point. You'll need all your stamina and courage in your dealings with Hedda."

When she looked as obstinate as ever, Luke lowered his mouth to the side of her neck and left a trail of kisses. When

he looked at her again, her eyes were as green as her dress.
"Please, for me?" he pleaded.

Aimee bowed her head in defeat. "Very well," she muttered. Her head reared up as she added, "But when it comes
to something I really believe in, I won't be so docile."

Luke hugged her. "I know that, and I wouldn't have you
any other way." He presented his arm. "Come, you beautiful
woman, I want to show you off. You still need to meet my
sister."

When they walked into the dining room, they found the
family already seated. Aimee nodded coolly to Hedda. She
blushed when Joshua boomed, "About time, you two."

When Luke grinned shamelessly and winked at his bride, a
black-haired girl with hazel eyes chided, "You're as bad as
Father, Luke. Must you men always be so crude?"

Luke said dryly, "And I'm glad to see you, too, Marietta."

Marietta flushed and sent him an angry look, but she
bestowed a friendly smile on Aimee. Luke seated Aimee next
to her and sat on his bride's other side.

"I'm delighted my brother has married at last. I hope we
can be friends." She patted Aimee's hand, leaning back as
the first course was placed in front of her.

Aimee sighed in relief. She had one ally, at least. "Thank
you, Marietta. I hope the same." She sent a swift glance over
Marietta. Her sister-in-law was tall and slim, her movements
both graceful and quick. She reminded Aimee of a doe, wary
of threats of traps. Indeed, Marietta was someone she could
understand.

Aimee listened as the family talked, her eyes wandering
about the dining room. A magnificent chandelier blazed
above the oval, solid cherry table. Matching sideboards were
set with the same red marble as the cream marble floor. An
enormous oriental rug lay under the table, its muted reds,
greens and golds a perfect backdrop for the silk brocade on
the chairs. The china and cutlery cabinets were fronted by
etched beveled glass doors.

Like the surroundings, the food was perfect. Aimee had
never tasted fresher carrots, fluffier rolls or more piquant
glazed ham. And with every bite she took, her foreboding
grew. Sigrid had always been the domestic one. She'd paid
little attention to Ingrid's lectures on how to be a good
housewife, an oversight she now regretted. Her thoughts

returned to the table when Marietta introduced a new name into the conversation.

"Jeremy is not as bad as . . ."

Luke snapped, "I'll not have my digestion spoiled by the sound of that name. I thought you'd given up defending him."

Marietta retorted, "That shows how little you know of me." She bit her lip when Joshua's head snapped up in warning.

He demanded, "Is that where you go when you disappear? If you're seeing that scoundrel Mayhew again, I'll see him ruined." Marietta paled and sipped her water.

Aimee's eyes narrowed at the name. It sounded familiar, "But isn't Jeremy Mayhew your son, Hedda?" she asked in confusion.

Hedda's features tightened. Suddenly, she looked old. "Yes, he is my son, to my everlasting shame. As you know, Luke and Marietta are my stepchildren."

Aimee opened her mouth, but Luke squeezed her arm under the table in warning. Aimee returned to her food, more curious than ever why the Mayhew name provoked such a strong reaction, first, from her parents, now, from the Garrisons.

After a time, Hedda queried, "And how do you like your new home, my dear?"

Aimee's fork clattered to the table as it slipped from her hand. She smiled, and steadied her reply. "It's beautiful. It must require a great deal of time to manage. How clever you are to do it so well."

Hedda relaxed. "Not at all. My start was rather shaky, I assure you. That's why I want things to be different for you and Marietta. You will work hard and follow my advice, won't you?"

Marietta leaned close to whisper, "When she's like this, the best thing to do is acquiesce, then go about your business."

But it was not in Aimee's nature to be so devious. She straightened and dabbed her mouth with her napkin. "I will do my best to carry out my duties, ma'am: I can promise no more. If I find your advice sound, I will take it. If not, I will do my duties as I see fit."

Luke groaned behind his napkin. He looked at his father,

and wasn't surprised to see him grinning, his eyes shifting in deep concentration as he glanced from one to the other as if attending a tourney. Luke cleared his throat.

"Ah, Hedda, I was wondering if you'd assist Aimee in hiring a maid?" As diversions go, it was not very successful.

Hedda nodded. But her cold blue eyes remained fixed on Aimee. "And your experience is so great that you know better than I how to run such a home?"

Shaking her head, her gaze was as direct. "No, I didn't say that. But I think it best we understand one another from the outset. I learn quickly, and I welcome your guidance—but not your orders. I am inexperienced, but not stupid, and I will not be treated as such by you or anyone."

Hedda's eyes froze a little more, then she sighed, and the blue glaze changed. "I can't blame you for that, child. I don't like it when anyone tries to order me about, either." This time, her eyes fluttered to Joshua, wiping the grin from his face.

Aimee stifled a smile as she agreed, "Yes, men do tend to be arrogant, don't they? Luke and I had some lively times before he finally learned to ask rather than command." Hedda's eyebrows shot up in surprise, and she couldn't refrain from smiling. They each took an enjoyable bite of ham, seemingly unaware of their spouses' frowns.

Hedda swallowed, intent on probing further. "Perhaps men are arrogant because they fear women will rule the world one day. We are, you'll agree, more intelligent. At any rate, we could hardly make a greater mess of the world than they have."

Aimee nodded in solemn agreement, ignoring the masculine gasps of outrage. "Yes, I have always thought so. Tell me, have you ever attended one of Susan B. Anthony's meetings? She seems a woman of uncommon perception, from what I've read, and I'd be interested in meeting her."

Hedda's eyes kindled. "I've always wanted to attend one of her meetings, but somehow my husband has always found something pressing for me to do at the time. Now, isn't that a strange coincidence?"

Joshua snapped, "Don't be foolish, woman. You're happy enough as you are. I don't see you as a second-class citizen; you're first in importance to me. Isn't that enough?"

Luke took Aimee's hand, a grimace on his handsome face. "And the same holds true for us."

Aimee flushed and jerked her hand away. "Do you think we'd suddenly be less important to each other if I was allowed to vote? I'm a thinking human being first, a woman second. All I ask is recognition of that."

Hedda nodded vigorously, waving a hand to forestall another angry comment from Joshua. "My thoughts exactly, Aimee."

They finished the meal with more discussion of the suffragettes, then Hedda rose and invited, "Let's go to the parlor and leave these two cavemen to their cigars." She swept her skirts haughtily aside and exited, head high.

Aimee wrinkled her nose at Luke—when she was safely at the door—and retreated. Marietta rose languidly, shrugged, and followed.

Clapping his hand to his forehead, Joshua groaned, "Luke, good God, what have you done? Once those two become friends, we'll be helpless against them. Our lives will never be the same again." But his mouth twitched, and his black eyes glittered with humor.

Luke grinned. "They're birds of a feather, all right. But I have a feeling we'll be the ones to get our tail feathers plucked before they're done."

And, indeed, in the parlor, Aimee and Hedda shared a long, engrossing conversation about the politics of being a woman.

Marietta stifled a yawn when urged to join in. "Leave me out of your plans. I'm happy with things as they are." She stretched, excused herself and went to bed.

Aimee and Hedda smiled, really smiled at each other for the first time. Hedda said, diffidently, "My dear, let me repeat, sincerely this time—welcome." She held out her hand.

Aimee swallowed a lump in her throat and squeezed Hedda's hand. "Thank you, Hedda. I will try not to disappoint you." As she met Hedda's smiling eyes, for the first time Aimee dared to believe she would be accepted here after all.

Her spirits fell again when she retired to their suite. She blushed as she looked at the chest where she and Luke had ignited such passion beyond her wildest fantasy. She retrieved the towel, which lay pooled on the floor where they had tossed it, and set it in the hamper. What was she to do? She sank into a chair and propped her elbows on her knees so she could rest her chin. With every intimate encounter she became less her own person. Exactly as she had always feared, she was losing her independence. Luke's happiness mattered now as much as her own.

Oddly, she found she didn't resent the change. She wanted to make him happy, *wanted* to be the wife he needed. If she had to lose a little freedom in the process, it was an acceptable sacrifice. She valued what he valued. It wasn't as if trying to fit into her new role would compromise her character in any way. Not really. If she wanted to win his love, what else could she do?

Luke desired her, obviously. He admired her character and intelligence. Other marriages were founded on a far less solid base. Surely if she strove to be the kind of wife he wanted, he'd come to love her in return? Aimee removed her clothes, resolving to hold her tongue and be patient. She would do whatever was necessary to keep Luke happy. As she climbed into bed, it never occurred to her that denying her own needs would plant seeds of resentment that would flower into bitter fruit.

Chapter Thirteen

Aimee would never forget those first hectic days in New York. They were frustrating, exciting, but above all, they were challenging. She faced each day with courage and resolve, aware that her future with Luke hinged on how well she fulfilled Hedda's expectations. So she delved within herself for more tact, patience and maturity than she had ever believed she possessed.

She saw little of Luke. He was negotiating a new business partnership; she was occupied with her household duties. But when he returned in the evening from the Fulton Street office some twenty blocks away, he always quizzed her about her day. She informed him truthfully that she found the pace absorbing both inside the house and outside on New York's bustling streets.

Slowly, the strangeness of the big city traffic congestion, soot-lined streets and aggressive pedestrians became as much a part of her world as the hills of Bergen had once been. Aimee was rather proud of her adaptability, but she was amazed at her patience with Hedda.

Hedda introduced Aimee to her new responsibilities as she did everything—with verve, decisiveness and self-confidence bordering on arrogance. She didn't suggest that Aimee check to be sure the linens were properly pressed and scented with roses; she ordered it. She didn't recommend the frequent turning of the mattresses; she demanded it. And when they discussed menus, so they could hand one of the servants a week's worth of suggested groceries, she stated that Joshua liked beef on Wednesdays, lamb on Fridays, shellfish on Saturdays, and so on.

For the most part, Aimee bit her tongue on the retort she sometimes longed to make and nodded at each command. She trailed after Hedda, making notes, and kept her caustic remarks to the margins of her pad. Some of Hedda's ideas seemed outmoded and rigid to Aimee, but she bided her time. She had to win Hedda's trust before she could design the household to run more efficiently, tailored less toward the whims of one individual.

Sometimes Aimee looked in the mirror, wondering if she saw a stranger there. Ingrid certainly would have been amazed at her malleability. Wryly, Aimee realized her love for Luke motivated her to learn the womanly pursuits she'd always scorned under Ingrid's uninspired lectures. If she was to be the wife he deserved and win his love, she had to learn these duties. So Aimee stifled the reservations she felt and worked earnestly toward that goal. Where she had been bored, now she was attentive; where she had been rebellious, now she was resolved; where she had been hesitant, now she was confident. If, in the depths of her being, she balked at the new shackles placed on her, she would not admit it, even to herself. Not for the moment.

Her patience soon bore fruit. She had the satisfaction of hearing Hedda praise her diligence in front of the family when they circled the dinner table a week later.

Hedda complimented her. "My dear, for someone who claims to know little about running a household, you've learned very quickly. In a week or so I may even leave everything to you and devote myself to some of the things I've always wanted to do but never had time for."

Joshua beamed at Aimee before turning to his wife. "That's something I never thought to hear you say. Every time I suggested you hire a housekeeper, you always told me you enjoyed overseeing affairs too much to trust it to anyone else."

Hedda waved a dismissing hand. "That was before Luke brought home such a lovely, intelligent bride to help me. I can trust her, but I would not feel comfortable depending on a stranger." She hesitated, then asked, "Aimee, would you prefer to engage a woman? Irene, the head housemaid, is very helpful, but if you'd prefer, I will help you interview applicants."

She looked possessively around the dining room, and Aimee could see that Hedda hated the thought of a stranger running her household. Aimee shook her head. "No, I rather enjoy my new duties. I would be bored with nothing to do, and I have a few . . . suggestions that might make things a little easier."

Hedda's head snapped up at this. "Oh yes? May I ask what?"

Aimee answered airily, "Oh, nothing specific as yet. Just a few ideas." She took a small bite of beef, it being Wednesday.

She hid a smile when Joshua chewed for a moment, then muttered to himself, "Beef again. Feel like I'm in the military sometimes." When Hedda glared at him, he sighed and subsided. Aimee dropped her eyes to hide the humor glimmering there.

She jumped when Luke drawled in her ear, "I see that glint in your eye, woman. What mischief are you brewing under that angelic smile?"

Aimee wrinkled her nose at him and started to speak, but, just in time, swallowed and answered demurely, "Nothing disastrous. I just plan to alter a few things, that's all."

Luke frowned at her stifled response. In fact, she had acted oddly for several days. He missed her sassy responses. He put the back of his hand to her forehead. "Aimee, are you feeling well?"

Aimee looked puzzled. "I'm fine. Why?"

"You seem . . . different. Less lively, somehow."

Looking away, she colored. Of course, he had noticed her changed behavior. She squirmed under his searching appraisal, hoping he wouldn't probe further.

Joshua distracted him from Aimee's averted face by suggesting gravely, "Luke, let's take our brandy to the study. I have something I must discuss with you." After a last thoughtful look at Aimee, Luke rose to follow his father, but stopped when Marietta's voice piped in.

"Wait, there's something I want to discuss with you."

Joshua and Luke looked at her warily, then sat back down. Aimee was sitting next to Marietta, so she saw her sister-in-law fumbling with the dinner napkin in her lap. Aimee looked at each of the Garrisons, wondering at the tension in their faces. What was wrong?

Marietta began, "Father, Luke, I spoke with Jeremy Mayhew the other day." When Luke and Joshua stiffened, she added hastily, "We met accidentally in the street. He told me he had planned to open a passenger line between Norway and America, only to find that you have done so before him. That seems an odd coincidence to me. Did you do it deliberately?"

Luke snarled, "That's none of your affair, miss. What I want to know is how you just *happened* to meet him?"

Marietta's brows lifted. Their eyes wrestled before she answered sarcastically, "That's none of your affair, sir."

Luke sputtered with rage, but Joshua waved him to silence. He put his hands flat on the table and leaned toward his daughter, his powerful body vibrating with controlled anger. "You, young lady, had better not be seeing that wastrel again. He'll not ruin you as he's ruined others. Need I remind you of what will happen if you defy me on this?"

Marietta paled, but her defiant posture didn't change. "Jeremy never 'ruined' the chit. She chased him and then put it about that he'd . . . forced her. She is accepted by New York's 'finest' so it's obvious who you'd believe. Besides, if you're working against him anyway, why shouldn't I see him?"

Luke rose and rounded the table to jerk her chair around to face him. He shoved his face into hers. "We've done nothing to him that any other competitor wouldn't. But we can, and will, ruin him if we find out you're seeing him. Understood?"

Marietta's cheeks colored. Her mouth worked with rage, but Luke's deadly gleam stopped her short. She nodded shortly. Without another word, the Garrison men strode out of the room, oblivious to Marietta's contempt and Aimee's shock.

Marietta turned to Hedda, who had sat white-faced and silent through the argument. "They opened the line deliberately, didn't they, Hedda?"

Hedda's voice cracked. "I fear so, child. But they want only to protect you."

Surging to her feet, Marietta released her rage. "They want vengeance on an innocent man! They sicken me!" Tears in her eyes, Marietta fled the room.

Hedda rested her head on her hand in such weariness that Aimee decided not to probe. This was twice now the Mayhew name had evoked fireworks. First, in her parents, now, in the Garrisons. Hedda was obviously too upset to badger, but Luke would surely reveal why the Mayhews were so despised. After all, Jeremy was Hedda's son. Surely whatever he had done could never be deemed terrible?

Hedda rose, trembling. "Aimee, I'm feeling tired this evening; I think I'll retire early. I guess I really am getting old."

Aimee kissed Hedda's cheek. "Of course, go ahead. But I beg leave to tell you, ma'am, that I only hope I age as gracefully."

A little color returned to Hedda's pale cheeks. "What a sweet child you are." She smiled.

"Goodnight, Aimee. In the morning I'll show you the mixture we use to polish the woodwork."

Aimee sat in the silent splendor of the dining room, feeling oppressed by the luxury around her. There were deep, dangerous undercurrents swirling under the surface peace and intimacy of the Garrison household. Aimee had never seen Luke so relentless, Joshua so stern, or Hedda so sad. What was it about Jeremy Mayhew that stirred such strong emotion?

Aimee fretted. She realized that she had thrown herself into her new role so vigorously that she had stifled her own urges in the process. Luke's harsh treatment of Marietta had seemed strangely discordant, and unlike him. And he had shared little with her about his business concerns since arriving in New York. Maybe he hadn't discussed his affairs with her because he didn't believe she was capable of understanding the complexities.

On the heels of that thought came one that disturbed her almost as much. She had been so determined to win his respect and admiration that she'd thought of little else since her arrival. Now that she had won Hedda's approval, she wondered at the cost. Yes, she wanted to make Luke happy, but not by abandoning her own principles. There was a fine line between enjoying the luxury around her and becoming obsessed with it.

She realized suddenly that she wasn't doing anything truly important.

She had seen for herself the deprivation lurking in this

great city. Urchins every bit as thin and ragged as any in London lingered in the streets, dancing, singing or selling trinkets to anyone kind enough to pause. And, unfortunately, affluent and poor alike were usually too busy to pause. Aimee had tried to share her concerns with Hedda, to no avail. Hedda was a kind woman, but she was too busy to do more than toss coins at the children. Aimee brooded over her rich custard, wondering if she would become the same, wondering if she really wanted to become a permanent fixture of the Garrison family if it meant submerging herself entirely in the details of the household management.

In the study, the mood was even more somber. Luke listened grimly, then demanded, "When did you learn of this?"

"Just today, when I was checking in some silver cargo myself and opened one of the crates to find it empty. A search turned up nothing. Unless you had them moved to another warehouse . . ."

"No, I didn't. Are you saying someone is stealing from us?"

"It looks that way, Luke. Tomorrow, I want to do an inventory to see if anything else is missing. We should probably consider hiring an armed guard."

Luke shook his head emphatically. "No, if we do that, we'll scare away the thieves and never catch them. Have you told anyone else?"

"No, I thought it advisable to keep it as quiet as possible. I haven't even told Tom yet."

"Good. Why don't we do the inventory ourselves, the next several nights? If more is missing, we can alternate working the warehouses at night. Surely the thieves aren't bold enough to attack in broad daylight."

Joshua tapped his chin thoughtfully. "Sounds like a good idea. I'll check our employee roster with the police to see if we've hired any suspicious characters of late." Joshua lowered his voice to add, "I needn't tell you not to mention this to Hedda. She'd come down hard, and her fuming would hardly aid a quiet investigation."

Luke agreed wryly, "And the same goes for Aimee. If I know my willful wife, she'd try to solve the mystery herself, and I want her kept safely out of the way. The fewer who know about this, the better."

Having retired to their suite, his willful wife reflected

darkly that learning to be a compliant wife was the hardest task she had ever undertaken. Even more frustrating, she suspected that Luke *preferred* her contrariness over her attempts to please him. If that wasn't just like a man. He did nothing but complain about her defiance, but if she bit her tongue and inhibited her nature, he scrutinized her sadly and diagnosed fever.

Aimee moodily shrugged into her nightgown. She picked up Luke's hairbrush and strolled to the window. When a sound drew her attention, she looked out. A tall, cloaked woman quietly descended the steps and peered down the street. Her hood fell back, and Aimee recognized Marietta. A carriage soon drew up. A very tall man got out, blond hair gleaming under the carriage lamps. He lifted her into the vehicle. They drove away.

Aimee stared after them so intently she didn't hear Luke's approach. She started when he caught her waist in his hands and yanked her back against him.

"Sweet, you look like a moonbeam standing there in your filmy gown, with all that silvery hair streaming down your back. Can you possibly be real?"

As if in doubt he gingerly cupped her breast. "Yes, you're soft and warm, and very much alive." He turned her to face him and whispered into her mouth, "And very much mine." He fastened his mouth over hers and kissed her hungrily.

Aimee dropped the brush and wrapped her arms about his neck, all her fears melting away under the heated caress. But when he tried to lift her and carry her to the bed she pulled away. "No, Luke, wait. I want to talk to you."

Luke's quick breaths slowed when she led him to a settee in the moon-washed sitting room. She folded her hands in her lap. "Luke, I'd like to involve myself in city affairs, if you've no objection."

Luke recoiled, frowning. This was sudden, unexpected. "What do you mean?"

"Would you mind if I joined a local society and helped organize an orphanage? I read in the paper that charities are seeking assistance. . . ."

Luke cut her off by kissing her lips. "I admire your compassion, sweet, but I don't think it wise. In fact, I would prefer that you not travel far from the shopping districts, at least not alone. And I certainly don't want you to have contact with disease-ridden street urchins."

She averted her head and Luke tensed, waiting for a tirade. When none came, he tilted her chin toward him. "Aimee, when Hedda leaves the household to you, you'll have plenty to do, what with your other obligations. You'll be satisfied."

Her huge eyes reproached him with the words she longed to say. *And what satisfaction can I give to my conscience?* She was disappointed, frustrated, angry, but she pushed the feelings to the back of her mind. She shifted away from him and rose.

"Very well, Luke. I'll accept your decision, for now." She rose to drift over to the window again. She drummed her fingers on the sill, debating whether she should mention seeing Marietta. She was certain the man Marietta had met so stealthily was Mayhew. However, she didn't want to make an enemy of her new sister-in-law without understanding why she sneaked away from the house to meet the man her family detested. It would be best to question Marietta first.

Aimee's mouth firmed with decision. She would not be put off in this, at least. If she was truly to be part of this family, she must know their scandals as well as their triumphs.

She whirled to face him. He was still sitting, watching her with a puzzled frown. His frown deepened when she asked, "Luke, what is it about Jeremy Mayhew you and Joshua hate so much?"

Luke rose. "I don't want to discuss him with you, Aimee. He's an evil man, as his father was, and he's caused both Hedda and this family a great deal of grief."

"But if he's Hedda's son, what has he done that's so terrible?"

"Made improper advances to my sister, for one. Marietta is not Hedda's daughter. I don't mean 'improper' in that sense. He also ruined an innocent girl. Borrowed money he had no intention of repaying. I'm convinced he would have ruined Marietta if we hadn't been able to intercede." When she opened her mouth to question him again, he shook his head adamantly. "That's all you need to know. The rest of the story is ugly, and I don't want to upset you with it. I would ask that you not mention any of this to Hedda. Her wounds aren't healed, even after all these years." Luke turned away and began removing his clothes, closing the subject.

For Aimee, however, the subject was not closed. She

turned to get into bed, her mouth quivering in hurt. Why didn't he trust her? He had broken down all her walls against him, yet he refused to let her do likewise. He relegated her only half of the role she wanted: wife and lover. She longed to be confidante and helpmate as well, a partner in every sense of the word. Why wouldn't he allow it?

Luke got into bed beside her and pulled her wooden body against him. He wrapped both arms about her and kissed the hollow of her neck. "Darling, I only want to protect you. Surely you see the danger you'd put yourself in by working in an orphanage. Have you considered that you might even bring sickness home to the rest of us?" When she didn't answer, he continued more forcefully, "As to the other, well, I guess the subject is very sensitive for me. I despise Mayhew and don't even consider him a worthy topic of conversation with you. Discussing it only stirs up ugly memories we're all better off forgetting."

When there was still no reply, Luke frowned. It wasn't like her to accept his decisions without argument. They were for her own good, of course, but that had never swayed her before. He gently turned her to face him.

She looked at him at last, but he couldn't see her expression in the gloom. Her voice seemed calm enough. "I believe you think you're doing what is best for both of us. But I just wish I felt more . . . useful. More a part of the family."

Luke grazed her cheek with a kiss. "You are the most important part of the family to me. As for feeling useful . . . Darling, would you like to help me next week? I'm hosting a small dinner at one of the city's finest hotels and I would welcome your assistance. I've noticed how astute you are about human nature, and I have a few doubts about the man I'm meeting. We plan to open up new business avenues together, but I'm not certain he's completely honest. I would welcome your appraisal of him."

"Of course I'll come with you. I'll be glad to offer what little support I can." What little you'll let me, she longed to add tartly, but reigned in her impulse.

Luke frowned at the bland response. "Aimee, won't you tell me what's troubling you?" He kissed the rim of her ear, smiling when she shivered.

"I've told you what's troubling me, Luke, but since you obviously put no credence in it, there's nothing left to discuss." Aimee turned her head, dismayed at her shrewish words. She didn't see Luke's relieved smile.

"Ah, that's my girl," he teased. He ran a hand up the back of her smooth leg. "But I don't want to argue with you right now. I can think of a far nicer way to settle our dispute." He pushed her down and inched her gown up about her waist. Then he lowered his body over hers.

Though Aimee answered his demand, she knew that nothing at all had been settled. Her own restrictions closed in on her, chafing her until his wandering hands soothed the irritation away. Long after he fell into contented sleep, she lay awake.

She wondered what he and Joshua had discussed in the study. Her mouth twisted bitterly as she knew it would do no good to ask. She had just served all the purpose she had for him. Aimee tried to deny the ugly suspicion, but the more she brooded, the truer it seemed. If he cared for her, for Aimee the woman instead of just Aimee the body, surely he would confide in her? Even when he asked for her help, it was for her womanly intuition rather than as a true partner whose opinion carried weight.

She was even more upset at his refusal to discuss Mayhew. To be shielded from business matters was bad enough; to be denied the facts behind a tragedy affecting the family was intolerable. Luke's refusal to tell her the details indicated a lack of intimacy she could not bear. She had been put off long enough, first by her parents, now by the Garrisons. She was curious, yes, but she also deserved to be told the truth.

Perhaps Marietta would be more willing to discuss the matter.

Hedda visited friends the next day, so Aimee had a perfect opportunity to broach the subject. After lunch, she followed Marietta to the parlor. She sat down next to her, pouring tea while Marietta worked on her embroidery. Aimee eased into the subject by shaking her head at the quality of the society men she had met during her outings with Luke and Hedda.

"I've never seen such a dandified lot in my life, even when I was in London. Are all the men here so . . . uninteresting?" she said in perfect English, laced with a slight accent. Marietta always admired Aimee's command of the English language.

Marietta nodded. "Most of them. The men my family find acceptable, I find incredibly boring. There are a couple, however . . ." As if aware she had said too much, Marietta bent over her work again.

Aimee took a sip of tea, set the cup precisely in its saucer and asked gently, "Is Jeremy Mayhew one of them?"

Marietta's head jerked up. She started to shake it, but when she looked into Aimee's warm, understanding eyes, she bit her lip and nodded instead. "Yes, unfortunately for us all."

"Why unfortunately?"

"Surely you know my family will never accept him. Hedda—my stepmother—is his mother, but she views him as a horrible mistake she made when she was young. My father and brother blame him for things he's not responsible for. They all believe he's ruthless. It isn't fair. I *know* Jeremy. They don't. He's as honorable, in his own way, as Luke. But they'll never believe it." Marietta stabbed her needle forcefully into the fabric.

"What has he done to make them hate him so?"

Marietta tossed the hoop away and wrung her hands. "Very little, personally. I know the girl he supposedly ruined, and I don't think he ever encouraged her, much less touched her. He's still trying to pay back the money he borrowed, but he's fallen on hard times and hasn't been able to scrape together the funds yet. But what condemns him utterly in my father's and brother's eyes is what he did to Hedda long ago, when he was a child. He chose his father over her. There was a scandal around the time Hedda met my father. I don't know everything, but it seems Hedda's husband, Samuel Mayhew, was allied with Hedda's brother Bjorn in an export business. Apparently Mayhew was a jealous, difficult man, and I suspect Hedda's marriage was unhappy. Then the partners discovered they were being stolen from. At first, neither man suspected the other, but when Bjorn hid one night to try to discover the culprits, Samuel Mayhew appeared to direct the removal of the cargo. Bjorn confronted him and was killed, Samuel claimed accidentally. Hedda believes differently. Tom Payton, Bjorn's first mate, witnessed their argument, and he testified at the trial that Bjorn fell onto the grappling hook accidentally. The jury believed Samuel's assertion that he was removing the cargo to keep it safe. Hedda believed he was trying to cheat Bjorn."

Aimee rubbed the goosebumps on her arms. "Isn't Tom Payton the manager of the family warehouse now?"

"Yes, my father hired him when he left Mayhew's employ after the trial."

"But if Samuel was absolved, why was Hedda so convinced he was guilty?"

"He and Bjorn had been arguing a lot about Samuel's treatment of Hedda. The partnership was on the verge of breaking up. Under the terms of their agreement, Samuel stood to collect less than Bjorn. Hedda adored her brother, and, when the thefts stopped with Bjorn's death, it was easy for her to blame Samuel, for he showed little remorse. To make matters worse, when Hedda left him and took Jeremy, who was a boy at the time, Jeremy ran back to his father. He never believed his father to be guilty. Hedda tried to coax him back, but Samuel won custody because Hedda's clerk's salary barely covered her own expenses. By this time, she had also met my father, and Samuel painted him in a very ugly light to the court. The final indignity was that, when Bjorn died unmarried, his share of the business went to Hedda, and so to Samuel." Marietta leaned back and closed her eyes, obviously upset at recounting the story.

No wonder the subject was so touchy. How terrible the experience must have been for Hedda, Aimee thought. "But why do they blame Jeremy? He was just a boy at the time."

Marietta moved her head from side to side in despair. "I don't know. I do know that Hedda tried to see him after the court hearing, but Jeremy was very cold to her. She was extremely upset, and, after a while, she gave up trying to visit him. She was in love with my father by this time, but Samuel refused to grant her a divorce. She defied society and lived with him anyway until Samuel died. He had heart failure."

At last Aimee understood why her parents had refused to discuss the subject. How they must have disapproved of Hedda. Aimee suspected that if Hedda hadn't been respectably married at last, they wouldn't even have considered the alliance, no matter how dire their straits. "And now she, Luke and Joshua blame Jeremy for the pain Hedda suffered all those years."

Marietta straightened up. "I suppose so. Jeremy won't make excuses, even to me, but I do know he believes his father was innocent of all charges."

"If that's the case, he's probably as bitter as they."

"Yes."

Aimee covered Marietta's hand with her own. "I'd like to meet Jeremy. Are you still seeing him?" When Marietta recoiled, Aimee added softly, "I won't betray your confidence, even to Luke."

"Yes, I'm seeing him. He wants me to marry him, but I'm afraid if I do that my father and brother will have him hounded out of New York. They wield a great deal of influence here, and Jeremy's business is already suffering."

Aimee watched Marietta closely as she spoke, sensing other unspoken reservations. She patted Marietta's hand and rose. "Thank you for talking to me. I hope you'll let me accompany you to meet Jeremy sometime."

"The very next time. I promise. And thank you for not criticizing me or condemning Jeremy out of hand. I'm glad to have you for a sister." The warm smile they exchanged was a comfort to them both.

After this meeting, Aimee felt closer to the women of the family. She better understood both Hedda and Marietta. Conversely, she became impatient with Luke and Joshua. In their overprotectiveness, they both devalued women's strength and condemned a possibly innocent man to an outlaw role.

Aimee's role of compliant wife became harder to fulfill, especially when Luke disappeared several nights in a row and made lame excuses about visiting friends when she quizzed him. At first she couldn't believe he'd see another woman. His nightly passion for her was too strong. More than likely he was involved in a secret business deal he wasn't ready to reveal. Oddly, she found this explanation almost as upsetting. Would he continually shut her up like a hothouse plant, bringing her out into the real world only when he had people to impress?

Aimee's reservations about her marriage changed to outright resentment the next day when she accompanied Luke to Lord & Taylor's. The store sat at the intersection of Broadway and Grand, an appropriate locale for a store that was grand indeed. Built of white marble, lavishly ornamented, its wide windows displayed a quality and variety of goods Aimee had seldom seen, even in London. The firm's growing reputation was beginning to rival that of A. T. Stewart & Co.

Aimee was always fascinated by the hurly-burly activity on Broadway, Manhattan's longest thoroughfare, but today she was distracted by Luke's stiffened arm and a feminine voice.

"Luke! I didn't know you had returned. How wonderful to see you again!" A voluptuous brunette with eyes as big and blue as delft saucers strolled up to them, eyeing his well-muscled torso suggestively.

After an uneasy pause, Luke stirred. "Hello, Claire. I've been back for some time, and I thought surely you'd heard. . . ."

Claire dismissed Aimee with a look and cooed, "Heard what? I've only just returned myself from Europe."

Luke cleared his throat, wishing himself leagues away, but he answered steadily, "This is my wife, Claire. Aimee, this is Claire Sutton, an old . . . friend."

Aimee noticed that significant hesitation. Here was the type of woman he had pursued before their wedding. She examined Claire closely and grew dismayed. The woman had a voluptuous body, feminine guile, self-assurance and stunning beauty. If Luke cared nothing for these qualities, as he claimed, why had he dallied with a woman who possessed them in such abundance?

Aimee couldn't control her catty satisfaction when the woman paled and staggered back. She recovered quickly and sent a dismissing look up and down Aimee's slim figure.

"Why, how . . . wonderful for you. May I congratulate you on a most . . . unusual bride, dear Luke." She raked another denigrating look over Aimee, stepping up to take Luke's red cheeks in her palms. "Just a little kiss for the groom," she purred. She pulled Luke's head down to kiss him full on the lips.

Aimee was too mortified by the scandalized looks of the pedestrians to notice that Luke did not respond, or that his hands were not gentle as he pried her away. "Same old Claire," he said with something approaching disgust. He took Aimee's arm and led her into Lord & Taylor's.

When he tried to explain his relationship with Claire on the way home, Aimee interrupted him. "It doesn't matter. I should probably get accustomed to meeting your vengeful inamoratas."

Luke was a bit insulted by her easy acceptance. He would long to tear any man limb from limb who dared to kiss Aimee. His clasp tightened on her arm at the mere thought.

He glared at a man who looked at Aimee's pretty face a mite too long.

Consequently, he missed the pain in the glance she shot up at him. Old fears rose up to haunt her, wailing in the shadowy corners of her mind.

When Luke's late excursions continued, Aimee's softer feelings hardened at her sense of betrayal. Luke was her husband, she loved him, but he didn't own her. She'd done everything humanly possible to make him happy, and he repaid her with half-truths. Why should she force herself into the constraining mold forged by Hedda and her son?

By the time they attended the Ferguson ball, Aimee was in a rebellious, ugly mood. Again, Luke had been out late. Again, he evaded her when she confronted him. Aimee was so angry she snapped at the young maid Hedda had hired, then she sighed, apologized, then admired the elegant coiffure the girl had arranged.

"Thank you, Emma. You are very talented." Aimee looked into the mirror and turned her head from side to side, studying the coronet of braids the girl had fashioned around a French pleat. The golden cords woven into the braids matched the trim on Aimee's cream satin dress. The heavy material was embroidered in strange, spiraling circles of gold thread that reminded Aimee of old Viking ornaments she had seen. Its stark design set off the beauty of the fabric. The tiny puff sleeves were bordered in gold. The tight-waisted skirt flared gently at the bottom, and the bustle, looped in golden cord, pulled the material so tight Aimee blushed to see how her figure was revealed.

Hedda entered, resplendent in ice blue taffeta bordered with silver lace. She stopped still at the sight of Aimee, a huge, pleased smile on her lovely face. She walked around her daughter-in-law, appraising her from every angle.

"My dear, you look as beautiful as I knew you would when I selected that material. It's a perfect background for your fair beauty. You look like a Viking princess, and I have the perfect touch to complete the effect." She opened the velvet case she carried. She clasped a necklace around Aimee's neck.

Aimee gasped. The gold spiraled delicately around her neck, matching the pattern on the gown. Large, perfect rubies were inlaid at each intersection of the spirals. A heavy pendant, depicting a small dragon in flight, hung suspended from the chain. It had blood-red rubies for eyes. Hedda held a pair of matching earbobs to Aimee's ears and added a ruby bracelet to her gloved wrist. She stood back, cocked her head and nodded in satisfaction.

"Joshua thought I was crazy when I ordered this made for your wedding present, but I knew it would look magnificent on you. You'll make these painted belles seem colorless and boring. I can't wait to see the look on Luke's face."

Even Aimee was amazed at her appearance. She looked regal, almost fiercely beautiful, in the barbaric finery. The half-wild look that had fascinated Luke from the beginning had never been more apparent, only now a new element glimmered there. Something she couldn't define, but which made Luke's black eyes smoke with passion when he entered to see if she was ready. Their gazes locked. Hedda smiled and urged the maid away with her, closing the door behind them.

Luke's eyes caressed her leisurely, paused at the dragon brooding on her breast, then settled on her mouth. He strode forward to pull her back against his chest. His smoky gaze raked over her as he murmured huskily, "You make me want to find a bear rug to throw you down on." He ran his hands over her shoulders, down her arms and insinuated his fingers between hers.

Breathing unsteadily, he backed away and ordered, "Stay close to me tonight. You'll take all the bucks by storm in that gown. I don't know what my mother was thinking of to dress you so for your first ball."

When she looked puzzled, he growled, "Look in the mirror, Aimee. Can't you see how sensual you look? You'll make every man there long for you."

Startled, Aimee looked at herself again, and she finally realized what was different. She no longer looked like a girl. Her mouth had a full sensitivity it had never had before; her eyes radiated the look of an experienced woman who enjoyed receiving and giving pleasure. That look, allied to the proud tilt of her head, was accented by the dress and jewelry. Aimee flushed and turned away.

His jaw set, Luke escorted Aimee downstairs. The others awaited them in the salon, Joshua magnificent and virile in black tails and top hat, Marietta gypsy-dark and lively in pink silk.

Luke snapped at Hedda, "I realize you want Aimee to

make an impression, but are you sure this is the right one?"

Hedda shrugged. "I wanted to set her apart from the others." She looked at Aimee again and smiled, obviously pleased with herself. "I've certainly done that."

"I won't enjoy my evening if I have to watch other men ogling my wife."

"Then I suggest you stay at her side to keep them from becoming too bold," Hedda retorted.

Aimee bridled at being discussed as if she weren't there. She wasn't a doll to dress up to impress Hedda's friends. Even worse, all Luke cared about was another man encroaching on his possession. She felt torn between despair and anger. He cared nothing for her. The thought of her attempts to win him filled her with self-disgust. Why should she betray the values of a lifetime to give happiness to a man who didn't appreciate her?

Joshua put a gentle arm around her shoulders and whispered, "Aimee, no one will make you come to the ball tonight if you'd rather stay home. Hedda means the best, truly. You'll be subjected to some malicious gossip tonight, I'm afraid, and she's merely trying to give you self-confidence in dealing with it."

When Aimee met his understanding eyes some of her resentment faded. "I appreciate her concern, but I'm not afraid. If Luke's friends don't accept me as I am, then I don't care if they accept me at all."

Joshua squeezed her shoulders. "That's the spirit. Every day, it becomes clearer to me what a wise decision Luke made in marrying you. You are a delight to me, Aimee. I couldn't wish for a daughter-in-law who would make me prouder."

Marietta, eyes sparkling, added, "You'll make every debutante there green as their money when they see you, Aimee. What an evening this will be!" She linked Aimee's arm and led her to the door, her excitement infectious.

Aimee's nerves felt soothed by their support as they climbed into the carriage. Luke played with her hand, but she ignored him and stared out the window.

The drive from Washington Square was brief, for the Fergusons lived but a few blocks up Fifth Avenue. Lights blazed from the stately brownstone. Conversation buzzed from the open windows. The sounds of an orchestra stirred

Aimee's soul, she loved the rich full tones of brass and string
instruments. She had made a good impression on Swedish
royalty, so what was there to fear from New York's elite?

Her hand was steady on Luke's arm, her jaw firm, when
she ascended the steps by his side. The women surrendered
their wraps, the men their hats, to a servant. They walked to
the ballroom, where they chatted briefly with their host and
hostess. Aimee cast her glance over the glittering crowd.
Women were attired in the latest Paris fashions, men in suave
and sophisticated black suits. Extravagant bouquets and
garlands of flowers graced every available nook and cranny
of the immense ballroom. The white marble floor reflected
back gilded molding and gas lights, while plush benches
covered in red velvet lined the walls, inviting the weary to
rest.

When the majordomo announced them, the milling crowd
below went still. A hush descended as the guests turned to
stare at the foreigner who had stolen New York's most
eligible bachelor. A few gasps echoed as both men and
women ogled Aimee's striking figure. When Aimee tipped
her chin and remained unruffled, they slowly turned away
—all except one man. He sauntered to the stairway with the
assured stride of one who cares nothing for society's laws. He
leaned indolently on the bannister, watching them descend.

Aimee stared back, fascinated with his resemblance to . . .
Luke, perhaps? Though physically quite opposite, he reminded Aimee of her husband's animal energy. His bright
golden head held the same proud angle; his pale gray, almost
silver eyes displayed the same fearless arrogance that often
infuriated Aimee. His tall frame was slimmer than Luke's,
but he had the same muscular grace and animal sexuality that
challenged any woman between the ages of fifteen and
seventy. He boldly appraised the graceful curves so vividly
accented by her tight gown. His smile was wicked, sensual.
He winked into her curious eyes.

His expression changed when he glanced behind her at
Hedda and Joshua. Something deep and painful flickered
there, but all emotion fled when he looked at Luke. His face
became as blank and secretive as a priory wall. Luke would
have brushed by him with no more than an icy stare, but the
man wheeled and straddled two steps to block their path.

"Not so fast, Luke. Even you aren't intolerant enough to

cause a scene here. Can't we spend time in the amenities?"
His musical baritone would have been enchanting if it had
lacked the razor edge.

Luke's tone was as sharp. "Amenities are for those civil-
zed and courteous. You fail on both counts, Mayhew."

Mayhew bowed sardonically. "You should know, Garrison. *Like* calling to *like,* so to speak. But then I don't have
your wealth and position to cover my sins, do I?"

Aimee's heart leaped. So this was the man so reviled by
the Garrisons. She looked pleadingly at Marietta, hoping her
sister-in-law could stop this scene, but she also seemed
stunned.

Luke hissed, "You've squandered your opportunities,
Mayhew, and you've only yourself to blame for your
failure. . . ."

The blond man interrupted harshly, "Myself, or the Garrisons, who will do anything to ruin my family name?" He cut
off Luke's retort by turning a brilliant smile on Aimee.
"Aren't you going to introduce me to your bride?" he
challenged. When Mayhew picked up her hand to kiss it,
Aimee felt how rigid he was with anger.

Luke snorted and mocked, "I'd as soon introduce her to a
wharf rat, Mayhew. Out of the way."

Luke elbowed Jeremy aside. Mayhew's white teeth
gleamed in a snarl at the insults. His hands doubled into fists.
Aimee closed her eyes so she wouldn't have to see them
connect. A frigid voice stopped both men in place.

"Enough, Luke, Jeremy! This is Aimee's debut into society, and I will not have it spoiled by your infantile wrangling!"

The blazing chandelier above their heads shone down on
Hedda, accenting her tall, imposing form and strong face.
Like a wise Athena meeting out justice, she looked sternly at
her sons, forcing them to behave. Luke's rigidity relaxed, but
Jeremy's fists clenched more tightly together. His eyes drilled
into Hedda's.

Aimee glanced from one to the other, wondering which of
them would be the first to yield. Neither had blinked when
Marietta hurried down the steps to hiss, "Now is not the time
to quarrel. We're causing a stir. Come, Jeremy, let's dance."
Marietta linked her elbow through Jeremy's and tugged him
to the ballroom floor.

Luke cursed softly as Jeremy led Marietta into the first

waltz. Marietta flashed her brother a smoldering, defiant look before smiling at her partner. Joshua sighed and shook his head at his daughter.

Hedda, her cheeks colored, turned to her stepson. "Luke, why don't you introduce Aimee?"

Luke nodded shortly. He led Aimee around the perimeter of the room, introducing her. Aimee was mulling over the scene she had just witnessed and didn't notice the interest she incited. Almost without exception, the men were admiring, even envious, as they appraised her glittering blond beauty. Most of the women were polite, a few were warm, but some of the younger girls nodded coolly when she was introduced.

Aimee barely noticed their rudeness. She knew the reasons for Marietta's suspicious absences and anger at her brother; she knew the reasons for the Garrisons' hostility. Somehow, now that she had met Jeremy, the two motivations more than ever formed a dichotomy in her mind. Marietta was as strong as the other members of her family, and Aimee could not believe she would be enamored of an amoral, ruthless man. She was still puzzling over the matter when a familiar voice interrupted her thoughts.

"Darling, so wonderful to see you again. When are you going to call?" Claire glided up and put her hand on Luke's free arm.

Luke tightened his grip on Aimee when she tried to move away. "My calling days are over, Claire," he said coldly.

"That doesn't keep you from dancing, does it?" She didn't give him a chance to refuse. She put her hand imperiously on his arm and led him to the dance floor.

Aimee watched Luke's hand rest on the woman's waist. Was it her imagination, or did his fingers move in a light caress? She tried to swallow her suspicions, but they lay in her stomach like stones. She had little time for jealousy. She was quickly surrounded by a swarm of gentlemen pleading for a dance.

She watched Luke whirling about the floor, turned away and bestowed a dazzling smile on a handsome young man. "I would be delighted, sir." She followed his movements fluidly, never giving a thought to her leg. When he confided that he had traveled the continent and admired Scandinavian lands most, he ignited her genuine interest.

"Indeed? I've heard many visitors find Norway the most

beautiful country they've ever seen."

He nodded in agreement, then teased, "But as far as cities go, I think I prefer Stockholm to Christiania. I've never had finer coffee or seen prettier women." He rolled his eyes in admiration.

Aimee's smile became still warmer when she saw Luke smiling at Claire. She cocked her head and trilled, "Oh, Bergen has much more to offer than good coffee and pretty women. We have some of the oldest churches on the continent and unique ports. Did you know my father is preparing to open a passenger line between Norway and America?"

The young man, as involved in New York's busy shipping world as most of the other guests, eagerly asked for more details. When the music stopped, he led her to a bench and listened as she described the schedule.

"They'll sail once every six weeks, carrying passengers and cargo from Bergen to New York, then back again. My father's ships will devote more space to the steerage section than is usual. That's where the real money is to be made, he's informed me more than once."

By now, Aimee was surrounded by curious gentlemen, and several gasped at such heresy. The latest trend in steamers was to see who could offer more luxury to big-name, affluent guests, lured aboard to ignite free publicity for the liner. That most lines made their profits by keeping their lowest berths fully booked was a fact seldom advertised.

"Isn't that a dangerous approach?" asked one elderly, pompous-looking man. "What if our economy goes sour and attracts few immigrants?"

"What if it does? First-class passengers will also limit their travel. Even if they don't, their patronage is not enough to guarantee a prosperous voyage. Besides, poor economic times are often worse in other countries. Little has discouraged immigration since your Civil War ended. I foresee no change in this trend."

Several of the younger men looked impressed with her logic. Most of the older gentlemen looked scandalized at such unfeminine boldness, though one of them nodded admiringly. "You have an uncommon head for business, young lady. It's a pity you're not a man. Your father could have used your help in his line, no doubt."

As if cued, Luke elbowed his way through the men to her

side. "You'll forgive me for disagreeing, Danville. I would be grieved to find my wife a man."

The men laughed heartily. Danville said, "It would be a waste indeed. Beauty and brains in a wife is a rarity, Luke. You are as lucky in love as you are in business."

A new male voice intruded on the scene. "By chance, or by design, I wonder?"

Jeremy Mayhew strolled up to join them. Aimee noticed that the other men moved aside for him as naturally as they had for Luke, but their smiles were stiff and unnatural rather than welcoming.

"What is that supposed to mean?" Luke asked softly.

Jeremy put one hand in his pocket and jingled his change, smiling affably. "Why, nothing in particular, unless you have something to hide. I've always wondered why you Garrisons prosper when the rest of us don't. Could it have anything to do with your connections?"

The gentlemen inched away from Luke, looking warily from one man to the other. Indeed, Luke took one step forward, but Aimee put all her weight on his arm to hold him in place.

She inserted breathlessly, "Perhaps it does, sir. Healthy relations with other shippers are important to any line. It might behoove you to look to your own."

Everyone looked back at Jeremy. His hand created a bulge in his pocket as he clenched it. "Perhaps I would, if allowed to. Somehow, I seem to be viewed with suspicion wherever I go. I wonder why?" His eyes smoldered at Luke.

Luke patted Aimee's hand in gratitude for her deft intervention and drawled, "I guess shippers are an uncommon judge of human nature." Luke's mouth stretched into a taunting smile. "By the by, Mayhew, did you know we've entered into a partnership with Aimee's father to open a Norwegian-American packet? We expect to begin operations very soon now."

Aimee stiffened, appalled at Luke's cruelty. He knew very well Jeremy was aware of it. His only intent was to humiliate the man in front of his peers. She tried to draw her hand away, but Luke would not allow it.

All watched Jeremy closely. It was common knowledge that he hoped to use his last two ships for exactly such a venture, but his ships were not fitted yet. They were disappointed at Jeremy's reaction. Aside from a tightening of his mouth, he reined in any further display.

He waved a hand, a sardonic yet admiring gesture. "Bully for you," he said. "May I wish you all the success you have wished me." After a glittering look at Aimee, he whirled and strode away.

Making their apologies, Luke encircled Aimee in his arms and spun her into a waltz.

She glared at him. "That's a fine way for a man to act who sets so much store by the amenities."

Luke flushed at the deserved barb and almost stepped on her foot. "Amenities be damned. I'll take no lip from that degenerate." His tone softened. "But thank you for your support. Your comment put him in his place far better than I could have."

"That was not my intent. I merely meant to advise he not go about with such a chip on his shoulder."

Luke narrowed his eyes in displeasure. "What do you care? He's earned his reputation as a troublemaker. I don't want you near him, do you understand?"

A few days earlier, Aimee might have refrained from comment, but now she was in no mood to suffer his arrogance, particularly when she spied Claire watching Luke hungrily from the arms of another man. "I understand all too well. You want me to be a submissive little wife without a thought in my head but that of pleasing you."

Luke's mouth dropped open. He recovered swiftly. "It's you I'm thinking of. I don't trust Mayhew with any woman, especially my own wife. Don't waste pity on one who doesn't deserve it."

They waltzed locked in hostility. Luke wheedled, "Come, sweetheart, you're much too beautiful to argue with. Smile at me, please?"

"Like Claire, Luke? That's all you care about, isn't it? Smiles, having your own way, a woman to climb on at night." Vaguely Aimee realized that she was throwing off her compliant role with a vengeance, but the pressures of the last few days were too much.

Suddenly, Aimee couldn't even bear his touch. She pulled away from him to hiss, "I won't swallow my pride any longer. I've tried, but I can't stand this anymore!" Her eyes blind with tears, she left him standing, white-faced and shocked in the midst of the swirling dancers. Aimee ignored the curious stares and whispers and sliced through the crowd to the rear veranda.

She leaned against the wrought-iron rail and bent her head, trying to regain control of herself. She wavered between self-contempt and anger at Luke. How weak and stupid of her to let any man control her life. Despite how much she had longed to pretend otherwise, Luke was no different from other men. She wondered now if he had been with Claire those nights he had disappeared.

No matter how much she loved Luke, she simply could not subjugate the instincts of a lifetime and ignore her own needs in order to please him. She had tried to be content with the half-life he had given her: material wealth, security and passion. But it was not enough. Such a life made her feel half a person. She was not whole without him, but she was not there at all without her old self.

The arguing voices took awhile to penetrate her misery, but the loud slap jolted her into awareness. She heard Marietta's tearful voice. "You're as bad as Luke! You don't own me. We're not married yet. I'll dance with whomever I please!" Aimee turned to see the pink form of Marietta as she ran into the ballroom. Jeremy appeared out of the shadows next, his hand to his cheek, his mouth twisted in pain.

He froze when he saw her. His hand dropped to his side. He gave her a deep, mocking bow. "Well, well, the Viking princess has escaped her fierce protector. Aren't you afraid a rascal like myself may carry you off?"

Aimee didn't flinch at his sneering smile, for she sensed a pain in him that surpassed her own. "No, I'm not afraid of you. I have never been one to judge someone unfairly, and you've yet to prove yourself a rascal in my eyes."

His sneer faltered, but he stepped to her to tower above her in challenge. "Brave words, indeed. Shall we put them to the test?" He put his arms around her and stared insolently into her face.

Aimee shook her head and gently pried his arms from about her waist. "It's not me you want to hurt. I won't let you use me to get vengeance on my family."

He flinched, then he stepped back and roared a bitter laugh. "Clever little girl, aren't you? It's a pity the rest of the Garrisons lack your perception." He propped his arms on the railing and stared sullenly into the shadowy garden. The sounds of a rushing fountain could be heard in the distance. The music inside turned light and airy.

Aimee leaned next to him. "Have you considered that your behavior invites the very condemnation you struggle against?"

He jerked his head around to glare at her. "I'm damned if I'll excuse myself to you or anyone. The stigma attached to my name is no fault of my dead father's or mine. It's largely a creation of the Garrisons to excuse their theft of my mother. In those circumstances, I owe them no consideration. I'm the one with a grievance. And you wonder why I refuse to cower before the mighty Garrisons?"

A ball of pity coiled in her stomach. Instinct had told her from her first seeing him that Jeremy was more than the Garrisons believed. She was becoming convinced that her judgment was on the mark. The throbbing pain in his voice was too real.

She nestled a soft hand over his clenched fist. "If that's true, then the Garrisons would be the first to regret their intolerance. Despite what you may think of them, my husband and his father are just men, and if you can prove yourself innocent, they'll do everything they can to make amends."

Jeremy looked at her suspiciously. He relaxed when he realized she was sincere. "There's no way to do that, now. The trail is twenty years old and far too cold." He smiled at her genuinely, warmly, revealing the charm that had bedazzled Marietta. "But I appreciate your forbearance. It's nice to know there's one Garrison, at least, who is kind enough to have an open mind."

"Don't you mean two?" Aimee teased, patting his hands and releasing them.

Jeremy straightened away from the railing. "No, I mean one," he said curtly. He bowed and walked back into the ballroom.

By the time the family climbed wearily into the carriage, Aimee's head was aching. She let her hand rest limply in Luke's, refusing to meet his searching gaze. Instead, she watched Marietta. Her sister-in-law's cheeks were flushed, her eyes bright, but Aimee suspected she was animated as much by anger as enjoyment. Whatever had she and Jeremy quarreled about?

When they reached their suite, Aimee calmly removed her clothes and prepared for bed, ignoring Luke's steady gaze. Luke waited until they got in bed to pounce.

"Aimee, I want an explanation for that little scene you treated me to. What did I do to deserve it?"

Aimee flung an arm over her eyes. "Must we go into this now?" she asked wearily.

He fixed her arm above her head so he could watch her face. "Yes."

Very well, she decided. He wanted truth? He would get it in spades. She struggled to a sitting position, fluffed the pillows behind her back, then folded her arms and began. "I'm amazed you even need to ask. How do you think it makes me feel to have nothing of you but your body and your wealth? I have a good mind. Even my father used to discuss business with me more than you do."

Luke sighed with relief and sat cross-legged before her, a smile playing about his lips. He enjoyed the contrast of her militant stance against her filmy bedgown and reams of hair flowing down her back. "As usual, my love, you have misunderstood me. I merely wanted to give you time to settle in before burdening you with more. I respect your intelligence more than any woman I've ever known. Why do you think I asked for your help a couple of nights hence?"

Aimee eyed him suspiciously. "You intended to share your concerns with me after I had 'settled in'?"

Pinching her cheek lightly, he teased, "Yes, you stubborn little vixen. If I'd simply wanted a compliant body, I could have wed a dozen times or more."

Aimee's arms fell to her sides in shame. "I'm sorry, Luke. I guess I can be too hasty, at times. Will you tell me where you've been the last few nights?"

Hesitating, Luke replied evasively. "Attending to a little crisis that has recently erupted. You can't help with this one, Aimee. I'm sorry, but it could be dangerous for you. That's my only reason for withholding the full story, I swear. I just don't want you involved."

Squeezing her eyes shut, she despaired. He told her he trusted her, respected her, then did the opposite. Her eyes were sad as she looked at him. "And what else do you not want me to know of? Your affair with Claire, perhaps?"

Luke scowled and rose to his knees. "Don't be ridiculous. I lost interest in her long before I met you. I've been as direct with her as I know how. Can I help it if she persists in embarrassing herself?"

"You didn't look embarrassed tonight when you were dancing with her."

"No, and neither did you when you danced with all those panting young bucks who tried to look down your gown."

Aimee gasped and rose. Without another word, she snatched her pillow off the bed, removed one of the quilts and marched into the sitting room.

Luke was too stunned to move at first. But when she banged the door between them, he leaped off the bed and flung it open again. Aimee, who was just settling down on the longest settee, gasped at his fierce face. He bent and gathered her up, quilt and all. He strode back to their bed and threw her down on the mattress, where he pinned her with his body.

"I'll fight all you want, but when the words are done and the lights go out, there's only one place you belong. In my bed. Forget this at your peril."

Aimee squirmed furiously, but couldn't budge him. Her hands were trapped by the quilt, so she couldn't even scratch him. She retaliated with the only weapon he left her—her voice. "You bastard! You tell me how much you respect me, then expect me to believe it when you show such disregard for my wishes? You won't even confide your family affairs, and I surely have a right to know them. Why should I listen to you? Tell me, why?"

Luke opened his mouth, snapped it closed on the only reply that would have appeased her and settled on his own side of the bed. He turned down the gas lamp and answered tiredly, "Because I'm your husband, and any 'disregard' I show is for your own good. Now, meet me in the study tomorrow at one and I'll share with you as much of my business affairs as you can stand to listen to."

He turned away and punched his pillow to relieve his frustration. Why, after everything, did she always think the worst of him? He had longed to reassure her with his love, but she always kicked him away. She had acted so oddly since they reached New York. First she was unnaturally calm, almost docile, now she spat at him like a wildcat. What had he done to incite such behavior? Though he felt a bit heartened by her jealousy, he was disgusted at her suspicions about Claire. Did she really believe he could savor her body, then betray her by bedding another woman, particularly one as tawdry as Claire?

Aimee bit her lip to stop her tears. She wasn't sure what to believe. She adored Luke with every beat of her heart, but she knew now marriage involved much more. It involved respect, trust, sharing. . . . Was she unrealistic to want more than sensual passion?

Chapter Fourteen

WHEN AIMEE ENTERED the study, she found Luke bent over
the elaborate desk. He drew her eyes like a beacon, as vital to
her as the sunlight streaming through the window. The sun's
merciless light put Luke's gleaming black hair, aggressive
chin and nose, long, masculine hands into clear relief. She
almost rushed to him to babble out her love. She would do
anything, say anything, to make him happy. She hated the
conflict that had, for the first time, denied them a night of
pleasure. Heat curled in her stomach as she remembered how
it felt to awaken in his arms, her body warm and moist from a
night of love.

Aimee closed her eyes and leaned against the door, weak
with love, struggling to regain her resolve. If she followed her
heart this time rather than her mind, they would never be
happy. She would resent his hold on her more each day until
he learned to return the full measure of her love. If he did.

Aimee took a deep breath and walked forward. "Luke,
what was it you wanted to tell me?" she asked calmly, seating
herself in front of the desk.

Luke started and glanced up. He felt himself beaming like
an idiot at the mere sight of her. Deliberately, he called up
memories of her stubborn resistance last night. It would
never do for her to learn of her power over him until she was
ready to return the love that made him ache to have her right
here on his desk. His loins stirred at the image. He

pulled his chair closer to the desk and gestured her over.

His reply was equally composed. "I want to tell you what I've been occupied with lately and explain our main enterprises."

Aimee leaned over his shoulder, her breast brushing him and her fragrance filling his nostrils. He shook himself from the dizziness entrapping his head, then showed her the financial data on his potential business partner, Victor Gleason. "He had his own boat awhile back, but his business was too small to survive our touchy economic times. He was recommended to us by Tom Payton, our warehouse manager. The partnership would confer benefits for each of us. We could have our ships towed at a much reduced rate and still earn our portion of the profits; he will have the extra capital he needs to stay in business, and we would, of course, recommend him to our business network."

"It sounds like a sensible arrangement," Aimee conceded. "So what are your reservations?"

Luke frowned, tapping his pencil against the desk. "I can't quite define them myself. There's just something about the man that gives me pause. I've had him investigated and found nothing, but still . . ."

Aimee nodded. "I understand. Instincts are almost as important in business as the financial details."

Luke couldn't stand being so close to her without touching her. He caught her waist to plop her into his lap. "And that, my Norwegian witch, is exactly why I want you to meet him. I've never met anyone with better instincts than yours."

They talked about business for another hour. The majority of their holdings, Luke explained, was in shipping, but they had shares in one of New York's largest banks. They also owned several rental properties and were considering investing in the new hotel where they would dine on the morrow. Interested as they both were in the subject, their position was not conducive to a calm business exchange. Luke's words became more and more disjointed, Aimee's attention less and less acute as the touch of her soft buttocks against his groin reminded them of the abstinence they had endured the last two days.

Luke ended the discussion by chewing her ear lobe. "And that is all the admiration you'll get from me this day for your fine mind, vixen. Right now, I'm far more interested in your fine body." As he spoke, he shifted her weight to the chair so he could lock the library door, then returned to prop her back on his aroused lap.

Aimee linked her arms around his neck and leaned against his shoulder, casting him an alluring smile. He leaned down and caught her lips hungrily, drinking in her softness, stoking the fire in them both. She moaned against him, glad she had averted her eyes at the last minute so he wouldn't catch the love in them. For now she wanted to sink into a sea of sensation.

The kiss they shared began lightly, but their emotions were too highly wrought for it to end that way. Luke kissed the corner of her lips and found her tongue there to meet him and lead him inward to the sweet cavern of her mouth. They groaned in unison, their hands wandering, seeking pleasing curves and angles. When clothes got in the way, they brushed them impatiently aside, too eager to disrobe. In minutes, Aimee was moist and aching to be filled; Luke was hard and hungry to oblige.

He shoved the papers on his desk aside and lifted her gently atop, but even when he was nudging the warm gate of her body, he controlled his ardor and studied her flushed face. "If this is too crude for you, love, we can go upstairs. But I confess I've been fantasizing about this since I looked up and saw you today." His head swam as she blinked in a passionate haze, and groaned her hunger.

"You're not the only one who fantasizes, dear husband. I can't look at your hands without remembering how they feel on my body. I don't want to wait. . . ."

Sighing her name, he entered her almost before she finished speaking. He gave her ample opportunity to enjoy his touch as he brought their fantasies to a brilliant fulfillment. And, when he slumped against her, spent, all was right between them again.

They straightened their clothing, giggling like adolescents. Luke found one of his father's reports wrinkled beyond repair, a suspicious stain on it. He rolled his eyes, muttering, "Now how the hell will I explain that to him?"

He whisked the report into the desk, looking so like a guilty little boy that Aimee couldn't resist kissing him. When he reached out to grab her, she danced away. Laughing, she taunted, "That's your problem. I came in here with nothing on my mind but business. Can I help it if you don't have the same concentration?"

Luke put his hands on his hips and mock-glared at her. "I never had problems with my concentration until you came in. And I didn't notice you arguing with my change of subject, either."

Aimee patted a yawn. "I was too polite to admit to boredom." The sidelong glance she sent him was so seductively provocative that he stalked her across the room.

Laughing, she shot out the door and up the stairs. Their playful mood set the tone for the remainder of the day. They bathed one another leisurely, dressing in casual summer attire. Business be hanged, Luke decided. Aimee was too distracting in this flirtatious mood for him to concentrate anyway.

A hand crossed gallantly over his heart, he bowed. "I am at your service, Mrs. Garrison. There's something I've been wanting to teach you."

She looked interested. "What?"

Eyes glittering, he drawled, "I'll never forget how I felt when I saw you standing with a pistol in your hand. I shuddered for days over the horrifying thought of what would have happened had you missed. Would you like to learn to shoot?"

Aimee's eyes lit up. "Oh, yes. Will you teach me?"

"Yes, if you'll promise to follow my directions exactly. And, above all, you must not tell Hedda. She would be appalled."

The afternoon found them in the rear, high-walled garden. Wisteria clung tenaciously to the red brick walls. A riot of flowers bordered the macadam walkways. Everywhere, there were roses: pink, white, red, gold and shades in between.

Aimee rolled up her sleeves. She watched Luke load the heavy Colt Patterson revolver, unload it, then hand gun and ammunition to her.

"The first thing any marksman must learn is how to hold and load a gun. And, for God's sake, *never* point it at anything you don't intend to shoot, loaded or unloaded."

The pistol was unwieldy, but she followed his instructions and loaded it easily enough. Luke almost laughed at the incongruous look of her delicate hand against the weapon, her fine features set with concentration. She beamed at him when she was finished.

He tweaked her nose. "Now, here's the proper way to hold it." Luke sprawled apart his feet, then braced one hand against the other to steady his aim. Smoothly, he squeezed the trigger, aiming at one of the bottles he'd set up on a bench against the wall. Aimee started as it exploded.

He turned back to her, smiling. "See how easy it is?"

She swallowed when he handed the gun to her, but nodded gamely. He put his arms around her to help her get the proper position, then he stood back. Aimee gritted her teeth, refusing to admit how much she hated the heavy feel of the gun in her hand. Pugnaciously, she straddled her feet as Luke had and braced the gun. She took a deep breath, held it as he suggested and fired.

The afternoon sun peeked through the tall elms as if curious about the spectacle. A blue jay squawked in outrage at having his habitat invaded by the rude clamor. With an agitated fluttering of wings, it flew away to safety.

The shot hit the wall a good three feet above the bottle she'd aimed at. Chagrined, Aimee lowered the gun.

"That's all right, Aimee. It takes awhile to learn. Try again."

Aimee spread her legs a bit more. She pinched her mouth in concentration and fired again. A clump of dirt in front of the bench leaped into the air.

Luke scratched his head. How could her aim be so far off? He coached her on the correct posture and grip again, then stood back. Luke groaned when this shot lopped off the main stem of one of his mother's favorite rose bushes. The plant sagged to one side.

Aimee's face was fiery with embarrassment. She tried to hand the gun back. "It's hopeless."

He shook his head in puzzlement. "I can't understand why you're so far off the mark. You seem to be doing everything right. Try it once more."

He positioned her hands around the Colt and shifted to one side so he could see her face. Her tongue went to the side of her mouth. Her eyes narrowed as she aimed. She fired. . . . Luke's mouth quivered in amusement, but the laugh died as the shot hit an iron planter and ricocheted.

He grabbed Aimee and dove for the ground, though it was a futile gesture, knocking the pistol out of her hand. They had heard the unmistakable ping of broken glass. Luke looked up warily. He sank back on the ground with a groan when he saw where the bullet had gone. His mother's custom-designed porch door fixed with a stained glass window had a hole bored into its center. She couldn't have done better if she'd been aiming.

Aimee heard the noise as well and sat up, looking toward the bench. Finally, she'd hit it! She scowled when seeing the bottle still sitting upright. Luke clasped her chin and turned it to the porch door. Her eyes widened. She bit off one of the curses she'd heard him use and slumped down next to him.

Luke pulled Aimee into his arms, teasing, "Such language! Don't worry, sweet. You can't be good at everything. I don't think Wild Bill Hickock will feel threatened by you." When she frowned, he elaborated, "He's a famous marksman."

Glancing at her sidelong, he drawled, "But there is one suggestion I'm sure he would give you." She looked curious. He put his lips to her ear and whispered, "You might try keeping your eyes open when you fire."

The eyes in question closed in disgust. "I wondered why I could never see where the shot went." She was so disgruntled that Luke could no longer contain his mirth. Aimee looked offended for a moment, then her face lit up with a grin. Laughing together, they stood.

They inspected the window and eyed one another guiltily. Luke swept away the signs of their activity, pocketed the gun and caught her hand. "I'm not looking forward to telling Hedda about this. What do you say we visit the park first?"

Aimee had not yet had the opportunity to see Central Park, the largest city park in America. She nodded eagerly. When they entered the house, Luke put the gun back in the gun case and rang for a carriage.

On reaching the park gate, Luke slowed the carriage to a crawl. A stern-looking policeman, dressed in a sedate gray uniform, waved them through the gate, admonishing, "Don't drive too fast and obey all the park rules." Luke tipped his hat in acquiescence.

He drove the open carriage slowly through the grounds so Aimee could see the varied scenery. He explained, "You'd never believe it now, but when work began in 1858, this land was nothing but scrub brush, sand and stagnant pools. I used to come watch the workers when I was a boy. My father was one of the original private citizens who fought for the Park. He believed New Yorkers of all class would need space for play, enjoying nature and plain relaxing. The site was chosen because it is in the center of the city. Isn't it lovely?"

Aimee turned glowing eyes to him. "Oh yes. Everything

looks so real it's hard to believe it was all man-made." She turned from side to side as they inched along the carriage path.

A rock ridge divided the center of the grounds into three distinct types of scenery: a miniature alpine region, a water region and a long sweep of lush lawn. Luke halted the carriage, helping Aimee down so they could explore the grounds. They ascended a broad flight of stairs near the 59th Street entrance, coming out on a great mall where people of every persuasion strolled.

A young nanny pushed a carriage with twin infants in it. A butcher, still wearing his apron, tossed a ball to his son. A flirtatious young couple dressed in the latest fashions strolled arm in arm. A tired-looking seamstress hurried by, pins stuck in the cushion around her neck. Two sailors tried to draw the attention of a group of girls shepherded by their school mistress.

Aimee was as fascinated by the diversity of people as by the scenery, so she barely noticed when Luke led her down three flights of stairs to the esplanade below. The splash of water caught her attention. She looked ahead and drew in her breath in awe.

A magnificent fountain towered above their heads. Its pedestal was set on two squares superimposed one upon the other to form a star. Water cascaded into a round pool. Luke put his hands on Aimee's shoulders and pointed, murmuring, "Look over there."

Aimee followed his finger, to a sixty-foot high waterfall plunging into a lake. The water was spanned by bridges busy with pedestrians. Rowboats dotted the lake. Some were rowed by straining young men showing off for their girls; others were piloted by fathers eyeing their adventurous offspring warily.

Strolling about on the greensward stretching before them, they savored this togetherness and enjoyed God's—and man's—bounty. There was a disturbance up ahead. Luke automatically tightened his arm around Aimee's waist to pull her away.

Standing on tiptoe, Aimee tried to see past the crowd of onlookers, but she wasn't tall enough. She followed Luke's guiding hand, but when a child screamed, she pulled away and ran into the crowd before Luke could stop her. The people, mostly men, were already dispersing.

One muttered to another, "T'weren't much of a fight. That little bastard looks like he ain't long for this world." The burly man shook his head with pity, but walked on.

Dusting his hands, a big youth spat on the ground and strutted away with a muttered, "Trash."

Aimee glared after him, then knelt on the ground next to a ragged, crying boy with a bloody nose. When she put her hand on his arm, he shrank away. Terror glinted out at her behind his watery blue eyes set in a gaunt face.

Her large, floppy hat shaded her features. Without a care for the harsh glare of the summer sun, Aimee jerked it off and smiled at him reassuringly. Luke put his hand on her shoulder and tried to make her rise, but she shrugged him off.

"It's all right, let me see your nose," she said gently to the boy. She pulled her handkerchief from her sleeve and dabbed at the blood.

He looked confused by her concern. His eyes flew to Luke's irritated face. "Ain't nothin' lady. I've had worse," he said, wiping the tears out of his eyes, returning Luke's glare through dirty strands of brown hair.

"Where is your mother? Can we take you to her?" Aimee asked, looking about.

The boy rose and dusted off his threadbare clothing as if he hadn't heard. He staggered a little. Aimee supported him, ignoring Luke's impatient tug on her arm.

"I'm not leaving until you let us take you home," she told the boy softly.

He turned his head to snap at her, but swallowed the words. The green eyes smiling at him were gentle, sympathetic and concerned, not pitying. It was the first time he could remember anyone showing him such kindness. He felt tears rising in his throat, but forced them manfully back.

"I ain't got no home," he said baldly, turning his head away.

Aimee's eyes watered, but she merely said calmly, "Well, then you must come with us. I'm sure my husband can use a good, strong boy like you. Would you like a job?"

Aimee met Luke's eyes, a plea in them. He looked appalled, angry, but when her tears threatened to spill, he sighed in resignation. He looked over the boy, assessingly. Strong, hah! He'd need a month of good meals before he'd be strong enough to pull a weed in the garden. He agreed,

"Yes, I have need of an assistant for my gardener. Are you interested?"

The boy seemed stunned. He replied harshly, "I ain't got no ex-ex-"

"Experience?"

He nodded. "I been livin' in the streets fer three years. Thievin' if I have to," he added defiantly. He pulled away from Aimee to brace his legs and goad Luke. "Do you still want me?"

Luke's mouth softened in admiration. Poor in material wealth this lad might be, but he was rich aplenty in spirit. Luke found himself giving the boy enough coins for a meal and his address. "We'll expect you this evening," he said firmly.

The boy clutched the coins and turned away. He paused, looked over his shoulder and muttered, "Thank you, ma'am. My name is Bob." He sauntered away, still unsteady on his feet but with some direction in mind.

Aimee threw her arms around Luke, pulling his face down to cover it with kisses. "Thank you, thank you, darling," she caroled joyously.

Luke swallowed the lecture he'd been about to deliver and enjoyed the feel of her in his arms. She gave him a kiss so long and sweet that even the thought of Hedda's expression when that child knocked on her door didn't bother him.

The walk back to their carriage was leisurely. Aimee's spirits felt lighter than they had in many a day. She had finally given back a tiny portion of the good fortune she'd experienced. Even more satisfying was Luke's capitulation. When the boy had stood up to him, he'd been almost as eager to help. She'd convert him to her way of thinking yet.

Aimee was lost in thought when Luke pulled on her arm to halt her, calling, "Tom! I have someone I want you to meet!"

A tall, red-haired man started and whirled from his conversation with a small, plump man. Aimee saw a flash of consternation in his eyes, then he smiled and strode forward with outstretched hand. "It's good to see you, Luke. Is this lovely lady your new wife?"

Luke led Aimee proudly forward. "Indeed. Aimee, this is Tom Payton, our warehouse manager." He looked at the small, plump man with blond hair and blue eyes behind Payton. "And this is Victor Gleason, an associate of mine."

Aimee shook their hands, appraising each man. Payton's eyes were a pale, piercing blue, very astute, very . . . Aimee couldn't pinpoint the other expression in them, but something about him made her uneasy. She looked at Gleason, noting his weak mouth and sweaty palms. He seemed nervous, easily agitated. She wondered what the two men had been discussing.

Luke talked to Payton about the rich shipment of silks and spices he was expecting from China in a couple of weeks. "We'll need to make room for the crates. I want them put in our most secure area, so move whatever is there." Luke turned to Gleason. "I'm looking forward to our meeting tomorrow. I should be able to give you my decision soon after. My wife will be dining with us, if you've no objection?"

Gleason shook his head. "No, not at all, I'll be charmed," he said heartily.

When they had taken their leave, Aimee peeked over her shoulder and studied both men. They were drilling Luke's retreating back with steel-like glances, and exchanging whispered words. She turned quickly around, chilled. Something was very wrong; she felt it. She was in a haze on the drive back to Washington Square. She debated sharing her suspicions with Luke, but she had nothing concrete to convey. She should give Gleason the benefit of the doubt. She'd watch him closely at dinner.

They walked in the house to find Hedda grilling the servants. "I'll have no more evasions. I want to know who, how and when my window was ruined." She bore holes with her eyes into the line of uniformed servants, but none murmured a word.

Luke cursed to himself and went forward to confess, but Aimee stayed him with her hand. She walked forward and admitted, "I broke the window, Hedda. Don't blame the servants. I was learning how to shoot and er, miscalculated. I can pay for a new window out of my allowance. I most humbly beg your pardon."

Hedda's outraged stance softened at Aimee's confession. She looked stunned, but merely sighed. "Never mind, child. I was never quite satisfied with the way that window turned out, anyway. Now I have an excuse to replace it."

The servants dispersed with grateful glances cast at their new mistress. Looking thoughtful, Hedda retreated to the study to sketch a design for the window.

Only Luke remained in the hallway to eye Aimee's demure expression suspiciously. "Humbly beg her pardon, eh? What drivel! You wouldn't know humility if it hardened into rock in front of your nose."

Aimee's mouth quivered. She looked up at him, revealing mischievous eyes. "Perhaps not, but Hedda's no longer angry, is she?"

Luke tried to look stern, but he couldn't hide his amusement. "You're learning, sweet, you're learning. You're changing the running of the household so slowly Hedda hasn't even noticed; you mute her anger such that she wonders why she was mad; you have Father and Marietta singing your praises to the skies; you have me eating out of your hand and missing you whenever we're apart. What will you do next? Decide to run for president?"

A musical laugh answered him. "No, of course not." She turned away, tossing over her shoulder, "But I may become a suffragette like Susan B. Anthony." She hurried up the stairs, laughing harder at Luke's horrified expression.

And shortly before dinner, when Bob appeared, Aimee appeased Hedda's anger with the same tact and skill. Luke watched, torn between admiration, amusement and foreboding as Aimee wheedled Hedda into hiring Bob to work in the garden. If, at the tender age of eighteen, she was so capable of changing everything and everyone around her, how would she be in the years of her prime? Luke gulped down his wine, trying to smother the thought.

They retired early that evening, passion rushing as hot and wild between them as their first time. Luke waited until he thought Aimee was asleep, then he rose and dressed quietly.

Aimee kept her eyes closed as he kissed her cheek. When she heard the door shut, she sat up in bed, buried her face in her hands and wept. After the blissful day they had shared, the empathy between them about Bob, she had hoped Luke's nightly absences would cease. The sound of a carriage retreating echoed back her foolishness.

Aimee tried to comfort herself and stem her tears, telling herself she was wrong. Luke would never leave her still flushed with passion and go straight to the bed of another woman. But what other explanation was there? What business could entail such nightly, secret meetings?

So much for passion and caring, she thought bitterly. She had let Luke take her like a slattern in full daylight in the study, meeting his ardor with sensuous lunges of her own. She flushed as she admitted she hadn't *let* Luke take her; she had taken him as well. But that encounter and the happy day that followed were still not enough to hold him.

Aimee was wiping her eyes with the sheet when someone knocked on the door. She cleared her throat, lay back down and pulled the covers up. "Come in."

She was surprised to see Marietta appear in the doorway, then approach quietly. "I saw Luke leave, Aimee. I'm going now to meet Jeremy. Would you like to come?"

Aimee's first instinct was to say yes. Her second was worry about Luke's reaction. He had ordered her to stay away from Jeremy, and his fury would erupt uncontrollably if she defied him. Aimee gritted her teeth. Her eyes were still red from crying. If he betrayed her, did she owe him all her loyalty? Yes, she answered herself. Marriage is not always easy, always convenient. Sometimes one partner had to give more than the other. She'd not done all she could to make her marriage work. Did she dare defy him on this one thing that she sensed would anger him most? Hesitating, she peered at Marietta's face in the gloom.

She had caught something in Marietta's voice that troubled her. She ruminated, "I wonder if it's your idea to ask me or Jeremy's?" Marietta bit her lip. "I thought so. Won't you tell me what's wrong between the two of you?"

Marietta began to shake her head, but when Aimee turned up the gas lamp and eyed her steadily, she sat down on the bed. "We've argued a lot lately. I always thought Jeremy was different, that he would allow me to say what I want, do what I want, but I think I'm wrong. We're not even officially engaged yet, and he had the gall to scold me for flirting with other men. All I did was dance with the baron."

Aimee lifted an eyebrow. She remembered Marietta's ardent response to the handsome young Austrian nobleman she danced with at the Ferguson ball. The young man had a sweet, gentle charm that reminded her of Gere. Marietta had been fascinated by him. She couldn't blame Jeremy for objecting. She probed, "Marietta, are you sure you want to marry Jeremy? Or are you more interested in defying Luke and your father?"

Marietta bridled. "Of course I . . ." She twisted a corner of the bed hanging and admitted, "I honestly don't know. There was a time when I was eager to marry him, but now . . . I've begun to notice other men. Jeremy has been almost as arrogant as Luke lately."

"Has it occurred to you that it's you who's changed, not Jeremy?"

Marietta looked stunned, then pained. "Are you telling me I've been infatuated? That I've given Jeremy false hope all this time?"

Aimee took Marietta's hand. "Not at all. I'm sure you've never been deliberately cruel. No doubt you thought yourself in love with him at the time." She added softly, "However, I fear the effect will be the same on Jeremy, regardless of your intent."

Marietta rose to pace up and down. "Now I understand why I've begun to dread our meetings. I'd been hemmed in for so long by Luke and Father that Jeremy was the perfect avenue of escape. Oh, I feel sick. God, how will I tell him the truth?" She came back to the bed to take Aimee's hands in hers. "Please, please, dear sister, come with me. It will be easier on both of us if you're there."

"I don't agree, Marietta. Jeremy's pride will be hurt. It's best you tell him alone."

Marietta's lips trembled. She choked, "I care for Jeremy, truly. I won't blame him if he's furious. It seems he gets nothing but pain at the hands of Garrisons." She went to the door, but Aimee called her back.

"Perhaps I can wait in the carriage, out of hearing. If he knows you're not alone, he'll be less inclined to be . . . hasty."

Marietta flew back to the bed and embraced Aimee. "Thank you. I'll wait downstairs in the carriage."

Aimee pulled out a dress at random. It wasn't until she'd put it on that she realized it was one of her most daring gowns. Of pink gauze, it was so sheer it followed each of her curves like loving hands. The bodice was high, but yoked in ice pink chiffon from throat to scooped neckline, making her revealed bosom enticing as pink pearls. Dark pink ribbons tied the gathered, elbow-length sleeves and bustle ruffles. Aimee shrugged and threw on a light summer cloak. She'd be covered, and Jeremy would probably never see her anyway. Aimee closed off the lamp and went down to meet Marietta.

Jeremy lived on New York's east side. The streets were full of refuse, pigs poking through the gutters, adding their stench to the foul smell. Tall tenements with peeling paint, rotting doors and sagging timbers surrounded them in a small canyon. Even at this late hour, people were in the streets. Young toughs sauntered down the board walk; worn-looking men and women stomped toward their work in the sweathouses of the wealthy.

Aimee pulled her cloak tighter with icy fingers when curious eyes followed their progress down the road. Aimee asked nervously, "Are you sure he wanted to meet you here?"

Marietta nodded, her eyes as disturbed as Aimee's as she, too, absorbed the poverty around them. "We've never met at his rooms before. But tonight he asked me to come to him. I'm not sure why."

They halted in front of a small building that seemed a little cleaner and newer than the rest. The coachman opened the door for Marietta. He was stiff with disapproval, but, after a haughty look from his mistress, he stepped aside and let her descend. Marietta gestured for Aimee to follow.

"I don't feel comfortable leaving you here alone. You'd better come, too. You can wait while I speak to Jeremy." Marietta strode up the steps with more confidence than she felt. Aimee followed reluctantly.

Jeremy answered the door on the first knock. "You're late. . . ." He scowled when he saw Aimee. "What's she doing here?"

"I asked her to come." Marietta walked past him, pulling Aimee in with her.

Aimee looked around at the old but expensive furniture. An original oil painting framed in gilt hung above the massive claw-footed divan. Aimee even recognized a vase from the Ming dynasty sitting on a fine cherry wood table. She was puzzled. If Jeremy was wealthy enough to own such things, why did he live in such a poor neighborhood?

Marietta suggested, "It might be best if we go to your room to talk. I have something private to say."

Jeremy smiled sardonically. "Filled with passion at last, my love?" He swept her a mocking bow. "Lead on."

The door closed behind them. Aimee wandered about, trying not to listen to their conversation, but the walls were thin. When their voices rose, she couldn't help but hear.

"I've been waiting for you to get up nerve enough to be honest with me. I've known for weeks that you'd changed your mind. Why do you think I asked you to come here alone? I wanted you to see exactly what you'd be getting. I guess I was wrong about you. You aren't any different from the rest of your clan."

Marietta's voice was tearful. "That's not true, Jeremy. I never minded that you were struggling to save your father's business. I would have lived with you in worse surroundings than this if I'd loved you." Her voice became soft, defeated. "I don't want to hurt you, but I know now I never loved you. We'd both be miserable if we married and pretended otherwise. Besides, if you're honest, you'll admit you never loved me either. I was a convenient vehicle of revenge to get at my brother and father."

There was a long, painful silence. Then, in a voice no longer hostile, Jeremy said, "Thank you for being honest with me, Marietta. I will always treasure the good times we had together."

"And I, Jeremy. Now, we'd better be getting back before Luke returns and finds us gone. . . ."

The door banged open. Marietta hurried out, rolling her eyes at her stupidity in introducing Luke's name. Jeremy stalked after her.

"Mrs. Garrison, so nice of you to visit," he said nastily, pronouncing Aimee's name like an epithet.

Aimee's anger stirred as she recalled how she had defended this man to Luke. She had done nothing to earn his contempt.

She stood arrow straight and answered coolly, "Thank you, Mr. Mayhew. It's a pity you couldn't make the visit enjoyable." She turned a snubbing shoulder to him and followed Marietta to the door.

The despairing words seemed torn out of Jeremy. "God, I'm sorry. I'm becoming as bad as Luke, condemning others out of hand. Please forgive me."

Aimee turned to meet eyes so weary that her anger melted. She took an impulsive step toward him, instinctively trying to assuage his pain. "Of course I forgive you. I'm desperately sorry for my husband's harshness to you. I know Marietta thinks he's wrong. From the little I've seen of you, I would agree. But why do you goad him to think the worst?"

Jeremy brushed a hand over his forehead. "What good would it do? Luke grew to manhood hating the Mayhew name as much as my father . . ." He snapped his mouth shut.

Aimee probed, "Yes, as much as your father what?"

Jeremy muttered, "Never mind. You'd better go before your absence is discovered."

Slumping into a wing chair, Jeremy poured himself a small drink. Aimee met Marietta's troubled eyes. She inclined her head toward the door, whispering, "Go on home. Send the carriage back for me. We all need to get to the bottom of this, or it will continue devastating your family and Jeremy."

Marietta looked doubtful, but she saw the determined set to Aimee's jaw. She shrugged and left.

Jeremy's mouth turned down as he heard the door shut. Thinking himself alone, he rested his head on his hand, his very bones weary. He started and spilled his whiskey when a soft, resolute voice sounded.

"Marietta will send the carriage back for me. But I will not leave until you start at the beginning and tell me everything you know about the night Hedda's brother was murdered."

Jeremy was obstinate at first, but Aimee's genuine concern finally pried the words out of him. "My father was anguished when Bjorn died. He was as baffled by the thefts as Bjorn was. That last cargo was one of their most costly, and he truly was trying to keep it safe when he had it removed. The jury believed him, but Hedda didn't."

He set his barely touched drink down and rubbed his chin, conceding, "His behavior did not encourage her belief. I see that now, though I blamed her as much as he did at the time. He was a stubborn, reserved man who always found it difficult to voice his feelings. He was devastated when Hedda refused to believe him. Being a proud man, he covered up his hurt with bitterness." He clenched his fists on his knees. "You know the appalling irony of it? My father loved Hedda passionately to the day he died. She still thinks, even now, that he hated her."

Aimee was disturbed. The Garrisons had been incredibly blind and unjust. Shouldn't she, the newest Garrison, help right the wrong that had been done? "The only way to solve the problem is to discover the real thief. If we can get proof, Hedda will have no choice but to believe you."

Jeremy looked hopeful, then sagged against his chair. "I tried that, shortly after my father died. I couldn't discover a thing. The evidence was damning against him. The thefts stopped with Bjorn's death. No, it's hopeless. Besides, I won't be in New York much longer. My father drank himself to death, and our business suffered as a result. I've only been able to hold on to two ships because no one will advance me more credit. My only hope was this idea I had to open a passenger line. Luke has put a stop to that. Now that things are over with Marietta, I intend to sell everything but one ship, pay my debts and strike out on my own."

Aimee winced, wishing she hadn't been the means by which Luke had tightened his stranglehold on his enemy. For the first time, she wondered if revenge had motivated Luke to marry her, as much as desire. She shoved the thought away. Now was not the time to worry.

She leaned forward, unaware when her cloak gaped open and revealed the seductive gown. "But don't you see? If we can gain proof, then the Garrisons will not only stop persecuting you, they'll help you refinance your line. Isn't it worth the chance?"

Jeremy looked at Aimee, noting the excited flush in her cheeks, the sensuous mouth, the intelligent, alert eyes. His eyes dropped to her bosom. A Garrison or not, she was a fascinating woman.

Jeremy dragged his eyes away from her bodice to her face. "Perhaps there is a chance," he muttered.

Aimee was too excited by his agreement to notice his double meaning or the strange look in his eyes as he led her to the door.

PART V

❧❧

These demons have cast an evil spell, but the race of the gods in their armor bright can trample to chaff the deceits of hell.

—Johan Sebastian Cammermeyer Welhaven, "Norway's Highlands"

Chapter Fifteen

LUKE WATCHED THE dawn's birth broodingly. The sunrise suited his mood, reflecting the colors of passion: gold, violet and red. Gold as Aimee's eyes, violet as the lilacs crushed in his hand, red as the enraged blood that surged in his body. Luke had returned early from the warehouse, eager to be with Aimee when she awoke. He brimmed with such good spirits, he decided to set aside pride and admit his love. Surely the woman who responded to him with such passion cared in some small measure for him? Boldly, he decided to test his theory. He grabbed a handful of flowers from a front bed and burst into their chamber, intending to confess his love by scattering flowers and kisses on Aimee's petal-soft skin.

His romantic dream became a nightmare when he was met by a cold empty mattress instead of warm arms. He had prowled through their rooms, unable to believe she was gone. Stunned, he crushed the flowers in his hand and went to the window in a haze of pain. He struggled to deny the ugly suspicions forming in his mind, but his disappointment and sense of betrayal overcame him. Aimee must be meeting another man. There was no other explanation for her absence. What social obligations could possibly call her out in the dark of night?

Her strange, moody behavior of late fit the pattern of a bored wife. He groaned through bloodless lips, every nerve screaming with frustration. Was he as stupid as other men, as easily fooled by a woman's duplicity?

Smoldering black eyes watched Aimee's weary descent from the carriage thirty minutes later. Luke listened to her furtive steps, the soft opening and closing of the door. Slowly, he turned, biting his tongue to control his rage. One chance, he'd give her.

When she removed her cloak, he winced at the sight of the gown she wore. It was one she had never felt comfortable wearing at home, yet she dressed in it for a clandestine meeting. He took another step before, with an immense effort at self-control, he wrapped his arm about the bedpost to anchor himself.

The movement caught Aimee's attention. She gasped in dismay at the sight of him, then smiled uncertainly. She was unable to see his face. The window was behind him, but something in his posture sent a chill up her spine. "Good morning, Luke. I was just out with Marietta. She asked me to accompany her on an, er, social call."

Luke's bland reply disturbed Aimee more than if he had become angry. "Strange, I didn't see Marietta alight with you."

"No, Marietta came home earlier. I . . . had something to attend to."

"Indeed, madam wife?" He put ugly stress on the title. "And what might that be?"

Aimee worried at her lip. If she told him the truth, he would be furious; if she said nothing, he would be furious. Only for an instant did she consider lying. She lifted her chin defiantly. She had done nothing wrong. In fact, her aim was admirable. She would give him the same explanation he had given her and see how *he* liked it.

"Something I can't share with you yet, but nothing dishonorable. Can't you give me the same trust you demand of me?"

Luke took a deep breath. He searched her pleading eyes, then let the crushed flowers in his hand fall to the floor. Indeed, how could he demand total trust from her if he didn't return it in kind? The black wave of jealousy and betrayal receded, but left nothing in its wake. His tone was lighter, but still grim when he answered, "Very well, Aimee, I'll question you no more for now. But what the devil were you doing that required you to dress like that?"

Aimee glanced down at herself, reddening as she realized

what had held Jeremy's eager attention toward the end of their talk. "I grabbed the first gown I came to. I intended to keep my cloak on, anyway."

Her complexion matched the gown's rose trim. She turned her head away, rekindling his suspicions. What a romantic fool he was, he told himself scathingly. Thank God he'd not blurted his feelings, for it was quite obvious she did not return them.

Luke watched Aimee closely for the rest of the day, but she seemed normal. She discussed menus with cook, watched Bob at his duties in the garden, coaxed Hedda into designing a less ostentatious window for the porch, running the household as efficiently and cheerfully as had become her wont. She never left the house.

Luke tried to dismiss his suspicions, but, once born, they took on a life of their own. If only she would return his love, he could forgive her anything, he told himself. But he felt less secure of his place in her life than ever. His insecurities were devastating to a man who had never known self-doubt.

Aimee knew he watched her. She was hurt by his lack of trust. She had always felt confident of his respect for her morality, if not for her intellect, but now he stripped even that comfort away. Angry, she said nothing, letting his suspicions eat away at him.

By the time they left for the dinner with Gleason, their smiles were strained. Each sensed the chasm between them, and each felt helpless to bridge it.

The meeting was held at one of Fifth Avenue's grandest, newest hotels. The interior was ornate with Italian marble cornices, columns and floors. Cloud-soft divans and chairs sat in discreet groupings throughout the lobby, with huge potted plants set off to the side. The restaurant off the lobby was an elegant blend of cream tablecloths, blue velvet chairs and azure carpet.

Gleason rose at their entrance. He bowed to Aimee. Aimee curtseyed and sat down in the chair Luke held for her. She said little during the rich meal, listening and watching. Gleason was both hearty and frank about his hopes for the partnership.

Too hearty and frank, Aimee reflected. No good businessman showed all his cards before the hand was played. As the evening wore on, Aimee's suspicion about Gleason increased. But what could it be?

Over the creme brulee she tried to draw them out. "Mr. Gleason, from what I hear, the tugboat business has not been good of late due to the recent decline in shipping traffic into New York. My husband always tells me it's wise to diversify your business. Forgive a woman's curiosity, but have you other interests?" Aimee's smile was sweet and innocent, but she squeezed Luke's hand meaningfully under the table.

Gleason, surprised, looked at Luke. He allowed his wife to take part in business discussions? He was relieved when Luke frowned at Aimee's impertinence.

"Aimee, I'll not have you interfering in matters that don't concern you," Luke reprimanded.

When Aimee's lip trembled, Gleason said hastily, "No, no, quite all right. I have no other major activities at the moment." Gleason dusted off his vest with nonchalant fingers, so he didn't see the look Luke and Aimee exchanged. Gleason was not a good liar, but the mere fact that he found it necessary to do so was telling.

They took their leave of Gleason, Luke promising to send his decision by messenger within the next few days. It seemed to Aimee that Gleason looked nervously about as he rose in good-bye. Aimee strolled out of the hotel on Luke's arm.

"What do you suppose he's trying to hide?" Aimee asked softly.

Luke gave the barest shrug. "I have no idea, but I'm afraid my instincts tell me quite loudly he's not to be trusted."

"I agree totally, Luke. You'd be wise to look farther for a partner." Aimee tugged her ear and gasped in dismay. "I must have lost an earring. I'll be right back."

She hurried into the hotel, her suspicions confirmed by what she saw. She ducked behind a huge plant. Gleason passed her, deep in conversation with Tom Payton. She heard one sentence before they were out of earshot, and the whispered words made her neck prickle with alarm.

"Garrison is as cagey as ever, Tom, and it'll slow things up considerably if he refuses the deal. . . ."

Aimee waited until they had exited before she dashed into the restaurant, picked up her earring from where she'd dropped it and hurried out again, praying the men had not seen Luke standing alone. She breathed a sigh of relief when she found Luke waiting in the carriage. She glanced down the street to see Gleason and Payton walking on opposite sides, as if they had never met so soon after the dinner.

If Aimee had needed further confirmation for her suspicions, their reluctance to be seen together would have supplied it. She attached her earring and scrambled with more haste than elegance into the carriage.

"Luke, I just saw Gleason and . . ." Her voice trailed off at the grim look on his face as he stared down the street.

"I know. It seems an odd coincidence that, after recommending Gleason to me so highly, I've seen Tom talking to Gleason twice in a rather secretive manner. Add to that the fact that so much is missing from . . ." Luke stopped abruptly. He rapped on the ceiling with his cane. The coachman clucked to the horses.

Aimee's eyes narrowed. "Missing from what?"

Luke smiled ruefully. "Never mind, Miss Busybody. I'm just talking to myself. May I compliment you on your assistance at dinner? I'd wondered why Gleason was so interested in getting involved in the tugboat business at this competitive time, but I couldn't devise a polite way to ask. You played the part of innocent so well I don't think he's even aware of what he let slip. I wonder what his real reason is for approaching us?"

Luke talked for the entire journey home, but Aimee didn't answer. She eyed him steadily, wondering what he was keeping from her. He praised her acuity on the one hand and denied her the sense to exercise it on the other. The distance that had been briefly spanned by their camaraderie widened again.

When Luke came to bed that night, Aimee pretended to be asleep. And, for only the second time since reaching New York, Luke did not pull her back against him to shelter her in his strong arms. They stayed on their own sides of the wide bed, struggling to breathe naturally to hide the desolation that kept them awake and miserable despite their lack of sleep.

When Luke rose several hours later to dress, he made no attempt to quiet his movements. Aimee didn't pretend not to watch. He turned at the door.

He said harshly, "I'll be back by morning. Will I find you here waiting for me?"

Aimee had been handed a note from Jeremy on their return. He suggested she come to his rooms that night to help him go over old newspaper accounts of the trial. Aimee had intended to wait until morning, but pain knifed her at seeing

Luke leave her yet again on a mission he didn't trust her enough to share.

Too upset to speak, eyes downcast to hide her tears, she shook her head.

Luke's expression grew bleaker. He balled his hands into fists and stormed out, slamming the door behind him. Aimee slumped against the pillows, tears burning her cheeks.

Aimee suited her dress to her mood and went downstairs. By the time the sleepy Clancy answered her summons, she had gotten a grip on herself. Only someone who knew her very well would have read the despair behind the clear green eyes. Aimee was surprised to find Bob waiting next to the coachman when she went outside.

His thin, adolescent body stood tall as he said laconically, "I heerd you was goin' someplace. It ain't safe this late. I want to come with you, ma'am."

Aimee was touched. She tousled his hair, smiling as he blushed. "I shall welcome your protection, kind sir," she said with a graceful curtsy.

He swept open the carriage door and helped her in. Clancy shook his head in disapproval at such familiarity between mistress and lowly gardener's helper and clambered onto his perch, unaware of the rider who followed them at a safe distance.

Bob and he were equally horrified when they reached their destination. Bob looked uneasily about when he got out and helped Aimee descend. He sighed with relief when Jeremy immediately opened the door and came out to meet Aimee. He shook his head at Jeremy's invitation to come in.

"Nope. I'll wait here to help Clancy if there's trouble."

Jeremy raised an eyebrow at Bob's slight build. Aimee shook her head and he swallowed the comment springing to his lips.

Jeremy ushered Aimee into his rooms and took her cloak, frowning a little at her pale face and sober black gown. "Would you like a glass of wine, Aimee?"

"No, thank you, Jeremy. The sooner we get this done, the better. Where are the articles?"

Jeremy tossed a folder on the table in front of the couch. Aimee sank to her knees and began to read. Jeremy eyed her bent head, wondering at her harsh tone of voice. Why was she so subdued this evening? He had hoped to charm her at their next meeting, but she was giving him precious little opportunity. Glumly, he sat down next to her and picked up a clipping.

A few minutes later Aimee exclaimed in surprise. Jeremy peered over her shoulder at the article, but he was distracted by her perfume and the warmth of her body. He had to strain to make himself listen to her.

"I know one of the men mentioned in this article as the man Tom Payton sent for the police the night Bjorn died. What was Victor Gleason doing on Bjorn's ship in the middle of the night?"

Jeremy was all ears now. He chased an elusive memory. "You know, I vaguely remember my father arguing with Bjorn about using Victor as their tugboat operator. He didn't trust the man, but Bjorn insisted his services were the cheapest he'd seen, since Gleason had just started in business."

Aimee propped her elbows on the table and cupped her chin in her palms. She stared into space, remembering Luke's slip, "Add to that so much is missing from . . ." Aimee's heart beat faster as the first piece of the puzzle fell into place. Could it be that thefts were occurring at the Garrison warehouse just as they had from Bjorn and Samuel so many years ago? It would explain Luke's late absences. It would explain why she instinctively distrusted both Gleason and Payton. It would explain Gleason's comment to Payton.

Aimee winced. And it made her anger at her husband contemptible and unjust. Instinctively, she knew he had not shared this with her because he was concerned that she'd involve herself, just as she was doing now. She had repaid his concern with accusations and evasions of her own. Aimee swallowed down her self-disgust and surged to her feet.

She threw the article back on the table and turned to Jeremy. "I must return home, Jeremy. There's something I must check on. We can meet again tomorrow, at the Park, during the day. Say, three o'clock? I think it's best that we don't meet at your rooms any longer."

Jeremy escorted her to the door, protesting, "But what have you discovered? I have a right to know."

"I'm not certain yet. I hope to tell you tomorrow." Aimee exited so hastily that she tripped on the steps. Jeremy caught her in his arms. Aimee calmly waited for him to release her, but to her astonishment he crushed her to him.

His eyes burned into hers like new-minted silver ingots.

"Aimee, I know you're not happy with Luke. How could you be? He's too arrogant to give you the care you deserve. . . ."

Aimee pushed at his chest, but he wouldn't yield. "You're wrong, Jeremy. He's given me all any woman could wish for, and I repay him with clandestine meetings with you. Let me go!" Jeremy released her reluctantly, and Clancy and Bob, who had started forward to assist her, relaxed back against the carriage.

Each of them was too intent to notice the lone horseman on the street. His white Arabian was a startling contrast to the soot-darkened buildings behind him. Strong hands held the reins in so tightly that Polaris tossed his head in protest at the unusual rough treatment. Had Luke been close enough to hear what was being said, his fury would have been appeased. But he was not, and a rage greater than any he'd ever known almost choked him as he watched his wife lie in the arms of the man he despised. He had been on the point of bursting in on them when she finally emerged. His expression did not change even when Jeremy released her. He checked his watch. They hadn't been alone for long, but it was long enough. . . . He swayed in the saddle at the images filling his tortured mind.

Aimee straightened her cloak and said through her teeth, "I want to help you, Jeremy, but if you once more force your attentions on me, I will never meet you again. I will not be used as your pawn to avenge yourself on my husband. Is that clear?"

Jeremy was tempted to tell her the truth. That he had entered this game with her wondering cynically if she really wanted to help, or if she was a spoiled lady seeking excitement like Marietta. But she showed no interest in anything but the clippings, and he could only conclude that she truly wanted to help clear his name. He still wasn't certain of her underlying reasons, but he knew he could never use her as he had originally intended. She deserved better. Indeed, he wanted to give her better. And when he caught her in his arms, he had not thought of her as a Garrison. She had been only a woman who drew him with her combination of soft strength and young wisdom as no other female had, including Marietta.

Jeremy inclined his head sardonically, hiding his bitter anger at Luke Garrison for being as lucky in his marriage as in everything else. "Clear, madam. I will see you tomorrow at the fountain on the esplanade."

Aimee returned home deep in thought. She had to tell Luke where she had been and why. He would be angry when he discovered she was trying to help Jeremy, but if Payton and Gleason proved to be thieves, even he would have to admit that they had likely been the culprits years ago. They would work to solve the mystery as they should have from the beginning. Aimee hummed, looking forward to the day when both Hedda's sons could meet in friendship rather than hatred. The thought never crossed her mind that Luke would not believe her explanation.

Aimee yawned and pulled her dress over her head, deciding she had time for a few hours' sleep before Luke returned. She was standing in chemise and stockings when a soft, deadly voice rasped against her bare skin.

"Where have you been?"

Here's your chance to make things right, Aimee told herself staunchly. She took a deep breath and turned to face her husband, but her eyes widened at the look on his face. His jaw worked, his cheeks were flushed and his eyes blasted her with such fury that she took a step back and held her petticoat in front of her as if it could protect her.

Her voice trembled when she answered, "I'll tell you where I was, Luke, but please try to understand why I did it. . . ."

An ugly laugh interrupted her. "I understand well enough. You're bored with my devotion and have no care for the honor of the name I bestowed on you. I saw you with Mayhew with my own eyes. . . ." He clamped his teeth shut over the name he almost called her.

Aimee was puzzled at his words, but she was glad he knew about Jeremy. She couldn't bear any more deceit between them. She took an impulsive step toward him. "I'm glad you know the truth, Luke. I never intended to deceive you, but I was afraid you'd forbid me to see Jeremy again if you knew I hoped to . . ."

Luke's control was shattered by Aimee's total lack of shame. In one great stride he was on her. He ripped the petticoat out of her hands and caught her shoulders so tightly she winced. He snarled, "You're right. I absolutely forbid you to see him again. I'm not sure I'll be able to forgive you as it is, but if you betray me again I won't be responsible for my actions." He stepped away from her as if he couldn't bear the sight of her, ripped a blanket and pillow off the bed and tossed them on the divan in the sitting room.

"It would make my skin crawl to bed down with you this night, so you'll sleep in there," he ordered coldly. He proceeded to strip his clothes off as if she wasn't there.

Aimee stood rooted in place, a humiliated flush burning her good intentions away. She had expected anger, but never this wrath. He wouldn't even let her finish her explanation. Aimee whirled and marched into the sitting room. She curled up into a tight ball, biting her lip in confused pain. She got as little sleep that night as she had the previous one. She rose with a pounding headache that would worsen as the day progressed.

Aimee's confusion changed to fury when she overheard Joshua and Luke discussing the matter the next morning. She was in the study, kneeling before the sofa facing the fire, inspecting the upholsterer's work, when the two men entered. Aimee fell back to the floor instead of rising when her name was mentioned.

"What the devil is the matter between you and Aimee, Luke? You've been dancing around each other for days, and this morning at breakfast you didn't exchange a word." Joshua's frown deepened when his son ignored the question and stared out the window with eyes bleak as a winter landscape.

He slammed his fist down on the desk. "Dammit, boy, I want an answer!"

Luke's mouth worked, and his reply was so soft that Aimee barely heard it. "What would you do, Father, if Hedda cuckolded you?"

Joshua sat in stunned amazement. Aimee shook her head, certain she must have misunderstood Luke. He could never believe such a thing of her.

Joshua apparently had more faith in her, at any rate.

"Balderdash!" he scoffed when his wits returned. "Aimee would never do such a thing!"

Luke rubbed his tired, burning eyes, muttering, "That's what I tried to tell myself when I found her missing two nights ago. She asked me to trust her, and, fool that I was, I decided I didn't have the right to demand her faith if I didn't give it."

"She still doesn't know about the thefts, then?"

Luke sighed, dropping his hands. "No. I haven't had a

chance to tell you yet, but I'm beginning to suspect Tom may be behind them." At Joshua's exclamation, Luke explained how he had met with Gleason. He revealed his suspicion that the tugboat operator was Tom's partner. "You know how busy the river traffic is. Since Tom has authority to check all cargo in and out, no one would question it if he loaded a barge and Gleason towed it away."

"But I thought we used Simmons for all our towing. Gleason doesn't even have his own boat."

"He's been renting one until we came to a decision, and Tom convinced me to give Gleason a chance since we were considering going into partnership together. I suspect the reason we've discovered nothing at night is because they've been stealing us blind in broad daylight."

Joshua cursed, infuriated at the betrayal by a man they had been uncommonly generous to, but he soon saw he'd lost his son's attention. He bit back the demand that they take action. Luke had something even more worrisome on his mind at the moment. They would get to the bottom of this soon enough. If Payton was guilty, God help him. He took a deep breath to throttle his fury.

"Go on with your explanation. We can discuss this later."

Luke's hand shook a little when he ran it through his hair. "I didn't go to the warehouse last night. I followed her." He slowly turned his head to look at his father, his eyes so despairing that Joshua rose to put out a hand to comfort him. Luke clutched that hand like a lifeline.

"She went to Jeremy Mayhew's lodgings and didn't emerge for quite a while. When she did, he embraced her." The quiet words echoed devastatingly. Joshua searched helplessly for something to say to counteract them.

Aimee bit her knuckle to keep herself from springing up and shrieking at her husband. How could he believe such a thing of her? She had no idea how the scene had looked from Luke's vantage point. Her love for him was as much a part of her as her eyes, her skin, her hair. If she betrayed Luke, she betrayed herself. The ugliness of the thing he believed of her pierced her to her marrow, and she barely heard the rest of the conversation.

"Luke, you must talk to her about it. There is surely some other reason. Marietta may be involved. She's entranced by the baron now, but it could just as easily have been Mayhew a week ago. You know how easily bored she is. Aimee might have been trying to protect her."

Eyes closed, skin pasty white, Luke shook his head. "No, I taxed her with it, and she admitted as much and didn't have a whit of guilt."

"That does not sound like Aimee at all, Luke. She must have misunderstood you. Think carefully. What exactly did she admit to?"

Luke combed through his tangled thoughts, and he realized Joshua was right. Aimee had said she was glad he knew the truth, but she didn't ask for a divorce, or say she was leaving him. She said only she was afraid he'd forbid her to see Jeremy again because she hoped to . . . Hoped to what? That was surely an odd way to tell your husband you were having an affair with another man.

"She didn't really admit to anything except seeing him, come to think of it. But why else would she be meeting him?"

"That's puzzling, I admit. There's only one way to find out. Ask her."

Luke rose with more vigor than he'd shown all day. "Thanks, Father. I'll do that right now." He hurried out the door.

Aimee heard Joshua heave a relieved sigh before he, too, left. Aimee rose calmly, dusted off her skirts and after a moment, left the study as well. From the entry hall, she went out the front door. Her face was taut as she hailed a cab and went to Central Park. She had intended to send a note to Jeremy suggesting they contact one another through messenger rather than upset Luke so, but now nothing on earth would have made her miss this meeting. Aimee's lungs pained her with every breath, her eyes burned with tears she refused to shed and her head throbbed with the knowledge that her husband believed her a whore, but her stride was determined when she walked down the esplanade to meet Jeremy. She was more resolved than ever to prove his innocence. Her almighty husband would suffer for his hasty judgment.

She told Jeremy succinctly of her suspicions, and why, concluding, "I overheard Joshua discussing the thefts with Luke. In both cases, years ago and now, two men were involved: Gleason and Payton. Coincidence or conspiracy? That's what we have to discover." Aimee went on to share Luke's suspicions.

A strange note crept into her voice when she spoke her

husband's name. Jeremy eyed her curiously, but she did not elucidate. Jeremy agreed, "Everything you say makes sense. Payton was in almost as trusted a position as Bjorn. He often handled the unloading himself after docking. But one thing puzzles me. Why would he give such impassioned defense of my father at the trial? Wouldn't he have been better off letting Father take the blame?"

"What benefit would there have been to him for Samuel to be dead or in prison? No one suspected Payton, and it seems to me his purpose would be served far better by assisting the rumors that Samuel was guilty of theft, if not of murder. Halting the thefts with Samuel's inheritance of the company was a perfect way to implicate someone else, particularly if he was ready to stop. How much did the partners actually lose?"

Jeremy said slowly, "It was a large sum indeed. And you know, I've heard sailors question how Payton lives so well on a warehouse manager's salary. It was always assumed he'd made wise investments. . . ." His voice trailed off.

Aimee dipped a hand into the fountain and touched her cool fingers to her aching temple. She collected her straying thoughts. "Then, if Payton decided to thieve again, he could have let Samuel take the blame. Tom was left to seem honorable in his defense of the very man who had killed his captain. Did the Garrisons not hire him shortly after?"

Jeremy scowled in growing fury at the way his father had been used. His answer came through gritted teeth. "Yes, and my mother worked at the warehouse office with Tom. I can only wonder what poisonous things he must have said to her. But why would he wait so long to begin stealing again?"

Aimee frowned, puzzled. "I can't answer that. Possibly he was afraid to since Samuel died. Or maybe he's been stealing for years but this is the first time he's been caught. I'll question Hedda and see what I can discover."

Aimee found the family arguing about her disappearance when she returned during dinner. Hedda snapped at Luke, "She didn't tell me she was going anywhere! Can't she take a step without your knowledge?"

Aimee closed the door and leaned against it, unutterably weary. She was in no mood to confront Luke, but she couldn't let him take out his anger on Hedda. She straightened her simple linen dress, lifted her chin and entered the fray.

Silence descended, hot and heavy, when she stepped into the dining room. Aimee took her usual place beside Luke, apologizing coolly, "Forgive me for being late. I was unavoidably detained." She spread her napkin in her lap and sipped daintily at her soup, ignoring Luke's grinding teeth.

He leaned close to hiss, "I want to see you in the study immediately after dinner, *wife*." He received a disdainful nod in return.

Hedda looked from Aimee to Luke, then at Joshua. He shook his head, warning her not to interfere. She smiled brightly. "Well, and what are we having for dinner this evening, Aimee? I never know what to expect anymore since you've upset my schedule."

Aimee put her spoon down carefully. "Do you mind that I've changed the menus a little, ma'am? It seemed most efficient to take advantage of the freshest and least expensive fare rather than stick to a schedule. Tonight, I believe we're having lamb. The new butcher I've discovered is just starting out, and he made us a wonderful bargain on some rather exotic cuts of meat. . . ."

As if cued, the kitchen maid came out with a fragrant platter of leg of lamb surrounded by a mint sauce pool. Hedda tasted the succulent meat and sighed with pleasure. "You have my leave to change my schedule in whatever way you see fit, child." She leaned over the table to whisper loudly, "Just between you and me, I was a little tired of beef on Wednesdays, anyway." Everyone laughed, and some of the tension around the table eased.

When Marietta enthused about her baron, Joshua smiled indulgently. "And who will it be next week?" Marietta looked hurt. Joshua patted her hand. "Perfectly natural for a young girl to try her wings. I'm only glad you've lost interest in young Mayhew at last."

Marietta shot a glance at Aimee. Luke intercepted it, and he also saw how his wife started slightly at the mention of Jeremy's name.

Aimee smiled when supposed to and seemed to eat heartily, but Luke noticed she spent most of her time raking her food around. Very little of it found its way to her mouth. He felt no more appetite, but forced himself to eat. He would not let her put him off food. She'd turned his world upside down. That was enough. Luke excused himself as soon as dessert was served, pulling out Aimee's chair.

She looked at him indignantly, but set down her dessert fork, lemon torte still clinging to it. She nodded to the curious family members and preceded Luke from the room, her spine straight as a grand duchess's. Luke wanted a fight? She'd be happy to give him one. It was the only way she could think of to keep her pain at bay.

She whirled on him the minute he closed the study door. "Where is your hood and crucifix, dear *husband?*" She looked around, as if surprised. "What, no stake to tie me to? How do you expect to conduct an inquisition without one?"

Luke felt like a fish out of water, and indeed, his mouth gaped like a gaffed mackerel's. She was acting like the one with a grievance, as if he had no right to question her absence. The hope that had surged through him with Joshua's encouragement died a painful death. Anger leaped up out of its ashes like a phoenix.

He strode forward to lift her chin and snarl, "Don't tempt me. A husband had absolute power over his wife in the days of the Inquisition. I'm beginning to see the advantages." His hand slipped as if by accident to her throat, the long fingers a caressing threat.

Aimee flung back her head. "Go ahead, Luke. I won't struggle or cry out. Punish me for the imagined wrong I've done you." Her eyes blazed with defiance as she met his stony gaze, and for one instant, his hand tightened. Then he turned away with an oath.

"If you've done me no wrong, why are you so defensive?" he intoned, head averted to hide the pain.

Because I hate you for believing such a thing of me, she longed to cry out. Aimee cupped her head in her palms, certain it would throb its way off her shoulders any minute. Dully, she answered, "Because you've given me no chance to redeem myself. I'm tried, convicted and condemned without a word in my own defense."

Luke turned slowly. He went to the divan and sat down, clasping his hands on his knees. "Very well, Aimee, I'm listening. Where have you been?"

If Aimee had been in less pain, if the light had not been behind Luke, she might have noticed the almost pleading look in his eyes. But she was too upset to care about anything but ending this tormenting interview as quickly as possible.

"It's useless," she whispered in despair. She braced herself, and taunted, "You want the truth, Luke? I left for a clandestine meeting with the man you hate most in the world—Jeremy Mayhew. You wanted confirmation of my duplicity? You have it. Now go wallow in it." She ran out the door, harsh sobs trailing behind her.

Luke sat as if turned to stone, but the fire in his mind and heart violently attested to his human frailty. He sat there unmoving for minutes on end, wondering how it was possible to feel such pain and live. That night, he moved his things to a guest bedroom, widening the rift between them to a chasm nothing could bridge.

Chapter Sixteen

A COOL FALL breeze entered the ballroom doors, fanning Aimee's heated cheeks. She smiled flirtatiously at her partner and let him lead her in a polka. Her gown was ruby red lace, the shoulders nonexistent, the bodice barely decent. It was caught on both sides with black silk roses, revealing a black silk underskirt. Tiny black and red silk roses peeped through the mass of curls piled on her head. Never had she been more beautiful. Never had she drawn more men's eyes. And never had she been more miserable. The one man she wanted to attract, the one man she had worn this daring gown for, avoided her.

Since Luke had moved to another bedchamber two weeks ago, the situation between them had deteriorated. If he spoke to her at all, it was scathingly. When Aimee's initial hurt and anger subsided enough for rational thought, she realized she was almost as much at fault as Luke. She should have told him the real reason she was meeting Jeremy instead of allowing him—even encouraging him—to think the worst.

Whenever she tried to catch him alone, however, he found a pressing need to be elsewhere. One night she'd even gone to his chamber to talk to him, only to find the door locked, the room silent to her entreaties.

Aimee was astonished at his behavior. Luke was not a man who avoided arguments. If he believed she had betrayed him, it would be more in character for him to beat her, divorce her or lock her up. Indeed, she would have preferred the beating over this icy condemnation. Hoping to force Luke's hand, she wore this daring gown to Marietta's engagement ball and matched her behavior to its sultry promise. She flirted outrageously with each of her partners, laughing huskily at their bold sallies. But, aside from one burning look when he first saw her, Luke ignored her and flirted just as audaciously with the many beauties he had known before his marriage. He never glanced at her, and, if she hadn't known better, Aimee might have suspected he was afraid to face her. She dismissed the idea as ludicrous.

Had she read Luke's thoughts at that moment, she wouldn't have been so certain. Luke was aware of her every movement. Out of the corner of his eye, he watched her match her steps to her partner's, cheeks rosy, gold eyes sparkling like aged champagne. He gritted his teeth to keep from rushing forward and demand she inch up that damned bodice. It was no lower than many others, but Aimee's display belonged only to him. Was this her way of communicating her scorn? She dipped and swayed to the music, a dancing pillar of flame that ignited an inferno of confused emotions in him: rage, pain, disgust, love, but, above all, fear. Fear of losing her; fear that if he was with her alone he would be unable to control his conflicting urges to strangle her, rape her or plead for her love. No, he had to understand her behavior before he dared face her and relax his tight hold on his emotions.

He was no longer certain of her unfaithfulness, for he'd followed her to a meeting with Jeremy. She'd been business-like rather than ardent as they met at the Park, and she had Bob with her.

He went home torn between hope and rage at the kiss Jeremy had placed on the back of her hand. Logic warned that Aimee could have no reason for meeting Jeremy other than the obvious one. But his months with her had given him too healthy a respect for her morality for him to accept that without incontrovertible proof. Her very goading of him to believe it comforted him, for Aimee would react so if hurt. Thus he bided his time, considering explanations as suspect as his own emotions. The next time she went to Jeremy's rooms, he would burst in on them. If he found what he feared, God help them all. . . .

After the dance, Luke went to the refreshment table.

Joshua caught his arm. "Luke, everyone is talking. You must dance at least once with Aimee."

Luke glared at his father over his cup of spiked punch. "Don't interfere in this, Father. Leave me to handle my marriage as I see fit." Luke put the cup down. If he touched her, felt that soft body that he still ached for nightly against his own, he'd lose what little control he had left.

Joshua was exasperated with both Luke and Aimee. Neither of them would talk to him or Hedda, and their hostility was ruining Marietta's engagement ball. Joshua hissed, "And a damned poor job you're doing of it. Why the hell won't you at least talk to the girl? This isn't like you, Luke." When Luke met his eyes with stony rejection, Joshua sighed and tried another tack.

"Hedda told me Aimee has been questioning her about Tom. Why would she do so if she knew nothing of the thefts?"

A bitter little smile played about Luke's lips. "I don't think I know my wife any longer. I'm not even sure I know myself." Luke poured himself another glass of punch and forced his thoughts away from Aimee. "So far Gleason has revealed nothing since we hired him. He was not pleased we decided against the partnership, but he appreciated our loan. I can't help wondering if we're not helping him to steal from us."

Joshua lowered his voice. "I know, Luke, it goes against my grain too, but making him our exclusive operator is the best way to keep an eye on him. Do you suppose they're waiting for the China shipment to make a move?"

"Possibly. I think we should arrange to be there early the day it arrives, but tell Tom we're going in late. We can hide in your office and watch as they check it in."

"That's an excellent idea, Luke. Nothing would please me more than catching the scoundrels in the act. I'll alert the police."

Luke nodded, his eyes wandering around the room. He froze, his cup halfway to his mouth.

Joshua nodded in agreement, following Luke's stare. He frowned. Aimee was laughing up into Tom Payton's face, tapping his arm with the red lace fan that matched her gown. What the devil was she up to?

Aimee had approached Payton casually, visiting with other guests until she reached him. When he looked down at her in surprise, she said gaily, "Sir, I've been wanting to talk with you for an age. I'm eager to learn more about Luke's business, but he's too busy to show me the warehouse. I was wondering if you might find the time?"

Payton lifted an eyebrow at the request, but he bowed. "I would be honored, Mrs. Garrison, provided your husband has no objection."

Aimee appeared to consider it. "No, I don't think he does, but I'll check with him to be certain. What would be a good time?"

"Shall we say tomorrow? In the afternoon?"

So whatever they planned was to take place later. "That is not a convenient time. My calendar is full until two days hence," she said smoothly.

Payton's mouth tightened. "What a pity. I'll be too busy at that time with a large shipment we're expecting."

Aimee dropped her eyes to hide her excitement. "Really? Is it a valuable one?"

Payton shrugged. "We handle such shipments all the time."

Liar, Aimee thought. She knew from Hedda that the steamer returning from the Orient would be loaded with silks, spices, priceless art works, ivory and jade. Hedda had told her this was to be the most valuable single shipment in years. Aimee unfolded her fan and wielded it vigorously.

"I'd love to see it. But if you insist, I'll wait until Luke can take me," she pouted.

Payton relaxed. "That would be best. May I make it up to you in some small way?"

Aimee laughed and tapped him on the arm again with her fan. "Indeed you may, sir. This country dance is one of my favorites."

Payton bowed and presented his arm, and only Aimee knew she had to steel herself to touch it. It was the last dance of the evening before Joshua closed the ball with the engagement announcement. The guests clapped and toasted the couple with champagne. Aimee bit her lip, wondering how Jeremy would take this news.

Still, she was happy for Marietta, who seemed content for the first time in Aimee's memory. Aimee offered her congratulations after the guests departed. She hugged Marietta and smiled at the handsome young baron. "I wish you every happiness. I'm only sorry you'll be living so far away, but I've heard Austria is beautiful."

Marietta returned the embrace, whispering for Aimee's ears alone, "And I wish you the same, dear sister. Though my coxcomb of a brother doesn't deserve you. Why don't you tell him the real reason you're meeting Jeremy?" Marietta had badgered the truth out of Aimee after that first meeting.

"I would, given the chance." Smiling brightly to hide her trembling lip, Aimee turned away. She almost collided with a broad, familiar chest. She looked way up into Luke's eyes. His searing eyes lingered on her bodice. She said haughtily, "Excuse me," giving him a wide berth as if he were a stranger she didn't quite trust.

Hedda stopped her before she could reach her room. Aimee rubbed her forehead tiredly. "Yes, Hedda, what is it?"

"Aimee, it's time we talked." The soft words brooked no refusal.

"Must it be now? I'm so very tired." Aimee swayed in genuine weariness, but Hedda did not yield.

"Yes, now." Aimee found herself escorted to Hedda's private sitting room overlooking the garden. It was a pretty chamber, redolent of flowers and wax. Aimee's eyes went straight to the small portrait of Luke as a boy. He sat astride a pony, and the confident, vibrant smile was so reminiscent of the man that she closed her eyes in pain, wondering if he'd ever look at her like that again.

Aimee's unhappiness touched the soft heart Hedda kept so well hidden, but she steeled herself. She and Joshua had given the children two weeks to settle their differences. It was time to intercede.

She sat down on the yellow brocade couch beside Aimee and took her hand. "Aimee, I can't talk sense into my son. You are the only one who can end this impasse. Please tell me truthfully why you are meeting Jeremy."

Jeremy. Not my son. Why was Jeremy always the one at fault? She jerked her hand away from Hedda's. "What? Don't you believe I'm consorting with the evil Jeremy Mayhew, the man you almost refuse to even acknowledge as your son?"

Hedda paled at the condemnation in Aimee's eyes. "There are things you don't understand, Aimee. And no, I don't believe you are betraying Luke."

Disarmed, Aimee leaned back and closed her eyes. "I'm

sorry, Hedda. I appreciate your belief in me. It's a pity your son doesn't share it."

"Please tell me why you meet with . . . my other son, Aimee. If you do, I'll tell you why Luke dislikes him so."

Aimee clasped her hands in her lap and said baldly, "I don't believe Jeremy is any more ruthless than his father was. I am seeking now to prove Samuel's innocence, with Jeremy's help."

Hedda looked astonished. "But how can you possibly prove such a thing after all these years?"

"That's what Jeremy said. I must admit, I wasn't hopeful until . . . Hedda, has Joshua told you someone has been thieving at the warehouse?"

Hedda started. Her eyes narrowed in anger. "No, he did not. Why would he keep such a thing from me? We discuss all aspects of his business."

"Probably for the same reason Luke didn't tell me. Out of some misguided male attempt to protect us," Aimee said tartly. Their eyes met in exasperation. When Hedda took Aimee's hand again, her clasp was returned.

"But what has this to do with Jeremy?"

Aimee explained their suspicions about Payton and Gleason. When she had finished, Hedda frowned. "So that's why you were asking me about Tom. Do you really think I'm so gullible that Tom could poison my mind against my husband? I had good reason for believing as I did. Samuel never even bothered defending himself to me. He seemed to hate me and lose all interest after he inherited the business. I never loved him, I admit it. And after I met Joshua . . . But even so, I would have stayed with Samuel, for Jeremy's sake, if I'd believed him innocent, and he'd wanted me. Instead, he poisoned my own son against me."

Aimee hated distressing Hedda, but it was time she knew the truth. "Jeremy told me Samuel was a stubborn man who was too proud to defend himself to you, especially after you met Joshua." Her voice softened, but it had to be said. "He also said Samuel loved you to the day he died. That's why he would never agree to the divorce."

Hedda looked stunned. Her mouth trembled. She covered it with her hand, mumbling, "My God, if that's true . . . and Samuel was innocent . . . no wonder Jeremy hates me."

Aimee put her arm around Hedda's taut shoulders. "He

doesn't hate you, Hedda. There was a time when he might have, but he's old enough now to realize Samuel was at fault too. By the time he did, of course, it was too late. You were already estranged, and Joshua and Luke were doing all they could to ruin him."

Hedda shook her head in denial, tears streaming down her face. "I'll never be able to live with myself if what you say is true."

Aimee wiped Hedda's face with her handkerchief. "That's the wrong attitude. You should be happy to have the truth come out at last. You can meet your son as you should have all these years—with open arms."

Hedda blew her nose. "You're right, of course. Oh, Aimee, we Garrisons have a lot to answer for. I never realized how proud we'd become until you came to us. Now you've risked your marriage to right *our* wrong. You've made me see so much I was blind to before." Hedda bent her head, twisting the handkerchief between her fingers. "I'm . . . sorry for being so uncaring. I realize the emptiness of my own life, and yearn to do more. I . . . have a friend who is organizing an orphanage. I've donated funds, but I realize now that's not enough. Would you like me to tell her we'd both like to help?"

Aimee hugged Hedda, tears burning her eyes. She had accomplished something, at any rate. "That sounds wonderful. Now, please tell me why Luke detests Jeremy so."

Hedda's bright expression dimmed. "You've seen the way Jeremy taunts Luke?" Aimee nodded. "It's been like that since they were boys attending the same school. Luke has always been possessive and protective of those he loves. When I moved in with Joshua, I filled the needs his real mother never had. He . . . adored me. He saw, even as a boy, how unhappy I was about Jeremy, and he naturally blamed Jeremy since he thought I could do no wrong." Hedda smiled wryly. "He knows differently now, of course, though I don't believe he loves me any less.

"Their competition deepened as they aged. And when Marietta met Jeremy, it was the last excuse Luke and Joshua needed. I tried to stop them from influencing their friends, but the Mayhew name was already . . . tarnished by Samuel's drinking. He'd lost much of his business by the time Jeremy took over. And, since Samuel's reputation was not good, our circle tended to view Jeremy in the same light, especially after the incident with that girl. That is one rumor I scarcely credited, at least."

Hedda framed Aimee's face in her hands and smiled at her tenderly. "So, my dear child, when you met Jeremy secretly, it was like waving a red flag in front of a bull. I'm surprised at Luke's restraint, actually. He must love you very much."

Aimee closed her eyes, swaying with longing. "I pray you're right, Hedda." But I don't think you are, she thought.

Hedda stood briskly. "Now, I'll go get Luke so you can tell him the truth. . . ."

"No, not yet. I'd intended to tell him, but now I must wait two more days. If Luke knows what I'm really doing, he'll forbid me to go to the warehouse." Quickly she explained her suspicions about the China shipment. "I'll tell him then, I promise. But I must see this through. For Jeremy's sake."

Hedda nodded reluctantly. "I suppose you're right. But I want to come with you."

"Jeremy won't like that, Hedda. He'll argue about my going, but he'll need me to flush out the truth. The police will be there, and Jeremy to witness their confession and guard me from any harm. The truth will finally emerge, and old wounds will eventually heal," she said, then leaned forward. "But please, Hedda, promise me you won't mention a word to Joshua or Luke."

Hedda was reluctant, but Aimee finally coaxed her into agreement.

Aimee had no need to avoid Luke for the next two days, for he was seldom home. She told Jeremy of the shipment at their scheduled meeting, and their plans, and after a brief argument, he agreed.

"I'm going, Jeremy. We've come too far together for me to back out now. It's not fair of you to even ask."

He glared at her, but her wounded look was a persuasive argument. "Oh, very well, but it will be dangerous. Payton keeps a man on guard at the warehouse entrance at all times. I think I may know a way to get by him." Jeremy explained his plan. "But if you can't think of a safe way to distract them, while I climb into a crate to hear their confession, then leave. I'll not have you endangered, even to clear my father's name."

Aimee's eyes sparkled. "I know just the dress to wear.

Bob, do you mind helping? It could be dangerous."

Bob grinned infectiously. "Heck, this is nothin' after what I was used to." Bob wandered off to feed the pigeons.

Aimee hesitated, then blurted, "Jeremy, I told Hedda the truth."

He stared blindly over the verdant lawn. "Did she believe you?"

"I think so. If we obtain proof tomorrow, so will Luke and Joshua."

Jeremy turned to look at his small champion, a much more stalwart defender than even Marietta had been, and, instead of elation, he felt sadness. Vindication was bitter-sweet, for the price of redeeming his name would be all hope of winning Aimee. The sun illuminated her silvery hair and creamy complexion, tempting him to take her in his arms and confess he no longer cared what anyone believed except her. She had sneaked up on him, this winsome girl. He had intended her to be the instrument of his revenge on the Garrisons. Instead, she had disarmed him, vanquished his hostility with her sweetness. He gritted his teeth to keep from pleading with her, Come away with me. Let me love you better than Luke ever will.

But he was not a man afraid to face unpleasant truths. The warm smile she bestowed on him was lovely, but held only friendliness. She saw no man but her devil of a husband. As usual, Garrison had won. There was nothing to do but end it, sail away and pray the wind and the sea would erode her indelible image.

Jeremy took her hands. "Thank you, Aimee Garrison. You are a beautiful woman, inside and out. Luke is the luckiest man in the world." He kissed the backs of each of her hands, then the palms, so tenderly Aimee's eyes filled with tears. He strode away decisively.

He did not look back, so he didn't see her dash her tears away, set her mouth in her best obstinate look and stride away as resolutely.

The apartment was luxurious. Heavy red velvet drapes muffled the toots of boats on the river. Gas lighting gleamed off surfaces of polished ebony, mahogany and cherry. Ivory and jade figurines were arrayed on shelves on the silk-papered wall. Tom Payton, wearing an expensive smoking jacket, sat in his favorite chair next to the window watching the river traffic.

Soon he could leave this stinking river for the salons of Paris and the tables of Monte Carlo. This next shipment was the largest the Garrisons had ever received. It was a perfect time to make one last rather large "adjustment" in the ledgers and quit while they were ahead. He didn't much care for the way Luke and Joshua had been watching him lately. They had no reason to suspect anything, but he'd be a fool to even chance it.

Payton rose and went to his bedroom to begin packing. If Victor already had the buyers he claimed to have, then they should be able to dispose of the merchandise within a couple of days, long before the Garrisons had a chance to do a complete inventory. Tom smiled and carelessly tossed a new, expensive Irish linen shirt into his trunk. He turned at a knock at the door. High time he arrived!

He let Victor in. "Why are you so late? What news have you?"

The rotund Victor took off his hat to fan his sweating face. He glared at his partner. "It's fine for you to complain, sitting here in your fancy apartment while I do all the dirty work."

Tom raised an eyebrow and returned to his packing. "But I'm the one who takes more of a chance, since it's my signature on those ledgers. You have to earn your thirty percent."

"I want to talk to you about that. Since this is our last job, I think I should get more. You're not the only one who wants to retire in comfort."

Tom turned slowly to face his partner. His expression did not change, but the way he ran his hand through his red shock of hair made Victor pale. "Indeed? But I'm afraid I don't agree. I masterminded the whole operation. You'd still be repairing engines if it weren't for me. Though I admit Samuel couldn't have played into our hands better if we'd hired him. The old fool." His contemptuous tones changed to his usual self-satisfaction. "Besides, if my plan hadn't worked so beautifully, we wouldn't be in such clover now. No, Victor. It's no time for you to get greedy, or else I may just leave a little . . . incriminating evidence behind when I leave."

Victor met Payton's chilly blue eyes, blustering, "You'd better hope the younger Mayhew never discovers what you've done. I saw him beat two men to a pulp single-handed in a tavern once."

"What *I've* done? You're in this right up to your fat elbows, Victor. Now, tell me who our buyers are and where we're to meet them with the goods."

The next afternoon, Aimee strolled along the docks with Bob as if she hadn't a care in the world, but inwardly she quaked as she grew closer to her destination. The rendezvous was drawing near, and the hour of her reckoning was on her. Jeremy would be somewhere near the warehouse as they had planned, ready to breach the guarded door and climb into a cranny, or crate to hear Payton expose himself. Her only weapon: her subtle sensual arts which could devastate a man with Payton's bloated self-opinion.

So she wore her most feminine dress: tiny row upon row of pink lace, a huge bow over her bustle in the back. The matching pink parasol made her look even more unscheming and helpless. It would, perhaps, serve another purpose as well.

She ignored the rude whistles and catcalls from the sailors she passed, forcing her fears down by absorbing the sights. This was her first visit to the South Street seaport docks. They made Bergen's cramped port seem roomy. Everywhere there were warehouses, countinghouses, lumberyards, coal-yards, firewood yards. Faded signs along the street advertised sailmakers, tugboaters, shipping offices. Out in the river, hay barges and boiler yards floated. Tugboats tooted up and down river, towing barges and boats.

When she arrived at the large, immaculate Garrison ware-house, she took a deep breath. She'd deliberately timed her arrival. She had fifteen minutes to work on Payton while Jeremy fixed himself in place to hear the truth unveiled—if things went as she hoped. She gave Bob a jaunty thumbs up sign and went to rap on the warehouse door.

A growled, "Who is it?" barely penetrated the thick wood. Aimee put her mouth close to it and called, "It's Mrs. Garrison. I have an appointment with Mr. Payton." There was the sound of a heavy bolt being shot back. A burly workman opened the door a crack.

"He didn't tell me about it," he complained.

Aimee tilted her head haughtily. "Does he acquaint you with all his appointments?" When the man still hesitated, she said imperiously, "Stand aside. I'm Mrs. Luke Garrison and this is partly my warehouse, after all. Now fetch Mr. Payton immediately."

Grumbling, the man stood back and let them in. He shot the bolt back, but when he turned to get Payton, Aimee opened it again quietly, just enough so that it barely cleared the door but would still seem fastened to the casual glance. Breathing a little more steadily, she watched the workman walk down the warehouse to Payton and Gleason, who were working with two huge piles of crates. She watched unobserved for a moment, but they seemed to be doing nothing untoward. Gleason called off numbers, Tom checked them off on the list he carried. When the workman spoke to Tom, he looked up and scowled.

Aimee held her ground, ignoring her quivering knees when he walked toward her. "Good afternoon, Mr. Payton. I'm so sorry to intrude, but I had to come to the area and thought I might stop by briefly." Aimee looked around at the rows of shelves, neatly arranged, the steam-operated elevator, the dollies and large carts. She wandered away from the door as if fascinated. The guard resumed his post, eyeing Bob, who remained rooted at the entrance.

Payton hurried after her, reprimanding, "You shouldn't be here, Mrs. Garrison. We're very busy. I must ask you to leave."

Aimee pretended not to have heard. She peeked inside a half-open crate on a lower shelf. She squealed in delight and pulled out a bolt of luminous green silk. She set her parasol down and held it up in front of her.

"How does it look? Do you think it flatters my coloring?" She batted her eyes.

Payton pulled the silk away and stuffed it back. "Yes, yes, lovely. Now, please . . ."

But Aimee interrupted again, this time diving into a crate that held Irish crystal. She flicked it with her fingernail and smiled in delight when it reverberated with the sound only the finest lead crystal makes. Every time Payton tried to usher her to the door, Aimee darted away and nosed into something else, or interrupted with a question. When he was red-faced and too frustrated for caution, Aimee peeked at her watch. Five more minutes. She picked up her parasol and hurried over to where Victor still worked with the crates.

Aimee didn't see the flutter of a curtain at a darkened office window as a strong hand almost ripped the fabric. "Dammit, I should have locked her in our room. The little fool could get herself killed. We've got to stop her." Luke took an agitated step toward the door, but Joshua gripped his arm.

"He wouldn't dare harm her here. We can intervene before he can get her away. Let's watch awhile longer. She's up to something, and it seems to be working. Do you see how nervous Payton looks? We've hidden all morning and haven't seen a thing unusual. Let's give her a chance."

Luke clenched his jaw over the need to snatch Aimee away to safety, but he couldn't argue with the sense of Joshua's words. Swallowing down his fears, he nodded. "A few more minutes."

Payton grabbed Aimee's arm and whirled her to face him, suspicion darkening his face. "You are interfering with my work. If you don't leave, I'll have to have my man usher you out."

Aimee twirled her parasol idly. "Odd. You talk almost like a man who considers himself an owner rather than an employee. I would have thought it was your duty to suit my convenience rather than the other way around." Aimee saw his eyes narrow further at her change in tone, and she was satisfied.

She glanced at her watch again, peeked at Bob and lowered her parasol. He took his cue and backed into a pile of crates set back from the door. Two toppled with a crash. The workman cursed and went to jerk him away and right the crates. Out of the corner of her eye, Aimee saw the door move. She turned away, forcing Payton to move to confront her. When Jeremy was safely inside, she rested the parasol's tip on the ground and held it braced in front of her like a sword. She hoped it was much sturdier than it looked.

Luke and Joshua saw Jeremy slip inside while Aimee distracted Payton. Joshua met Luke's eyes, relief in his own. "I'm glad we came, for this reason alone. Of course. We were stupid not to see it. Aimee has been helping Jeremy, not . . . consorting with him. Payton must have had something to do with the thefts years ago as well." Joshua met his son's eyes, and the expression he saw there touched him deeply.

Luke slumped against the door as if, free of the unbearable

weight he'd carried for weeks, he no longer knew how to balance himself. He took a deep breath, then reached for the handle.

"No, wait, let Aimee proceed. We owe her that."

Luke looked at his father impatiently. "Don't you think I know that? Look at them. They won't notice if we slip out. I want to hear as well as see and be ready to help Aimee if Payton turns vicious."

From the other side of the warehouse, Jeremy watched and listened as well, his face working with anger and worry. He was on the verge of plunging in and devil take the hindmost when he saw Luke and Joshua slip outside their office and ease along a row of shelves until they could overhear. He had to turn away from the look on Luke's face. The pride and love he read there pierced Jeremy to the heart, pinning him to the floor. Luke had the right to feel such things. He didn't. If anyone had to intervene to save Aimee, it should be Luke. Thus, Jeremy stayed where he was, vaguely aware that something momentous had just occurred within him. For the first time in a long time, he'd done something selfless. In spite of the pain it caused him, he felt good.

And so Aimee faced Payton, unaware of her new audience, her concentration solely on the aquiline, ruthless face before her.

She glanced at the time again. The police should arrive in two minutes. Aimee shed her artless look, meeting Payton's cold eyes with contempt in her own.

"You don't care who you hurt, or how, do you? How many people besides us have you stolen from?"

Payton stiffened. "I don't know what the hell you're talking about."

"Don't you? Jeremy Mayhew won't believe you. I certainly don't. We figured out days ago that you and Gleason must have been involved in the thefts that ruined Samuel." When Payton's eyes flickered, Aimee's last remaining doubt dissolved. She went on, her voice ringing now with conviction. "It was all your idea, wasn't it? You took advantage of the hostility between Bjorn and Samuel to rob them, didn't you?"

Payton leaned back against a crate. "Get on with it," he ordered Victor, who was watching in horror. When Payton gestured, the guard left his post at the door and approached.

None of the three had seen Bob slip out the door to wait for the police.

Payton turned back to Aimee, smiling pleasantly. "They say curiosity kills the cat, my dear, and you have much the look of one." When Aimee seemed unmoved at the threat, he turned nasty. "Do you know what it's like to take orders, orders, from others who grow rich from your work? Bjorn and Samuel obtained many of their contacts through me and Victor, and we got a pittance in return. Hell yes, we took advantage of their feud. But I must say, Samuel couldn't have played into our hands better. Removing the cargo that night was the last proof Bjorn needed of his partner's greed. I saw the fight. It *was* an accident. Samuel *was* removing the cargo to keep it safe. So I testified at the trial, as was the honorable thing to do."

Aimee swallowed down her disgust. "You don't know the meaning of the word. You only told the truth because it suited your purpose. Samuel dead was a far less efficient scapegoat than Samuel alive, drinking himself to death because of what seemed to others as guilt."

Payton nodded his head in mock admiration. "You're smart, I'll give you that. Why don't you tell me what else you've figured out?"

Aimee took a deep breath and gripped her parasol tighter. Her eyes swept over the ceiling as she played for time and listened for the sounds of approaching feet. "One of the things I couldn't understand was why you stopped your thieving after the trial," she began, coughing. Her mind churned, putting the pieces together, while creating time until the police arrived. "At first I thought you were afraid of being discovered—Samuel wouldn't steal from himself after all. But now I understand why. You were in the Garrisons' employ. You didn't stop your stealing. You merely switched victims."

Luke and Joshua met one another's eyes in bitter fury, as much at their own carelessness as at Payton's thievery. Luke had heard enough. He took a stride forward, eager to get his hands on Payton and make Aimee safe, but again Joshua stayed him. "Let her finish, boy," he mouthed.

Luke nodded reluctantly and turned back to listen. This was Aimee's moment. After his ugly suspicions, he owed her this. Gritting his teeth, Luke waited.

"You seemed so noble to everyone. How hard was it to further poison Hedda against Samuel?"

Payton shrugged. "It wasn't difficult. She already resented him. Yes, I must say I owe a lot to Samuel Mayhew. Hedda felt sorry for me and urged Garrison to hire me. Because she trusted me, so did he. It was so easy to list more losses due to water damage each year. They have such volume they never doubted my figures."

"You've been too greedy lately. You were discovered weeks ago. I think I've even begun to understand how you did it." Aimee had been watching the other two men work. "These two piles of boxes are identical, are they not? You selectively substitute boxes with like numbers for the real ones. Only when they're shipped to the buyers, or a total inventory is done, will it be discovered that they hold rocks, wood, or something else equally worthless. Correct?"

Payton applauded her. "Correct. It's a pity the Garrisons will never know what an astute girl you are. Are you foolish enough to think I'll let you go free?"

Aimee smiled nastily. "Are you foolish enough to think I'd come here alone?"

Just then a bell sounded outdoors, signaling the arrival of the police.

Payton straightened abruptly, shock on his face. Then all affability fled as his true nature surfaced. Aimee shivered as she watched his cobra-hooded face turn ugly and he hissed, "You interfering little bitch. You'll not live to see them." He whipped a small pistol from his coat.

Everything happened at once.

The police swarmed in. Aimee swung her parasol up in a vicious arc, knocking the gun from Payton's hand just as he reached up to grab her as hostage. Luke and Joshua leaped from behind the shelves, as warehouse hands in Payton's employ appeared to thrust themselves into the melee. Gleason dropped his chart list, bleated like a terrified lamb and fled. Joshua went off in hot pursuit. Luke gathered himself to tackle Payton, but the workman stepped in front of the manager and caught Luke against his massive chest.

Payton cursed, grasping his aching wrist. Recovering quickly, he took a menacing step toward Aimee. Jeremy bolted from behind the wood pile he had crawled behind to protect her, since Luke was preoccupied: he lunged out and grabbed the man. Aimee, noting the hammerlock Payton employed, brought the parasol up over her head and down on the man's balding head. The delicate sticks splintered, leaving Payton dazed among the pieces. He released his grip on Jeremy, and passed out.

Jeremy leaped to his feet, brushing off warehouse floor sawdust, with a look of admiration in his eyes. He went to stand beside Aimee. "You little fiend, I might as well not have come," he growled. But Aimee didn't hear him. She was fretting as she watched Luke battle the guard. How much had he heard? Did he understand now why she had been seeing Jeremy?

Meanwhile the five policemen who had swarmed into the building were engaged in rounding up the several warehouse hands who had materialized when they heard the first cries. They waved their bobbie sticks threateningly, and after a few skirmishes, the men complied.

Aimee watched the man-to-man combat with growing fear. Luke punched his assailant in the belly. He recovered quickly and slammed a right into Luke's jaw. Aimee winced, but Luke rebounded quickly. He set his teeth and catapulted into the man, head first, knocking him to the ground. He straddled him and landed two crushing blows to his chin, knocking his head back against the stone floor. The guard went limp. Luke took several gasping breaths, then he stood and stepped shakily toward Aimee.

Aimee took several steps to meet him, her hand out in supplication as she tried to read his face in the shadowed warehouse. Joshua was occupied with tying up Gleason; Aimee and Luke knew of nothing but each other. Only Jeremy saw when Payton suddenly reared up from the floor, the pistol in his hand and hatred in his face. He leveled it first at Aimee, then, as if he realized she'd be easier to escape from, he swung it toward Luke.

Jeremy had time only for a wild, "Look out, Luke!" before he launched himself at Payton. Aimee, Luke and Joshua turned in time to see the pistol go off. Stunned, they watched as Jeremy slumped to the ground, a stain spreading on his shoulder. Payton shoved him aside and leveled the pistol again, but by now Joshua was close enough to reach him.

His face black with rage, Joshua brought his fist slashing down on Payton's arm, knocking the weapon away. Joshua smashed his other fist into Payton's nose. There was the sickening crunch of broken cartilage and a gush of blood.

Howling, Payton fell to his knees. Luke grabbed up a rope and quickly tied Payton's hands behind his back. Only then did Joshua back off, for, even in his fury, he wouldn't hit a bound man.

Aimee dropped to her knees beside Jeremy. Blood gushed from the hole in his shoulder. She fumbled in his pocket for his handkerchief and pressed it over the wound, tears of gratitude and worry in her eyes.

"Jeremy, Jeremy, why did you do it?"

Jeremy smiled weakly. "I couldn't let Payton kill the man you love, Aimee. If I can't have you, I at least want you to be happy."

Aimee's tears flowed hotter. She kissed the top of his head. "Thank you from the bottom of my heart. Now lie quiet. We'll send for a doctor immediately. You'll be fine." She eased Jeremy's head into her lap to stroke his brow. She didn't see the large figure who came to stand over her. Jeremy had eyes only for the lovely face bending over him. He reached up to run a finger over her wet lashes.

"Don't cry for me, little love. This is a moment to celebrate, and I assure you I'll live to see it."

Luke couldn't see Aimee's eyes, but he saw Jeremy's expression with devastating clarity. It was a look he recognized. It was his own when he looked at her—that of a man totally possessed by love.

The world that had been so bright only moments before went dark, and Luke turned away and went for a doctor. Another police vehicle arrived, and men in blue rushed in. Their shouts as they wrestled the captured warehouse hands outside counterpointed the mourning inside. Joshua finished tying up the workman in time to see the expression on his son's face. Luke never even heard him when he called his name, for his ears echoed with Jeremy's endearment, "little love, little love . . ." Why would he call her that if she'd given him no reason? Perhaps they'd started meeting for honorable reasons, but what if Aimee had come to care for Jeremy as more than a friend she wanted to help?

Bob joined the melee, and a short while later, Luke returned with the doctor. Joshua let Luke make explanations while he supervised Jeremy's removal.

He took Jeremy's hand after the doctor had examined him. "We owe you a great debt, Jeremy," Joshua said gruffly. "We've wronged you heinously, and you repay us by saving

ke's life. Everything is clear to me now, and I've never felt
e such a fool. Samuel never stole anything, did he?"

Jeremy tried to shake his head, but couldn't. He winced.
No, sir. But until your daughter-in-law vowed to help me, I
asn't able to prove it." He groaned as the doctor helped
m to his feet.

Joshua shook his head at Aimee, but his eyes were soft and
ving when he tugged her into his arms. "You stubborn little
ol, you could have gotten yourself killed. You and Hedda
e two of a kind."

Aimee laughed tiredly into his chest. "As you'll discover
hen you get home. Hedda is angry with you for not telling
er the truth." Aimee's eyes went to Luke. He was watching
er strangely, but when she looked at him, he whirled away.

Joshua tightened his arm around her. "He'll come around
s soon as you're able to talk with him. We'll stay and
raighten out this mess. I want you to take Jeremy home and
ut him in our best guest chamber."

After helping the doctor get Jeremy in a cab, she held him
her arms on the trip home, cushioning him against the
olts. Hedda met them at the door.

She paled when she saw Jeremy's wound, but, characteris-
cally, took charge instead of asking questions. She showed
e doctor to the only bedroom on the ground floor, sent the
aid for towels and hot water and insisted on helping with
e bullet removal.

When the doctor protested, she said tartly, "He's my son.
's my duty as his mother." She tousled Jeremy's hair as she
ad when he was a boy, smiling down at him so tenderly that
imee's eyes watered. "And I *want* to help. I don't want
nything to harm him, ever again."

Aimee noticed she hadn't even asked for explanations. Her
yes met Jeremy's and she realized he, too, caught the
ignificance of that. Jeremy sank back against his pillows with
sigh, giving up without regret his struggle against the
other he'd always loved.

When Marietta returned from shopping, she hurried in to
ee him, concerned. He was almost asleep, but he brushed
side her sympathy. "I'll be fine. Congratulations on your
ngagement. I hope you'll be very happy."

Marietta sighed with relief and held his hand until he slept.

When Joshua returned several hours later, Aimee and
Hedda barraged him with questions. He held up his hands,

laughing, "Can't a man have a bite to eat to fill his achin͏ belly?"

Hedda crossed her arms over her bosom and glared at hiͭ one foot tapping. "More than your belly will ache if you donͭ explain what happened immediately. It's the least you owͤ me after deceiving me all these weeks."

Joshua went to her contritely. "You're right, love. Comͤ into the study and I'll talk to your heart's content. But firsͭ how is Jeremy?"

Hedda softened. "Sleeping peacefully. He'll be fine, thͤ doctor said."

Joshua sighed with relief. "Thank God. Come, ladies, I'ͮ a story to tell." He led them into the study and closed thͤ door.

After they were seated, Joshua began, "Payton wouldn͏ say a word, but Gleason broke after Luke threatened ͭ charge him as an accomplice to attempted murder. Paytoͭ and Gleason were not content with the salary of honeͣ seamen, and they concocted a scheme to take advantage ͦ the hostility between Bjorn and Samuel. They were ingenͤ ious, I have to give them that. Whenever a valuable shipmenͭ came in, they'd mark identical crates with the same numberͣ loading them with rocks and substituting them for the reͣ ones. They'd always leave several of the original crates on thͤ top of each group, so, when they were checked, it woulͩ seem nothing was missing unless each box was openeͩ Gleason would tow the boxes away along with his legitimatͤ cargo. Bjorn and Samuel discovered the thefts sooner beͭ cause Tom had less control over imports. Wholesalers conͭ tacted them when their promised merchandise didn't arrive."

Hedda interrupted, "You mean he's been stealing from uͣ all these years?"

Joshua met Aimee's eyes. "You tell her, child. We owͤ finding out the truth to you, so this is really more your storͧ than mine."

Aimee nodded sadly. "Yes, Hedda. He admitted as mucͪ to me. He was selective, until lately. Since he kept the bookͣ at the warehouse, it was easy for him to list an amount eacͪ year as loss from breakage or water damage. Why didn't yoͧ ever question the amount, Joshua?"

"The sum was high compared to other shippers, but wͤ believed our large volume to be the cause."

"How much have they taken?" Hedda growled.

"We're not sure yet, but I imagine it will amount to tens of thousands of dollars."

Hedda spat, "I want them prosecuted to the fullest extent, Joshua. Their thievery is bad enough, but they deserve the worst for what they did to Samuel and Jeremy."

Joshua pulled Hedda into his arms, patting her back. "Yes, love, they'll pay, don't worry. But I think we're almost as guilty as they are for our intolerance. We must make it up to Jeremy in every way possible. I only regret it's too late to do the same for Samuel."

Joshua extended his hand to Aimee. She sat down next to him and was clasped in his other strong arm. "And this young lady is courageous as a man. I wonder how long it would have been for the truth to come out if it hadn't been for her? You should have seen the way she pried his guilt out of Payton, Hedda."

Aimee waved a dismissing hand. "He thought he didn't have anything to lose. His poor opinion of women was his downfall."

Joshua watched Hedda and Aimee smile at one another. He dropped his eyes to hide a twinkle when he drawled, "Doubtless he'll have many years to reflect on his foolishness." He deliberately kept his voice so even that Aimee looked at him quizzically, uncertain whether he was sincere or not.

Hedda scolded, "Don't tease the child, Joshua. We owe her a great deal."

When Joshua looked repentant, Aimee smiled at him with her own brand of mischief. "You and Luke would have solved things fine without my help." Following his lead, she left her tone bland. "You were already at the warehouse, after all." Her voice roughened. "Where . . . is Luke?"

Joshua looked at Hedda. The worry in her eyes was reflected in his own when he answered, "He stayed at the warehouse to begin an exhaustive inventory. We'll open every crate this time, not just selective ones."

Luke climbed the stairs, his eyes gritty with tiredness, hoping he could finally sleep. He had worked like a fiend at the warehouse in an effort to obliterate the image of Aimee cradling Jeremy in her arms. The knowledge that Jeremy was innocent complicated matters greatly. He had been told personally by the banker who had lent Jeremy funds that

Jeremy had promised to repay them after the sale of his ship. The certainty that he had been instrumental in Jeremy's defeat compounded his guilt. Luke felt sick at his behavior toward the man who should have been, indeed deserved to be, treated like a brother. On top of everything else, Jeremy had saved his life. Much as he tried to deny it, conscience voiced the only honorable course: if Aimee loved Jeremy, he must step aside.

And so he told himself, over and over as he opened crate after crate. But repetition made the knowledge no more palatable. Every time he envisioned Aimee in Jeremy's arms, the emerald ring he'd given her replaced by another, Luke was filled with rage toward Jeremy for stealing the woman he loved, and Aimee for choosing another over him. Right or wrong, honorable or dishonorable, Aimee was his, would remain his to the day she died. Whether she loved him or not, he could not let her go. She was the foundation of his life, the woman he had sought for almost thirty years. Without her all he had achieved, all he yet hoped to do, would crumble into dust.

Luke removed his clothes in preparation for bed, resolving to make Aimee forget her infatuation with Jeremy. He was frowning blackly in renewed anger at the thought when a sound drew his attention. He turned, his powerful body nude.

There she stood, back against the door, watching him with those unwavering green eyes that haunted him night and day. His eyes swept over her. Her hair was a teasing drape over the breasts and shoulders revealed by the sea-green wisp of a nightgown. Slim, delectable, she was all woman, the woman he had teased and taunted into life and for whom he suffered now because of her power over him. He groaned and turned away to hide the desire that surged hot in him. It had been so long. . . . Why, why, did she come to him now, when he was struggling with jealous anger?

Aimee's heart pounded in her chest at the sight of him. He was so beautiful, so much a man. Her hands tingled with the need to reacquaint themselves with the plains and valleys so arousingly revealed to her. Aimee licked her lips and forced herself to think calmly. He was still angry with her, and she had to find out why before giving free rein to her desire.

"Luke, why are you angry? Surely you understand why I was meeting with Jeremy now. The hatred you all felt for the

Mayhews was as unhealthy for you as for them. It was vital to clear their name. I did it for your sake as much as for Jeremy's." When her soft pleading brought no response, she went to him and laid her hand on his arm. "Luke, please listen . . ." She gasped when he rounded on her and caught her shoulders in a crushing grip.

"It was for *my* sake that you held him as tenderly as a lover, full of concern for him and caring not a whit that I was safe?"

Aimee opened her mouth to deny the charge, but he railed on, "Well, love him you may, and perhaps he even deserves you more than I do. But you, madam, are married to *me*. You are my possession, to do with as I will. You'll see neither Jeremy, nor another man ever again. Your nights will be spent only with me, where you belong. Understand, wife?" He shook her a little, anguished at the white, shocked look on her face, appalled that even now, angry as he was, he longed to fling her on the bed and take her until the world and all their troubles ceased to matter.

Every word drove into Aimee like spikes, entombing her foolish dreams. He didn't care for her at all. Even after the laughter, the fights, the pain they'd shared, she meant no more to him than a possession. She was a female for his use, not an individual who deserved consideration and respect for her own abilities. Her efforts were for naught. He could never love her because she meant no more to him than the horse he rode or the boots he wore. Perhaps he was incapable of the kind of love she felt.

Aimee jerked away from him and stood to her full height. Her voice came soft and deadly. "Yes, Luke, I understand. At last I understand." She reached out to brush the male flesh that ignored his will and strained toward her. "This is your only interest in me. You don't care about what I want, whether I'm happy, as long as you can command me to service you as bedmate and housekeeper. That's why you never share business matters with me, that's why you so readily believed I was unfaithful to you. You have no respect for me as an individual." Aimee's voice rose with each word. Shaking, she turned away to get a grip on herself, missing Luke's appalled expression.

How could she misunderstand him so completely? He wanted only to keep her with him, no matter what he had to do. He took a step toward her to correct her misinterpretation, but she took a deep breath and faced him again. His words died at the look on her face. No matter what life had tossed her way, she had accepted the challenge and tried to learn from every defeat. But there was no spark in her eyes now. No hope for the future. Only bitter acceptance.

"I want you to know nothing ever happened between Jeremy and me. You are the only man I've ever desired, but I can't live with a man who views me only as a possession. I'd lose all self-respect and become your whore instead of your lover, your toy instead of your wife. I can do that for no man—not even you." She went to the door, pausing with her hand on the knob. "No matter how much I might love you," she whispered, tears streaming down her cheeks at last. The door closed softly behind her.

Luke stood stunned, wondering, hoping he'd heard her right. Aimee loved him? The weight of the world fell off his shoulders. He leaped for the door. He'd taken three great strides before he remembered he wasn't wearing a stitch. He was sweaty and grimy from his long day. A jubilant smile stretched his weary face as he decided he'd have a quick bath so their reconciliation could proceed once explanations were done. Humming, he ran the bath water.

Aimee threw a few clothes into a small case. She rubbed angrily at the unstoppable tears and sat down to pen a hasty note to Joshua and Hedda. She removed the ring from her finger. For a moment, she looked at it, gleaming in the gaslight with a promise that had proven false. A harsh sob escaped her as she recalled the words she'd once spoken to him with such conviction: "I won't ever leave you again, not unless you send me away." Tonight he *had* sent her away by proving he returned her love not in the smallest portion.

She placed the ring on top of the note. She whipped her fur-lined cloak over her gray serge dress, grabbed up the case and the reticule filled with her recent quarter's allowance, and went softly down the stairs and out the door.

She walked to Broadway, still busy even at this time of night, and took a cab to the wharf. She purchased a ticket on a steamer that sailed for London on the tide. From there she could buy a ticket for Norway. Maybe the clean, cold breeze of home would bring life back to her numbed body and mind and make her eager to feel again.

Luke entered their bedroom when Aimee didn't answer. At first he was puzzled at the empty bed, but then the note on the bureau caught his eye. A prescient chill running up his spine, he picked up the envelope addressed to his parents. A metallic jingle alerted him. He bent to the floor. There lay the ring he had twice placed on Aimee's finger. A strangled groan caught in his throat, Luke ran out the door, praying he'd get the chance to put it back on her finger again.

But Aimee was gone. Joshua helped him look for her, but they found no trace at any of the hotels. By the time they discovered which steamer she had booked, it had sailed for London. Joshua feared for his son when they returned home. He flung off his father's hand, and, tears in his eyes, barricaded himself in the study.

Luke sat with his head in his hands, wondering if the whispered words Aimee had spoken had been conjured up by his longing, or if they had been real and he'd sent her away by his own folly. For hours he sat there, so buried in grief he barely heard Joshua's entreaties, or even Hedda's. Near dawn of the next day, a younger, more irritable voice penetrated his fog of misery.

"Dammit man, open up unless you want me to pass out here in the hall and bleed all over your blooming rug," Jeremy ordered crossly.

Luke rubbed the tears out of his eyes, took a deep breath and opened the door. Jeremy seemed not to notice his ravaged face as he staggered into the room and sat down with a sigh of relief.

"You Garrisons are the stubbornnest group of people it's ever been my misfortune to meet. Aimee most of all."

Luke's head swiveled around at mention of that name. Jeremy chuckled dryly. "Thought that would get your attention. Wipe that ugly look off your face. My knowledge of Aimee stems from our friendship, nothing more. I admit if it'd been up to me, I would have known her far better, in every sense of the word. . . ." When Luke hovered over him, fists clenched, Jeremy patted a yawn and continued, "But it wasn't up to me. Aimee is smarter than any woman I've met, but she has a blind spot where you're concerned. She loves you more deeply than you can ever deserve, Garrison. I didn't get a bullet in my shoulder to see her suffer. Go after her and go down on your knees to her, if necessary."

Incongruously, Jeremy's insulting words brought a grin to Luke's face. He sat down next to Jeremy, tiredness soaking in. "Hell, even when you try to be kind, you're obnoxious,

Mayhew." He sobered. "I admit I don't deserve it, but please tell me honestly. Does Aimee really love me?"

Jeremy had his eyes closed and seemed not to have heard him. Only when Luke repeated the question, his voice strained, did Jeremy answer. "You're right, you don't deserve it. But yes, she loves you." When Luke's face lit up like a Christmas candle, Jeremy drawled, "But even the best of women have been known to be feeble-minded at times."

Luke was too busy basking in the glow of the revelation to hear him. He turned to Jeremy and held out his hand. "Jeremy, I never thought I'd live to hear myself say this, but you have my everlasting gratitude and my deepest apologies for my behavior. I was only trying to protect those I love, but that's no excuse."

Jeremy shook his hand. Luke said, "Oh hell, why not. You're my brother now."

And, to Jeremy's astonishment, he found himself enveloped in a hug. He stared at his grinning brother when he was released, for once at a loss for words.

Luke went to the door, tossing over his shoulder, "I've got plans to make, but I want you to know that my father and I want to recompense you for your losses. He can discuss the details with you." He hurried out.

Jeremy leaned back against the couch, his eyes on the fire, but his mind filled with a slim, silver-haired image. "Aimee, sweet love, be happy," he whispered shakily.

After Luke had taken the smallest of their idle steamers and sailed for Norway the next morning, Joshua talked to Jeremy. To his amazement, he found Hedda's eldest son obstinately opposed to the loan.

"No, I've lost interest in the export business. All I ask is a fair price on the ship and warehouse I have left. I intend to take the other ship and sail away, offering my services as courier or conveyer to whoever is willing to pay for them." And the more danger, the better, he added to himself.

Joshua argued hotly, but Hedda took him aside and intervened. "No, let him go. It may be best, now that Marietta's getting married." Joshua finally agreed. So Hedda, Joshua and Marietta kissed Jeremy good-bye several weeks later.

If Hedda's whispered, "God speed, my son. May the winds of good fortune blow behind you and lead you to happiness," had another meaning, only Jeremy and Hedda were aware of it. He kissed his mother's cheek.

"I'll be fine, Mother. I'll write when I can. Give Aimee my . . . best wishes." Hedda met his eyes compassionately and nodded. They watched his cab disappear into the distance, then went back in to tensely await word from Luke.

PART VI

*All that is good, if two can share, has double
sanctity and worth. That life's deep longing
should be sated, when soul in soul is recreated,
that is the greatest joy on earth.*

—Bjørnstjerne Bjørnson, "Love Song"

Chapter Seventeen

AIMEE PULLED HER cloak tighter about her shoulders as she jumped down from the *karjol*. The snow was falling and the mountain wind this November was bitterly cold. Still, the bleak landscape had a beauty all its own. Icicles graced the barren limbs of the trees like charms on the arms of scrawny maids. Far below in the valley, smoke rose, curling up and about the tiny chimneys to be whisked away by mountain winds.

Aimee turned her face into that wind, welcoming its icy bite. She had arrived home yesterday, delighting her family. She knew Sigrid and Gere had married, but she'd been thrilled at the latest news that Sigrid was expecting a child.

She kissed her sister, teasing, "Soon you'll have a little one to worry about, as you used to worry about me."

Sigrid had opened her mouth to comment on her sister's haggard appearance, but Ragnar shook his head. She responded brightly, "And when will you greet us with similar news?"

Aimee put one hand over her abdomen. "I think I already have similar news," she whispered. The realization of her pregnancy had hit her when she was sick the entire, smooth crossing. The knowledge made her future even more frightening, though she was comforted that she would always have a part of Luke. She smiled and nodded at her family's congratulations, but inwardly she cried at the knowledge that the child she carried would never know its father, for she had no intention of telling Luke. She was too weak yet to give him such a hold on her. She might agree if he tried to make her return.

Ragnar cornered her after the gay, celebratory meal Ingrid had hastily arranged. "And what has put such a sad look on that pretty face, *datter?*" he questioned gently.

Aimee tried to turn away, but he caught her chin and made her look at him. "Come, child, I see you're hurting. There is a new maturity about you that delights me. I despaired of ever seeing my younger daughter such a strong woman so sure of herself, when she was running wild in the hills. But at what cost have you learned so much?"

Aimee sagged against his strong chest and wept. He stroked her hair, clucking to her as he had when she was a child. He led her to the sofa and listened to her halting explanation of much that had happened.

His face darkened with anger at Luke. "I can't believe he treated you so unfairly. Are you sure you understood him?"

Aimee rose to pace up and down. "I understood his words well enough. And I have no reason to doubt his sincerity. It explains too much." Her face crumpled as she remembered yet again that last ugly confrontation. She ran to Ragnar, fell before him and buried her face in his knees.

"Oh *Far,* I don't know if I can bear it. I loved him so. I still love him so, though sometimes I almost hate him. He helped me learn so much. I tried so hard to make him happy. Why can't he love the person he's helped me become?" Ragnar looked down at his daughter's fair head, an expression on his face that boded ill for Luke.

As she wandered the hills now, Aimee wrapped her arms about her body, thinking again of the life slumbering within her. Poor little one, to be seeded and live only to reap the bitterness of a failed marriage. It wasn't fair. With the thought came sounds that snapped Aimee's head up in a frantic search. The yowls of a cat in pain. . . .

Luke approached the Lingstrom house in a far more nervous manner than he had months ago. He dismounted, tied Polaris to the gate familiarly and stuffed his shaking hands in his coat pockets. Trying to walk confidently, he banged the door knocker, hoping Aimee's stop in London had been brief, and waited for the door to swing open.

Ragnar himself appeared. Luke's heart sank at the glare he received as a greeting. For a minute he thought Ragnar would slam the door in his face, but the older man stood stiffly aside. Luke entered, watching him warily.

Ragnar growled, "If it's Aimee you're seeking, you've some explaining to do before I let you near her."

Luke nodded ruefully and followed the erect back into the living room. "What do you want to know?"

"One question above all—do you love my daughter?"

His face would cow any man into lying, Luke decided. But he, thank God, had no need to lie. "I love your daughter, Ragnar, more than my own life. That's not to say I deserve her. I've made a terrible mess of things."

Ragnar unbent enough to smile an agreement. "Tell me your side of what happened."

And so it was that just as Aimee knelt a few feet away from a small lynx who was struggling to escape the trap that bit into its foot, a shadow blocked the watery sun. Aimee looked up with a gasp—into Luke's face.

This time, he carried no club. This time, there was no air of arrogant challenge about him. This time, he looked contrite, hungry for the sight of her and very unsure of himself. He didn't scold her. He dropped to his knees beside her. "Let me help you open this, love," he said huskily.

Aimee turned back to the cub, almost dizzy with the longing to throw pride and caution to the winds and fling herself into his arms. She had no way of knowing that Luke's need for the same thing was just as strong.

The cub growled and swiped at them as, together, they released the spring on the trap with a tree limb, and stepped back as the wounded beast ran away. The wound was only a surface wound, and the fresh snow would act as a balm to speed its healing.

Aimee dusted her hands off, straightened her hood, cleaned the snow off her cloak, then looked into the warm glow of her husband's eyes. He seemed so different. Almost . . . humble. Aimee scoffed inwardly at the word, but it fit his sheepish expression. He hadn't railed at her for putting herself in danger, or for leaving him. That was not like the Luke she knew at all.

"Why have you followed me?" she asked finally, when he didn't speak.

He put his hands behind his back and cleared his throat.

"To ask you to come back with me. To . . . tell you that I am ashamed of my behavior. To thank you for the risks you took for my family. To . . . apologize for my hasty words to you before you left. I can only say that I was half crazy with weariness, anger, guilt, desire, and . . ."

Aimee's heart surged to life for the first time in over three long weeks. She peered at his bent head, yearning to run her fingers through his hair and smother him with kisses. But she longed more to hear the words she prayed he would at last speak. "And?"

Luke's head jerked up. He looked her in the eyes, his expression a torment of worry, doubt and . . . "Love. I love you as I never dreamed it was possible to love a woman." Luke couldn't see Aimee's face, for she had pulled her hood up against the wind. She evinced no reaction whatever as the avowal he'd practised for weeks came out clumsily. In a panic, he dropped to one knee before her and took her hand.

He peeled the glove away and kissed the back of her hand, the palm and each finger, smothering her skin with the words of devotion that she had dreamed of so long. "I can't sleep because you're not there . . . I can't eat because you're not there . . . I can't even walk without remembering how sweet it is to swing your hand. Please, please forgive my foolish pride and come back with me. I'll never order you around again. I'll never hide anything from you. You can attend every business meeting with me, you can even pick the clothes I'll wear. . . ."

That was too much. Aimee teased, laughter running under her commanding tone like a vein of gold, "If I want you to wear plaid trousers with a checkered coat, you will?" Luke nodded uncertainly. "If I speak up at your business meetings, you'll let me talk, even if I'm wrong?" Luke opened his mouth, snapped it shut and nodded once, reluctantly. "And you'll let me help with an orphanage?" Luke nodded again. "You'll let me do whatever I want?"

Luke's eyes narrowed as he finally caught the laughter shining in her voice. He shifted, devilishly uncomfortable with this humiliating position, but he'd stay here until he froze solid unless she agreed to come back with him. Feeling like a jack-in-the-box, he nodded again.

Aimee nibbled on one finger, deep in thought. "There is one thing I'd really like to do." When Luke looked inquiring, she pushed her hood back, cocked her head on one side and miled sweetly, "Become a suffragette."

Luke surged to his feet, growling, "No, dammit, I'll not ave my wife . . ." He broke off as she went into peals of aughter.

He heaved a great sigh of relief and reached for her. She luded him, chortling, "You looked so funny like that. It's obvious you've never known a moment's humility." Aimee lanced behind a tree to avoid his long arms.

He made to step one way, then swooped around the other and tackled her when she fell for his dodge. He cushioned her all with his long body, sighing with happiness at the feel of her at last against him.

"Don't you have something to say to me, wife?" he demanded. When she lifted a haughty eyebrow, he softened his tone. "Please, Aimee. I need to be sure of your love as much as you need to be sure of mine."

Aimee buried her cold nose in his neck and kissed the pulse throbbing there. "I love you, my tender devil. I thought I would die when I had to leave you."

Luke lifted her chin. "Don't ever leave me again." He removed her ring from his pocket, placed it on her finger and kissed it. "See that stays there this time. I'm damned tired of finding it lying on top of notes."

He helped her to her feet, demanding, "Well, are you ready to come home where you belong?"

Aimee thought about teasing him again, but there was a vulnerable look to his strong face that touched her deeply. She kissed his cheek. "Yes, love, I am."

He smiled, the grin stretching slowly until it reached ear to ear. When he had her safely in his arms he drawled, "Good. If I'd had to eat any more crow I would have choked."

Aimee struggled against him, and, laughing, he lowered his mouth over hers, soothing her annoyance in the way they both liked best. The kiss they exchanged was a penance, a promise and a pledge, and it chased the last of the shadows away from each of their hearts.

When they could breathe again, Aimee peeped up at him. "I have a gift for you."

He looked only mildly interested. "Indeed? Nothing you can give me can make me any happier than you already have."

Aimee removed the glove on his right hand, smiling mysteriously into his puzzled eyes. She took his hand inside her cloak to her soft stomach. "Even this?"

Luke's cocky grin quivered. His hand shook where it rested against her. "Aimee?" he breathed.

She nodded. "Yes, love. In the summer."

He paled as he remembered how he'd tackled her to the ground, then went even whiter as he remembered how she'd helped him free the lynx. "Dammit, woman, you'll be the death of me yet if you don't learn to be more careful!"

Aimee leaned against him in utter contentment, letting him rail on. When she decided he'd blown off enough steam, she interjected, "I'm certain you'll see I'm careful from now on. Not that you'd order me around, of course, unless it was for my own good." She looked at him provocatively, deciding she'd even change his mind about her becoming a suffragette —eventually.

He smiled, grinned, and then he was laughing. He cupped her cheeks in his hands, kissing every inch of her face. "You know me too well, love. Ah, we're two of a kind." They smiled at each other in perfect accord, aware they'd have it no other way.

Luke spoke her thoughts. "Maybe that's why we're so happy together. We've some interesting stories to tell our grandchildren, with more to come, no doubt."

"No doubt," Aimee agreed serenely. She took his arm and walked with him into that future.

Sweeping
Stories
of Captivating
Romance

Highly Acclaimed
Historical Romances From Berkley